How lucky we are.

"Bring us about, Sulu," Kirk said. "Rahda, don't wait for my order. Fire the second you have a clear shot."

The Indian officer spared only a glance over her shoulder. "Aye, sir."

"They're coming around again, Captain," said Medeiros. "They're trying to get in behind us."

Kirk leaned forward in his seat. "Don't let them do that, Sulu."

The lieutenant did not reply, his attention focused on his controls. His piloting prowess was evident both on the viewscreen and the astrogator as the *Enterprise* maneuvered over, under, and around the Klingon vessel, searching for an avenue of attack while denying it to its adversary.

Medeiros warned, "They're firing again!"

The effect of the second strike was not as pronounced, thanks to Sulu's skill, but the *Enterprise* still trembled beneath the force of at least one disruptor striking its shields.

"Glancing blow to starboard shields," said Medeiros, who was gripping the edge of the science console with one hand while using the other to brace himself against the station's sensor viewer.

Sulu cast a quick look over his shoulder to Kirk. "Bringing us about."

"Firing!" called out Rahda.

STAR TREK®

THE ORIGINAL SERIES

LEGACIES: BOOK 3

PURGATORY'S KEY

Dayton Ward & Kevin Dilmore

Based upon *Star Trek*
created by Gene Roddenberry

POCKET BOOKS

New York   London   Toronto   Sydney   New Delhi   Usilde

Pocket Books
An Imprint of Simon & Schuster, Inc.
1230 Avenue of the Americas
New York, NY 10020

This book is a work of fiction. Any references to historical events, real people, or real places are used fictitiously. Other names, characters, places, and events are products of the authors' imaginations, and any resemblance to actual events or places or persons, living or dead, is entirely coincidental.

™, ®, and © 2016 by CBS Studios Inc. STAR TREK and related marks and logos are trademarks of CBS Studios Inc. All Rights Reserved.

This book is published by Pocket Books, an imprint of Simon & Schuster, Inc., under exclusive license from CBS Studios Inc.

All rights reserved, including the right to reproduce this book or portions thereof in any form whatsoever. For information, address Pocket Books Subsidiary Rights Department, 1230 Avenue of the Americas, New York, NY 10020.

First Pocket Books paperback edition September 2016

POCKET and colophon are registered trademarks of Simon & Schuster, Inc.

For information about special discounts for bulk purchases, please contact Simon & Schuster Special Sales at 1-866-506-1949 or business@simonandschuster.com.

The Simon & Schuster Speakers Bureau can bring authors to your live event. For more information or to book an event, contact the Simon & Schuster Speakers Bureau at 1-866-248-3049 or visit our website at www.simonspeakers.com.

Manufactured in the United States of America

10 9 8 7 6 5 4 3 2 1

ISBN 978-1-5011-2277-4
ISBN 978-1-5011-2278-1 (ebook)

For Gene Roddenberry

*Thank you for giving us such a wondrous sandbox
in which to play.*

Historian's Note

This story takes place early in the year 2268, several months after the *U.S.S. Enterprise*'s mission to ferry Federation diplomats to the conference on the neutral planetoid Babel ("Journey to Babel"), and immediately following the Romulan attack on the planet Centaurus (*Star Trek: Legacies*—Book 2: *Best Defense*).

One

Pivoting on her heel and flattening the wooden training *bat'leth* as she lifted it from its resting place on her left shoulder, Visla swung the weapon with her right arm and let its heavy blade arc across her body. The impact against her opponent's simulated blade made her arm shudder but she ignored it. Instinct guided her to her left and she ducked under her adversary's counterattack, feeling the rush of air as the training weapon sliced through the air above her head. Adjusting her stance and raising her own *bat'leth* in preparation for another attack, Visla realized something about her counterpart's movements was not quite right.

"Mev!"

The response to her command was immediate, with her opponent, Lieutenant Koveq, halting his own movements and returning to a basic ready stance. With both hands, he held his *bat'leth* before him, cutting edge pointed toward the deck plating.

"Commander?"

Visla eyed him. "You do not attack me with full force. Why?"

"I do not understand," replied Koveq, his heavy brow furrowing in confusion. "This was to be an exercise interval."

"I have no wish to be coddled like a child." Feeling her grip tighten on her own weapon, she relished the anger flowing through her for another moment. "Attack me. Spare none of your strength and skill."

Regarding her with obvious doubt, her weapons officer replied, "Are you certain, Commander?"

It was not an unreasonable question, Visla conceded. Her subordinate was well trained in close combat, both with bladed weapons and his own hands. He outweighed her by a considerable margin, and there was no denying that his brute physical strength was superior to her own. There also was the simple fact that she had engaged Koveq in this exercise as a training bout, for which there were rules and protocols in order to reduce the number of preventable, even stupid injuries.

She cared nothing about any of that today.

"Stop questioning my orders, attack me!"

In response to her command, Koveq said nothing more. His expression darkened and Visla recognized the determined set to his jaw. He raised his *bat'leth* blade, angling the weapon so that the end to Visla's left was higher and tilted toward her. With skill born from countless hours of training and actual combat, he advanced, neither rushing his movements nor offering any insight into what he was planning. Visla felt her pulse quicken in anticipation, and she could not resist a small smile of satisfaction as she hefted her blade and began stepping to her right.

She expected Koveq to feint to his left before launching an assault to her left flank, but the weapons officer surprised her by lunging left, shifting the angle of his *bat'leth*, and then continuing with his original attack angle. Visla brought her blade up and over in time to block the strike, by which time Koveq was pivoting away, using his momentum to swing his weapon with one hand back toward her head. She parried that attack, backpedaling to give herself maneuvering room, but her subordinate had already gathered himself and was charging again. She started to counter his move, but he spun at the last instant, turning away from her blade as she took one step too far and overextended her reach. Koveq's *bat'leth* swung across his body, and Visla felt the sting of the training weapon across her back. The force of the strike pushed her off her feet and she stumbled, stopping her fall with her free hand and pushing herself back to her feet.

"*Mev*," said Koveq, dropping his *bat'leth* to a carry position that indicated he was neither attacking nor defending.

Visla glowered at him. "I did not command you to stop."

"I know, Commander. As the ship's combat training officer, it is my prerogative. This exercise is concluded."

"Why?" She used her forearm to wipe perspiration from her brow. "You were winning."

"Training is not about winning or losing, Commander," said Koveq, his voice calm. "It is for learning."

Growling in irritation, Visla shook her head. "You sound like a Vulcan when you talk like that."

"Despite their annoying tendencies to incessantly ramble about subjects of little consequence, Vulcans are quite adept in the fighting arts." Crossing the room, Koveq paused before the bench that angled outward from the training room's slanted bulkhead. There, he retrieved a towel and began to wipe down his training *bat'leth*. "I have studied some of their unarmed combat disciplines. There is much to learn and to admire."

Her ire rising, Visla held up her own simulated weapon. "Before I find a way to kill you with this toy, what does any of the nonsense you spout have to do with anything?"

Setting the *bat'leth* on the bench, Koveq turned back to her. "The Vulcans are masters of opening their minds to new ideas and new ways of doing things. For this reason, they are most adaptable to almost any situation, including combat. It is this attitude that facilitates their learning and their ability to meet any challenge. For one to learn, one's mind must be attuned to the task at hand. Your mind is elsewhere, Commander."

She was opening her mouth to respond when Visla caught herself. Several heartbeats passed before she took a step backward, drawing a deep breath and letting the wooden *bat'leth* drop from her hand. The weapon clattered as it struck the metal deck plating. For the first time since entering the training room, she smiled and released a small laugh.

"You understand that not even my first officer is permitted to address me in such a manner, and I actually like him."

The comment elicited a deep belly laugh from the weapons officer. "Yes, but you have entrusted me with being the keeper of your conscience, Commander. It is not a responsibility I take lightly. You are obviously troubled, and it affects your focus."

Though Visla valued his counsel, there were times when Koveq's calm, unflappable demeanor made her want to drive his face into the nearest bulkhead or simply fire him from one of the ship's torpedo tubes. When he spoke to her this way, it only heightened her annoyance because she knew he was well aware of the source of her anger.

"You know I hate it when you cloak your words," she said, reaching for the *bat'leth* she had dropped and returning it to its place with the other training weapons on the far bulkhead's storage rack. "Say what you wish to say, Lieutenant."

Moving to stand beside her, Koveq placed his own weapon on the rack. "You are conflicted. You are grateful that your son lives, and yet you feel that he, much like yourself, has had his honor taken from him through forces over which he has no control. You fear that he will be reduced to a mere servant of the Empire—fated to serve in obscurity, with no opportunity for advancement, commendation, reward, or respect."

Her jaw clenching as she listened to her trusted friend, Visla turned and punched the bulkhead. The force of the strike did nothing to damage the metal plating, of course, though she felt the satisfying jolt of pain in her hand even through the heavy leather glove designed to protect it. Still, the punch produced a dull echo in the wall, and she imagined the reverberation carrying through the entire skeleton of her ship. Then she laughed at the absurdity of such thinking.

You and I, we are both stubborn. We never buckle. We never surrender.

While this old bucket might be well beyond its prime, the *I.K.S. Qo'Daqh* still retained some measure of mettle and pride. The D5-class battle cruiser was a relic, an obsolete deathtrap that should have been consigned to scrap a generation before Visla even was born, but it possessed a history filled with both glory and shame. The latter, of course, was all that mattered, along with the dishonor brought to it and the Klingon Empire in a battle fought and lost decades earlier. Like the battle, the commander of that ill-fated campaign, Visla's grandfather, had been all but erased from official records, and no one she knew had spoken aloud of that ignominious day. He had never spoken of it, preferring to shoulder the burden of humiliation in silence until the end of his life.

Under almost any other circumstances, the *Qo'Daqh* would have been destroyed, but someone somewhere decided that it retained some small portion of value. As those who had crewed it were consigned to disgrace, so too was this vessel damned in similar fashion. It was forever barred from performing anything save the most menial of tasks, let alone taking any action that might see its honor and legacy restored. Anyone sent to serve aboard it did so knowing that the Empire held them in the lowest regard, and that was especially true of the Klingon condemned to its captain's chair. It was to be Visla's punishment for having the temerity to be born into a house that had dishonored the Empire.

"My son was already doomed to follow me down the path of disgrace," she said, moving from the weapons rack to where she had left a coarse canvas towel lying on the nearby bench. "It was his misfortune to have me as his mother. His shame is only compounded now."

Visla had not slept since receiving word the previous evening that the *I.K.S. HoS'leth*, the cruiser to which her son, K'tovel, was assigned, had been lost in battle against a Romulan ship near the planet Centaurus. The location of the battle was interesting, given that peace talks had been under way between envoys from the Federation and the Klingon Empire. The *HoS'leth*, under the command of a renowned Klingon general, Kovor, had fought the Romulan vessel with the unlikely assistance of a Federation starship, the *U.S.S. Enterprise*. Details of the encounter remained unreported, though Prang, the Klingon attaché assigned to Councillor Gorkon during the peace talks on Centaurus, had told Visla that the confrontation was an outgrowth of some important discovery on Usilde, a remote world in the Libros star system. Prang had not offered any other information, leaving Visla to speculate that whatever had been found on that planet, it obviously was of great interest to the Romulans as well as the Klingons and the Federation.

Further, someone had deemed that discovery to be of sufficient value to spur General Kovor to ally himself with the captain of the Federation ship, James Kirk. Visla had found this hard to believe, considering what she had read of the Earther's recent engagements with other Klingon vessels. Those encounters had earned him scorn as well as grudging respect within the High Command. Numerous ship commanders had already made clear their desire to engage the human captain in combat, to see if the reports of his tactical prowess and guile were true. For her part, Visla suspected the accounts had been embellished to mitigate the incompetence of the Klingons who had suffered defeat at Kirk's hands.

As for the *HoS'leth*, all Visla knew at this point was that a group of survivors from the destroyed cruiser awaited pickup on the planet Centaurus, and that K'tovel was among them. How her son and his shipmates had evaded their vessel's destruction during the battle also was a question that would remain unanswered until the *Qo'Daqh* arrived to retrieve them. Visla was already anticipating the reaction she would receive from the Klingon High Command when it was learned that K'tovel was among the *HoS'leth* survivors.

More dishonor upon our house.

"I have read the report," said Koveq. "Though it lacks detail, it is obvious that the Starfleet captain acted without regard for our traditions. The *HoS'leth* crew, including your son, were prepared to die with their vessel, but were robbed of that prize. This should be taken into account when passing judgment upon the survivors."

Wiping her face with her towel, Visla scowled. "And how likely is that to happen?" She shook her head. "No. The High Command has never squandered an opportunity to remind my family of its place. They will not do so here, and the insult is only compounded with me being sent to retrieve them. It is an endless cycle, Koveq, and one from which there is no escape." Pausing, she regarded him for a moment. "How is it that you don't allow your feelings to spill forth? You have also had your honor stripped away. Does it not anger you?"

"My dishonor is by my own hand, Commander." The weapons officer stared at the metal deck plating. "I hesitated in battle. It was my first time facing an enemy, and one might look to youth and inexperience as an explanation, but the simple fact was that I was afraid. That fear kept me from acting, and that failure resulted in the death of two warriors. I live with that knowledge, and with each new day I try to be a better warrior than I was the day before, but I know that I can never atone for that mistake. All I can do is work to ensure it never happens again."

Visla nodded. Like her and Koveq, every member of the *Qo'Daqh*'s crew had such a story, some failing or shortcoming that was viewed as having brought discredit to the Empire. There were other ships just like this one, filled with castoffs and rejects who ultimately possessed but one purpose: die so that other warriors, better and more honorable, might live to fight another day.

We shall see about that.

"You and I are of similar mind, my friend," she said. "I

have no concerns over restoring my own personal honor, as doing so is not within my control. However, that does not free us from our duty as warriors, and if that means correcting an insult directed against the Empire, then that is what we should do."

Koveq eyed her with confusion. "I do not understand, Commander."

The intercom panel near the training room's entrance emitted a series of beeps before a deep male voice said through the panel's speaker, *"Bridge to Commander Visla."*

Smiling at her trusted friend, Visla said, "You will understand in due course, Lieutenant." She gestured for Koveq to follow her to the communications panel, and she pressed the unit's activation control. "This is Visla."

"I apologize for interrupting your personal exercise period, Commander," said Woveth, the Qo'Daqh's first officer, *"but we have received a subspace message from the Klingon High Command. They are demanding to know why you have not acknowledged our orders to set course for Centaurus."*

Visla exchanged a glance with Koveq, whose brow again had furrowed.

"That is because we are not going to Centaurus, Lieutenant," she said. "Plot a course for the Libros system and engage at maximum speed. Once we are under way, notify me with our time of arrival."

A pause was Woveth's initial response, and Visla thought she could hear him breathing through the open channel. Then the first officer said, *"Commander, I do not understand. Did I fail to note a change in our orders?"*

"No, Lieutenant. This is at my discretion, and I accept full responsibility. We will discuss it in detail when I return to the bridge. For now, execute the course change."

The first officer, obviously confused, nevertheless offered no resistance. *"Understood, Commander. Plotting the new course."*

"Excellent." Visla pressed the panel control to sever the communication.

"Commander?" Koveq was making no effort to mask his skepticism. "An unauthorized deviation of our course will not go unnoticed by High Command."

Visla nodded. "Quite true. My hope is that they will not notice our attempt to redeem the *HoS'leth* crew and restore the honor taken from them."

"The crew." Koveq's eyes narrowed. "Including your son."

"Yes, including my son." Visla turned to face her weapons officer. "Do I have your loyalty, Lieutenant?"

Koveq nodded. "Always, and without question, Commander."

"Good."

Feeling the all but imperceptible tremor in the deck plates beneath her feet that signified the *Qo'Daqh* was increasing speed and drawing more power from its engines, Visla allowed herself a smile of satisfaction. She, her misfit crew, and her dilapidated vessel were going to seize back for the Empire and the *HoS'leth* that which had been taken from them by one foolhardy Earther.

James Kirk would pay for his insolence.

Two

First the lights flickered. Then the artificial gravity wavered just enough to throw Kirk off his stride. He reached for the nearby bulkhead just as the omnipresent drone of the *Enterprise*'s warp engines changed. Even with inertial damping systems, Kirk still felt himself just for the briefest of moments pulled toward the front of the ship. The sensation faded in the same abrupt manner it had been conjured, its only lingering effect a slight shifting in his stomach.

Not alone in the corridor on deck five, Kirk exchanged confused looks with the dozen or so crewmembers visible in this stretch of curved passageway. He was just moving toward an intercom panel when the system's whistle filled the air, followed by the voice of the *Enterprise*'s first officer, Commander Spock.

"Bridge to all personnel. The ship has unexpectedly dropped out of warp. Engineering is already assessing the situation. All damage control teams, submit updated reports to your department heads. Stand by for further instructions."

Kirk let him finish before thumbing the companel's switch. "Kirk here. What happened, Spock?"

"Mister Scott reports continued problems with the warp drive, sir." As always, the Vulcan's speech and tone were formal as he conveyed information. *"He has also reiterated his advisory with respect to other damaged systems. Repairs in those areas will be delayed while he addresses the warp engines."*

Releasing a sigh, Kirk reached up to rub the bridge of

his nose. It had been less than twelve hours since the *Enterprise* had taken a pounding at the hands of a Romulan warship, and Commander Scott and his team of engineers had spent almost every minute since then attempting to heal the starship's various wounds. First and foremost, the *Enterprise*'s warp drive had suffered thanks to the protracted battle, along with the ship's deflector shield generators and a host of other, smaller yet still important systems that had experienced overloads and burnouts thanks to the Romulan vessel's disruptor weapons. Even a gifted magician like Montgomery Scott had found himself hard-pressed to accomplish all of the needed repairs.

"What's our present position?" asked Kirk.

Spock replied, *"We are still traveling at full impulse power, maintaining course for the Libros system."*

Sensing what was coming, Kirk said, "You can spare me the calculations for how long it'll take us to reach Usilde at our present speed."

"Very well."

There was a pause, and Kirk imagined he could see his first officer standing at his station on the *Enterprise* bridge, his right eyebrow cocked as he pondered being denied a chance to offer up his computation in exacting detail. The silence stretched to the point that Kirk began to regret his attempt at levity. While his friend was willing on most occasions to play along with his captain's very human tendency toward jocularity, the stresses of recent events certainly must be weighing on him. Worrying about his father, Sarek, and his former shipmate Captain Una—who both remained trapped in the mysterious parallel universe that connected to their own thanks to a wondrous technology discovered on the planet Usilde—had to be wearing on the Vulcan, though no one but his closest friends would even notice the strain. Spock, as always, carried himself with an all but unflappable composure, but Kirk had known him long enough to see tiny cracks forming in his friend's armor.

"I'm sorry, Spock. I was only trying to . . . I'm sorry."

"The effort is neither unnoticed nor unappreciated, sir." Such a response, Kirk knew, carried a risk of being perceived as overly emotional and perhaps even a concession to his human half. That the first officer had offered it was an indicator of the emotional strain he was experiencing, regardless of his Vulcan control. *"Shall I have Mister Scott contact you with a revised repair estimate?"*

"No. I think I'll go down to engineering and get a look for myself."

"Acknowledged. Spock out."

Severing the communication, Kirk sighed again. The thought of sitting on the bridge staring at distant stars as the *Enterprise* limped through the interstellar void held no appeal for him. Likewise, he had had no interest in waiting for updated repair estimates, and he had no intention of trapping himself behind his desk and dealing with reports or the other administrative debris that came with being a starship captain. Besides, if he did that, then he would be forced to answer what he imagined were several communiqués from Starfleet Command wanting to know just what the hell he thought he was doing. After all, he had set the *Enterprise* on course for the Libros system from Centaurus without first receiving authorization. He had acted within regulations, notifying his superiors of his intentions and taking advantage of the discretion and latitude Starfleet granted its ship commanders with respect to any number of decisions. Still, heading into a potential interstellar incident did not typically fall within those parameters.

Main engineering was chaos.

Standing in the open doorway leading into the spacious chamber that was the heart of his ship, Kirk surveyed the scene before him. Wall panels lay about the deck, along with tools and components or pieces of larger components. Men and women in Starfleet uniforms and jumpsuits were climbing ladders, crawling into access conduits, pulling the innards out of consoles, or simply sitting in the middle of the floor while working on some piece of equipment. Kirk could not remember ever seeing engineering in such a state of disorder.

Montgomery Scott stood at the center of the maelstrom, guiding the efforts of all those around him. The chief engineer's arms waved in different directions, pointing subordinates to this control panel or that access opening or to retrieve a particular tool. Behind him and beyond the protective grille separating the engine room's main floor from the massive plasma conduits that fed energy to the starship's warp nacelles, it was dark and lifeless. Normally the plant pulsed with restrained power, but now all was still, feeling to Kirk as though the ship had fallen into a state of deep slumber.

"Damn," he said, trying to take it all in.

Noticing his captain's presence, Scott offered one last instruction to a waiting junior engineer before stepping away from the bedlam unfolding around him and moved toward Kirk.

"Captain, I didn't know you'd be paying us a visit."

"My ship's not working, Scotty," replied Kirk as he stepped farther into the room.

The engineer's mouth tightened, and he nodded. "Aye,

sir, it's a bit of a mess at the moment, but we're on top of it. I expect to have warp drive back within the hour."

Crossing the main work area, they walked past the large dual matter-antimatter integrators. Kirk noted that access panels had been removed from both of the oversized components and junior engineers were working in and around them. A pair of legs was visible on the deck near one of the integrators, their owner lying on his or her stomach and stretching to reach something inside the crawlspace. As the two men drew closer to the protective grille, Scott gestured toward the dark, inert plasma conduits.

"It'll require a cold restart, of course, and once that's done, if you could go easy on the girl for a bit, I'd be grateful."

Kirk frowned. "I can't promise anything, Scotty. I don't know what we're going to be up against once we reach Usilde. We can't afford delays. The Klingons certainly aren't waiting around. Every minute we're out here, their people on Usilde are working to figure out the Jatohr citadel."

"Aye, I understand." Scott looked about the cavernous room that was his realm. "I can't say I'm happy with the current situation, sir. Some of the repairs we need are better suited to a starbase or even a dry dock."

"We have to play the cards we're dealt." Though perhaps not to the same exacting level of detail as his chief engineer, Kirk was still aware of the issues plaguing his ship. The skirmish with the Romulan vessel near Centaurus had been brief yet costly, as much from direct damage inflicted by the enemy ship as the evasive tactics he had been forced to employ. The list of damaged or compromised systems had been as long as it was varied, and it was in all honesty a true miracle that Montgomery Scott and his team of engineers had held the *Enterprise* together during the pitched battle. Now Kirk was asking Scott and his people to perform yet another miracle and heal the wounded starship before he was forced to take it once again into harm's way.

"Aside from the warp drive," said Kirk, "what's the status with the rest of the repairs?'"

"I've got teams crawling through every Jefferies tube and maintenance shaft on the ship, sir. I've ordered my people to triple-check every system even if no damage was reported, just to be sure." Scott reached up and wiped his forehead with his shirt sleeve. "We'll do everything we can to make her shipshape, Captain. We'll need to put in to a starbase once all this is over."

"I promise. In the meantime, coordinate with Spock and pull people from wherever you can find them to pitch in and help."

Scott forced a smile. "Already doing that, sir." He gestured toward the center of the room and the hive of activity taking place around them. "Now, if you'll pardon me, sir, I'd like to get back to it."

"Don't let me keep you, Scotty." Kirk eyed the room and the engineers. "Tell your people I appreciate their hard work."

"Aye, sir. That I will."

The engineer took his leave and returned to the numerous other demands on his attention, making his way toward one of his subordinates and the console on which the younger man was working. Kirk watched their exchange for a few more seconds before turning and heading for the exit, knowing the group of talented specialists would accomplish more if their captain chose not to hover over them.

Get out of their way and let them get back to work.

Three

Black smoke swirled with tan sand and light dust, billowing toward her. The cloud towered above her, a murky curtain steadily shrouding the distinctive features of New Athens University. Students and faculty members walked about, on their way across the campus with its fincly tended landscaping and structures of utilitarian design, seemingly oblivious to what was coming to engulf them.

Amanda Grayson watched the oddly familiar cloud advance.

Thickening tendrils loomed over her, extending from the drab cloud and blotting out the clear blue sky. Reaching out, Amanda plunged her bare hand into the cloud, staring as the dust wafted up her arm like an unwelcome glove, though she did not move. As the dense, undulating mass moved to envelop her, she saw none of its residue upon her, and neither did she feel grit against her flesh. Each breath came with no difficulty, and she let the cloud's opacity overtake her.

Then there was nothing but silence and diffuse brown light, and Amanda brought her outstretched arm to her side. Despite the fact that she stood within it, the cloud existed apart from her. She sensed nothing but the dim illumination around her. Then she closed her eyes, closing herself off even from that.

My wife.

Faint words, but hearing them shocked her enough to open her eyes. The cloud remained around her without physical effect. Amanda stood still, holding her breath and straining to hear the voice—or anything else—again. Had she imagined it? She took a step forward, perceiving the action on an intellectual level though nothing about her surroundings changed. The cloud's presence swallowed any evidence of her movement. Another step forward offered no further clues.

"Sarek?"

My wife.

A bit louder this time, just enough to convince Amanda that the voice was no wishful manufacture or trick of the wind. Those were words.

His words.

Hope flaring in her heart, Amanda stepped forward yet again, sensing herself flailing her arms though she realized now that neither they nor the rest of her body was visible. There was only the cloud. Her attempt to dissipate it or move beyond it was fruitless. Frustration mounting, Amanda willed her arms straight out in front of her and ran. She sensed her feet moving, with speed and grace across unseen ground, and she hurtled herself in a direction she had no way of determining.

"Sarek! Where are you?"

Gulping in deep breaths of air that was free of dust, Amanda ran. Had she strayed from her course, wherever it was the voice was leading her? Any attempt to turn or change direction was met with more of the unremitting cloud swirling around her.

"Sarek! I'm here!"

My wife.

Helplessness and futility were overwhelming her, and

Amanda dropped to the ground. Flogging the dirt beneath her hands, she cried. She drew a breath to scream—and caught herself before it left her lungs.

"No," she said. "I cannot lose control. Sarek will find me."

Pushing herself to a sitting position, Amanda rested on the ground, drawing her legs underneath her. She forced herself to slow her breathing and turn her mind inward, just as her husband had instructed uncounted times. Rather than struggling to interpret any distinguishing shapes in the light, she unfocused her gaze and her mind.

And then she noticed it.

All around her, the dull browns of dust were giving way to warmer shades of blue and violet, cutting through the drab light and its feeble attempts to pierce the cloud. There was a sensation of relief, but Amanda did her best to suppress the feeling. She maintained her inward awareness, refusing to let the omnipresent cloud overwhelm her. Slowly and uniformly, the cloud retreated from her as if she were newly encapsulated in an expanding dome of clarity. She first was able to see her whole body, then, as the cloud retreated from the space surrounding her body, she could see her full stride as she walked. While the ground offered no characteristics to confirm she was moving, Amanda grew in confidence that she now was gaining dominance over this state of being. She halted and let the dome expand from her even more, growing quickly to the size of a room, then a house, then a courtyard. It crept outward until at a distance it revealed a lone motionless figure clad in black robes. The figure raised one hand, beckoning to her. She gasped, sure of whom she had just seen.

"Sarek!"

Amanda jerked herself awake, her breaths coming fast and shallow as she sat up in her bed. It took her a moment to recall that she was not in her bedroom in the home she shared with her husband on Vulcan. Instead of familiar furnishings, mementos, and other decorations, she saw plain gray bulkheads and the divider screen separating the sleeping area from the sitting room in her guest quarters. She placed a hand over her heart, feeling its rapid beats already beginning to slow, and she forced herself to regain control of her breathing.

Reclining once more on the bed, Amanda closed her eyes and searched her memory for that last image she could recall from her vivid dream. The vision of Sarek, his dark robes contrasting against the drab cloud in which he stood, teased her, but she could not bring the image into full focus. On an intellectual level, she realized the dream was an involuntary mashing of random elements pulled from her subconscious, but her heart told her there was more here.

Much more.

She had not merely dreamed about her husband; she had sensed him, in that way only she could do, thanks to the unique, intimate bond they shared. Was Sarek alive? Had he somehow managed to reach across the odd barrier or void separating him from this universe, as Spock had explained? As quickly as the thoughts conjured themselves, Amanda felt doubt encroaching upon them. Perhaps she was suffering some odd side effect from the sedatives given to her by Doctor McCoy. She would have to speak with him.

Giving up on the attempt to recall her dream imagery,

Amanda rose from the bed and made her way from the sleeping area. Other than the steady thrum of the *Enterprise*'s powerful impulse engines, the room was silent, and for the first time, she began to regret the solitude she had requested.

As though sensing her thoughts, her room's door chime beeped for attention.

"Come in," Amanda called out, and the door slid aside to reveal Doctor Leonard McCoy. He was dressed in a less formal, short-sleeved version of the standard Starfleet tunic and had brought a tricorder with him.

"Mrs. Sarek," said the ship's chief medical officer, by way of greeting.

Offering a smile, Amanda replied, "Hello, Doctor. Is this a house call?" McCoy's expression brightened, but only somewhat, and Amanda could sense that the doctor was putting on a polite front.

"I thought I should stop by and see how you were feeling. Yammering into an intercom panel is a little impersonal for me. I hope I'm not disturbing you."

Amanda stepped back from the door, gesturing for McCoy to enter. "Not at all. I can't sleep."

Stepping into the room, the doctor frowned. "Having trouble? I can prescribe something else."

"No, that won't be necessary. In fact, I think I'll be fine from now on without any extra help." She motioned for him to take one of the chairs positioned around a small table in her room's sitting area. "I should probably get dressed, instead of lounging around in my pajamas," she said, her other hand toying with the folds of her sleeping robe.

McCoy's grin widened as he moved to stand next to the proffered chair. "To be honest, when it comes to Vulcan fashion, I can't tell the difference between a ceremonial robe and a bathrobe." Then his expression changed. "That's not to say you don't look presentable, ma'am. Forgive my manners."

The comment made her chuckle. It was an indulgence she often declined at home, but did allow herself when in the company of her fellow humans.

"If it's any consolation, I can't tell the difference most of the time either."

For the first time, McCoy seemed to set aside his forced facade and allowed himself a genuine laugh. After a moment, he said, "Wow, I needed that. Thank you, Lady Amanda."

"Please, just Amanda. I try not to stand on formality unless circumstances absolutely require it." Realizing that McCoy's gentlemanly nature would keep him standing until she took a seat, she moved to the chair opposite him and lowered herself into it.

"Only if you call me Leonard," replied the doctor. He sat in the chair opposite hers, placing the tricorder in his lap.

Amanda nodded. "It's a deal."

"How are you feeling?"

She paused a moment to consider the question. Her cuts and abrasions had been treated and healed, and the fractured rib, arm, and leg she had suffered were now knit. There was no longer even residual pain from those injuries. The only remaining physical evidence of the wounds she had suffered during the furious Romulan attack at New Athens University were singed wisps of her silvery hair and a dull ache from the array of bruises she had endured. Even that was fading, and she had declined further medication for that discomfort.

What did remain, however, were her memories.

"I know that look," said McCoy. "It's pretty common with people who've been subjected to a traumatic experience like you saw on Centaurus."

"It was certainly a first for me." Each shard of recollection stabbed at her psyche, delivering shocks of pain and realization that jarred and disoriented her with the same force as the strafing runs to which she and so many others had been subjected during the attack. The terror had gripped her and refused to let go, punctuated by repeated plasma blasts with enough force to rip the breath from her lungs even as her body was peppered with shrapnel and stone. The sounds of shattering glass, tortured metal, and the screams of the injured rang in her ears and in her mind. Closing her eyes did nothing to keep away images of billowing clouds of debris as buildings collapsed upon themselves, and neither did it obscure the bodies that had been strewn about, broken and bleeding. Included among those victims had been her beloved husband, Sarek, who had risked his life to rescue a delegation of Klingon ambassadors from a university dormitory moments before it was reduced to rubble.

And then he was taken from me.

"Amanda?" prompted McCoy.

Clearing her throat, she said, "I can still hear and see everything. I remember being next to Sarek, looking around to see whether it was help or another attack that was coming." She recalled how, despite his own injuries, he had remained stoic and strong in the finest Vulcan tradition as he saw to her. Then he had yielded to unconsciousness. Even her throat seemed to ache, parched from the dust and from her repeated calls for assistance. She still saw Joanna McCoy, who had come to help her with Sarek, mere moments before the searing white light had appeared from nowhere, enveloping her husband and the young woman as though wiping them both from existence.

"When I saw Sarek and your daughter disappear," said Amanda, "I was overwhelmed. The idea that he'd been taken from me without warning was too much to bear." She had fainted, a response for which she now was grateful. So much of her remaining time on Centaurus was a blur to her, including the initial treatment of her wounds by triage teams. One memory to which she had clung was that of seeing Spock walk toward her as he emerged from the surrounding crowd of those injured and providing care. In that moment, she released all of the shock, grief, pain, and despair welling within her in an unfettered display of raw emotion. Spock had weathered the outburst in a manner that would have made his father proud, assuming Sarek ever admitted to such a thing, but it was her son's next words, so simple and yet so powerful, that had given her renewed hope.

Sarek might yet live, Mother.

Amanda seized the words, replaying them over and over in her mind. Spock had told her that Sarek and Joanna, along with numerous other people, had been subjected to the same phenomenon and were not dead. Instead, they had been transported into a separate, parallel universe. Whether they could be retrieved was unknown, but the *Enterprise* was committed to that goal. Since the starship's departure from Centaurus, her son and other members of the crew had been working tirelessly toward finding a way to rescue her husband and the others. All Amanda could do now was wait and hope.

"How are you handling all of this, Leonard?"

As though caught off guard by her question, McCoy

shifted in his seat. After a moment, he replied, "To be honest with you, not as well as your son. There are times when I wish I could channel some of that Vulcan emotional control. In my line of work, it'd sure come in handy."

Once more, Amanda laughed. "Spock's told me that you can become quite . . . passionate when it comes to practicing medicine."

McCoy frowned. "Spock talks to you about me?"

"Occasionally, during our infrequent subspace messages. I have a tendency to pry, and every once in a while he throws me a small morsel of information so that I'll leave him alone." Adjusting her position in her chair, Amanda said, "He usually settles for telling me a little about his crewmates, rather than talking about his work. I actually like that, since I like to hear about who's out here with him. It's nice to know that he has such good friends who care for him. When you first were serving together, he told me a bit about you."

"I'm afraid to ask what he said."

With a sly smile, Amanda replied, "Did you know he had to consult the ship's computer banks to look up the word *hobgoblin*?"

Blanching, McCoy shook his head, then offered a sheepish grin. "You'll have to forgive me. I can be a bit . . . enthusiastic with my word choices."

"So I've heard." Reaching across the table, Amanda put her hand on his forearm. "Don't worry about it. You certainly didn't offend him, and he knows that deep down, you don't really mean it. Besides, he heard quite a bit worse growing up on Vulcan with a human mother."

"I can imagine," said McCoy, a sympathetic look crossing his features.

Amanda pulled back her hand. "However, those aren't

my stories to share. So, if you wouldn't mind keeping that to yourself, I'd appreciate it."

"Fair enough." Holding up his tricorder, he said, "Anyway, since I came here to see how you're doing, I should probably get on with it."

Extracting a small scanner from the tricorder's storage compartment, the doctor rose from his chair and moved to stand next to her. Both devices hummed and whined as he waved the scanner over her arm, then her leg, and finally her torso.

"You're sure you're feeling all right?"

Amanda mulled over her response. On Vulcan, such questions were not routinely asked by Vulcan physicians, including those versed in the treatment of humans. However, she recalled from her previous visit to the *Enterprise*, during her husband's heart difficulties, that McCoy preferred a more informal, sometimes holistic approach to diagnosing his patients. Rather than relying on the wondrous, even miraculous devices that assisted him, he supplemented their findings and actions with old-fashioned observations of mind and body and—on occasion—spirit.

"I'm feeling much better, actually. You and your staff have taken wonderful care of me."

McCoy asked her to take a series of deep breaths, and as she did so he continued waving the scanner along her left side where her rib had been injured.

"Any pain?" he asked.

"Nothing I can't manage."

"Good." Nodding in apparent satisfaction, McCoy deactivated the scanner and returned it to its compartment in the tricorder. "You took quite a beating."

"Physically, yes," Amanda said. "Emotionally, I believe we both have."

His gaze lingering on his tricorder, McCoy cleared his throat. "Well, I can't argue that."

"Your daughter, Joanna. She seems like a remarkable woman." Amanda had learned the identity of the woman from Nurse Chapel while undergoing final treatment in the *Enterprise*'s sickbay. Though she had been cared for by doctors on Centaurus, the damage to the New Athens hospital had prompted Doctor McCoy to order her transported to the *Enterprise*. This was more than acceptable to her, as she had already decided that she could not wait there while her son and his shipmates set off for parts unknown in a desperate bid to rescue Sarek and the others. She wanted to be on the *Enterprise* if and when that miracle occurred. As for Joanna McCoy, it was only upon learning of her connection to the ship's chief medical officer that Amanda realized why the doctor had seemed so tense and distracted in those first hours after the ship's departure from Centaurus.

McCoy nodded. "She's the one thing I'm most proud of; the one thing I can say without doubt that I got right."

"She's just like you," Amanda said, motioning for him to retake his seat. "Your passion, your desire to help others regardless of the risk. I watched her on Centaurus. She didn't hesitate, not for an instant, and I'm absolutely certain it's because of her that I'm alive. Me, and Sarek . . . wherever he is."

McCoy forced a smile. "Thank you. That's kind of you to say."

"You believe they're alive, don't you?"

"I'm . . . I'm not sure."

Again, Amanda laid her hand on his arm. "I am. I believe it with all my heart. Just as I believe that your daughter is there, with my husband, caring for him just as she cared for me."

Moving his arm, McCoy grasped her hand in his. "I'll borrow a little of that hope, if you don't mind, and I'm sure Joanna's just as grateful to have your husband as he is for her."

Amanda smiled. "Gratitude? Remember who we're talking about. Let's settle for his acknowledgment of her competent performance as a nurse."

Despite what had to be heavy thoughts troubling him, McCoy's smile returned. "Right. How silly of me." He squeezed her hand once before releasing it. "I feel a little better now, thanks to you."

She nodded in understanding. For the first time since boarding the *Enterprise*, she felt real hope that all would work out for the best.

"No. Thank you, Leonard."

Four

He had been sitting at his desk less than a half hour, and already Kirk felt his eyes beginning to glaze over. If he were to list the various aspects of his duties that he would do away with given the chance, reviewing status reports of any sort would have to be his top choice.

Status reports from the *Enterprise*'s department heads were necessary, of course, as Kirk took a keen interest in every aspect of his ship and crew. Though he might not understand every facet of every piece of equipment or task undertaken, it was critical that he not shirk his responsibility to be engaged to the maximum possible extent. He relied on the expert opinions of his senior staff and other crew members to help fill the gaps in his knowledge, but he did not allow that to be a substitute for actual engagement with the people under his command.

Having dispensed with those reports, he now was reviewing the latest message traffic from Starfleet Command. The constant stream of communiqués relayed from headquarters could not be avoided, and while being mindful that the information such reports contained was important, it remained an often mind-numbing process. Not for the first time, Kirk found himself stealing glances at his bed. It was a tempting thought, he conceded. He had not slept much over the past couple of days due to the stress of the *Enterprise*'s current situation and the repairs Mister Scott and his engineers were continuing to address.

You can sleep later.

For now, there were the reports and his coffee. Kirk thanked whatever deity who might be listening that the food slot in his quarters was back up and running, providing him constant access to that marvelous elixir. Drinking from his second cup since sitting down, Kirk sighed and returned his attention to the reports and computer data cards littering his desk.

Salvation came in the form of his door chime, and it was with more than slight relief that Kirk said, "Come in."

The single door slid aside to reveal McCoy, who stood in the corridor with arms crossed. Kirk noted a tricorder slung over his friend's left shoulder.

"Are they fixing this ship, or just building us another one?" said McCoy.

"Bones," said Kirk, smiling in greeting. "What can I do for you?" It was the first time he had seen his friend since informing him and the rest of the ship's senior staff that they would be returning to the Libros system.

"I got tired of looking at the walls of my office and thought I'd take a walk." The doctor stepped into the room and allowed the door to close behind him. "Then the ship started acting up, and I got curious. Took a peek in engineering." He shook his head. "Scotty's got his boys running every which way."

Unlike many medical and science professionals assigned to starships that Kirk had encountered over the years, the *Enterprise*'s chief medical officer was not the sort to lock himself in sickbay or a lab and pretend the rest of the universe did not exist. With no restrictions preventing him from accessing any part of the ship, he preferred to wander the *Enterprise* corridors when time permitted such opportunities, interacting with the crew who called the vessel home. Assessing their mental and physical well-being in this way was—at least in the doctor's opinion—far more helpful than within the more formal atmosphere of an examination room.

Today, however, Kirk suspected his friend was roving about because it aided his own mental health.

"How are you holding up?" he asked, waving his friend to the chair on the other side of his desk.

Unlimbering his tricorder, McCoy placed the device on the desk before dropping into the seat. "All things considered? I'll get by. It's the not knowing part that eats at me."

It was McCoy's nature to be anxious about the welfare of anyone, and that compassion had been tested on numerous occasions just in the time he had served aboard the *Enterprise*. Unlike those previous missions, even those that had brought with them great peril to the ship, its crew, and the handful of shipmates he counted as close friends, this situation was far more personal. His daughter, Joanna—along with Ambassador Sarek as well as Councillor Gorkon of the Klingon High Council and the commander of a Klingon battle cruiser, General Kovor—was caught up in the latest chapter of a mystery that had begun nearly two decades ago.

The current situation had been put into motion weeks earlier, with an unusual and unexpected visit to the *Enterprise* by a former member of its crew, Captain Una. Her ties to the starship dated back to its earliest missions under its first commanding officer, Robert April, for whom Una had served as a junior lieutenant. After April was succeeded by Christopher Pike, she received a promotion in rank and became the ship's first officer. Later, after Pike's transfer of the *Enterprise* to Kirk, Una eventually received her own promotion to captain, as well as her own command, the *U.S.S. Yorktown*, her current assignment. Despite the years that had passed, it was her bond with the *Enterprise* and both of its previous captains that had brought her back, with a most unusual purpose.

Una had taken from Kirk's quarters an alien artifact entrusted to him by Christopher Pike, and to Pike from April. The artifact, the Transfer Key, was the central piece of a much larger and far more powerful piece of technology. Eljor, an alien scientist, had devised a "transfer-field generator" for the purpose of moving his people, the Jatohr, to this universe from their own, which was in its death throes. That effort had been focused on Usilde, a planet in the Libros system to which the *Enterprise* currently was headed.

"I can't believe you and Spock kept this secret to yourselves all this time," McCoy said. "I know there are things you don't always tell me, for one reason or another, because it's classified or whatever, but after everything we've been through, it's hard to believe you'd still be carrying something like this around."

Kirk replied, "It wasn't personal, Bones. This is just something that's been handed down, from captain to captain. If all had gone according to plan, I'd have passed the damned thing to the next captain and gone on my merry way."

The Key and its origins had been discovered by Captain April during the *Enterprise*'s original visit to Usilde. Eljor's transfer-field generator had taken the form of an immense construct the Jatohr called "the citadel," which was the landing point for Jatohr making the transition between universes. Though Eljor's reasons for creating the device were well intentioned, the first Jatohr to make the transfer from their own universe had immediately taken to colonizing the planet and beginning the lengthy process of terraforming it to suit their own needs. This had come at great cost to the world's existing ecosystem as well as its indigenous inhabitants, which included a sentient species, the Usildar. Further, the planet was to serve as a beachhead, a foothold in this universe from which the Jatohr could expand to other systems and perhaps inflict similar damage to other worlds.

Along with the immediate danger the Jatohr posed to the Usildar, the larger threat the transfer-field generator represented in both universes had compelled April and his crew to assist Eljor in returning his own people to the realm from which they had come. Eljor had sacrificed his own life, entrusting to April the Transfer Key, without which the transfer-field generator could not function. The doorway between universes would remain sealed, so long as the Key was kept safe. Eljor wanted to prevent the Key and the generator from being used for further exploitive or destructive purposes, and April had promised to uphold the Jatohr scientist's final wishes.

To that end, the captain had held on to the Key, rather than surrendering it to Starfleet's research and development branches for study, thereby protecting it from possibly falling into the wrong hands. April stored the Key in a sealed compartment in his own cabin aboard the *Enterprise*, and upon his transfer from the ship, it had become Pike's secret. Both Pike and Una would continue to safeguard the Key and its secrets until it became Kirk and Spock's turn. In time, Kirk had expected he would turn over the Key to whoever followed in his footsteps as the next *Enterprise* captain.

"Do you think Joanna and Sarek may have found

Captain Una?" asked McCoy. "I keep wondering what the odds of that might be."

"There's no way to know, Bones, but if there's any consistency to how the Transfer Key operates, they may well have all ended up in the same place." Kirk had no evidence to support his theory. Instead, he was relying on his gut and no small amount of faith. Even Spock, following his own renewed examination of the alien device, had been unable to provide an answer in this regard. "Spock's still trying to find some answers. If anybody can figure out how that thing works, it's him."

McCoy grunted. "I know. Just don't tell him I said that, all right?"

"Your secret's safe with me." Kirk could not help a small smile, as he was happy to see his friend's spirits lift even the smallest bit. "Besides, he has just about the same stake in getting to the bottom of this as you do."

"Maybe even a bit more," replied the doctor. "After all, Una's almost like family to Spock. For a while, she might have been closer to him than Sarek. At least before he and Spock buried the hatchet."

Captain Una's theft of the Transfer Key from Kirk's quarters and her subsequent flight from the *Enterprise* had all been motivated by personal guilt. During their initial survey of the planet eighteen years earlier, Captain April and his crew, including Lieutenant Una, had discovered that the Transfer Key could also be used to remove individuals and small groups from this universe and send them to the Jatohr's home universe. Una's landing party, and later four members of the *Enterprise*'s bridge crew, were targeted. At the time, there was no way to know if they had survived the transition or if they could be retrieved. From that day forward, Una, who had narrowly escaped the fate that befell her landing party, felt responsible for what happened to her shipmates, whether they were dead or, at the very least, beyond any hope of rescue.

She might well have shouldered that burden for the rest of her days, but then she learned about the *Enterprise*'s encounter with a peculiar ion storm and the transporting of Kirk—along with McCoy, Montgomery Scott, and Lieutenant Uhura—into a parallel universe that in many ways mirrored their own. After reviewing Kirk's detailed accounting of that incident, Una realized that her friends might well have been subjected to a similar experience.

Armed with this information and after her stealing of the Transfer Key, it had not taken long to surmise that she was taking the Key back to Usilde. Complicating matters was the fact that in the intervening eighteen years, that sector of space had become a point of dispute between the Federation and the Klingon Empire. Tensions were high between the two powers, and any sort of incident might be enough to trigger an interstellar war. It also was arguable that Captain Una's actions had alerted the Klingons to the presence of the Jatohr citadel and exposed its advanced technology as something worth the Empire's interest. With the citadel and the transfer-field technology residing within the challenged region, it was paramount that neither Una nor the Transfer Key fall into Klingon hands. Kirk and the *Enterprise* had prevented that, but not before Una made the decision to transport herself into the Jatohr's universe in a bid to find and retrieve her long-lost crewmates. Supporting her plan, Kirk also agreed to her request for the *Enterprise* to return in sixty days with the Transfer Key and activate the generator, in the hopes of retrieving her and her friends from a predetermined location.

"I only wish Una would've just asked me for help," said Kirk. "She could've at least asked Spock, and he would've asked me. It's not like we're strangers to contravening Starfleet or going against orders to help a friend." Spock had taken that concept to an extreme a year previously, when he had elected to transport his former captain to Talos IV, the one planet to which Starfleet forbade travel upon penalty of death. The details of that incident had been classified, but Kirk knew that Spock's decision, no matter how contemptible it may have been toward Starfleet regulations, had been the correct one for Pike's well-being. Would the Vulcan hesitate to help Una, another former shipmate whom he respected? Not for a moment, and neither would Kirk, if only he had been asked.

"And if she had asked," said McCoy, "we might've avoided all that other trouble."

Despite the complications offered by a Klingon presence in the system and on the planet, Kirk had vowed to honor Una's request. Then the Key was stolen by a Romulan spy, Sadira, who had been disguised as a human, Lisa Bates, serving as Kirk's yeoman. Sadira had escaped with the Key to a Romulan vessel that had been trailing the *Enterprise* from Chippewa Prime. Because of this, Kirk felt that he had failed in his duty and betrayed the trust of Captains Pike and April.

The Key had resurfaced far sooner than he expected, during the peace negotiations between the Federation and the Klingon Empire on the planet Centaurus. Sadira had used the alien device to remove key members of both delegations, apparently transporting them into the Jatohr's universe and perhaps to the same place where Captain Una's shipmates had been banished. This was followed by the removal of Ambassador Sarek along with Joanna

McCoy. The revelation of the Transfer Key and the power it wielded had derailed the peace talks, bringing the quadrant that much closer to war as the Klingons accused the Federation of murdering their representative, Councillor Gorkon.

Though Kirk and the *Enterprise* were able to recover the Transfer Key following a pitched battle with Sadira and her Romulan warship, he was forced to reveal the truth of the Key and the transfer-field generator to the Klingons in order to prevent the Empire from seeking retribution for Gorkon's loss. Any pretense of civility had been swept away as the Klingons realized the awesome military applications for the Jatohr technology. Though the Klingons had already seized the Jatohr citadel, without the Key, their efforts to take advantage of the technology would be thwarted. Still, Kirk did not rule out the possibility of Klingon scientists eventually finding a way to engineer a suitable replacement for the missing component. Left with little choice, Kirk had ordered the *Enterprise* back to Usilde in the hopes of keeping the citadel out of Klingon hands and preventing all-out war with the Empire. Failing that, he hoped to rescue Captain Una, Joanna, Sarek, Gorkon, and everyone else trapped in the parallel universe.

That's not too much to ask, is it?

McCoy said, "I can't imagine Starfleet Command's very happy with you right now. Any word from them about your sudden change of plans?"

"That's putting it mildly." Kirk glanced to his computer terminal. He had reviewed the latest missives from Starfleet, demanding to know his intentions for returning to the Libros system. With Klingons orbiting Usilde and the planet still in dispute, the entire situation was a powder keg, and the *Enterprise* was the fuse. Things only grew more complicated after factoring in the Romulans and their intentions to sow chaos no matter what.

"They're not happy that I'm holding on to the Transfer Key," he said after a moment. "They understand why Usilde is important, and not just from a strategic standpoint with respect to the Jatohr technology. But we can't wait to save Captain Una and the others." He gestured toward the computer terminal. "One of the reports I read came from Starfleet Intelligence. It seems the Romulans are backing off, at least for now."

McCoy frowned. "Backing off?"

"Based on a report sent from an agent working deep undercover within the Romulan Senate, the praetor isn't very happy with how things turned out with Sadira." Kirk sighed. "Losing one of their ships in a very public and embarrassing way and having nothing to show for it isn't exactly what he had in mind."

"Maybe we should send him some flowers."

Kirk smiled. "Not a bad idea. Anyway, we know that sort of thing isn't how the Romulans like to do things. According to the agent's report, the Romulan government is taking a wait-and-see approach so far as Usilde is concerned, but they're obviously very interested in the Jatohr technology."

McCoy said, "Well, at least they'll be out of our hair for a little while. This situation is sticky enough with the Klingons looking over our shoulders." He shook his head. "Espionage and all that silliness isn't why I joined Starfleet, you know."

Turning in his chair, Kirk opened a small cabinet set into the low wall dividing the two rooms of his quarters and extracted a curved bottle and two glasses.

For the first time, a hint of McCoy's familiar humor showed in his eyes. "Are you buying me a drink, sailor?"

"You're not the only one with good prescriptions," said Kirk, pouring a healthy dose of Saurian brandy into both glasses before offering one to McCoy.

Leaning back in his chair, the doctor replied, "You're learning." He downed the brandy in one swallow, drawing a deep breath and closing his eyes. After a moment, he said, "Nope. I still feel like hell." He sighed. "I'm worried about her, Jim. I'm worried about all of them."

"So am I." Kirk leaned back in his chair. "We'll find them, Bones."

McCoy eyed him across the desk. "How can you be so sure?"

"Because the other option is to let them stay there, and I'm not going to let that happen while there's the slightest chance we can save them."

He hoped the words carried enough conviction to comfort his friend, but to Kirk they sounded hollow. Suppressing a sudden feeling of uncertainty, Kirk downed his own brandy.

They were alive. Kirk could feel it, but what could be happening to them in that other universe?

Five

Opening her eyes, Joanna McCoy was greeted by the twin suns of another world.

She flung her forearm across her face, attempting to block out the whiteness of the cloudless sky. Inhaling warm, dry air into her lungs, she coughed. Then she forced herself to take a second, slower breath, and this one hurt far less. After allowing her eyes to adjust to the bright light, she pulled her arm from her face and used her hands to push against the ground beneath, raising herself to a sitting position. Only then did she venture a second look at the strange environs in which she now found herself.

Nothing looked familiar. This was not Centaurus. Gone was the destruction wrought by the Romulan attack. In its place was nothing but a flat, desolate landscape. The ground itself was unremarkable, dry and salt-streaked, and the only visible terrain feature was what appeared to be a hazy, distant mountain range. Where was she, and how did she get here? The last thing Joanna recalled was the chaos of the attack. Like so many others, she had been rushing to help the numerous wounded people scattered around her. Then she remembered the odd sensation, washing over her body. What happened after that?

"Hello," said a voice from behind her.

Scrambling to her feet, Joanna spun toward the voice, and found herself staring at a middle-aged Vulcan male. "Hello," she blurted. As she scrutinized the Vulcan, whose dark robes stood in stark contrast to the plain's arid, colorless soil, she realized she recognized him. "I'm Joanna. Joanna McCoy. Do I know you?"

"I am Sarek of Vulcan. I have only just awakened myself."

Sarek. Joanna replayed the name in her mind. *I should know Sarek. We're supposed to be together. I think he . . . needs me for something. Why isn't my brain working?* "Ambassador Sarek, of course. Do you know where we are?"

"No," replied the Vulcan, "though this is not Centaurus."

Centaurus. The attack. Sarek. He was . . . wait . . .

"You're *hurt!*" Joanna started forward, extending her hands to assist him, then stopped herself when she realized that neither he nor even his clothing bore any evidence of the injuries she knew he had sustained. "Well, you *were* hurt."

"I appear uninjured. I assure you I am well, though I must confess that I am unable to explain why that is so."

"On Centaurus, you were hurt. I was treating you for internal bleeding." She reached up to wipe her forehead. "At least, I think I was?"

Snap out of it, Joanna. Think!

"You are correct," said Sarek. "However, I assure you that I am no longer suffering from such injuries."

"I don't get it."

Sarek replied, "Neither do I, but I am continuing to consider the possibilities."

"I'm going to guess that we're not dead." Joanna studied their surroundings before her gaze returned to Sarek, who had not moved. "Are we?"

"I have no reason to believe that is the case," replied the Vulcan.

Joanna nodded with new conviction. "Good. Okay, then. And you're sure you're feeling all right?"

"I am certain."

Instinctively, Joanna reached to her hip. Instead of the portable medkit she normally carried while working the floor at New Athens University Hospital, her fingers brushed only against the hem of her tunic.

I didn't have it with me. I had to borrow one from Nett to . . . to treat . . .

"What happened to the woman I was helping?" Joanna looked around, but only she and Sarek were here on the bleak plain. "She was injured too."

Sarek said, "My wife. She is not here. I do not know where she is. I can only assume that she remains on Centaurus."

Remembering that she was dealing with a Vulcan, Joanna took solace in Sarek's self-control even in the midst of this bizarre situation. No doubt he had his own innumerable questions about their present location, how they had come to be here, and what had happened to everyone else who had been in close proximity during the attack. She did not doubt he was concerned for his wife, but his command of his emotions, like most Vulcans, was all but absolute.

"Well, if we're not dead," she said, "and we're not on Centaurus, then where the hell are we?"

"Unknown," said Sarek. "Without more information, speculation would be illogical." He gestured to the soil around them. "However, we are not the first to be in this place. This ground appears to have been disturbed by foot traffic. Someone has been here, and recently."

Joanna frowned. How had she not noticed that before? Now that Sarek had pointed it out, she saw light footprints marring the otherwise undisturbed dirt. There were several sets of tracks, with many looking as though someone had wandered in and around the immediate area, just as she had done while trying to orient herself. She imagined someone, another man or woman, attempting to get their bearings before seeing the mountains in the distance. With that in mind, it took her a moment to find the various trails of barely discernible footprints heading off in that direction.

"What are the odds that we'd wake up in the middle of this wasteland, where other people have traveled?" she asked. "Please tell me I'm not the only one who finds that just a little weird."

"You are not alone," replied Sarek. "It is most unusual."

Gesturing toward the distant mountains, Joanna said, "Looks like they went that way. It seems as good a plan as any. Besides, we need to think about finding some shelter and fresh water, and getting ourselves out of the sun." She glanced upward. "Suns."

Sarek replied, "Agreed, though it may prove an arduous journey."

"It's not like we have a choice." Drawing a deep breath, Joanna realized something else. "On the other hand, I feel fine. I'm not tired."

"Like you, I do not feel fatigued, and neither am I hungry or thirsty."

Frowning, Joanna pondered this. Her own throat was not dry. She glanced to the suns. "I don't even feel hot. I guess things could be worse."

"Indeed."

The pair walked in silence, and Joanna used the opportunity to study their surroundings. She saw no vegetation, or even a rock formation, but instead unrelenting flat terrain. The sunbaked, pale gray soil was broken up by expanses of fine, white crystalline powder, in which the tracks left by unknown travelers were more visible. Might this once have been an immense ocean, gone to dust millennia ago for reasons unknown? *Even a former seabed would feature some terrain features*, she thought.

"How are you feeling, Ambassador?"

Sarek, who had established an efficient stride that was not too difficult for her to match, replied, "I am feeling well, thank you."

"Me too, and that's what's odd." It was not something she had realized until they had walked some distance. "I should be hot, or at least feeling some fatigue in my legs or back, but I don't. I'm not even winded." Casting a glance toward the Vulcan, she said, "It makes sense that you'd be fine. You're a Vulcan." She gestured to indicate their surroundings. "You're used to these environs."

"I am." He regarded her. "I infer from your observations that you are similarly acclimated?"

Joanna chuckled. "Hardly. Centaurus is pretty temperate in that department."

When Sarek said nothing in reply, she elected not to try to force further conversation, choosing instead to concentrate on keeping pace with the Vulcan as they proceeded across the plain. She guessed they had been walking for less than thirty minutes, though without a chronometer there was no way to be sure. How long was a day on this planet? As far as she could tell, the suns had not moved since their arrival, but she could not be certain of that, either.

"My wife."

The words, the first ones spoken by Sarek in some time, startled Joanna, and she jerked her gaze from the interminable pallid soil stretching out in front of them to regard the ambassador. His hands were clasped before him, and he held his arms by his sides as he continued to walk. For the first time, she realized that his eyes were closed. How long had he been doing that, and how had he managed it without stumbling or veering to his left or right and possibly stumbling into her?

"Ambassador?"

Instead of responding to her, Sarek continued walking, his eyes still closed. Joanna noticed his lips moving, though he said nothing else she could hear. Was this some kind of sleepwalking? She knew that Vulcans possessed exceptional senses of direction and awareness, but this was unlike anything she had seen before. It occurred to her that he might simply be lost in thought, trying to occupy his mind rather than be transfixed by the unrelenting sameness of their surroundings. Perhaps he was meditating, as she knew most if not all Vulcans did for a variety of reasons.

"My wife."

So quiet were the words that Joanna almost missed them. Now he was beginning to worry her. Reaching out, she stopped just short of resting her hand on his arm. She noticed that his brow was furrowed, as though he was in deep concentration. Had he become so immersed in meditation or whatever he was doing that he did not realize he was speaking aloud?

"My wife."

This time the ambassador stopped walking, and when he opened his eyes Joanna noted his confusion. He was acting as though he had emerged from deep slumber, and upon noticing her staring at him, he straightened his posture.

"Forgive me," he said. "I was . . . overcome by the most peculiar sensation."

"Are you all right?"

Sarek paused a moment, as though considering his response. "I am at a loss to explain the experience, except to say that it felt very much like the bond I share with my wife."

From her studies of their culture, Joanna knew that Vulcans were telepathically joined to their mates and, depending on individual proficiency, could sense or even communicate if they were in proximity to each other. There were numerous stories about just how great a distance could be bridged in this manner, but Joanna herself had never put much stock into such things. Further, she doubted that the ambassador's wife possessed the telepathic talents to achieve such a feat. She decided that he must have been meditating and he had spoken aloud when his thoughts turned to her. Given their present circumstances, she felt Sarek could be forgiven for what some Vulcans might view as a lapse in discipline. Besides, if it helped him to stay focused as they made their way toward their destination, then she certainly was not going to take issue with it. After all, they still had a long way to go before they reached—

"Wow."

Sarek asked, "What is it?" Instead of replying, she looked first to him and then to the distant mountain range.

The mountains were closer. *Much* closer. Their foothills appeared to be shrouded by trees, which doubtless would provide shelter.

"How the hell did that happen?"

"We seem to have made much better progress than would seem reasonable given our foot speed," said the ambassador.

Joanna nodded. "No kidding. How long have we been walking?"

"I am uncertain." After a moment, Sarek added, "I find myself unable to calculate elapsed time in this place, nor even to estimate it."

"That's unusual for you, isn't it?"

Sarek replied, "It is. Most interesting."

Ahead, the mountains and the welcoming forest at their base waited. Joanna wondered what they might find.

What the hell kind of place is this?

Six

B'tinzal hated this cursed planet, along with everything and everyone associated with it. Well, almost everything.

Thinking about it, she supposed she should have welcomed the thick, unremitting rainforest and the oppressive heat accompanying it. After all, it reminded her of the jungles of the Kintak region on Qo'noS, in which she had spent many seasons hunting as a child. Those were pleasant memories, made all the more so by the fact that her father and grandfather had flouted the conventions of her village by taking a female offspring to hunt, rather than leaving her to tend to the home and livestock. With no son to which such traditions could be passed, her father had seen to it that she was as prepared for adulthood as any male child.

Despite what preliminary sensor readings had conveyed regarding this planet's indigenous wildlife, B'tinzal so far had seen nothing on par with the wild *targs*, *krencha*, and other big game animals she had pursued on those hunts so long ago. She was tempted to set off into the wilderness, armed with nothing but her trusty blade, and see for herself what challenges this world had to offer.

Perhaps another time, she reminded herself. For now, this planet offered only one thing of interest: the alien construct.

B'tinzal stood on the terrace overlooking the compound that had become the center of operations for the

Klingon contingent on the world known as Usilde. The first rays of morning sunlight were filtering through the trees, illuminating the large section of forest that had been cleared away by construction equipment to form an open compound. Six buildings of varying size had been erected here in hasty fashion, using thermoconcrete and other semipermanent construction materials. The camp was encircled by an intrusion control barrier to defend against local predatory wildlife, which seemed to exist with abundance in the surrounding forest. All of the buildings arrayed around the makeshift courtyard were single level, with the exception of the one housing her quarters as well as the camp's command center. This was her favorite time of day, before the buzz of activity seized the encampment. Other Klingons were already moving about, tending to their first tasks of the day, and in the distance B'tinzal could see soldiers moving to and from the guard tower standing at the compound's far edge.

Just visible through the trees north of the camp and rising from the center of the vast lake was the enormous dark metal hull of the bizarre fortress. Enclosed by a circular wall that extended sixty meters out of the water, the citadel was dominated by the towering central column that supported a collection of saucer-like modules, which grew ever smaller toward the top of the column and culminated in a large domed saucer. A cluster of sensor and communications antennae sat atop the uppermost saucer. It was striking, even beautiful in its own way, and had proven to be as infuriating as it was mesmerizing.

"Good day, Professor."

Her reverie disrupted, B'tinzal turned from the terrace to see her assistant, Kvarel, standing in the doorway. The young Klingon wore a dark coverall garment of the sort favored by the rest of the science contingent.

"Good day to you," replied B'tinzal. "Am I to surmise that you bring a message at this early hour?"

Kvarel nodded. "Yes, Professor. Captain J'Teglyr demands a new status update on our progress."

"You mean since the one I sent him before retiring last evening?" B'tinzal shook her head. "Why am I not surprised?" Though she led the survey team that had been dispatched here, overall responsibility for the mission still fell to Captain J'Teglyr, commander of the orbiting warship *I.K.S. Vron'joQ*. A traditional warrior, J'Teglyr had little use for anyone who did not wear a uniform and even less regard if that individual happened to be a female. Like many in his chosen profession, the captain failed to see the importance of anything that did not directly further the goals of conquest. To him, this assignment was a distraction at best and a punishment at worst, even though it held the potential to bring something of great value to the Empire.

His expression hardening, Kvarel said, "He does seem to be making these requests with increasing frequency."

"I suspect he is receiving similar commands from his own superiors." B'tinzal allowed herself a mischievous smile. "It is difficult to summon much in the way of pity for the captain. I did warn him that this likely would be a rather time-consuming endeavor." She gestured over the terrace toward the compound. "He apparently feels the need to justify the time and resources devoted to establishing our little expedition."

What had begun as a simple scientific mission had been escalating toward what B'tinzal knew would be a full-scale occupation of the entire planet. In her view, such formal appointments as the military garrison and the command post were not needed, as she was the ranking member of the survey team, with only a small security contingent to provide protection for her and her colleagues. Even that was perhaps more than was necessary, given that the indigenous sentient species, the Usildar, posed no real threat.

Nevertheless, Captain J'Teglyr, who followed his orders without question, had set into motion the take-over of the planet. Most of the local inhabitants of nearby settlements had already been gathered into camps and dispersed to carry out various tasks, such as clearing areas of the surrounding forest to make way for a larger, more permanent base. Plans were also in motion to subjugate the rest of the Usildar population, though that would require considerably more personnel to accomplish. B'tinzal could see the point to such effort, of course; the claiming of Usilde would provide yet another source of valuable mineral ores and other natural resources to be used by the Empire and in particular to feed the ever hungry Klingon military apparatus. Of equal or perhaps even greater value was denying this same opportunity to the Federation. The planet offered little else, though its strategic location would at least be helpful in disrupting the Federation's ceaseless expansion efforts.

Then there was the citadel.

It taunted her, just as it had done every day since her arrival on this world. Its creators were not to be found, and those Usildar who had been here to witness its construction had been less than helpful when asked to describe its builders or purpose. Only in the vaguest terms had they been able to offer the knowledge that the citadel was a gateway for aliens from another universe, the Jatohr, who planned to take Usilde as their new home and had begun terraforming the surrounding region to suit their needs, much to the chagrin of the Usildar.

That scheme, however far along it had developed, had been disrupted by the actions of a Starfleet captain and his ship, some years ago. The result of that intervention was the apparent killing or removal of the Jatohr who had made the transit from their universe. B'tinzal suspected that the Earther captain and his crew had found a humane way of removing the Jatohr threat rather than killing them outright, but no Usildar had yet been able to corroborate her theory. As for the machine, it had been rendered largely inert, at least with respect to its supposed primary purpose. Whatever portal or doorway it was able to conjure had been closed, perhaps permanently, leaving only the device itself and whatever secrets it might contain.

It was those secrets that so intrigued the Empire and had brought B'tinzal here. The mission she had been given was a simple one: study the citadel and determine to what use the Empire might put it. Surely, a device of such power had more than one purpose, or could at least be modified to serve other needs? If that was true, then the machine was proving to be most uncooperative in that regard.

Sooner or later, B'tinzal thought as she gazed through the trees to the silent, defiant citadel, *you will surrender*.

"I will respond to the captain's request in due course," she said, leaving the terrace. "Come. Let us proceed with the day's work." Despite the frustrations she had encountered with her attempts to study and understand the alien contraption, the challenge it presented could not be denied. Patience and perseverance would triumph; of this, B'tinzal was certain.

It took only moments to walk across the compound

and to the edge of the lake in which the alien fortress resided. B'tinzal used the opportunity as she did each day to admire the citadel's marvelous construction. Getting into the fortress had proven to be a challenge in the beginning, with its primary point of access being several underwater entrances through which transport craft entered the bottom of the complex. Once B'tinzal and her team had arrived on station and the Klingons established a long-term presence here, steps had been taken to facilitate getting to and from the citadel. A deployable field transporter had been set up near the guard post at the lake's edge and was controlled by one of the soldiers from the security garrison, and it was there that B'tinzal and anyone else with business inside the fortress was beamed into what had been identified as a courtyard of sorts within the alien complex's towering fortifications. Only after the first reconnaissance teams had made a survey of the citadel's interior had this area been found, which was otherwise inaccessible from outside the structure itself. Though the first group of Klingons to take charge of the complex had employed scattering fields to prevent unauthorized transport to and from the structure, B'tinzal had dispensed with that security measure, at least for the time being. The fields could be reactivated in the event a Starfleet ship or some other party was discovered to be attempting a covert infiltration, which Captain J'Teglyr and the *Vron'joQ* were supposed to prevent.

We shall see if the good captain is up to that task.

The transporter deposited B'tinzal and Kvarel inside the quad, and from there it was a short walk to the structure's master control room. It was a multitiered chamber, with four distinct levels all connected by a network of ramps. At the room's center was the tall, cylindrical shell housing this portion of the massive transfer-field generator that was the very reason for the existence of the entire complex. Consoles were arrayed in a circle around the shell's base, positioned so that their operators could monitor activity on the display screens set into the curved bulkheads. Like so much else of the alien construct, the generator was inactive.

This area had become an amalgam of Jatohr and Klingon technology, with members of her team working at tables littered with computer terminals, portable scanners, and other devices. The equipment had come from the *Vron'joQ*, and several of the display monitors and other components pulsed or hummed with life. In contrast, most of the consoles that were part of the room's original setup were inert. Only a handful of indicators were active, and it had taken B'tinzal and her people several days to discern that these displays corresponded to different autonomous systems functioning deep within the citadel. The entire complex reverberated with a low yet distinct power, the purpose of which remained a mystery. Sensor scans had revealed that the citadel's inner mechanisms were in a constant state of reconfiguration, all taking place without any apparent oversight or concern for the Klingons or anyone else in their midst. To B'tinzal, it was as though the fortress was the physical manifestation of a computer program, carrying out whatever instructions it contained until that process was completed or interrupted.

It is as if the machine lives.

Any chance that she might escape Captain J'Teglyr's notice disappeared when B'tinzal felt her communicator buzz for attention. Stepping off the portable transporter pad, she removed the bothersome device from a pocket of her coveralls, allowing herself a sigh before activating it.

"This is B'tinzal."

"Did your servant not inform you that I am waiting for a status report?" boomed J'Teglyr. B'tinzal thought the Klingon ship commander seemed even more irritable than normal.

"Good day to you, Captain. Yes, I did indeed sleep well, as that is all that has transpired since my last report."

"The Klingon High Command grows weary of this lack of progress, and I grow weary of enduring their wrath."

Deciding that further antagonizing J'Teglyr would be amusing though unproductive, B'tinzal said, "I share their frustrations, Captain, and yours. The alien device has resisted our efforts to force its operation. As you know, at least one vital component is missing." Without the Transfer Key, as it was called by its Jatohr creator, the transfer generator seemed incapable of functioning. Complicating matters was the knowledge that the Key was in the possession of James Kirk, an Earther known to many Klingons. Such reports were strengthened by the latest information from High Command, which reported that Kirk and his ship were now en route to the Libros system.

Such guile. It is as though Klingon blood flows through his veins.

Kirk would not easily surrender the Key, and at this point B'tinzal was uncertain just how far the High Command would push against Starfleet and the Federation to obtain it. Was this alien contraption worth inciting a war? Klingon warriors needed little reason to fight, but B'tinzal knew the political leaders who guided such decisions would not act without due consideration of all factors.

"We must face the unpleasant possibility that without the missing piece," she continued, "this is a puzzle that may remain forever unsolved."

"*You sound like a Vulcan when you speak that way.*" There was a sigh, as though J'Teglyr were composing himself before saying anything further. After a moment, he added, "*Our orders are clear, Professor: find a way to activate the machine and determine if it can be of any use to the Empire, or destroy it to keep the Federation from using it against us. At this point, I am leaning toward the latter of those two options.*"

"With all due respect, Captain, that would be a rash decision." B'tinzal began crossing to one of the room's inert control consoles. "Though our efforts to activate it have so far been unsuccessful, we have still learned a great deal. The technology contained within the mechanism offers boundless opportunities for research. There is still much this device can teach us."

There was another pause, and B'tinzal sensed that the captain was considering every word. Like many officers with lengthy careers, J'Teglyr had almost certainly given thought to how a situation might benefit him and his personal standing. Delivering a prize like the citadel to the High Command would be a noteworthy achievement for any Klingon, but even more so for an officer of J'Teglyr's rank and seniority. This surely would serve to advance him within the military leadership hierarchy. However, B'tinzal also suspected that the captain might have other, more selfish designs for the alien artifact. It would not be the first time that a Klingon warrior had sullied his honor for personal gain.

This idea seemed to be strengthened when he did something that was very much out of character. J'Teglyr said, "*Very well, Professor. I will tangle with the High Command yet again on your behalf. What else can be done to assist you?*"

B'tinzal chose to field the question without dwelling on any ulterior motives. "We simply need the time to properly study this device, Captain. I cannot offer a timetable for that. After all, this is a totally new technology."

"I would suggest a redoubling of your efforts." The discussion ended with an audible click, leaving B'tinzal to stare at her now dormant communicator.

Kvarel offered, "He never fails to instill confidence and inspiration in those around him, does he?"

The remark provoked a howl of laughter from B'tinzal as she returned the communicator to her pocket. "Indeed he does. I for one feel more than ready to conquer the day."

Whatever response Kvarel may have offered was cut short by shouts of alarm echoing from one of the corridors leading from the control room. Those working at various tables and stations turned in response to the cries to see a trio of Klingons emerging from the curved passageway into the larger room. One soldier, along with a member of B'tinzal's science contingent, was supporting another uniformed Klingon. It took an extra moment for B'tinzal to realize that the soldier's left leg had been amputated below the knee in apparently brutal fashion.

Looking to the Klingon scientist who was assisting the wounded soldier, B'tinzal said, "Tothar, what happened?" Even as she voiced the question, she suspected she knew the answer.

Tothar, with the other soldier's help, moved their wounded companion to a nearby workstation and set him on the floor, propping him against the console. Now B'tinzal could see that the leg had been severed below the knee and a crude tourniquet applied above the kneecap. Blood stained the makeshift wrap—which looked to have been made from a towel or rag—and the Klingon's trousers. The blood was a stark contrast to the dark, charred flesh that marred the soldier's stump. Someone, likely his comrade, had performed a hasty cauterizing of the wound in the hopes of staving off traumatic blood loss. It was a practical if barbaric method of emergency medical treatment, doubtless keeping with some arcane clause of the Klingon warrior ethos of which B'tinzal was unaware.

"This infernal contraption!" spat Tothar, waving back the way they had come. "It confounds us at every turn. Just when we think we have made the slightest measure of progress, it lashes out as though punishing us for our transgressions."

The Klingon who had aided Tothar with the injured soldier said, "We apparently triggered another of the mechanism's internal security features. We had successfully opened an inner passageway, and our sensor scans showed the presence of a large power generation facility. When we attempted to investigate, the machine began sealing off access to that area. All interior hatches were sealed." He gestured to his wounded comrade. "Kventok slipped and fell during our retreat and was caught by one of the hatches."

B'tinzal moved to the wounded Klingon, inspecting his damaged leg before casting a glance to the soldier. "What is your name?"

"Komaraq, Professor."

"Did you treat him in this manner?"

"Yes." The Klingon's expression did not waver. "It was the only way to prevent him from bleeding to death."

"It was excellent initiative," said Kvarel. "You likely saved his life."

The soldier's eyes narrowed. "To what purpose? His days as a warrior are almost certainly finished."

"Take him to the physician," said B'tinzal, gesturing to Komaraq and another soldier who had come in response to the alarm siren. "We will let him make such determinations." As the soldiers assisted their comrade toward the portable transport pad that would beam them outside the citadel, B'tinzal turned to Tothar.

"What else can you tell me about the new section you explored?"

Having had time to compose himself, Tothar replied, "It is as Komaraq said. We were working in one of the secondary control hubs, attempting to gain access to areas beneath the central power generator. One of the computer technicians had discovered a means of accessing a protected memory core and was able to decipher some of the information stored there. This in turn led to our finding a means of unlocking several interior passageways."

"But what might it be doing now?"

Tothar frowned, holding up his scanning device. "From what I can tell, a series of water-intake conduits has been opened at various points along the hull, beneath the lake's surface. The water is being drawn toward this new section. It could be for filtration or cooling, or both. Without a means of accessing that area, I have nothing but guesses."

"Is this the first time this has happened?" asked B'tinzal.

"The first since our arrival. It may well be a regular occurrence, at least as measured by the cursed beings who conceived and built this monstrosity."

B'tinzal nodded, processing this new information. Aside from the citadel's stubborn refusal to activate the universe-bridging portal mechanism that seemed to be its primary reason for existing, the alien construct had managed to defy almost all of their efforts to explore its inner sections. She had lost much sleep during her first few nights here, poring over the schematics compiled from the scans recorded of the citadel's interior. Much of the structure remained a mystery, as she and her team discovered that entire areas of the machine were composed of materials that defied sensors. These sections, she believed, contained the main power plant and other critical systems, providing energy to the mechanism responsible for generating the bridge between this universe and whatever realm the Jatohr called home.

It made sense that such technology would be located in a secure area of the structure protected by sophisticated systems to prevent intrusion and tampering. No active intrusion countermeasures had yet been detected, but B'tinzal was aware that the Jatohr had employed a form of remote-controlled drones to keep the Usildar population in line. B'tinzal had yet to see or hear of those sentries being seen within the citadel, leading her to wonder if all of the devices had been destroyed or rendered inoperative. Perhaps they were of limited number and would be used only when other measures proved ineffective? There was also the possibility that other security features were waiting for her and her people as they progressed ever deeper into the alien structure. As for the transfer generator itself, although it was accessible—for the moment, at least—it continued to rebuff all attempts at reactivation.

"The effect was like an emergency protocol aboard one of our ships," said Tothar. "Similar to a hull breach, which would trigger the sealing of adjacent compartments." He waved toward the citadel. "There are countermeasures of this sort throughout the entire complex."

B'tinzal shook her head. "It is as though this place

knows we are here to conquer it. Rather than bow to us, it wishes to fight." If the citadel had been a sentient being, she might even have admired it for its cunning. As it was, the fortress's actions only served to anger her.

"We must have the Key," said Kvarel. "Its creators appear to have been most thorough in this regard. It is obvious that this machine will continue to deny us until we provide the Key or some worthy substitute."

No such alternative seemed to be forthcoming, B'tinzal knew, which left her—and the Empire—with but one option.

Take the Transfer Key from the Earther James Kirk.

Seven

His eyes closed, Kirk listened to the sounds of his ship. There was the ubiquitous murmur of the ship's main engines, of course, which even with sound dampening carried through every deck plate and bulkhead, and reverberated ever so slightly across every interior surface. With his right hand laid flat atop the briefing room table, he could just barely sense that all but imperceptible tremor channeled across the surface.

There you are. Alive again.

Thanks to the untiring efforts of Montgomery Scott and his engineering staff over a period of more than seven hours, the *Enterprise* once again was soaring through space at a solid if not exceptional cruising speed. The chief engineer had cautioned against straining the engines, insisting on a cap of warp five until he could complete yet another thorough systems check. Scott, even more so than normal, was fussing over the ship with the intensity of a mother hen, but Kirk knew it was with good reason. The repairs, as effective as they were, were still not up to par with what the starship could expect on its next visit to a Starfleet repair facility. This point had been made repeatedly and with great passion on Scott's part, and it was Kirk's solemn wish that he would be able to respect his chief engineer's wishes.

You probably just jinxed the whole thing.

The sound of the doors startled Kirk from his moment

of solitude. Opening his eyes, he swiveled in his chair to see Spock, McCoy, and Scott entering the briefing room.

"Captain," offered Spock as he moved to take the seat to Kirk's left, where a computer terminal was positioned at the head of the table. McCoy and Scott claimed seats across the table from Kirk.

Leaning forward in his chair, the captain rested his elbows on the table and clasped his hands together. "Mister Spock, report."

The Vulcan nodded. "At our present speed, we should arrive in the Libros system in seventeen hours, thirty-four minutes."

"She's not exactly purring like a kitten," added Scott, "but she'll get us there, Captain." The engineer looked tired after the long hours he and his teams had been devoting to the ongoing repair efforts.

Turning his attention to the engineer, Kirk said, "Well done, Scotty, getting the warp engines back online. How are your diagnostic checks coming?"

"We're getting there, sir. Not that I like the results we're seeing. I know what you're about to ask, and I have to warn you that anything past warp five is begging for trouble. The engines will definitely need the sort of attention we can only get at a starbase."

His arms folded across his chest, McCoy asked, "And what about you? How are you feeling?"

"Ridden hard and put away wet, Doctor." Scott mustered a smile. "I promise I'm heading to my quarters for a few hours' sleep before getting back to it."

McCoy's eyes narrowed. "At least five. Doctor's orders." Before the engineer could protest, he added, "They can call you if they need you, but not unless the warp engines are about to explode."

"There's still a lot of work to be done, Doctor, and I don't like being away too long when my lads are still at it."

"I already know you've got them rotating through so everyone can get some rest," replied McCoy. "Now it's your turn." Then his voice softened. "You trained your people well, Scotty. Let them do their jobs."

Kirk chimed in. "They can mind the store for a short while. Give yourself a break."

He had reviewed Scott's status reports while waiting for his senior officers to arrive, and so already knew most of what his chief engineer had just reported. He was not happy with the update, but he also was aware that Scott was not being overly cautious or melodramatic.

"What about the other repairs?" asked Kirk.

Scott sat up in his chair. "The major systems are back to full power. All the overloads in the shield generators, weapons, and life support have been addressed. We've still got a few handfuls of burned-out circuits to replace, but most of those are in noncritical systems, and we're able to reroute power around them. We should have all of that taken care of before we reach Libros, Captain, but I'm still leery about what we might be up against once we get there."

"I'm working on that." Knowing he could not avoid it any longer, Kirk had transmitted a message to Starfleet Command, requesting help in the form of additional starships dispatched to the Libros system. With the *Enterprise* still not back to full operating capacity, he had no desire to take on alone any Klingon warships that almost certainly would be orbiting Usilde. He was still awaiting a response, which he knew would be packaged with all manner of questions regarding the actions he had taken up to this point, as well as his intentions. Kirk was not looking for a fight, but protecting the Jatohr citadel from being plundered by the Klingons was of paramount importance. Not only did the Usildar require protection from exploitation at the hands of the Empire, but the alien contraption was also the only means of retrieving Sarek, Joanna McCoy, Captain Una, and everyone else who had transported against their will into the other universe.

"All right," said Kirk, "we're going to get there, thanks to Mister Scott. What happens after that?"

Spock propped his forearms on the conference table, holding a pair of computer data cards in his hands. "Ensign Chekov and I have been continuing our study of the Transfer Key. We are limited, of course, in that we cannot disassemble the mechanism and risk being unable to properly put it back together. Even tricorder and sensor scans of the device's internal components have proven inconclusive. It is our theory that due to its origins in the other universe, its technology is at least somewhat incompatible with our own. Indeed, our scans of it and the Jatohr citadel support our hypothesis that the other universe may well be governed by a different set of physical laws. Still, we believe we have made some progress."

"Can it be adapted to our power systems?" asked Kirk.

Spock replied, "We will require Mister Scott to weigh in on our findings, but we feel that it is possible to adapt the Key to our warp drive and use it to power the device without the same ill effects that befell the Romulan vessel."

McCoy asked, "Can we use it to communicate with anyone in the other universe?"

"Unknown," replied Spock. "Analysis of our sensor and tricorder readings of the Transfer Key have so far revealed nothing that might be comparable to targeting or communications components. However, those systems are present in the transfer-field generator. Based on our findings,

I believe the only way to locate or contact anyone in the other universe is via the field generator, using the Transfer Key as our means of direct access." Spock placed the data cards on the table. "It is possible, perhaps likely, that our technology is incompatible with the physical properties of that realm. We are continuing to conduct further tests, including computer simulations that we revise as we learn more about the Transfer Key."

"I'm pretty sure I don't like the sound of that," said McCoy.

While Kirk trusted Spock's recommendations without hesitation, he was less inclined to put total faith in a computer's conclusions on what they might encounter. Simply put, Spock, Chekov, and the ship's computer needed more information from the source.

"What about a probe?" asked Kirk. Then, remembering to whom he was speaking, he offered a small smile. "Let me guess. You've already thought of this."

The Vulcan nodded. "It is our hope that we can equip an automated or remote-guided probe with the proper sensor components to record the effects of the other universe on our equipment. Ensign Chekov proposed this as a possibility. Again, Mister Scott's expertise will be most helpful, but that was to be our recommendation."

This was more like it, Kirk decided, though there would be issues even with this option. "The Klingons will be watching our every move once we reach Usilde. It's a safe bet that whoever's there knows by now that we have the Transfer Key, but I don't expect them to make any direct moves against us, at least not right away."

Spock replied, "The Organian Peace Treaty allows ships from both sides to be present in a disputed area, so long as we do not engage in combat."

"I'm not about to trust whoever we find there to play fair," said Kirk. "Besides, we've already seen that the Organians don't always take a keen interest in every little skirmish."

"Do you think they're even paying attention to any of this?" asked McCoy. "I mean, on the surface this seems like just any other disagreement about who lays claim to a single planet, but there's so much more at stake here."

"That's a good question, Bones." Kirk was grateful that his friend seemed to have regained at least some of his confidence and was once again making his opinions known, rather than allowing his concerns for his daughter to force him into silence and possible despair.

"Our mission to Capella IV made me rethink the Organians and the likelihood of involving themselves." The *Enterprise*'s visit to that world and its subsequent encounter with a Klingon emissary seeking to undermine Federation negotiations with the Capellans had been enough to tell Kirk that the Organians were not interested in managing every squabble. "They seem content to let us settle small-scale disagreements."

McCoy replied, "Right, but this is a little different. Maybe we just haven't tested the upper limits of their patience yet."

"Doctor McCoy's point is valid," said Spock. "This situation may well prove sufficient to test his theory."

That was enough to make McCoy lean in the Vulcan's direction. "You mean you're agreeing with me?"

Spock's eyes narrowed. "I believe I just said that, Doctor."

"We're obviously not counting on the Organians stepping in," said Kirk, "either to help us or tie our hands. Scotty, we'll need weapons and defenses at peak efficiency, no matter what it takes. Be ready to route power from wherever you need it. Don't even wait for my order, if it gets to that point."

The engineer replied, "Aye, sir. We'll be ready."

"We also can't forget the Jatohr." Kirk eyed his friends. "The impact of their arrival seems limited to Usilde, but we can't know for sure they'll be content to remain there. There's no way to know what the Jatohr might be planning, and they've had eighteen years to continue preparing for that door to open. Getting our people out is important, but we have to do it without aiding and abetting an invasion." According to the reports Kirk had read as filed by Captain Robert April and then-Lieutenant Una, the Jatohr scientist they had met on Usilde, Eljor, was worried that his people would never cease attempting to replicate the Transfer Key or find another way to activate the transfer-field generator and provide them passage from their universe to this one. Add to that the Klingons and their ongoing efforts to unlock the secrets of the citadel, and it was a recipe for catastrophe.

Nobody ever promised me this job would be easy.

"There is, of course, another concern," said Spock. "The Usildar."

Kirk nodded. "Agreed. They didn't ask for any of this, but we're involved now. Whatever we do, we have to look out for their best interests. It's not just what the Klingons might do to them and the planet, but also the damage that's already been inflicted by the Jatohr."

"Terraforming efforts to restore the planet's ecosystem could take decades," said Scott, "assuming we're even able to reverse everything the Jatohr did to alter the environment to suit their needs."

Kirk replied, "It doesn't matter how long it takes. It's the right thing to do."

"Without question." Spock straightened his posture, clasping his hands before him and extending his forefingers so that they touched, adopting what Kirk likened to a meditative pose. "However, any aid to the Usildar will be contingent on the Klingons and their intentions for the planet."

That was the question Kirk had been pondering almost from the moment the *Enterprise* had set course for Usilde. "The way I see it, the only thing the planet offers is the citadel, and for the moment, the citadel is useless to the Klingons without the Transfer Key."

The captain paused, drawing a breath. There was no easy way to say what had to be said. Glancing at McCoy, he added, "We may find ourselves facing a difficult situation with respect to the Jatohr citadel. If the Klingons find a way to exploit it, we might be left with no choice but to destroy it to keep it out of their hands."

"You mean before we can use it," said McCoy. "Before we can rescue Joanna and the others."

"It is a distinct possibility, Doctor," Spock replied. "If we are unable to make use of the citadel without Klingon interference, or if the Klingons attempt to take the Transfer Key from us, we will be left with very few options."

McCoy glared at the Vulcan. "I understand all of that, Mister Spock, but we're still talking about fifteen people trapped in that other universe." He threw his hands up. "And those are just the ones we know of. There may be more; innocent people thrown into whatever the blazes might be over there. We can't just leave them."

Unaffected by the emotional outbursts, Spock replied, "Doctor, it is important to remember that we do not know whether any of our people are even still alive. While the presence of those Jatohr who transferred into our universe strongly suggests that Sarek and the others survived transition to the other realm, it is not conclusive. We know very little about Jatohr physiology and nothing with respect to that universe."

Spock's matter-of-fact delivery did little to assuage McCoy's feelings. "Blast it, Spock. That's my daughter you're talking about with your detached, logical analysis."

"I am aware of that, Doctor." Then Spock drew a small breath and added, "I am sensitive to the emotional strain you are presently enduring." It was a rare display of empathy for the Vulcan; the equivalent of throwing his arms around the other man and offering a warm embrace.

Though tempted to say something to defuse what might fast be devolving into a war of words between the two men, Kirk opted to remain silent. Sympathetic to his friend's feelings, he also refused to believe that all of this was for nothing. Joanna and the others were still alive. He felt it, in his gut. For his part, McCoy seemed to hear and understand not only Spock's words, but also their unspoken meaning.

"Sorry, Spock," he said, shifting in his seat. "I know you're worried about your father too. I . . ." He stopped, casting his gaze down to the conference table, before shaking his head. "I'm sorry."

Kirk tapped his fingers on the table. "Don't worry, Bones. We're not giving up on Joanna or any of the others as long as there's the slightest chance we can get them back." The words "dead or alive" crossed his mind, but he was not about to say them aloud. Until given empirical proof otherwise, Joanna McCoy, Ambassador Sarek, Captain Una, and everyone else who had been transported into the other universe was still alive, waiting for the *Enterprise* to rescue them.

So that's what we're going to do.

The whistle of the ship's intercom echoed in the room, followed by the voice of Lieutenant Nyota Uhura.

"Bridge to Captain Kirk."

Reaching for the small control panel set into the top of the conference table, Kirk pressed the button to activate the three-sided display screen situated at the table's center. All three screens flared to life, coalescing into the image of the *Enterprise*'s communications officer.

"Go ahead, Lieutenant."

"Sorry to disturb you, sir," replied Uhura, *"but you asked to be informed when we received a response from Starfleet Command. Admiral Komack reports that the U.S.S. Defiant has been rerouted to join us in the Libros system. The Defiant's captain has already sent along a report that they expect to be on station within twenty-two hours."*

"Twenty-two hours?" asked Scott. "That's a wee bit of a gap to fill."

Kirk agreed, but there was nothing to be done about that now. Instead, he asked Uhura, "I take it the *Defiant* is the closest ship?"

"Yes, sir," replied the lieutenant. Her expression was one of regret. *"The admiral apologizes. He is trying to find another ship to send our way."* She paused before adding, *"There's another communication, Captain, addressed to your attention only."*

"I can guess what that one will say," replied Kirk. "I'll take it in my quarters, Lieutenant. Please send my acknowledgment of both messages to Admiral Komack. Kirk out." He tapped the control to terminate the communication before leaning back in his chair. "Well, you've heard me say this before, but it looks like we're on our own, at least for the time being." He looked to his chief engineer. "Scotty, you know what that means?"

The other man nodded, the fatigue in his eyes now seeming more evident. "We'll have the old girl squared away before we reach Usilde, Captain. You have my word."

"Good enough." Kirk rose from his seat, his senior officers responding to his nonverbal signal that the meeting had ended. "There are a lot of people counting on us, gentlemen. Let's make sure we don't let them down."

Eight

My wife . . .

Captain Una awoke, her mind flooding with the odd, unknown voice. Looking around the remnants of the now compromised prison cell, she saw that she remained alone except for her two former shipmates, Lieutenant Commander Raul Martinez and Ensign Tim Shimizu. The voice certainly had not belonged to either of them. Had she heard it or simply imagined it?

Where am I?

It took her a moment to clear her mind and recognize her surroundings. She had awakened slumped against the stone wall of the cell into which she and her companions had been confined but that now served as a simple shelter. Beyond the boundary of what had been the cell's far wall, twin suns shone brightly, illuminating the clear blue sky above a nearby lagoon of shimmering gray water. As she had noted before, her surroundings were conspicuous in their near total lack of ambient sounds.

How long had they been here? Despite her usual keen and precise capacity to track the passage of time, Una still found herself questioning that ability. Had it been days, or weeks? She glanced to her shipmates, who had been trapped here far longer. Somehow, the nature of this place seemed to exact an influence upon their minds that she had somehow managed to escape. While her thoughts remained clear, her friends appeared to suffer from the loss of all but the most recent of their memories. They would be of little assistance, she knew, in understanding their current situation and finding a way to return all of them to their proper existence.

My wife . . .

That voice. Was it real? Una thought she had dreamed it, or that it might be the result of some trickery played by her own mind as it worked to provide her answers. Pushing herself to her feet, she tried to retain some feeble grasp upon the words that already were fading from her mind. To whom did the voice belong? From where had it come? It was not a memory; of that she was certain.

"Did anyone else hear that?"

As her eyes acclimated to the daylight, she turned her attention to her colleagues, neither of whom had responded to her question. Shimizu, one of her closest friends going back to their days at Starfleet Academy, was sprawled across the cell's smooth floor. She looked at him with regret for their irretrievable loss: years' worth of shared experiences, career accomplishments, exploratory achievements—everything they had hoped their lives might be.

Slumped against the cell's opposite wall, Martinez sat with his arms crossed over his bent knees so as to give him a place to rest his head; his present state troubled her even more than Shimizu's. An able-bodied and highly capable leader during their shared service aboard the *Enterprise*, Raul Martinez had inspired confidence and no small admiration in the younger Lieutenant Una. At the beginning of their mission to Usildar, he never questioned Captain Robert April's orders for her to lead the ill-fated excursion to the planet's surface. She had spent years blaming herself for that day, continually revisiting her decisions and actions and how they led to the loss of the entire landing party to this mysterious universe. Seeing Martinez now only served to bring forth those feelings once again. After years existing in this inexplicable place, this once commanding presence with a bright future in Starfleet was the merest shadow of his former self.

She could not get them those years back, she knew, but she could get them home.

"Guys, we need to get moving."

Her words stirred Shimizu just enough that he rolled onto his back while Martinez did not budge. "Tim! Commander! Wake up!" When that did not work, she resorted to shaking them until they responded.

"What?" asked Shimizu as he reached up to wipe his eyes.

Una replied, "Time to go." Crossing to Martinez, she knelt beside him and placed a hand on his shoulder. "Commander, you need to wake up now."

Finally, Martinez lifted his head. "Captain, is everything all right?"

Una had to admit that his use of her current rank sounded odd.

"Nothing's wrong, I promise. We need to get moving."

In truth, if night in this strange realm had not fallen so quickly, Una might not have suggested the three stay in the cell to which they had been summarily relegated after meeting with the tyrannical Jatohr warmonger Woryan. Even after making one of its walls disappear as a demonstration to her companions of the potential mental powers they wielded in this realm, it had made sense to use the cell for shelter until daybreak. Her ability to make such a thing happen, to manipulate the elements of this world as she had trained herself to do, surprised her as much as it had her crewmates. It had not taken Una long to realize that one of the apparent debilitating effects of exposure to this realm was short-term memory loss.

Had her enhanced mental discipline allowed her to combat this affliction? There was no way to know.

"I heard a voice," she said. "Before, in my mind. A male voice. I'm not sure why, but I think he might be able to help us."

"I didn't hear anything," Martinez said.

Shimizu replied, "Me neither." He frowned. "Wait. You say you felt him in your mind?"

"Not exactly," Una said. "I mean, not fully, at least. I don't pretend to understand it, but I figure it must be somebody who's trapped here like we are. We need to find him, before Woryan does."

"Woryan," Martinez said, and Una felt a twinge of hope as he seemed to remember the alien's name and possibly their meeting with him in the Jatohr city across the lagoon from where they now stood. "We need to keep him from finding his own way back to our universe."

"Yes! Exactly, Commander," Una said. "So, let's get moving."

Shimizu said, "Wouldn't miss it." He flashed a familiar, welcome smile. "Where are we going?"

"I'm not sure," Una said, "but I have an idea for getting there."

Leading them out of their cell, Una proceeded to the edge of the gray, dreary lake. She crouched at the lagoon's edge, extended her hands over the water, and closed her eyes. After a moment spent in concentration, she focused on a single goal, as she had done the previous evening when she had made part of the cell wall disappear. Now she wanted to conjure something from nothing.

Concentrate. See it, and make it real.

"What the hell?" said Shimizu. "How are you . . . ?"

Una ignored him, though she did pause long enough to realize her suspicions about her friends' loss of short-term memory seemed to be confirmed. Setting aside that thought, she returned her full attention to her objective.

She opened her eyes when she heard the water start to churn, and she smiled. Emerging from the lagoon's depths was a dull metallic facsimile of an antigravity skid.

It worked!

"Am I seeing things?" asked Shimizu.

Martinez replied, "Only if I am. Where the hell did this come from, Captain?"

"It was my grandfather's," replied Una. "As a kid, I always loved riding it on his farm on Illyria." Despite it being designed for hauling equipment and crops, she had been allowed to use it for recreation when her work was completed. Its nose was dented and the paint covering its body panels was scraped and worn.

"And you just . . . wished it here?" asked Martinez.

Una nodded. "Something like that."

The key was belief, she now realized as she reached for one end of the skid's bed and pulled it toward shore, a simple task thanks to its antigravity properties. Between whatever physical properties governed this realm and her own advanced mental control, it seemed that almost anything might be possible.

Shimizu asked, "Does it work?"

"We're about to find out."

Climbing into the cab, she settled into the cushioned

bench seat. "It's just like I remember." With practiced ease, she thumbed the control to bring the sled's twin gravity nullifiers to full power. She smiled at the vehicle's signature peculiarity, a rhythmic tremor caused by output variations from the rear emitter that her grandfather never had been able to remedy.

"Unbelievable," said Martinez.

Una gestured to the bed behind the cab. "Climb on, and let's get out of here."

Once her friends were settled, she grasped the control grips and moved the sled forward. After an initial lurch, the vehicle glided onto the lagoon and across its smooth surface, and Una noted that the water remained undisturbed despite their passing. She recalled the phenomenon from her previous crossing of the lake. Something that had escaped her notice before now caught her eye: a tree line not far from the shore of the lake. It would offer them concealment from the Jatohr as well as shelter should they need rest. How she had missed a forest nagged at her thoughts for a moment, but she concluded it must be yet another aspect of the general unpredictability that defined this place.

"Where are we heading, Captain?" asked Shimizu.

It was a good question. Una had no clue as to the location of the owner of the mysterious voice in her mind. Might the same abilities that had allowed her to conjure the sled also be used to trace his presence?

Perhaps.

———

Watching the holographic image of the odd, graceless antigravity vehicle making its way across the lagoon, Anadac felt a wave of trepidation sweep through hir form.

Hir concerns grew not from the possibility that the vehicle's human occupants might realize they were being watched. The sentry globe providing the visual feed remained well above detection range. Neither were hir concerns rooted in the remarkable abilities exhibited by the being known to hir as Una, although Anadac never had seen such a power demonstrated by any being in hir lifetime.

Anadac had held hir breath the first time s/he had watched the image of the being raise the sled from the lagoon. However, upon repeated viewings of the incident with images as enlarged and enhanced as hir equipment made possible, the Jatohr scientist concluded the vehicle had not simply been raised from the water. Instead, s/he was convinced the vehicle had been *created* by Una, transformed from the material of the lagoon itself—or perhaps by nothing at all—by the human using some unseen means. Hir mind reeled with questions. Was this ability psychic in nature? Was Una the only outsider possessing this transformative power over the environment, or was it an innate trait of her species? Did such ability pose a threat to the Jatohr? Had Anadac just witnessed the first hints of an invasion force from the other universe?

Though these questions were concerning, Anadac was worried even more by the prospect of Woryan's response to this new revelation. There could be no doubt that the supreme leader would marshal hir forces in a bid to hunt down all outsiders. Anadac already had seen too many battles waged against the Usildar. Such brutality against other life-forms deeply disturbed hir as it did many if not most Jatohr.

And yet, conflict and tyranny were the way of things under Woryan, who gained power and position over the Jatohr by feeding their worst fears: life from elsewhere, perhaps from the very realm to which the Jatohr hoped to travel, proving a greater threat than even their own dying universe.

As a being of curiosity and discovery, Anadac had resisted such thinking. S/he had resolved never to raise arms against another and had managed to keep that pledge by serving Woryan's regime from a scientific station. S/he knew that once Woryan learned of Una's abilities, the supreme leader would use that to stoke still more fear of all outsiders. Once unleashed, Woryan would not stop until every outsider was eliminated.

There was no alternative, Anadac decided. S/he would keep this admittedly incomplete report to hirself, at least until s/he could make more observations and offer an objective explanation for the phenomenon.

"Anadac!"

The voice startled hir, and s/he utilized one of hir mechanical graspers to deactivate the image display. S/he turned hir head in time to see Zened, one of Woryan's top advisors, approaching hir. The bulky gastropod was gliding over the laboratory's smooth floor, albeit slowly.

"Your leader seeks an update on the portal's progress," said Zened without preamble.

Anadac sighed. The centerpiece of Woryan's plan to ensure the survival of the Jatohr was the construction of a transdimensional portal capable of forcing an opening between this world and their former stronghold on the Usildar's native planet. Since the entirety of the Jatohr occupiers had been flung here by the transfer-field generator invented by Anadac's fellow scientist, Eljor, Woryan wanted a means of exploiting its dimension-bridging abilities on hir own terms. However, such occurrences were infrequent and unpredictable.

To that end, Anadac had been charged with lead-ing the development of an anti-Key, as it were: a device capable of locking on to any activity initiated by Eljor's transfer-field generator. Instead of watching its transfer portal evaporate, Woryan instead wanted a way of holding the portal open at hir whim so that s/he might return to the realm from which s/he had been banished. Anadac did not relish the idea of creating a way for a despot and hir military force to invade a single planet, let alone an entire universe.

An effective scheme, s/he had learned, was to lie, but to do so with restraint.

"I believe I have determined the necessary frequencies and harmonics for our portal to achieve Woryan's goal," Anadac said. "What remains is to test the device, which re-quires us to be at the site of the incursions." S/he had suc-ceeded in identifying the likely location of these openings.

"Excellent," said Zened. "Woryan will be pleased with this news."

Anadac replied, "I would suggest tempering hir expec-tations. I cannot guarantee success on the first attempt. We still require information that I can gain only from an ini-tial, controlled experiment. Even a failure would provide data I can use to refine the mechanism."

The advisor seemed to fret over this notion, hir trian-gular mouth puckering while hir sensory tentacles quiv-ered in response. "Consider the ramifications any such delay is sure to cause."

"I have," replied Anadac, "and this is all dependent on when such a test can be conducted. That requires the doorway to open, an action that is entirely beyond our control."

"Even more incentive to be successful on the first attempt, Anadac." Zened shifted hir hulking form. "I will inform Woryan of your progress, and I also will inform hir that our return to the Usildar home world is imminent and that our preparations should begin with all due haste."

As Zened moved away, Anadac released another sigh. Engineering delays of this sort were becoming more problematic. Woryan possessed little patience, and s/he soon would demand greater progress and irrefutable results.

Returning hir attention to the image display, Anadac resumed hir observations of the human Una and her companions. The antigravity sled had completed its crossing of the lagoon and now was moving in slower fashion across more rugged terrain. S/he admitted hir scientific curiosity toward Una and the scope of her transformative ability now superseded hir interest in the portal's development. To meet this human and witness such demonstrations for hirself! What if such a meeting might lead to an unprecedented turn of power and influence across the realm? Might that be worth the risk such a meeting entailed? What if s/he could explain to the humans, and to Woryan, that invasion and conquest was not the only answer to the problems the Jatohr faced?

Yes, Anadac concluded. Such a goal was very much worth the risk.

Nine

"Finally. The last piece of the puzzle."

Bending over the antigravity sled, Ensign Pavel Chekov retrieved the sensor module and carried it to the workbench where his creation—his and Mister Spock's—sat waiting.

"Do you wish to do the honors, sir?" asked Chekov, holding out the component for Spock, who stood at an adjacent workstation along the *Enterprise* astrophysics lab's aft bulkhead.

Turning from the console, the Vulcan replied, "As you have overseen all of the configurations to this point, it seems appropriate that you complete the task yourself, Ensign." After a moment, he added, "Although I comprehend and appreciate the sentiment."

"Aye, sir," said Chekov as he turned his attention back to his work. The sensor probe rested horizontally atop the workbench. The bench was not part of the room's normal furnishings, but supplied for this purpose and currently positioned between the main viewscreen on the forward bulkhead and the central control console. Cylindrical and nearly two meters in length, the probe's central access panels had been removed, exposing the collection of tightly packed internal components.

Reconfiguring the standard telemetry probe had taken the better part of four hours, including the time required to transport the device along with the other necessary components from storage. It was Spock who had suggested using the astrophysics lab for this task, as it allowed the science officer to divide his time between assisting Chekov and studying sensor telemetry gathered from Usilde. Data from the *Enterprise* sensor logs along with Spock's own tricorder readings had been combined with information previously gathered by Captain Una years ago during her own encounter with the Jatohr transfer-field generator.

Leaning toward the probe's outer shell and reaching into the open compartment, Chekov set the sensor module into the small cradle that was part of the larger sensor array and snapped it into place. He finished the final connections before reaching for the small keypad affixed to the array's housing and activating the unit's power supply. The rest of the control panel flickered to life, and Chekov heard a low, dull hum as the array came online.

"That should do it, sir," he said, admiring his work. "Everything's installed according to your specifications."

Spock stepped away from his workstation and approached the probe. "You fail to give yourself appropriate recognition of your own contributions, Ensign. This was a joint effort."

Despite his best efforts, Chekov was unable to restrain a small smile of pride. "Thank you, sir." Since arriving aboard the *Enterprise* to serve as one of the starship's navigators, he had wanted nothing less than to carry out his responsibilities to the best of his ability. At the same time, the ensign knew that such a prestigious assignment would provide all manner of opportunities for expanding both his own continuing education as well as advancing his Starfleet career. While being a starship navigator carried with it no small number of challenges, being assigned to such a lengthy mission of exploration meant that he, along with the rest of the crew, would be among the first to encounter new worlds, new species, and new technology. The excitement of such possibilities was almost overwhelming, and Chekov intended to take advantage of every moment of his tour with this storied vessel.

After a few moments spent in silence while he examined the modified probe and its reconfigured innards, Spock said, "This is impressive work, Mister Chekov. Your cross-training and additional study efforts have served you well."

"Thank you, Mister Spock. Your guidance has been invaluable." He still did not fully understand why the first officer had taken such a keen interest in him, along with several other junior members of the *Enterprise* crew. Chekov had only recently made the switch from beta to alpha shift, putting him on the bridge when Captain Kirk and several other members of the starship's command crew were on duty. The bulk of his responsibilities revolved around the navigator's station and working in concert with Lieutenant Sulu and other helm officers, but Spock had with increasing frequency called him to the science station. There, the ensign had begun a sort of informal instruction as he monitored incoming sensor telemetry as well as assisted with requests to the ship's main computer. Chekov guessed that the Vulcan had reviewed his personnel file and noted his interest in bridge operations, with emphasis on sensors and ship security, and decided the young officer would benefit from additional training in these areas.

"Now that the probe reconfiguration is complete," said Spock, "our next step should be a thorough diagnostic test of our modifications. The multiple phase emitters in particular will likely require fine-tuning."

Chekov nodded. "I was just about to perform those

tests, sir. I've already written a new program for the computer to execute."

"In such a short time?" Spock's right eyebrow rose. "That is impressive."

Chekov felt his cheeks reddening. "I must confess I didn't do it all on my own, sir. Given the mission parameters you supplied, I instructed the computer to provide me with anything from the data banks that might help me quickly create both navigation and diagnostic procedures for the probe. The computer didn't take long to find something."

Crossing to the main console at the center of the room, Chekov dropped into the station's single chair and began activating a series of controls. In response to his commands, a pair of panels on the probe's outer hull slid aside. From within these recessed compartments emerged an angular strut, each bearing a cluster of sensor arrays. The struts rotated and locked into position, the motion accompanied by an affirming tone from Chekov's console. He input another set of instructions, and one of his station's display screens flared to life and began displaying a scroll of text as the ship's computer interpreted the signals now being transmitted by the probe.

"I do not recognize all of these modifications," said Spock. "Where did you get your additional information?"

Chekov replied, "I adapted the sensor configuration from other examples stored in the memory banks. At first I concentrated on standard Starfleet long-range reconnaissance probes, but then the computer gave me a model I hadn't considered."

He tapped another set of controls and the image on the console's monitor changed to a schematic of a sleek, almost arrow-like construct. The image was not from a current Starfleet technical database, but instead an older diagram the *Enterprise*'s computer had extracted from its memory archive.

"Interesting," said Spock. "The Nomad MK-15c. You based your configurations on this?"

Chekov nodded. "Partially, sir. The probe's original data-assimilation encoders and selective amplifiers are based on older technologies, of course. However, they were designed for long-duration deep-space exploration and the probability that the probe would encounter hazards during its journey."

He had spent several hours poring over all of the information the ship's computer could provide about the original Nomad probe, launched from Earth in the early twenty-first century to travel interstellar distances in search of other intelligent life. Most of what Chekov had reviewed was a refresher, as he had conducted a similar study when the *Enterprise* encountered the probe several months ago. The crew was startled to learn that the device had chanced upon a similar automated drone craft dispatched by an alien species, and the two probes had somehow combined to become a single unit. This merger had corrupted each device's internal programming, resulting in a flawed amalgamation that became destructive to anything it found and perceived to be "inferior." Captain Kirk and Mister Spock were forced to destroy the hybrid probe, but not before the first officer succeeded in collecting detailed sensor scans of the device's internal configuration.

"The acquisition sensors, predictive tracking screens, and amplifier screens of the original Nomad probe are very close to what we decided we needed for this probe," said Chekov. "I requested engineering and the quartermaster to supply me with similar components using modern materials. We're still making an educated guess as to what the probe will encounter once we send it through to . . . the other side, but based on what little information we have, I think she's ready, Mister Spock."

The Vulcan replied, "Agreed. Proceed with the diagnostic tests."

"Aye, aye, sir." Returning his attention to the control console, Chekov entered the necessary commands to begin the diagnostic procedure. Within seconds, the probe's responses to interrogation by the *Enterprise*'s computer began scrolling on the workstation's screen.

"Sir, are we sure this is even going to work?"

His gaze fixed on the viewscreen as he reviewed the diagnostic data, Spock replied, "There remain several variables with respect to the Transfer Key, Ensign. Mister Scott is completing the process of interfacing it with our power systems."

Chekov glanced to the workstation that had been the focus of Spock's attention these past few hours. A portion of the console had been removed, offering the first officer access to its internal power conduits and relays. Cradled within the maze of circuitry and other components was a box that was somewhat larger than an oversized book, and inside that box sat the Transfer Key, the alien technology that was at the heart of everything Chekov and Spock were doing here. Running from the box was a collection of power and optical data cabling that Chekov knew was not a normal part of the console's internal configuration; it had been installed by Spock with the assistance of the *Enterprise*'s chief engineer. For the moment, the Transfer Key appeared inert and wholly incapable of the feats for which it had been responsible.

Such a small thing, causing so much trouble.

"So far, we've only seen the Key used to transfer individuals." Chekov gestured to the probe. "This is obviously quite different."

Spock replied, "Based on what we know of the Transfer Key's abilities, as well as those of the transfer-field generator on Usilde, the process is somewhat similar to our transporter systems. Of course, there is the extradimensional aspect of the Jatohr technology, which we still do not completely understand." He reached over to tap one of the console's controls, halting the progression of the diagnostic data. "Power requirements may also prove problematic. Based on our observations, those requirements increase in relation to the size and location of the targeted subject. The greater mass of the subject or the farther the target from the device, the more power is needed."

There was also Spock's current theory that the realm the Jatohr called home may well be subject to physical laws different if not incompatible with those of this universe. Though Chekov had been the first to voice the suggestion of using a probe, he suspected Spock had already been thinking along these lines, yet had allowed his protégé to reach that conclusion on his own.

"There's still one outstanding issue, sir," he said, nodding toward the probe. "We can send it, but we don't have a way of calling it back."

"Nor will we be able to communicate with it once it is transferred," replied Spock. "We may be able to program an onboard interface with the Transfer Key and embed an instruction to send the probe back after a predetermined span of time, but that would require our sending the Key along with an untested probe."

"And risk never getting it back," Chekov said.

The first officer spared him a glance. "That thought had occurred to me, Ensign."

For a moment, Chekov chided himself for his comment. Hikaru Sulu, who was fast becoming his best friend aboard ship, had more than once kidded with him for his habit of "stating the obvious," and his apparent need to talk just to hear his own voice. Was this Spock's version of the same joke?

"What we really need is a second Transfer Key."

Spock replied, "I have studied the device enough to understand that we are unable to duplicate its functionality with our current level of technology. However, we may be able to use our technology to replicate at least some of its processes."

Chekov frowned. "I don't understand. You're saying you know how it works?"

"In theory. My review of Captain Una's original tricorder readings and her subsequent reports put forth a hypothesis regarding molecular harmonics. Atomic-level vibration frequencies are a constant in our universe. As a result, everything we experience exists on the same physical plane." Spock crossed his arms. "Speculate on the consequences of adjusting those frequencies within an object."

Pondering what he had just heard and restraining himself from offering a comment about how he was beginning to feel a headache coming on, Chekov replied, "The object would no longer be compatible with this universe. It might even cease to exist, at least as we know it. Like being subjected to a phaser set to maximum or a transporter beam interrupted midstream."

"Nothing so drastic, I hope," said Spock, "but hopefully similar to the properties exhibited by the Transfer Key. If we are able to replicate the harmonics utilized by the Key, even at a small, localized level, we may be able to align with the constants of existence in another universe, a realm present on top of our own but unreachable to us, just as communications are undetected on any frequency except for those to which we are tuned."

"You're suggesting we retune the atomic vibration frequency of the probe? Is that even possible?" It sounded farfetched, and Chekov was actually surprised to hear such a seemingly outlandish theory offered by someone of Spock's scientific renown.

"There are always possibilities, Ensign. How would you suggest proceeding?"

You mean besides bending the laws of physics?

Swallowing the nervous lump that had formed in his throat, Chekov replied, "Well, we would need to determine if there is such a perceptible shift in the physical state of someone or something sent by the Transfer Key. We'd need to know what frequency the device uses and try to match it."

"I will attempt to determine the necessary harmonic frequency," said Spock.

Looking to the probe, Chekov added, "We'd also need to modify the internal communications system so that the probe can transmit a programmed harmonic sequence."

The change in Spock's expression was so slight and so fleeting that Chekov almost missed it.

Is that approval?

"That seems a simple enough task," said Spock. "Begin those modifications immediately."

His gaze lingering on the probe, Chekov considered his next action. Yes, the modifications to the probe would be simple. It was just hardware, after all. Then his gaze fell once more upon the open console and the Transfer Key nestled within it.

What about those laws of physics you're hoping to bend?

That, Chekov knew, would be a much more formidable challenge.

Ten

Sighing in momentary contentment, Joanna McCoy rested with her back against the large tree that, like everything else in this place, was both familiar and yet alien. She pressed her spine against the tree's trunk, stretching her shoulder blades and enjoying the kneading of her muscles. It was a habit she had acquired while taking in the open air of the campus back on Centaurus, relaxing for a few precious moments between classes. The tree as well as the memories it prompted were comforting, but as she looked up through the branches toward the sky and its twin suns, she was reminded once again that she was a long way from home.

"I should be tired," she said after another minute spent in silence. She and Sarek had traversed the salt flats in broad daylight, but she felt neither fatigue nor thirst. Now the desolate expanse had given way to lush forest at the base of the mountains that had been their destination, and she felt as fresh as after a good night's sleep. Though her body seemed to be weathering the exertion, her mind certainly welcomed the idea of slumber.

That was likely not coming, at least until she and Sarek found shelter, so for now she rested. A few paces from her, his back to an adjacent tree and his hands clasped before him, Sarek knelt. She had been watching him for the past several minutes, his eyes closed and his brow furrowed as though in a deep meditative state. Only when his position shifted and he turned to look at her did she speak.

"How are you feeling, Ambassador?"

The Vulcan nodded. "I am well, thank you. I continue to experience no debilitating effects from our extended journey, which I find unusual and fascinating."

Physically, Sarek was in prime condition, and Joanna knew that their trek across the salt plain would not have affected him to any significant degree even without whatever mysterious properties were assisting them here. Instead, she was concerned about his mental state. The infrequent, short bouts of seeming distraction had continued as they walked, as though Sarek were attempting without success to meditate. The occasional calls to his wife, almost under his breath, had stopped, but it was obvious to her that Amanda was not far from his thoughts. She did not want to disturb these periods of apparent somnambulism, which Joanna assumed the ambassador could maintain indefinitely, so she remained silent during their journey. Upon reaching the forest, with new obstacles to impede their travel, Sarek had returned to full awareness, even taking the lead and navigating a path through the undergrowth.

Rising to his feet, Sarek smoothed his robes. "If you are sufficiently rested, I am ready to continue."

"Works for me." Joanna pushed herself to her feet, the involuntary groan she released being more from habit than distress. After a moment to ascertain his bearings, Sarek set off into the forest and she followed, walking in the direction of the twin suns. For the first time, she noted that they seemed closer to the horizon, rather than appearing to remain fixed in the sky as they had during this extended walkabout.

As she had during their passage across the salt plains, Joanna allowed her mind to drift while they walked, in a desperate bid to combat boredom. Not for the first time, she noticed the distinct lack of ambient noise as they proceeded through the forest. She heard her own footfalls along the uneven ground as she stepped on grass or leaves or fallen branches, and likewise she noted her clothing brushing against branches as she maneuvered too close to a tree or shrub. Meanwhile, there was no breeze rustling the treetops, no birds or insects.

Weird.

Opting to break the odd silence as she had at irregular intervals throughout the day, she asked, "Still feeling all right, sir?"

Sarek replied, "I remain well. However, I have noticed that you inquire about my well-being each time you initiate conversation."

A bit embarrassed, Joanna smiled. "I think it's a habit I picked up in nursing school." She shrugged. "Or maybe from my father. He's a doctor."

"Your father is Leonard McCoy, chief medical officer aboard the *Starship Enterprise*."

"That's right." Joanna eyed the ambassador. "I don't remember telling you that."

"A logical assumption," replied Sarek. "Besides what I gleaned from my own observations, you did introduce yourself as McCoy, and the *Enterprise* was in the Centaurus system at the time of the Romulan attack and our relocation to this place."

"Good point." She frowned. "Wait. Observations?"

"You exhibit mannerisms that are similar to those I recall seeing displayed by your father."

That caught Joanna by surprise. "I didn't realize you knew him."

There was a small pause before Sarek said, "I was a

patient under his care during a previous assignment that required me to travel aboard the *Enterprise*. His skills were most adequate."

Joanna could not help a small chuckle. "Adequate? I know that's probably high praise for a Vulcan, but I can imagine my father's reaction to hearing something like that." She laughed again. "I'd love to be around when he hears it."

"You may share that with him upon our return." Sarek said nothing for a few moments, and she once more fell into step behind him. His simple comment was enough to offer her at least some reassurance that they would indeed find a means of returning to Centaurus.

This situation is temporary. We'll figure it out.

"Nurse McCoy," said Sarek, his voice much lower in volume than before. He had also slowed his pace so that he once more was walking alongside her.

Instinctively, Joanna offered her reply in a softer volume. "What is it?"

"We are being followed."

"What?" Noting the Vulcan's demeanor, she forced herself not to begin looking around in search of anyone or anything who might be lurking in the vicinity. "Are you sure?"

"Yes. I estimate three to five life-forms have been moving with us, maneuvering among the tree canopy."

Despite her initial attempt at self-control, Joanna could not stop herself from looking up to the trees towering above them. She saw nothing to indicate anyone following them or staring at them. "What should we do?"

Sarek seemed to ponder this for a moment before saying, "I believe it is to our advantage to engage them sooner rather than later, particularly if darkness is coming."

"Sounds like a plan." When the ambassador said nothing else, Joanna asked, "Do we just shout at them to come out, come out, wherever they are?"

"A simple yet efficient course of action." Halting his advance through the forest, he turned back the way they had come and directed his attention to the trees. "Greetings," he called out in a loud voice. "We mean you no harm. We are lost and would appreciate assistance. I assure you, we carry no weapons."

Wincing at the bold admission, Joanna said in a hushed voice, "You didn't have to tell them *that*."

Sarek seemed unfazed by her remark. "It is the truth, although I am proceeding from the assumption that whoever or whatever follows us understands what we are saying. Regardless, honesty may well be the wise course."

"Always the diplomat?"

"You are correct."

Behind them, something heavy landed on the ground, and Joanna turned to see a lithe, long-limbed humanoid standing before her. His tanned skin was unadorned and nearly free from garments, and his hair was a shade of jade green that blended with the surrounding vegetation. He studied her and Sarek, his body tense as he shifted his feet, which Joanna noticed were bare and very similar in form to his hands, complete with opposable thumbs. Before she could say anything, more of the humanoids, similar in appearance to the first new arrival, dropped from the trees. They landed with grace, each of them wielding a stone-tipped spear.

"Um, hello," Joanna offered. The humanoid did not respond, but instead stared at her. His sole reaction to her words was to blink.

Speaking in a tone Joanna hoped their apparent stalkers would not find alarming, the ambassador said, "I am Sarek of Vulcan. This is Joanna of Earth. Can you understand me?"

To Joanna's surprise, the first humanoid nodded. "Yes, we understand." He gestured to the surrounding forest. "Are there others?"

"There may be others, yes," Sarek said, "but none with us now. We are new here, and we seek out others like us. Have you seen such beings?"

"Perhaps," replied the humanoid.

Joanna asked, "Do you have a name?"

Bringing himself up to his full height, the humanoid raised his hands to indicate himself. "I am Feneb, Ranger of the Usildar." Once more, he gestured to the forest. "The trees are our home now."

"Thank you for letting us travel through your home," she said.

"The others we seek look like us," added Sarek. "Have you seen them?"

Appearing to relax, Feneb replied, "We have. We travel with them. One is a very brave warrior and fights with us. He seeks others like him, and like you. So, we will honor his request and bring you to him."

"That is very kind of you," Sarek said. "Thank you."

Feneb clapped his hands three times, and Joanna watched as his companions began climbing the nearby trees, disappearing into the foliage. Feneb, however, did not follow.

"I will guide you."

Sarek nodded. "We are grateful for your assistance."

Matching the ambassador's stride as they followed Feneb deeper into the forest, Joanna could not help stealing glances into the treetops. Now that she knew what to look for, she was able to spot the other humanoids moving among the tree canopy. What had Feneb called them? Usildar?

"Feneb," said Sarek after a moment, "has this always been your home?"

"No. My people are of Usilde, not this place. Brought here we were, by the Newcomers, the Jatohr. They seek to control us, on Usilde and here. We fight to remain free."

"A noble effort," replied the Vulcan.

Feneb grunted in what Joanna interpreted as agreement. "Your people, your friends, they have spoken such words, but we cannot defeat the Jatohr. They are many in number, and their weapons are powerful. So, we hide. We strike when we must. All we want is to live in peace. We want Usilde but we will accept this world. Why must they take both?"

The question hung unanswered as shrieks of alarm drifted to them from somewhere farther ahead.

Feneb seemed to recognize the odd sound. He glanced up as if he wanted to take to the trees for speed and safety, but he remained on the ground. Then he gestured for them to follow him.

"Come," he said, calling out over his shoulder as he began running. "Hurry."

Now dashing through the forest, Joanna split her attention between Feneb, Sarek, and the uneven ground ahead of her. A rut or tree root here might twist an ankle or even inflict more serious injury, but both Feneb and Sarek seemed to run with no concern for such things.

She flinched as an anguished cry of frustration and rage pierced the forest air. Ahead of them, she saw Feneb coming abreast of something lying on the ground and realized it was another humanoid form, but it was not

Usildar. It took her a moment to see that the being was wearing a blue Starfleet tunic and dark uniform trousers.

"What happened?" She lunged toward the unmoving person who appeared to be a human male. Drawing closer to Feneb, she said, "Let me help!"

All but ignoring her, Feneb laid his hands on the human's chest. "Dylan-friend!"

He shifted to one side, allowing her to get closer to the fallen man, but Joanna saw that the victim was beyond help. Lying on his back, his gaze was fixed and the tip of his tongue protruded from his mouth. His open, unseeing eyes were streaked from hemorrhaging, and the purplish pallor of his skin denoted obvious internal bleeding. His chest seemed sunken, and Joanna pressed two tentative fingers against his rib cage, which yielded to her touch. "My god," she whispered. "It's like something crushed him."

"Nurse McCoy," said a voice over her shoulder, and Joanna looked up to see Sarek standing behind and to her left. He was pointing at something even farther ahead, among the trees. She looked in that direction and saw three of Feneb's Usildar companions standing at the crest of a low rise, hovering over what looked to be five additional bodies.

All but one of them wore Starfleet uniforms. The other corpse was an Izarian male dressed in civilian attire.

"No!"

She shouted the single word with such force that it startled Feneb and the other Usildar. Moving to join them, Joanna surveyed the victims. Each appeared to have suffered the same ghastly, unknown fate. One of the victims, a woman clad in a red tunic and dark trousers, also had burn marks on her face and hands. Feeling her breaths coming in rapid, shallow gasps, Joanna stepped away from the scene and put her hand to her mouth.

"Our friends," said Feneb. "Your friends. They are no more."

"Who were they?" asked Joanna. "Where did they come from?"

Sarek shook his head. "It is impossible to be certain. However, there is at least one curiosity." He pointed to one of the victims. "These are Starfleet uniforms, but of a type that is no longer used. This style was replaced some years ago by the current version."

"I would've never picked up on that," replied Joanna. "They all look the same to me. It still doesn't tell us who they were or how they came to be here."

"Feneb!"

Looking away from the victims, Joanna saw another of the Usildar waving toward them. He was gesturing at something beyond the rise that they could not see.

"Come! The fight continues! The warrior is ahead!"

"What fight?" asked Joanna, but the question was forgotten as Feneb and Sarek began moving toward the rise even as the other Usildar returned to the trees. The rustle of branches bowing beneath weight and motion was the only thing belying their movements before they disappeared altogether.

Joanna continued to chase after Feneb and Sarek, and as she advanced toward a clearing she could hear voices shouting along with the sounds of movement and perhaps things colliding with other things. By the time she caught up with the ambassador and the Usildar Ranger, the pair had reached the edge of a clearing, and she got her first look at what lay beyond.

What the hell?

Some distance ahead of them, a melee ensued.

Usildar bodies, more than Joanna could readily count,

littered the open ground. Others were running and jumping amid their fallen comrades, throwing spears and rocks and whatever else they could use as weapons. Their enemy appeared to be numerous hulking masses clad in what Joanna thought might be opalescent armored shells.

"They're giant slugs," she said aloud, not really caring who might hear her.

Two of the amorphous blobs were lying motionless and unattended while another pair fended off a handful of Usildar each. Despite their size and bulk, the slugs moved with surprising speed, defending against the Usildar's multipronged attacks. On the distant side of the clearing, another sizable armored gastropod was positioned at the controls of what Joanna took to be some sort of antigravity sled. The vehicle was hovering over the ground, green beams of energy lancing across the glade from an emitter at its front. One of the beams struck an Usildar fighter, arresting his movements before dropping him to the ground. To her right, another Usildar leaped from an overhead tree branch onto the sled, attempting to take its control handles from the pilot.

Joanna's eyes widened in fright as she tried to process the scene unfolding before her. "What are those things?"

"I do not recognize the species," replied Sarek. "Feneb, are these the Jatohr you spoke of?"

The Usildar nodded. "Yes. The Newcomers who took our home from us." He pointed to the battle. "I must go. I must fight."

"Wait," said Sarek. "We have no weapons. It would be illogical to proceed into battle unarmed."

Feneb growled, pointing to his fellow Usildar littering the glade. "I will take up the weapons of my people."

More movement from the field attracted Joanna's attention, and she could not help the gasp that escaped her lips. Without thinking, she grabbed Sarek's arm and pointed.

"Ambassador!"

In the midst of the skirmish, another figure had come into view. Standing head and shoulders above the Usildar, the humanoid was running toward the sled, which Joanna saw had been taken from its Jatohr pilot. Dressed in soiled, torn white robes, the new figure screamed in savage delight as the sled listed to one side and nosed into the ground. The crash tossed the Jatohr from its controls, but the Usildar who had hijacked it maintained his footing and stayed aboard. The new fighter stopped, raising a broad, bladed weapon above his head.

"The tide of battle turns! Now we take the fight to them!"

It was a Klingon.

"Councillor Gorkon," said Sarek.

Joanna stared in disbelief at the ambassador. "You *know* him?"

"Indeed I do. Fascinating."

Across the glade, the remaining Jatohr appeared to be retreating, with numerous Usildar giving chase. Standing before the antigrav sled, Gorkon lowered his weapon. Then, as though sensing he was being watched, he turned until Joanna could see his face. The Klingon smiled before releasing a loud, raucous laugh.

"Sarek!" Once more, he raised his blade, pointing it at the ambassador even as his smile widened. "Just like a Vulcan to show up once the fighting is over." Stepping away from the sled, he made his way across the open ground toward them. "It is good to see you, Ambassador."

Nodding, Sarek replied, "It is good to see you as well, Councillor, though I confess to not understanding how you came to be a part of this battle."

"It is a glorious tale," replied the Klingon. "One I'm happy to share over a fine meal, provided we can scrounge up something worthy of a warrior's stomach."

Joanna shook her head, still trying to absorb everything. "Tell me I'm not the only one who thinks this is all just a little too crazy. Better yet, somebody just wake me up and tell me I'm dreaming and that I'm late for class."

"You're not dreaming."

The new voice came from behind them, and Joanna whirled to see an older human female in a Starfleet uniform—at least, she looked human—emerging from the trees and walking toward them. Her dark hair framed her face, and there was a determination in her cold, blue eyes that Joanna found intimidating.

"Ambassador Sarek?" asked the new arrival, regarding the Vulcan.

"I am Sarek." He paused, glancing at Joanna before saying, "You know who I am?"

The woman nodded. "Indeed I do, sir." She cleared her throat. "My name is Captain Una. I know this might sound a little odd, even when you consider our situation, but I've been searching for you."

What?

All of this was becoming just a bit too much, Joanna decided. What was it about this place that had seen fit to bring them altogether, here and now? Was it simple chance? That seemed unlikely. Were their actions being guided by some unseen force or other being? She guessed that was possible, and perhaps not even so outlandish a notion, given their present circumstances.

Of course, it sort of begged the question: *What or who else are we going to find here?*

"You have been searching for me," said Sarek.

Una nodded. "Yes, sir. I know how this sounds, but . . . I heard you calling out to your wife."

"Interesting," said Sarek. "Then it seems we have much to discuss."

"Can we discuss it while we eat?" Gorkon snorted, his smile broadening even farther. "Battle makes me hungry."

Joanna released an exasperated sigh. "Are you *sure* I'm not dreaming?"

Eleven

"You want me to *what*?"

Uhura stood in the *Enterprise*'s astrophysics lab, her arms crossed as she watched Chekov with his arms buried up to the elbows inside an automated sensor drone that had undergone significant modifications. Had she heard the ensign correctly? Was he being subjected to a form of hazing ritual that was part of his being accepted by the starship's cadre of junior officers and that required him to make bizarre requests of the senior staff?

An odd and quite audible sigh escaped the probe's innards, which Uhura at first thought had come from Chekov. It took her an extra moment to realize that the escaping air had instead come from a pressurized compartment inside the probe. Extracting his hands from inside the device, the ensign turned and smiled at her.

"I said I'm hoping you can help me modify a subspace transceiver to send and accept sensor readings sent from another dimension."

Her eyes narrowing, Uhura replied, "Okay. That's what I thought you said." Stepping closer to the probe, she noted the presence of additional acquisition sensor modules as well as a second stereographic analysis component. "You're really beefing up this thing." Seeing a second power supply wedged into the device's upper access compartment, she said, "Is this an extra battery for the transceiver?"

Chekov nodded. "Yes, Lieutenant. Mister Spock and I

decided a dedicated power source for the transceiver relay was prudent, given the circumstances. That is, assuming it can function the way we need it to. I'm hoping you can help me with my backup plan."

"*Backup* plan?" Uhura asked. "Should my feelings be hurt here?"

Chekov smiled. "Not at all. It's just that given what we're about to try with this probe, I want to be as prepared as possible for the unexpected."

"Always a good idea, Ensign. So, what's your plan?"

Pointing to the probe's open compartment, Chekov said, "You know we're modifying this probe so that we can send it into the other universe. According to the theory Mister Spock and I have developed, we believe we can use the Transfer Key to relocate the probe to the same area within the dimensional realm where Captain Una and the others were sent. We're programming the probe's sensors to collect data and then recalibrate itself to send that information back through the link between the two universes."

Uhura tried to recall the theoretical physics discussions in which she had participated as a cadet at Starfleet Academy. The conversations had been spirited, and much of it was beyond her grasp of science and engineering. Her own intimate knowledge of subspace communications had kept her from becoming completely lost during such discourse. There were some scientists who even speculated that subspace was itself an alternate domain of existence, accessible only by faster-than-light travel. Even then, such a realm could not truly be explored, and therefore theories about it being a tangible, even inhabitable plane remained untested, perhaps for all time. In many ways, it was far different even than the strange parallel universe into which she along with Captain Kirk, Spock, and Montgomery

Scott had been transported. Though that reality mirrored this one in many ways, including another *Enterprise* and near-perfect representations of her friends and shipmates, everyone there seemed to be a darker, malevolent representation of the people she knew. Fate and good fortune had allowed them to return to their own dimension.

And now here they were, facing something like that yet again.

"Do you and Mister Spock really think you can transport that thing into the Jatohr's universe?" she asked.

Chekov nodded. "We are almost certain. The Transfer Key has already shown us it's possible, and Captain Una's encounter with the Jatohr scientist who created it tells us that we can certainly transfer people from there to here. Even if we're successful, we don't know how the other universe will react to anything we send across. Our regular communications equipment may not work properly. That's why I want the backup plan."

"Communicating across a dimensional barrier." Uhura was speaking more to herself than Chekov as she regarded the modified probe. "I suppose there are worse ways to spend my off-duty time. Let's get started."

Smiling, Chekov said, "Two-way communication is preferable, but even being able to receive a one-way feed from the probe is better than nothing. Still, it'd be nice to see what the probe is seeing, in real time. There's no way to know if there are any hazards waiting for it."

"Let's hope there's nothing like that, for the sake of Captain Una and everyone else trapped over there." Beyond just rescuing their friends and former *Enterprise* crew members, Uhura knew that retrieving Ambassador Sarek and Councillor Gorkon was vital if the Federation hoped to avoid further escalating tensions with the

Klingon Empire. She suspected they already were living on borrowed time and wondered how much longer the Klingon High Council or its military leaders would wait before deciding Gorkon was lost, and it was the Federation's fault. What Spock and Chekov were planning needed to be put into motion without delay.

Better get cracking, then.

"Okay," she said. "Tell me about this theory you and Spock have."

Several minutes passed as Chekov talked about molecular harmonics, vibrating atoms, and how changing the frequency of vibration could shift objects between dimensional planes. The ensign did a creditable job explaining it, and she understood most of what he was saying, but there still were aspects of the problem that eluded her. Uhura realized that she did not need to grasp every last detail. The Jatohr had already done that for her.

"The Transfer Key is able to change this frequency," she said, "and do so in a targeted manner, both in relation to the person or object being moved and a fixed point in the destination universe. You're saying this process is like a frequency we can't hear or that our sensors can't detect."

"That's the idea," he said. "What we need to figure out is whether an object present in one universe can receive a communication from an object in another."

"Why not? Communication can take many forms. Subspace carrier waves, old-fashioned radio signals, or even pulsing light or radiation across a spectrum." Uhura paused, considering what she had just said. "Hang on a minute."

Moving to one of the lab's auxiliary consoles, she dropped into the station's seat and reached for the rows of multicolored controls. It took her only moments to enter a command sequence to the ship's computer, and once her instructions were executed she activated the lab's main viewscreen. Uhura turned from the station just as the screen flared to life, watching as a computer-generated image coalesced into existence. It was a white graph superimposed over a black background, and a bright red line began tracing over the grid from left to right, arcing and dipping as it crossed the screen.

"Gamma rays?" asked Chekov after a moment.

Uhura nodded. "With a recursive modulating algorithm, we could transmit basic data in a form that we would be able to detect as it seeps between the dimensions. Once we have that, sending a matching harmonic signal back the other way should be possible. That second power source will come in handy for something like this."

"I'll also need to make further adjustments to the subspace transceiver, but that shouldn't take long."

Studying her impromptu solution, Uhura said, "It just might work. I don't know for how long or how powerful the transmission will be, but I may be able to boost the ship's communications array so that it can detect the signal."

Stepping away from the console, Uhura moved to the workbench supporting the probe. "Let's get a better look at this thing."

Chekov drew closer, preparing to assist her, but she was already peering into the probe's open compartment, her gaze tracing the internal circuitry paths and component configuration.

"This is some nice work, Ensign." Uhura found the communications components without trouble. Not for the first time, she applauded her decision to remain abreast of the inner workings of such components. This had often necessitated spending her share of time deep in the bowels of the ship's communications array or even sprawled on the deck underneath her console on the bridge to repair or replace burned-out components. She had never minded "getting her hands dirty" with the equipment, as Mister Scott said. Others might be content to leave such tasks to an engineer or assistant, but not her. Equipment repair and maintenance was just another part of the job, and it was this aspect that Uhura strove to teach the entire communications staff.

Behind them, the lab's doors slid open to admit Spock. The first officer was carrying a data slate, and his tricorder was slung over his shoulder. He paused in the doorway upon seeing Chekov and Uhura.

"Mister Spock," said Uhura.

The Vulcan nodded. "Lieutenant." To Chekov, he said, "Ensign, I have isolated the readings required to match the probe's frequency modulation to that of the Transfer Key. Have you completed reconfiguring the internal components?"

Gesturing to Uhura, Chekov replied, "I had an idea about one final modification and requested the lieutenant's assistance."

"I'm happy to help," said Uhura. "I know you've had a lot on your mind."

She hoped Spock would find her deliberate phrasing appropriate, not wanting him to think he may have displayed any emotional reaction to the current situation. It was obvious to even a casual observer that Spock had been under tremendous strain since the incident on Centaurus. Only someone who had served with him would notice the subtle shift in his normally stoic demeanor. It was obvious that he was concerned about Ambassador Sarek, and that it was these feelings—however controlled they may be—that now drove Spock to find a way to retrieve his father. Uhura knew that he and Sarek had only recently repaired a dysfunctional relationship that had stretched back nearly two decades. The resolution had come during the *Enterprise*'s mission to ferry the ambassador and a number of Federation diplomats to a vital conference. The tension between Spock and his father even during the brief moments Uhura had witnessed was palpable. Their differences had been resolved after Sarek had suffered a life-threatening heart attack that required surgery and a massive blood transfusion that only Spock could provide. It was the first step on a long path toward reconciliation.

"Your assistance is most welcome, Lieutenant," said Spock. "What have you determined?"

Uhura replied, "I think I've come up with a method of modulating gamma rays as carrier waves for altering molecular harmonics across the . . . well, whatever it is. A barrier? Conduit?"

"Interesting." Spock pondered the lieutenant's suggestion. "As Doctor McCoy might say under similar circumstances, 'Nothing ventured, nothing gained.' I will need to see your analysis, but the idea holds promise."

He reached with his free hand to his data slate, and Uhura noticed that he was holding a yellow computer data card beneath his left thumb against the slate's flat surface. Retrieving the card, he offered it to Chekov.

"These are my calculations for the variance in frequencies between the two universes. Program them into the probe's communications processor, after which we will carry out a final series of diagnostic tests. I will inform the captain that our preparations for the probe are nearing completion. Your work to this point has been exemplary,

Ensign." Turning his attention to Uhura, he added, "I have no doubt your expertise will prove invaluable, as well, Lieutenant."

"Thank you, sir," replied Chekov. Uhura had to suppress the urge to smile as the ensign beamed with obvious pride.

Spock departed the lab, on his way to the bridge to continue whatever preparations remained before the probe could be launched, leaving Uhura and Chekov alone in the astrophysics lab. To his credit, Chekov waited until the doors closed behind the first officer before releasing an audible sigh of relief.

"When I was a boy," he said, "I had a teacher who scared every one of his students. He was nothing compared to Mister Spock."

Putting her hand to her mouth, Uhura stifled a laugh. "He does have that way of making you feel like you're failing at everything, even when he's complimenting you, doesn't he? But you'll never learn more working with anyone else." Her gaze lingering on the doors, she added, "Besides, he must have a lot of trust in you, to let you head up this part of a project that's as important as this one."

Chekov replied, "We should probably get back to work, then."

"Agreed." Uhura smiled. "After all, these molecular harmonics aren't going to modulate themselves."

Twelve

"Bah! This is hardly a way to celebrate victory."

Lost in thought, Captain Una was startled by Gorkon's sudden outburst as the Klingon dropped another large piece of wood onto the campfire he and a few of the Usildar had prepared. Still grumbling under his breath, Gorkon moved away from the fire, perhaps searching for more wood to fuel it.

The fire pit surrounded by stones, presumably gathered from the surrounding forest, was the centerpiece of the improvised encampment created by the Usildar. Una, along with Sarek and the human nurse, Joanna McCoy, had accompanied Gorkon and his new friends here following the battle. The councillor and the Usildar had opted not to give chase to those few Jatohr that had survived the skirmish, choosing instead to regroup and assess their status. Little more than a collection of shelters created from whatever materials the Usildar could find within the forest, the camp's most interesting feature was its ersatz armory containing a diverse collection of spears, clubs, and other handcrafted weapons. The small arsenal had been augmented by a few blades—oversized swords that reminded Una of Klingon *bat'leths*—and other items salvaged from the small battlefield.

"Are you all right?"

The new voice made Una turn her gaze from the fire to see Joanna McCoy moving toward her. As the nurse lowered herself to sit on the ground on Una's right, the captain forced a small smile.

"I'm fine, thank you. Just . . . thinking."

"This place will do that." McCoy crossed her legs, then held her hands out before her, directing her palms toward the fire. "It's weird. I don't really feel cold, but the fire is still warm and soothing."

Una nodded in agreement. The fire had been unnecessary, at least for warmth. She felt no chill in the air and only registered the heat from the flames once she focused her attention on it. Still, it had provided illumination once darkness had fallen, while she had imparted to Sarek and Joanna everything she knew about this universe. She described her prior encounters with the Usildar, the Jatohr, and the enigmatic technology that was responsible for their current situation. Included in that part of the report was her mission to rescue her lost shipmates and the plot she and Captain Kirk had cooked up to secure their return.

"Ambassador Sarek tells me the Izarian was his military advisor during the peace talks on Centaurus," said Joanna. She paused, and Una sensed her hesitation. "Did you know the other Starfleet officers?"

"Yes. They were all former shipmates of mine, many years ago when I was a lieutenant on the *Enterprise*." She spent the next few minutes retelling the story of her first encounter with the Usildar, the Jatohr, and the transfer-field technology that had trapped her comrades here, rather than killing them as was first believed.

"I knew I had to do everything I could to rescue them." She let her gaze drift toward the fire. "As it happens, everything wasn't good enough."

Lieutenant Ingrid Holstine and Ensigns Dylan Craig

and Bruce Goldberg were killed by the Jatohr, after Una had ordered them to return to the salt plains that seemed to be the common arrival point for everyone transported to this universe. Una had been unable to find an explanation for that phenomenon, but at least it was something—some known if intangible quality—with which they could work. The trio died along with Lieutenant Karen Griffin and Petty Officer James Cambias, who had been part of her original landing party to Usilde eighteen years earlier. All five of them had been banished here by the transfer-field generator. Their deaths hurt her even more because Una thought she had found a means of retrieving them.

You still have the others to watch over. Your duty is not done here.

The thought made her glance to one of the primitive shelters, under which her other former crewmates, Shimizu and Martinez, were sleeping. Under an adjacent lean-to was Ensign Terra Le May, another member of her original landing complement, and Ensign Cheryl Stevens, a navigator who had been transported here directly from the *Enterprise* bridge. This place seemed to have had an odd, almost debilitating effect on them, which Una could not explain. Was it due to the circumstances of their transfer? Had they encountered something else here that had carried some unidentified side effect? If her friends had been compromised in some manner, was it treatable? What would happen when Una was successful in getting them back to their own universe? There was no way to know.

"Come!"

Gorkon's voice erupted from the darkness, interrupting her thoughts, and she looked away from the fire to where he stood among a small group of Usildar. "We must seek food and drink, so that we may feast and sing songs of our victory in battle."

Joanna shook her head. "Is he even hungry? I have no idea how long I've been here, but I haven't even thought about eating."

"I don't think it really matters," replied Una. "Klingons fight, then they eat and drink. Then they sleep it off, and then they find someone else to fight. Logic or reason seldom enters into the equation."

That made Joanna smile. "Where did you find him?"

"He found me. Apparently, he was transported from Centaurus just as you and Sarek were, and arrived at the same location out on the salt flats. He wandered toward the mountains like we all did, and somehow our paths crossed." She shook her head. "It makes absolutely no sense whatsoever that we'd all find each other so easily. I convinced him to help me find my people, after which we'd all head back to the landing point and await rescue. I didn't anticipate Gorkon taking such a liking to the Usildar we came across. They were preparing to launch an attack on that group of Jatohr. He just took charge and led the assault. That's when you found us."

"I didn't expect to do any fighting here," said Joanna.

"Neither did I, but it may come to that." Una studied the young nurse. "The Jatohr are nothing if not persistent, and we've seen indications that they may be massing forces on the salt plains. Given that their original intent was to transport to our universe in order to escape this one, it may be part of their larger plan. Time moves . . . differently here, so there's no way to know how long they've been preparing for this moment."

"Sarek has said something similar, more than once," said Joanna.

"Yes. Vulcans have a wonderful ability to grasp the passage of time. Years ago, I might've found it annoying, but here and now? I'm glad to hear it." Una had been hoping to discuss with the ambassador her issues attempting to keep track of time in this place.

Pointing to a cluster of trees at the edge of the encampment, Joanna said, "He's been doing that a lot since we got here."

In truth, Una did not require Joanna's help to know Sarek's location or even what he was doing. She could see him in her mind as clearly as if he was seated here next to her at the fire, and she had been sensing his presence since his arrival along with Joanna. Indeed, Una could tell that he was aware of her, and her thoughts regarding him, though she did not understand how that was possible. She was no telepath, and even if this connection was a consequence of their surroundings, why didn't she sense Joanna in similar fashion?

"Excuse me," said Una. Pushing herself to her feet, she crossed the camp, already able to discern Sarek's silhouette where he sat near the base of a large tree. The Vulcan knelt on the ground, his hands held clasped to his chest. His eyes were closed, but they opened at her approach.

"Captain."

"I apologize for disturbing you, sir." Una stepped closer, and at his unspoken gesture lowered herself to the ground next to him. From her vantage point, she was able to see the fire and Joanna McCoy, still bathed in its glow. Turning her attention back to Sarek, she said, "You know why I'm here."

The ambassador nodded. "You are able to sense my presence. You have heard me attempting to reach out to my wife. Most interesting. It confirms a theory I have been formulating. In this place, I am somehow able to amplify my thoughts, though I do not understand how this is possible, or why you alone are able to sense them."

"I'm not a telepath," replied Una, "but I am trained and experienced in a variety of mental disciplines." She smiled. "Growing up in the Illyrian colonies had its challenges and perks."

"The Illyrian colonies. Of course. That explains it. Perhaps the skills you mastered at an early age have provided you with an unexpected benefit here. That is quite intriguing. We may even conclude that despite the facility for psychic connection presented in this place, such activity remains out of reach for the unprepared mind. This might explain why, at least to this point, my attempts at outreach have not been perceived by our human or Usildar companions, or even the Jatohr."

Una replied, "Likewise, yours is the only other presence I've felt since my arrival."

"What else have you sensed?" When Una did not reply, Sarek added, "Forgive me, Captain. I realize the question may sound abrupt. I am curious as to any other insights or conclusions you may have drawn about our present circumstances since your arrival here."

Shifting to a more comfortable sitting position, Una said, "If you're asking where I think we are, I'm not sure." She gestured to indicate the surrounding forest. "I have reason to believe that none of this is what it appears to be."

"Explain."

"I don't believe this place exists, at least physically. Instead, I think we're all participating in some kind of . . . collective hallucination or simulation." When she said it aloud, Una realized it sounded more than a bit farfetched.

Sarek seemed to ponder this, but only for a moment. "A shared mental construct."

"Exactly. When my people and I were being held by the Jatohr, I began to realize that my perceptions were different than my human companions'. I don't know why, but as an experiment, I applied a lucid-dreaming technique I learned years ago, and the results were surprising."

Placing her palms on the ground before her, Una cleared her mind, then began to focus on a single thought. From her memories, she retrieved an image of a portable lantern that once had belonged to her grandfather. She had grown fond of it as a child, and she—along with her brothers, Hudek and Leighton—had often used it to explore the wooded regions around the family home on Illyria.

Concentrate.

She lifted her hands from the ground, and a moment later a red lantern, identical to her grandfather's, appeared from nothingness. It illuminated the space between her and Sarek, and by that light she was able to see the ambassador raise an eyebrow in obvious surprise.

"Fascinating."

Una cleared her throat. "I've also used it to make obstacles go away, including helping us to escape the Jatohr." She shrugged. "It's a bit draining, and to be honest, I'm still a bit skeptical about the whole thing." The light between them faded, and she was startled to see that the lantern had vanished. "Case in point. I stopped thinking about the thing, and it disappeared. I'm worried about losing my concentration at a critical moment and hurting myself or someone else."

"That is understandable," replied Sarek. "Like you, I had concluded that what surrounds us exists only as a communal illusion in our minds. However, I was unaware of the potential for it to be manipulated."

"Of course, if it's true, then it raises even more questions." Una gestured to herself. "While our minds are being occupied, somewhere and somehow, our physical needs are being met."

Sarek nodded. "And is it merely a natural phenomenon of our environment, or are we being influenced by the Jatohr or someone else? If it is the latter, then for what purpose?"

"All good questions." Una blinked several times to help her eyes adjust to the sudden return of darkness. "Here's another one: Were my shipmates really killed in that battle with the Jatohr or was that an illusion, too? If so, then where are they?"

Placing a hand on his chest, Sarek replied, "Perhaps they are with our physical bodies. Assuming this theory is correct, of course."

"Right." Una was thankful to have her suspicions confirmed by the ambassador, whose mental acuity and discipline far exceeded her own. "It's a lot to process." She sighed. "I don't even how to begin explaining this to the others."

"For the moment, the best course might be to withhold any explanations," said Sarek. "Such concepts are best absorbed gradually, when emotional responses can be better controlled. Also, the notion that nothing here is real may lead one of our companions to assume undue risks to themselves. We have seen what we believe to be death in this place. We are uncertain how such an ending might affect an individual's physical form."

"On the other hand," countered Una, "the more clear minds we have, the better our chances of figuring out how to get home." She looked toward the encampment. "I'd like to think Jim Kirk is doing everything he can to rescue us, but for all I know, we're on our own."

"Knowing Captain Kirk as I do," Sarek said, "I am convinced he along with my son will do everything in their power to assist us. They are both very determined individuals."

Smiling, Una replied, "You're not telling me anything new."

Thirteen

Alert sirens wailed in the narrow passageway, echoing off the metal bulkheads of the *I.K.S. Vron'joQ* in concert with flashing indicators spaced at intervals along the corridor. Those members of his crew he encountered looked intent as they moved with speed and purpose toward their assigned stations, but they all cleared a path for him as Captain J'Teglyr strode past.

"Attention," said a voice through the ship's internal communications system. *"Scanners have detected a Federation battle cruiser on an intercept course. The vessel's intentions are unknown. Stand ready at battle stations and await further commands."*

Reaching a junction in the corridor, J'Teglyr halted his advance and slapped the activation switch of a nearby communications panel. "This is the captain. What is our status?"

"We have energized defense fields, my lord," replied his first officer, D'jorok. *"I was preparing to bring weapons online."*

"Negative. Do not activate our weapons until I give the order. Maintain defensive posture until further notice, and continue scans of the Federation ship."

Ending the connection before D'jorok could reply, J'Teglyr continued his transit to the bridge. Along the way, he took the opportunity to inspect the level of readiness exhibited by those subordinates he passed. Even the youngest of his crew, a handful on their first deep-space assignment, appeared prepared for battle. J'Teglyr nodded as he made eye contact with individual warriors, conveying his approval.

Excellent, he thought, pleased to see that the prolonged period of relative inactivity while orbiting the useless ball of mud below them had not eroded their attention to duty.

He reached the pair of reinforced pressure hatches at the end of the corridor, which parted at his approach and allowed him access to the bridge. The ship's command center stood at the ready. The lighting here was subdued, and everything was awash in a dim crimson lighting that served to highlight the bridge's array of screens and other status indicators and controls. He glanced to his right and saw his tactical officer, G'peq, hovering over his console, his face bathed in the red glow of his station's sensor readouts.

"My lord," said Commander D'jorok, rising from the high-backed chair at the center of the room, "we are holding our defensive status. Weapons remain inactive."

J'Teglyr thought he sensed doubt in his subordinate, as though D'jorok might be considering questioning the wisdom of this simple order. In truth, J'Teglyr had expected the first officer to be uncertain, though he also knew the other Klingon would never take him to task here on the bridge, in the presence of the crew.

Deciding to help his second-in-command by not prolonging a potentially awkward silence, J'Teglyr said, "Your training and drills of the crew are evident, Commander. Well done." He gestured toward the bridge's forward viewing screen. "What is the status of the Federation vessel?"

"They are approaching at warp speed, my lord. If they hold to standard Starfleet protocols, they will drop to sublight upon entering the system and proceed on course at impulse power. With that in mind, I estimate the ship's arrival within the hour, my lord." D'jorok's eyes narrowed, and a small smile seemed to tease the corners of his mouth. "We have identified it as the *Enterprise*, Captain."

J'Teglyr could not help the sudden rush of excitement he felt upon hearing the name. "Kirk's ship."

So, the reports from the Klingon High Command were true, and the notorious Earther captain was making his way here after all. Those updates had notified J'Teglyr that the *Enterprise* had suffered significant damage during its battle against a Romulan warship near the planet Centaurus. How impaired was the vessel, if at all? The *Vron'joQ*, as a D6 battle cruiser, was in many respects an inferior vessel to the Starfleet ship currently approaching Usilde. High Command had informed him that at least one more Klingon vessel had been routed to the Libros system, but it was distant and would not arrive before the *Enterprise*.

"This Earther has quite the reputation," said D'jorok. "He should not be underestimated."

"I have no intention of doing so." Stepping away from his first officer, J'Teglyr began a slow circuit of the bridge's perimeter stations. In keeping with the ship's elevated alert level, every console was overseen by a crew member, and each was focused on their individual collection of status readings. J'Teglyr studied the information being fed to each console, noting the status of every system that would be critical to success should the need arise to engage the approaching Starfleet ship. Despite whatever tactical advantage the other vessel might hold, he was confident he could give the Earther captain a memorable fight.

Victory requires more than simply wielding the bigger weapon.

Sensing D'jorok standing behind him, J'Teglyr turned from his inspection and regarded his first officer. "You have concerns, Commander."

To his credit, the first officer looked around him to ensure his words were not overheard before replying, "I am curious as to why we do not bring our weapons to the ready, my lord."

For the briefest of moments, J'Teglyr wondered if his first officer might finally be challenging his authority. It was an absurd notion. In addition to being an officer of exceptional skill and determination, D'jorok was loyal, perhaps to a fault. He would rather die than betray his captain. On the other hand, the commander had made no secret of his desire to one day command a ship of his own, and his commitment to that goal was evident. How high did that ambition reach? Might J'Teglyr one day have cause for worry?

I hope not. I would truly hate having to kill him.

D'jorok's voiced uncertainty was reasonable, given the circumstances, and all things being equal and normal, J'Teglyr would already have given the appropriate order. However, relations between the Klingon Empire and the Federation were not equal for any number of reasons, just as they were certainly not normal.

"Given the constraints of the treaty forced upon us by the meddling Organians," said J'Teglyr, "we must proceed with care, so as not to provoke our self-proclaimed nursemaids."

He felt his ire rising at the mere mention of the enigmatic, noncorporeal beings who had inserted themselves into the Empire's growing conflict with the Federation. It had been less than a year since the Organian Ayelborne had appeared here on the bridge of his vessel, looking like a ghost conjured from the depths of a fevered imagination. One of J'Teglyr's warriors had attempted to shoot the intruder only to discover that it was some form of alien projection, the source of which could not be located. The officer also learned that his own disruptor pistol, along with every control on every station throughout the ship, had begun radiating a heat so intense that the consoles could not be touched. At the time, J'Teglyr recalled the odd contradiction of the heat not permeating the air around him, even as he and his crew were rendered helpless by the sudden phenomenon. Then came the Organian's boast about disabling both the imperial and Federation fleets in a similar fashion.

J'Teglyr and his crew listened in useless, silent rage as the alien claimed to be standing on the Earthers' home world as well as upon the sacred soil of Qo'noS. According to Ayelborne, the Organians had inserted themselves into the conflict between the Empire and the Federation, unilaterally deciding that there would be no war. Under the terms of the treaty they had imposed upon both powers, all disputes—including those of territory and the annexation of unclaimed worlds—would now require resolution in diplomatic fashion. That might be fine for the Earthers, and those who answered their call, but to a Klingon warrior such restrictions were suffocating.

In the months since the levying of the peace accords, there had been a few incidents of conflict between imperial and Starfleet ships. That those encounters had apparently gone unchecked by the Organians raised suspicions that the aliens might be playing an elaborate ruse, but there were those on the High Council who worried about retribution should the terms of the treaty be abrogated. As an officer sworn to obey the wishes of the Council and those appointed over him, it vexed J'Teglyr that he was bound to observe and respect such cowardly thinking.

If any gods remain, I hope they see fit to cast those spineless wretches into the depths of Gre'thor.

"But what of Kirk?" asked D'jorok. "I have read the reports, and while he has demonstrated an ability to fight, he does not seem one who would come seeking battle."

J'Teglyr nodded. "I agree, but that does not mean he won't come to the aid of those he feels are in need of rescuing. For instance, the primitives on the planet below."

Usilde was of moderate value from a strategic standpoint, and it possessed sufficient quantities of raw minerals to justify the effort to subjugate it. The indigenous population was of little consequence to the Empire beyond serving as a labor pool, but they were just the sort of weak, useless people to whom the Federation loved pledging unending support.

"Of course he will not come simply to fight," said J'Teglyr. "He is far too shrewd to attempt something so clumsy." Turning toward the bridge's main viewscreen, he regarded the image of Usilde as the planet turned beneath the *Vron'joQ*. "Along with his superiors, Kirk worries about the alien technology we now control. If he is coming, you can be sure that is his primary concern. The only question that remains is how far will he go in order to wrest it from our grasp?"

D'jorok said, "While we may have seized the alien device, we do not control it. At least, not yet." He scowled. "If that *petaQ* B'tinzal were not so useless, the machine might well be ours by now."

"I harbor no particular warmth for B'tinzal, but that does not mean she is wrong. Understanding an alien technology is not a simple task, even for someone supposedly possessing such skills." Though he did not enjoy dealing with the increasingly frequent interrogatives dispatched from the Klingon High Command, J'Teglyr was no fool. He understood the complexities of the assignment given to B'tinzal. The scientist might be bothersome, but it did not mean she was wrong when reporting the challenges she faced while trying to decipher the mysterious alien artifact.

"Besides," J'Teglyr said, his gaze lingering on the image of the blue-green world turning beneath his ship, "if B'tinzal is right, then the solution to our problem may at this very moment be delivering itself to us."

———

Talk about walking into the lion's den.

That and other cheerful thoughts marched one after the other through Kirk's mind as he sat in his chair on the *Enterprise*'s bridge, watching Usilde as the planet grew larger on the main viewscreen. The increase in size was an illusion, of course, generated by the starship's sensor array and the viewscreen's imaging processors. Even at their present speed, they were still some distance from the planet.

"We're secured from warp speed," reported Sulu from where he sat at the helm station, ahead and slightly to Kirk's left.

"Slow to half impulse and make your course for a standard orbit over Usilde," said Kirk.

Sulu nodded without looking up from his console. "Aye, sir. Time of arrival at half impulse is just over fourteen minutes."

Pushing himself from his chair, Kirk crossed to the red

railing separating the bridge's command well from the science station. "What about that Klingon ship, Spock?"

"Scanning," replied the Vulcan, who stood bent over the hooded viewer affixed to his console. A soft blue light emanated from the viewer and bathed his face. "Sensors indicate it is a D6 cruiser. Maintaining a standard orbit above the planet. It has raised its deflector shields, but I am detecting no signs of active weapons." He looked up from his controls. "Under normal circumstances I would say the *Enterprise* was the superior vessel, but given our present operational status, that might not be the case."

Kirk could not resist a small grin. "No faith in your captain, Mister Spock?"

Behind him, Ensign Chekov called out from the navigator's station, "Captain, shall we raise shields?"

It was a valid question. The Klingon ship's commander had justifiably raised his own vessel's shields, but Kirk found it telling that its armaments had not been brought online. An unusual move for a Klingon. However, the Libros system was in a contested area of space, with both the Empire and the Federation having equal claims to the region. That could change, in accordance with the Organian Peace Treaty, if either side demonstrated an ability to better develop any world claimed in the disputed area. Was this Klingon merely adhering to the tenets of the Organian agreement, or was there something else in play?

Only one way to find out.

"Negative on the shields for now, Mister Chekov," said Kirk. "However, raise them at your discretion if things take a dicey turn."

The ensign nodded. "Aye, aye, Captain."

Looking to his right, Kirk eyed his communications

officer. "Lieutenant, are you picking up any hails from the Klingon ship, or any other comm traffic?"

Uhura swiveled in her seat. "Nothing in our direction, sir." She reached up to pull the Feinberg receiver from her left ear that allowed her to filter through the varying number of incoming and outgoing signals. "However, once we dropped out of warp I did detect what was probably ship-to-surface transmissions."

"Well, that answers my next question," said Kirk. "They've still got people on the surface. Can you confirm, Spock?"

Hovering once again over his sensors, the first officer replied, "As expected, there are Klingon life signs inside and in proximity to the citadel. There are also larger concentrations of Usildar life-forms that are inconsistent with our last visit here." Spock pulled away from the viewer. "If the Klingons are following their normal procedures for occupying a planet with an indigenous higher-order population, then the likely conclusion is that the Usildar are being collected and gathered into internment and labor camps. This would be consistent with the increased mining activity our sensors have noted."

"What about the Jatohr terraforming efforts?"

"It has only been eight weeks since our previous scans, and I am detecting no appreciable difference from those readings." Spock added, "Of course, terraforming is a rather lengthy process."

Resisting the urge to comment on the first officer's stating of the obvious in the finest Vulcan tradition, Kirk instead regarded his friend with a knowing look that communicated the same sentiment and earned a raised eyebrow for his efforts. "Now for the big question: What's the status of the citadel?"

"Sensors are registering energy levels consistent with

the scans we conducted during our previous visit. I have found no indications that the transfer-field generator is active or has been since Captain Una last employed the device."

Kirk nodded. "The Klingons haven't figured out a substitute for the Transfer Key. Not yet, anyway."

"Obtaining even a rudimentary understanding of the technology involved in the device's construction would be a most time-consuming process, particularly without the actual Key available for study. It would be most unfortunate if it fell into Klingon hands, Captain."

Stepping up to stand next to his first officer, Kirk asked, "Is that your way of saying we should've left it somewhere safe, Spock?"

"I would argue that few such places exist." Placing his hands behind his back, Spock continued, "It is logical to presume that the Klingons waiting for us at Usilde have been apprised of our having regained control of the Key from the Romulans. Given their apparent failure to activate the transfer generator, they will doubtless see us as a target of opportunity."

There had been plenty of time during the journey from Centaurus for Kirk to contemplate all of this. Even with the Organian treaty in effect, he could not count on the commander of a Klingon vessel to abide by the agreement's forced stipulations, but there were other factors at play.

"If the Klingons here know what happened at Centaurus," the captain said, "we may be able to convince them that helping us retrieve Councillor Gorkon from the other universe is the right thing to do." He gestured toward the viewscreen. "It's a nice idea, anyway." Glancing to the communications station, he ordered, "Lieutenant Uhura, open a hailing frequency. Let's see if they're willing to talk this over."

A moment later, Uhura turned in her seat. "Hailing frequency open, sir."

Moving to stand in front of the helm and navigation stations, Kirk drew a breath and straightened his posture before calling out, "Klingon vessel, this is Captain James T. Kirk, commanding the Federation *Starship Enterprise*. Be advised that we are here on a rescue mission. We've noted and appreciate you keeping your ship's weapons inactive, and your sensors should have told you by now that my defenses are also down. We have no quarrel with you, and in fact would welcome your assistance with this rescue. Please respond." Once he was finished, Kirk looked to where Spock stood at the bridge railing. The Vulcan offered a small, approving nod.

Behind Kirk, Uhura said, "Captain, we're receiving a response. Onscreen." Without waiting for the order, the lieutenant accepted the incoming message and a moment later the image of Usilde vanished from the viewscreen.

Replacing it was the glowering visage of a Klingon officer, sitting in a high-backed chair. The image focused on him, with the rest of the bridge of the Klingon ship blurred as though to thwart any attempts at gleaning information from consoles or displays. The Klingon's black hair was cropped close to his scalp and high enough to reveal a large, smooth forehead. Thick, sweeping brows hovered over a pair of cold, dark eyes. A thin, trimmed beard accented the lower half of his face. He wore what Kirk recognized as the standard uniform for a Klingon officer in command of a warship, including a gold baldric worn from his left shoulder.

"I am Captain J'Teglyr, commanding the imperial war-

ship Vron'joQ. This planet and the surrounding star system have been claimed by the Klingon Empire, Captain Kirk. Your presence here could be interpreted as a hostile act."

Stepping away from the helm console, Kirk replied, "We both know that this system and planet are open territory under the terms of the Organian Peace Treaty. Determining ownership is a job better left to diplomats. As I said, I'm here for more immediate concerns, which benefit both our peoples."

J'Teglyr smiled. It was not a pleasant sight. *"Surrender the alien device you hold in your possession, and I'm willing to forgive your intrusion."*

So much for holding that card close to the vest.

Kirk replied, "That's also not a decision for me to make, Captain. We need the device as part of our rescue mission. It's a bit complicated, but—"

"I am aware of the device's function, Kirk." The Klingon's irritation was starting to show, fading the facade of composure with which he had begun the conversation. *"Just as we know what the fortress down on the planet is supposed to do, and that it will not work without the component you hold. What I don't understand is why I should care about a handful of humans who may be trapped on the other side of whatever door that thing is supposed to open."*

"Because it's not just my people who are trapped in that other universe, Captain." Kirk took another step toward the viewscreen. "At least two Klingons have been sent there against their will as well, including Councillor Gorkon."

This was enough to make J'Teglyr's eyes widen in surprise. *"Gorkon?"*

"I guess your High Command didn't tell you about that." Kirk held out his hands. "You can confirm this with them, if you'd like. I'll even promise to take no action until you've had a chance to do just that. We have a chance to do good here, Captain. I don't want a fight." He sighed, then offered a small, wry smile. "At least not today."

His last comment had the intended effect, and Kirk watched the Klingon's expression soften. "*Very well, Earther. I will contact High Command and verify your claims. Do not attempt to send anyone to the surface.*"

Kirk shook his head. "Actually, I have no need to do so." He cast another glance toward Spock before adding, "Our rescue plan is a bit more . . . complicated than that."

Fourteen

The lights flickered, and several of the alien control consoles blinked in rapid succession at the same time B'tinzal heard a low buzz that seemed to reverberate up through the floor and across the walls. Turning from the portable computer workstation she had set up in the citadel's master control room, B'tinzal inspected the rest of the chamber and saw the same effect playing out across other consoles. Even a few that until now had been dormant had come to life, each of them displaying an indecipherable string of alien script accompanied by a litany of flashing lights and indicators.

"What is that?" she asked, moving away from Tothar's station. The other three Klingons working with her exchanged similar glances of confusion and concern.

Standing at an adjacent console, Tothar replied, "It appears to be another security measure, Professor. Internal scanner readings are showing several interior hatches have closed, and I am unable to see anything within the sealed-off sections."

"Do we have people in those areas?" B'tinzal asked. Eyeing her console's status display, she noted that the affected sections were in proximity to the massive mechanism that was the heart of the alien fortress.

"Yes. Two of our people and two warriors." His fingers playing over his controls, Tothar added, "I am only detecting two life signs from that section." Turning from her station, B'tinzal bolted from the room. With Tothar following close behind, she plunged into the narrow, cylindrical passageway leading from the control center and deeper into the citadel. She had made this transit enough times that she had memorized the route, so it was with some surprise that B'tinzal ran through one final junction and into the corridor leading to the chamber that housed the largest components of the transfer-field generator and found herself staring at a new, large bulkhead blocking her path. Standing near the new barrier was another of her colleagues, Doctor Vurgh, and a Klingon warrior, Komaraq, B'tinzal remembered from earlier in the day. The young warrior had drawn his disruptor pistol and was studying the corridor and surrounding bulkheads, obviously on alert for new threats.

"Did you fire your weapon?" asked B'tinzal.

"No, Professor." He glanced at the disruptor in his hand. "It was an . . . instinctive reaction."

"Understandable, but let's not tempt whatever is controlling this alien contraption." B'tinzal had issued instructions to everyone working inside the fortress not to discharge weapons unless authorized or if no other option was possible in the event of an attack or other infiltration of the complex. Given the citadel's array of autonomic processes and its reactions to the presence of intruders in its midst, B'tinzal was wary of somehow triggering a more aggressive defense protocol than what they had seen to this point.

"What happened?" she asked.

Vurgh shook his head. "I'm not sure." He held up a portable scanner and gestured with it toward the bulkhead. "I was recording some new readings of the generator when this happened."

It was not even the first time today that something

like this had occurred. Two similar "modifications" of the citadel's internal configuration had taken place in different sections of the fortress, but neither of those instances was within this area of the complex.

"Do you believe this was in direct response to your scans?" asked B'tinzal.

The younger scientist replied, "I am not sure, Professor, though I do not believe in coincidence."

"What of the others?" Tothar pointed toward the bulkhead. "Are they in there?" He had brought his personal scanner with him and was in the process of adjusting its controls.

"Yes. We attempted to contact them via personal communicators, but it appears the transmission is being blocked, just like our scans." Vurgh gestured to the barrier. "It is not as though it was conjured from nothing. Just as with the other occurrences, the pressure hatch was triggered by something. It cannot just be our mere presence here, as we have been moving about the interior for some time. The only thing that makes sense is that the internal systems are reacting to specific actions on our part."

B'tinzal was not convinced. "Or, the structure is continuing to execute its own predetermined instructions and does not care at all about us." Her observations since beginning her study of the citadel would seem to bear out her theory, but she did not discount other factors in play. "Still, it is possible that in addition to these autonomous actions, it also is reacting to us. That might even explain the increasing frequency of these incidents. Perhaps the machine is reaching some milestone in whatever plan it is following, and it senses our presence as a threat."

"You make it sound as though the machine is alive," said Komaraq.

B'tinzal smiled at the warrior, recalling her own thoughts on the subject. "I suppose it is, after a fashion."

"I am detecting two life signs beyond the bulkhead," said Tothar after a moment. "The readings are faint, but that is likely due to interference from the structure itself."

"But you are still able to make scans," said B'tinzal. "Impressive."

Not taking his eyes from the scanner, Tothar replied, "I have been working on it for a while now. After all, there is still so much of the structure we have not yet seen."

This much was true. Despite their best efforts, B'tinzal and her people had been foiled numerous times in their attempts to penetrate deeper into the fortress. In addition to sections and compartments that already were sealed and resisted even the most intense sensor scans, there were the ongoing instances of the structure's interior reconfiguring itself. It was obvious to B'tinzal that the alien mechanism was operating for its own, unknown purpose. At least for the moment, she and her team appeared to be little more than the occasional distraction as it carried out its automated processes.

"If our scanners can be configured to better work in here," said B'tinzal, "then perhaps transporters can be modified to work as well." Though the field transporter outside the fortress was effective for moving to and from the structure's outer areas and some of its interior spaces, it was all but useless when trying to penetrate the citadel's innermost sections. Defeating this restriction would prove most helpful in the team's continuing research.

B'tinzal noted Tothar taking a step closer to the bulkhead. "Wait. Something is happening. The scans are shifting. I am detecting . . . weapons fire."

"Where?" Even as she asked the question, B'tinzal realized the foolishness of her own question. Her gaze shifted to the wall separating her from the blocked compartment. "Who is firing?"

"It must be K'troq," said Vurgh. "He and Komaraq were assigned to serve as security in this section."

Before B'tinzal could respond, she became aware of the new, low rumbling that began emanating from behind the walls around them. It also resonated through the floor, the vibrations working their way up and over her body.

"It is the same sound we heard before," said Komaraq. "We must move from here immediately."

Vurgh added, "He's right. We could also become trapped here."

Still eyeing his scanner, Tothar said, "These readings are much more powerful and widespread than anything we have seen."

"What do you mean?" asked B'tinzal.

"It is as though the entire structure is undergoing a reconfiguration this time." Tothar looked up from the device, and B'tinzal saw the uncertainty in her colleague's eyes, along with something else.

Fear?

Ahead of them, a hole appeared in the center of the bulkhead and the barrier began to dilate. The opening expanded until the entire wall retracted into the edges of the cylindrical passageway, revealing two Klingons standing inside the newly unsealed compartment. B'tinzal saw the soldier K'troq and another member of her science team, Z'teth. The warrior was wounded, his left arm hanging limp at his side as he backpedaled toward them. His right arm, wielding his disruptor pistol, was raised and he was aiming at something B'tinzal could not see.

Then B'tinzal's gaze fell on the soldier's target. Peering into the adjoining section, she saw four black metallic globes moving about inside the compartment. From the looks of their maneuvering, B'tinzal guessed the automated or remote-operated drones were attempting to envelop the two Klingons as a precursor to some kind of offensive action. Beyond them, another of the devices lay on the deck, its outer shell marred by the telltale sign of a disruptor beam from K'troq's weapon. It appeared inert, but now its four companions were pressing their own attack.

"Everyone retreat!" B'tinzal snapped, her hand reaching for the smaller disruptor she carried in a pocket of her jacket. Tothar and Vurgh, though scientists and unarmed, nevertheless remained nearby, regarding B'tinzal with uncertainty.

"And leave you here?" asked Tothar. "No. We cannot run like frightened children."

"We need to regroup," replied B'tinzal. "Courage is useless if we're caged down here like animals. Retreat to the control room. Now!"

The rumblings from the citadel's depths were louder here, but now they were accompanied by the high-pitched whine of the sentry globes. There were more of the infernal devices moving about the compartment now. At least seven or eight additional drones had joined the original complement. There could be more, but it was difficult to be sure, given that some were moving almost too fast for B'tinzal to track. K'troq was doing his best to keep the drones at bay, but he was outnumbered.

We all are.

Checking the setting on her weapon, B'tinzal used her free hand to push Tothar farther up the corridor, away from the sentry globes. She gestured toward her aide and

Vurgh. "I told you to get to the control room!" She stepped toward the open doorway, reaching for Z'teth's arm. "You as well. Evacuate this area."

The younger scientist's eyes were wide. "They emerged from hidden compartments in the walls. K'troq disabled one, but they are so fast."

"Move!" shouted B'tinzal.

A disruptor beam howled in the corridor, accompanied by a flash of brilliant light, and B'tinzal turned to see K'troq firing at another of the drones. The device was faster, arcing up and over the attack before diving straight at the Klingon. K'troq attempted to duck to his right but he was too slow, and the globe slammed into the soldier's chest. His entire body jerked and twitched and B'tinzal heard the sound of what likely was an electrical discharge being unleashed against him. Releasing a cry of shock and pain, K'troq staggered backward but did not fall. The globe, having backed away from the warrior, was moving in again but B'tinzal took aim with her disruptor and fired. A harsh green energy beam spat forth and struck the drone and the device stopped its advance. It shuddered for a moment before dropping to the floor.

"Can you run?" asked B'tinzal, splitting her attention between the remaining three globes and the injured K'troq. For the first time, she realized she needed to raise her voice to be heard over the muffled reverberations emanating from within the fortress.

The Klingon, still staggering from the effects of the attack, had not dropped his disruptor and even now was raising it to search for a new target. The trio of drones had moved back in the wake of losing another of their number, and B'tinzal was certain she could sense them plotting and scheming, looking for another opening. She fired at the closest device, but it seemed to anticipate her move, pulling itself up and out of immediate danger.

"They are taunting us," said K'troq, forcing the words between gritted teeth. He moved a few more steps backward, crossing the threshold of the bulkhead that had cycled open.

No, decided B'tinzal. This was something else. The drones, apparently operated by some central control mechanism that had eluded her and her team, showed signs of independent action and even decision making. This ability was likely governed by each unit's independent onboard computer software. Though she was not a computer expert, B'tinzal still had enough familiarity with the science that she knew she would spend many fascinating hours studying the alien devices.

Perhaps later. There are more pressing matters now.

"I think they're being cautious," she said, guiding K'troq back into the corridor, away from the compartment and in the direction of the master control room. "Perhaps we have damaged or destroyed enough of them that they are being judicious with their remaining numbers." There was also the possibility that a greater, even insurmountable number of the sentry globes were lying in wait, ready to strike.

Always an optimist.

Backtracking to the control room, B'tinzal noted that the vibrations coursing through the surrounding bulkheads were even louder here. All around her, lights blinked in rapid, chaotic fashion, as though experiencing an interruption from the citadel's massive power plant.

"Something new is definitely happening," B'tinzal surmised, though she had no idea what action the fortress might be taking. The structure's current reactions were unlike anything she and her team had yet encountered. Had they done something to trigger this new development? Was it even safe to remain here?

Once again studying his personal scanner, Tothar replied, "It is the same power readings we detected before, Professor. Water, along with silt and other sludge from the lake bottom, is being drawn through those intake valves. We still do not know the purpose for this action."

B'tinzal's attempts to track the water being pumped into the citadel had been defeated by the structure's continuing efforts to block scans of the interior. They had managed to acquire scans of massive storage tanks deep within the alien fortress, but tracking where the large volumes of drawn water went after that had proven fruitless.

"And the power readings?" she asked.

Tothar said, "They are much more intense than anything we have seen." He shook his head. "I have no idea how to explain it, except that there are power sources within the structure coming online that have been dormant to this point." Scowling, he deactivated the scanner, and for a moment B'tinzal thought her aide might hurl the device against a nearby bulkhead.

B'tinzal asked, "What about the main power generators?"

"Sealed off," replied Tothar. "Our scans are even more muddled than before. I can see indications of inner mechanisms in operation, but as always, their purpose or goal remains unknown. The thing has been relatively quiet since our arrival, and you have been using scanners almost the entire time we have been here. Why does the machine grow upset at us now?"

B'tinzal nodded. "A very good question, and one for which we have no answer."

The reports of weapons fire from behind them made B'tinzal turn to see Komaraq shooting at another of the sentry globes that had appeared near the entrance to the control room. His shot missed as the drone darted toward the floor before lifting again. The device then surged forward, striking Komaraq in his right arm and causing him to drop his disruptor. The weapon clattered to the floor and slid out of reach across its smooth surface.

"Move aside!" shouted B'tinzal, taking aim at the globe and firing. She also missed, and the drone flitted up and away. Looking past the injured but still conscious and upright Komaraq, she saw more of the sentries moving about in and around the control room, along with Tothar and others attempting to defend themselves. Her aide and Vurgh had found disruptors similar to her own in one of the equipment containers the team had brought with them from the *Vron'joQ*, and now they were attempting to assist the warriors. More sentry globes had entered the room, apparently coming from compartments or passages hidden within the bulkheads.

"We need to evacuate!" shouted Tothar, even as a dull, pulsating tone began to sound in the corridor. He waved toward B'tinzal. "Entire sections of the interior are being reconfigured. If we stay here, we will be trapped!"

B'tinzal gestured with her disruptor. "Outside! Everyone outside!" She had to yell to be heard over the mounting din in the passageway.

Ahead of her, K'troq was still firing at any drone that presented itself, but the devices were moving with such speed and dexterity that it was becoming increasingly difficult to target them. The warrior still managed to score a glancing blow against one of the drones, his shot just grazing its dark outer shell. The globe wavered in the air for a beat before dropping to avoid K'troq's next shot, then launched itself at him. It struck K'troq below his knees, sweeping his legs out from under him. The warrior collapsed to the deck, grimacing in momentary pain even as he rolled onto his side and fired his disruptor at his assailant. This time he was successful, striking a direct hit on the drone and sending it crashing into a nearby bulkhead.

"Well done," said Komaraq as he reached his companion and assisted him to his feet. The warrior turned his attention to B'tinzal. "Professor?"

Dividing her focus between the warriors and the other globes moving about the corridor, B'tinzal replied, "We cannot stay here. At least, not without reinforcements." She noted that the sentries now seemed to be holding their ground, no longer advancing on them the farther they retreated from the citadel's interior areas as well as the control room. While all of this was taking place, the structure was continuing to vibrate and rumble. It was similar to an earthquake, or perhaps the sensation of an ancient spacecraft preparing to propel itself toward the distant stars beyond the confines of this pitiful ball of mud.

"Evacuate!" B'tinzal shouted the command, catching the attention of everyone in the control room. "Head for the transporter!"

Having anticipated this order, Tothar was now standing before one of the science team's portable computer workstations. While holding a compact disruptor pistol in one hand, he moved his other hand across his console's array of controls.

"I am transmitting our data to the *Vron'joQ*," he called out. "We cannot afford to lose all that we have learned."

B'tinzal's first instinct was to tell her aide to ignore all of that, but Tothar was correct. They would need the information they had collected. Perhaps buried among all of that data was the answer to what they were now experiencing.

Two of the sentry globes appeared to decide that they had loitered long enough in the control room. Drifting away from their companions, the drones moved toward Tothar, who was still hunched over his workstation.

"Watch out!" warned B'tinzal.

She was joined by K'troq as they fired their disruptors, each striking one of the globes and halting their advance. First one and then another of the devices shivered in midair before dropping like stones to the floor, bouncing and sliding along the floor's smooth surface. The reaction of the other five globes in the room was immediate: they spread out and formed a circle. By then, Tothar had moved from his console and was following B'tinzal and K'troq from the control room and into the corridor.

Their escape route was blocked.

"The corridor has reconfigured itself," said K'troq, growling with mounting frustration. Gone was the curved, circular passage that would lead them out to the peripheral quad. In its place was solid bulkhead, and B'tinzal could hear still more rumbling behind the walls and beyond the ceiling and floor plating. Whatever was happening, they were trapped in the middle of it.

"The docking areas," she said. "We will get out that way. We will swim if we must." She recalled the route to the closest of the docking bays that provided underwater access to the citadel. While she and her team had not used any of those entry points for some time, they would without doubt serve their current purposes. "Follow me," she said, gesturing toward another length of corridor.

"B'tinzal!" The shout came from Tothar, who grabbed

her arm just as she saw another segment of bulkhead begin to move before them. It swung outward, blocking their access to the passageway before locking into place. More groaning of metal accompanied the movement, followed by what sounded to B'tinzal like a series of heavy clicks as other components were shifted to new positions.

Seams appeared in the floor plating, and B'tinzal saw the gaps widening as sections of the floor began retracting toward the walls.

"Back!" she shouted. "To the control room!"

It was too late. Another section of bulkhead had emerged from the ceiling, blocking their route back the way they had come. Segments of the ceiling now were pulling apart, offering B'tinzal an unfettered view up a narrow column that stretched into darkness. The corridor was becoming a shaft or vertical conduit, and the smooth bulkheads offered no purchase or safe harbor.

Then the floor beneath her disappeared, and she along with K'troq and Tothar fell into unyielding blackness.

Fifteen

"Fascinating."

Swiveling his command chair to face the science station, Kirk watched Spock continue to bend over his sensor readouts for another moment. When the Vulcan said nothing further, Kirk realized he was tapping his fingers on the chair's arm, and he forced his hand to remain still. Just as he was about to say something, Spock turned from his console.

"The citadel's power readings are increasing at a significant rate." Moving to stand before the curved red railing separating him from Kirk, the first officer added, "As with our previous attempts to scan its interior, I am unable to ascertain just what sort of activity is taking place within the structure, but these new readings are consistent with a startup sequence for the transfer-field generator."

Frowning, Kirk asked, "It's activating? Without the Transfer Key?"

"The Key was designed to operate independently from the field generator, but the larger mechanism cannot by itself generate the portal connecting the Jatohr universe with ours. Only with the Key can it complete the necessary computations to align the generator and select a transfer target and destination."

Kirk recalled how Captain Una had manipulated the alien controls in the citadel, instructing the machine to select her before she disappeared with but the press of a single button, hurled across dimensions from their universe toward that of the Jatohr. Where was she? Assuming she had survived the transfer, what had become of her and the others who had endured the same fate? What of Sarek, and Joanna McCoy, and Councillor Gorkon? Would Una be able to find them and bring them to whatever rendezvous point the field generator selected if and when it could be reactivated with the Transfer Key?

The questions, as they had for days, hammered at Kirk, partnered with concerns that had nothing to do with the fates of Captain Una and the others. With the Klingons in orbit above Usilde and on the surface, accessing the alien machine was going to be problematic. Even if the giant mechanism could be controlled from the *Enterprise* with the help of the Transfer Key, Kirk knew that the Klingons would not stand idle and allow him and his crew to carry out such a brazen act right before their eyes.

That's one way to put it.

The whistle of the ship's intercom system echoed across the bridge, followed by the voice of Ensign Chekov.

"Science lab to Mister Spock."

Activating the comm panel at his station, the first officer replied, "Spock here."

"Sir, it's the Transfer Key. I think you and the captain should see this."

———

The science lab, one of twelve aboard the *Enterprise*, was packed with all manner of computer consoles, worktables, storage lockers, and other cabinets and equipment. Kirk recognized some of the items here, and of those devices, the number he knew how to operate was only a small subset. This despite having enviable grades in all of the science classes he took at the Academy, and a host of assignments as a junior officer that required him to possess a working knowledge of a vast array of equipment. As he solidified his career path on the command track, his studies had become more specialized, and there were times when he regretted not keeping up with the latest advancements of computer, engineering, and other science technology.

Thankfully, he now had an entire crew of highly trained personnel to help him, such as young Pavel Chekov. Though formally assigned to the *Enterprise* the previous year as a junior navigation officer, the young ensign had demonstrated a keen interest in other facets of the starship's operations, including sensors, tactical systems, and internal security. Spock had taken notice of Chekov's off-duty study habits and recommended him along with a handful of other junior officers to Kirk for accelerated training in a number of subjects. According to Spock, Chekov was distinguishing himself in these extra courses and his duty performance since reporting aboard had been nothing short of exemplary.

"It started transmitting the signal after we dropped out of warp," said the ensign, standing at the table and gesturing to the Transfer Key. "The signal is on a very low frequency, sir. The only reason I saw it is because I've been subjecting it to a variety of scans and checks designed to detect even the slightest change."

To Kirk, the alien device looked as unassuming and inert as always. "And it's continuing to transmit even now?"

"Yes, sir," Chekov said. "It's a constant broadcast. I don't think we were supposed to notice it."

"Do you think the Klingon ship has picked it up?"

The ensign shook his head. "I doubt it, sir. They

would've needed the same kind of access to the Key that we've had, taken the same kind of sensor readings that allowed Mister Spock and me to modify our scanners to detect the signal in the first place."

Kirk looked to where Spock stood at the large control console dominating the lab's forward bulkhead. The Vulcan seemed engrossed in several of the station's displays.

"Spock?"

Turning from the console, the first officer said, "I have compared these readings to the sensor scans of the citadel we have been collecting since our arrival in the Libros system. According to the time codes, the signal from the Transfer Key immediately preceded the citadel's latest round of internal reconfigurations."

"Are you sure?" Kirk asked, then held up his hand. He offered a small smile. "I'm sorry, Spock. You'd think I'd know by now not to ask something like that."

"No apologies necessary, Captain." Spock clasped his hands behind his back. "It is a most unusual development."

"The Key did not exhibit this type of behavior when we took it from the planet," said Chekov.

Spock replied, "It is entirely possible that it was transmitting such a signal at that time, or perhaps something similar, and we simply did not know it."

"We hadn't had the chance to study it," said Kirk.

The Vulcan nodded. "Precisely. Even with all that we have learned with it in our possession, the Transfer Key likely possesses several qualities that remain unknown to us. Given this new development, I would advise caution as we proceed."

"That's good advice, regardless." Kirk sighed, folding his arms across his chest. "What about the Klingons on the surface? Can you tell what they're doing down there?"

Chekov said, "Our sensors show no Klingon life signs inside the citadel, sir. At least, not within those areas our scans can reach." He nodded to the first officer. "Mister Spock has been teaching me the finer points of configuring our sensors to detect readings beyond their usual range and specifications. Even with those modifications, we're still not able to scan the citadel's complete interior."

"But you can see that the transfer-field generator is online."

"Yes, sir. It's definitely active, though based on our earlier readings, we think it's operating in a lower power or standby mode. Definitely not at the capacity we saw during our first visit here."

Kirk considered this. "Like it's waiting for something. Instructions, or the Transfer Key itself."

"That is our current theory," said Spock. "We also believe that these new readings are connected to a report provided by a member of Professor B'tinzal's science team about how they were forced from the citadel."

The captain of the *Vron'joQ*, J'Teglyr, had wanted no part of the explanation Kirk provided about their rescue plan for Captain Una and the others. Instead, the Klingon captain had shunted the communication to the planet's surface, leaving Kirk to speak to a Klingon scientist who had assumed B'tinzal's duties following her apparent death inside the citadel. Kirk had listened as the Klingon conveyed the details of the alien complex's sentry globes attacking the research team. While he was sympathetic to the losses suffered by the team as they were evicted from the citadel, Kirk weighed that against the continued plight of the Usildar who remained under Klingon rule. That was an injustice that needed correcting, and Kirk wondered what if any influence he might exert on the Usildar's be-half.

And of course the Klingons will be thrilled to work with me.

"They'll be watching every move we make," he said. "Particularly now that they're on the outside looking in, figuratively and literally." They would, Kirk suspected, be watching and waiting for any opportunity to take advantage of the situation and try to seize the Transfer Key. The next steps taken to assist Una, and everyone else trapped in the Jatohr universe, would have to be undertaken with care.

"Is the test probe ready to go?" asked Kirk.

"Mister Scott and his team are making their final preparations now, sir," Chekov replied. "They expect to be ready for launch within the hour."

Nodding toward the Transfer Key, Kirk asked, "And you're sure you know how to work this thing and get it to transport the probe somewhere close to where we hope Captain Una is?"

"There is still a degree of uncertainty, of course," replied Spock. "Targeting the object to be transferred is a rather simple process, whereas the calculations to send it to a particular point in space within the other universe are a good deal more complex. However, I have had the computer analyzing the *Enterprise*'s sensor readings taken of the citadel during our first visit here, including the point when Captain Una transferred herself. With the computer's assistance, we are using those readings as a referent for creating a set of computations that I believe will place the probe in the same approximate area as the captain's destination."

"So, you're saying it's still a big guess as to whether we'll find her," said Kirk.

The comment elicited a raised right eyebrow from the Vulcan. "That is essentially correct, Captain."

"Well, I suppose there's really only one way to find out," said Kirk. "Have Scotty report to me when he's completed the probe's preparations. I want to launch it as soon as possible."

"I am finalizing a procedure to integrate the Transfer Key into our power systems," said Spock. "With Mister Scott's assistance, the installation should take very little time, and we should avoid the problems encountered by Sadira and the Romulan vessel."

Kirk nodded. "I'd appreciate that."

"What about the Klingons, sir?" asked Chekov. "Do you think they might try to interfere?"

Spock replied, "If all goes according to our plan, Ensign, they will not have an opportunity to take action against the probe."

"But that doesn't mean they won't take action against us."

———

It was not until her helm officer turned in his chair and regarded her with a puzzled expression that Visla realized she was absentmindedly tapping her fingers on the arm of her chair.

Now conscious of the involuntary act, the commander halted her fingers and pressed the palms of her hands against the armrests. Eyeing her subordinate, she asked, "Is there a problem, Lieutenant?"

K'darqa replied, "No, Commander." He paused, his gaze dropping for a moment to the metal deck plating as though deciding the wisdom of his next words, before returning his attention to her. "You appear troubled."

"Thank you for your observation. Should I feel the need to give voice to my inner turmoil, rest assured that yours are the first ears I shall seek out. Until such time as that unlikely event comes to pass, mind your station."

Stiffening in his chair, K'darqa offered a single, formal nod. "Yes, Commander." He turned his seat so that he once more faced his helm console.

Visla scanned the faces of the rest of her bridge crew, noting the furtive glances exchanged between the other officers, though none were cast in her direction. She did see at least one relayed from her first officer, Lieutenant Woveth, to Lieutenant Koveq. Her tactical officer appeared as unimpressed with the potential for distraction as she did, and she even heard him growl as he gestured for Woveth to return to his duties. Chastened, and unlikely to forget this fleeting insubordination, the first officer began once again stalking the *Qo'Daqh*'s bridge perimeter stations.

For her part, Visla was surprised by Woveth's breach of protocol, as he normally presented the very picture of military bearing and control, in particular when in the presence of subordinates. She watched him walk past several of the workstations, inspecting the displays and indicators on each console, and waited for him to look in her direction before silently indicating for him to join her.

"Lieutenant Koveq," she said, "you are in command until I return."

Rising from her chair, she saw Koveq's small nod of understanding before moving to the pressure hatch at the rear of the bridge. The doors parted, and she stepped into the connecting corridor. Woveth followed her and she waited for the doors to close, leaving them alone in the narrow passageway.

"Your eyes betray your uncertainty, Lieutenant."

Like most Klingons who possessed even the merest shred of honor, Woveth bristled at the very mention of the word "betray." His eyes narrowed, appearing almost like black slits in the corridor's dim, red-tinged lighting. What illumination there was reflected off the smooth skin of his bald head and his gold baldric. He stood at attention, his eyes locked on some point over her left shoulder.

"It was not my intention to give offense, Commander."

Visla offered a dismissive wave. "If I was offended, you would already be dead. As my first officer, it is your responsibility to bring to my attention any matter you feel may have a detrimental effect on the crew. I sense your concern. Tell me what concerns you, Lieutenant."

Drawing a deep breath, Woveth replied, "The rumors are circulating throughout the ship, Commander, regarding our change of course and that you have not formally acknowledged our abandoning the mission to Centaurus. There is worry that you may be disobeying orders from High Command and about what that might mean for the crew."

"Divided loyalties, Woveth?" Visla stepped closer, lowering her voice. "Are you warning me that I may have a mutiny on my hands?"

The first officer shook his head. "I have heard nothing to indicate anything of the sort, Commander. However, if there is to be no clarification of our present circumstances and the orders under which we are operating, the crew will soon grow suspicious."

He paused as they both heard the sound of heavy footsteps approaching them from a connecting corridor. A moment later, another Klingon appeared in the passage, looking surprised to see the ship's two ranking officers blocking access to the bridge.

"Commander," said the new arrival, his expression a mask of uncertainty.

Visla gestured toward the bridge. "Attend your duties." Despite the younger officer's best efforts, she still saw the momentary flicker of his eyes to Woveth as he passed. He nodded as he drew abreast of her.

"Thank you, Commander."

This time, it was Woveth who waited for the doors to close before speaking again. "As you can see, at least some of the crew have questions, even if such concerns are not given voice. They are unsure of their standing, both here, and with our superiors."

"You seek clarification." Visla pondered the word for a moment before lifting her chin and fixing Woveth with a stern glare. "Very well. We are presently operating outside the orders given to me by High Command. How do you believe we should present this development to the crew?"

Woveth stood ramrod straight, his expression offering no clue as to how he was processing this revelation. His eyes did not so much as widen, reinforcing her belief that his unflappable composure could still be counted upon, though recent events were still presenting a challenge to him as he worked to carry out his duties.

"Speak freely, Woveth," she said, after a moment. "You have more than earned that right."

For the first time, he broke his military stance and turned his head to look at her. "Is this departure from our orders necessary for the security of the Empire?"

"I am convinced it is."

"I believe you, Commander."

"But you remain troubled."

"I do." Woveth cleared his throat. "Based on the reports I have read, the *Enterprise* is en route to the Libros system. It is possible it has already arrived there. I am left to wonder if this has somehow motivated you toward the action you have taken."

Smiling, Visla replied, "You are very perceptive, Lieutenant."

"You seek to reclaim the honor taken from you."

"Correct, but not just from me. From everyone on this ship who so ably serves me, yourself included. So long as I am your commander, you will share whatever fate the High Command sees fit to inflict upon me." Visla paused, placing her hands on her hips. "Now, fate has seen fit to provide us with an opportunity to reclaim that which was taken from us while acting in service to the Empire. I would be a fool not to seize that chance."

More footfalls in the connecting passageways caused them to again halt their conversation. As she watched a pair of her crew members walk past, Visla cursed whoever was behind the decision not to give this ship a private space for its captain to engage in privileged conversation. There was her cabin, but that was not an option. The last thing that she needed at the moment was a rash of unsubstantiated rumors about a romantic tryst with her first officer. Besides, she had Koveq for such things, and Visla trusted her tactical officer's discretion more than Woveth in that regard.

She could see Woveth working through conflicting thoughts and emotions. He also had the misfortune to be born into a house that had somehow disgraced the Empire, thanks to the actions of an ancestor now long dead. Indeed, Woveth was the first male from his house in four generations to join the military. He had never disclosed his reasons for willingly entering into service for a regime that would never grant him even the slightest fraction of respect. Visla suspected he one day hoped to regain his family's honor, and perhaps he was forestalling direct action while waiting for the unlikely day when he would command a ship of his own. Or had he been biding his time until presented with a prospect like the one Visla now offered him and the rest of the *Qo'Daqh*'s crew?

"And if we fail?" asked Woveth.

"Then our fate will still be better than living out the rest of our days in shame."

"But what of High Command? Surely they will soon know your intentions. It is possible, even likely, that Captain J'Teglyr has already reported our approach and is wondering why such an unfit vessel has been sent to him as reinforcement."

Visla replied, "I am hoping that J'Teglyr will see that having any additional ship will prove useful against the *Enterprise*."

She had considered the difficulty when it came to dealing with J'Teglyr. First, there was the simple reality that his ship, the *Vron'joQ*, was not on equal footing with the Federation's heavy cruisers. Then, there was J'Teglyr himself. She had never met him, but Visla was aware of his reputation, which while not glowing was at least serviceable in the eyes of the Empire. Based on what she had read of his official missions, she considered J'Teglyr to be an unimaginative officer, prone to following rules and procedures to an exacting degree while leaving little room for imagination and innovation. Given the unconventional tactics exhibited by James Kirk, Visla believed that in a direct confrontation J'Teglyr would be outmatched. It galled her that a Klingon of his mediocre caliber held a rank greater than hers. Further, she scoffed at the notion that he was allowed to serve with honor while she was relegated to obscurity and ignominy for circumstances over which she had no control. Simply put, J'Teglyr was not up to the task of facing off against Kirk, let alone acting in the best interests of the Empire.

"Whatever I may think of him personally," said Visla, "he is an experienced and loyal ship commander, and he will see the virtue of greater numbers. Regardless of our differing standings, we are both warriors of the Empire, united against a common foe."

Woveth pondered this. "What if Captain J'Teglyr does not share your view of the situation?"

"Then we may have a problem."

Visla did not expound on her reply, but the rest of her answer was already beginning to trouble her, and her thoughts turned to K'tovel, who along with the other *HoS'leth* survivors still waited for her on Centaurus.

I swear on my life, my son, that I will allow no one to stop me from regaining our family honor.

Sixteen

Air buffeted the underside of the antigravity sled, and Anadac felt hir body swaying in rhythm to the vehicle's rocking as s/he guided it over the rocky uneven terrain at the edge of the forest. The journey might have been less erratic, had s/he not been dividing hir attention between the landscape ahead of hir and the imaging display on the sled's control panel. According to the tracking information s/he was receiving from the sensor drone, s/he was drawing ever nearer to hir quarry. It appeared that Una and her band of humans along with a group of Usildar had taken refuge within the forests at the edge of the salt lands. With the aid of a pair of sentry probes keeping watchful eye from the clouds, Anadac had managed to approach and covertly monitor the outsiders.

Keeping watch on Una and her companions was—in and of itself—a simple endeavor, though doing so without attracting other undue attention had proven much more difficult. Under the guise of traveling to investigate possible sites for testing Woryan's transfer portal, Anadac now led a half-dozen additional antigravity sleds, each one now fitted per the supreme leader's wishes for battle against the Usildar or any other perceived enemy. No member of the contingent knew of Anadac's ulterior motives, which made hir attempts at clandestine reconnaissance all the more problematic.

Behind hir, Anadac heard the signature whine of an

accelerating sled. A moment later, Cisdor, the leader of the research team's security contingent, pulled up alongside hir.

"We have traveled a great distance, Anadac," said Cisdor. "How much farther?"

Anadac replied, "I am uncertain." It was a lie, and one s/he offered without reservation. "The scan readings are fluctuating, making it difficult to pinpoint the precise location."

"Will we reach the site before the suns set?" asked the security leader. "I would prefer not to set up our base camp in darkness."

"I am unable to provide an exact estimate. I will know more once we reach the salt lands." Anadac looked again at the imaging display, and noted that Una and her companions seemed content to remain in their own encampment as nightfall approached. That was helpful, s/he decided. It would make monitoring them easier.

A shrill tone sounded from the control panel of Cisdor's sled, and Anadac recognized it as a communications alert. The security leader activated his own imaging display, and s/he and Anadac were greeted by the visage of none other than Woryan hirself.

"Cisdor!" There could be no mistaking the supreme leader's foul mood. *"There has been an attack on one of our patrol units in your sector. It appears they were ambushed by Usildar refugees. You are to suspend all assistance to Anadac's search efforts and redirect all of your assets to this emergency. I want the perpetrators found and punished at once!"*

Feeling a wave of dread beginning to wash over hir, Anadac said, "Woryan, are you certain of the responsible party? Perhaps it was not the Usildar, but instead some other—"

"It was the Usildar refugees," snapped Woryan. *"And they were aided by the other outsiders. Cisdor, the coordinates of the patrol's last reported location are being transmitted to you now. See to this personally. I want them dealt with."*

Cisdor replied, "Understood. We will move to intercept them at once."

Woryan did not even bother with the courtesy of a reply before hir image disappeared from the display. Even before the connection was severed, Cisdor was adjusting the communications frequency on hir control panel.

"Cisdor, to all units. Charge all weapons, and stand by for dispersal instructions." S/he spent the next moments outlining Woryan's orders and other pertinent information relating to the coming military action.

"No," said Anadac when the security leader paused. "Cisdor, please. Woryan's orders may be in error. Please do not do this."

Shifting hir bulk to regard Anadac, Cisdor replied, "Disobey a direct order from our supreme leader? Do you even understand the risk you take simply by suggesting such a thing?"

Anadac realized hir plea was not a defensible position, particularly with respect to Una and the other humans. How was s/he supposed to protect them—at least long enough for hir to speak with them and learn from them—while preventing a military unit from carrying out the commands given to them?

Attempting another tactic, s/he said, "We cannot lose sight of our mission. We are so close to conducting a successful test of the portal. Woryan has made that his top priority. *Our* top priority. We both know that Woryan's passion can divert hir thinking. It is important for those s/he trusts to protect hir interests."

"Zened was correct to warn me about you," replied Cisdor. "S/he assigned me to watch over you because you think you know better than Woryan."

"That is preposterous." Despite hirself, Anadac all but shouted the response. "Like you, I am dedicated to the safety and preservation of all our people. I am trying to help Woryan and all of us."

Cisdor's attention already seemed consumed by the coming task. "This is a discussion for another time. Perhaps it would be best if you and your research team waited behind while I lead my units to carry out Woryan's orders." S/he seemed to tower even higher in hir sled. "We will destroy those savages and anything else that dares stand against us."

The sounds of mechanized vehicles, energy weapons, and cries of terror and pain brought Una out of her makeshift shelter, wielding the spear she had fashioned with her own hands. She had only just finished stripping a length of tree branch and sharpening its tip using a rock she had found, and the weapon felt both alien and yet oddly comforting in her hands.

"What is it?" she shouted as she saw Ensign Cheryl Stevens running through the middle of the camp, warning everyone to get out of their shelters.

Stevens pointed back the way she had come. "The slugs!" she shouted, using the term she and the other *Enterprise* crew members had employed to describe the Jatohr. "They found us. They're shooting everything in sight!"

To her left, Una saw Sarek and Joanna emerge from

their own low-slung shelters made from tree branches and brush, both carrying spears like hers. Beyond them and armed as they were, Tim Shimizu was crossing the camp toward her.

"Martinez isn't going anywhere," he said by way of greeting. "He's in our shelter."

Worried that the commander might be at the mercy of Jatohr soldiers should they make it this far, Una forced herself to set aside her concerns and concentrate on the matter at hand. "We'll fall back and get him if they get too close." She gestured to Shimizu. "You're with me. Stevens, where's Gorkon?"

The ensign waved toward the forest from which she had come. "He ran to join the Usildar fighters."

"Of course he did."

Stevens had turned and was running back to the forest. "Le May's up there too. We have to help them!" Without waiting for a reply, she turned and ran back for the forest.

Looking to Joanna, Una said, "You stick with us."

Sarek said, "I am prepared to fight as well."

"I'd rather you watch our backs, just in case any of them slip past the Usildar." She nodded toward the shelter shared by Shimizu and Martinez. "And keep an eye on Raul."

"Very well," replied the Vulcan. "Be careful, Captain."

Una nodded. "You too." To Shimizu, Stevens, and Joanna, she said, "Let's go."

Following the sounds filtering through the forest and catching the odd flash of light between the trees, it took the small group little time to make their way to the scene of the skirmish, but the evidence of battle was evident even as they approached. They reached a small clearing and Una beheld the sight of a Usildar fighter facing off against a Jatohr battle sled. A bright green glow projected from the vehicle's prow bathed the barely clad fighter, and the Usildar writhed and screamed as he fought against the attack. Lifted from the ground, his body was twisted and then flung through the air to strike the wide trunk of a nearby tree. The fighter's body fell limp to the ground and lay still.

All around the clearing and even in the surrounding trees, Usildar hurtled spears and rocks that clattered uselessly against Jatohr armor. Those who dared to advance and challenge their attackers to close combat stood no chance against the superior Jatohr weapons or defenses. Una spotted Stevens along with Ensign Terra Le May, one of the members of her original security detail all those years ago. Both were fighting alongside a handful of Usildar, their human forms contrasting with the smaller, gangly beings, but doing little good against their adversaries.

"Look out!" shouted Le May, just before Una watched Stevens and several fighters near her become the next victims of an energy beam from a Jatohr battle sled, which picked them up and flung them into the forest. Stevens landed heavily on the ground, but Una was relieved when the ensign rolled onto her side and began pushing herself to her feet.

"Captain!" Joanna yelled. "We have to—"

"Stand fast," Una said, holding out her free hand. She looked to Shimizu. "We can't take them on like this."

"If you've got any ideas," replied the ensign, "I'm listening."

Before she could respond, her attention was drawn to the rear of a small formation of three Jatohr battle sleds as a dark figure emerged from the forest. It was Gorkon, sprinting across the short stretch of open ground and leading a group of Usildar. They approached the closest sled, and Gorkon hoisted one of the fighters up and over the sled's parapet, giving the Usildar an unobstructed attack as he thrust his spear into the Jatohr pilot's neck. The bulky soldier jerked away from the sled's console as the Usildar stabbed it again, and the sled itself pivoted on its axis until its forward weapons faced his companions.

"No!"

Una's cry went unheard as the energy beam spat forth from the sled, enveloping both Gorkon and his Usildar comrades. As the sled continued to turn, the group was pulled along by the beam until they were flung across the small glade to land near the trees at the clearing's edge. Scanning the area, Una saw that the skirmish was turning into a rout, with more than a dozen Jatohr sleds moving at will through the forest and shooting at anything in their path. Those Usildar who had not already fallen to their enemy were beginning to retreat, seeking whatever pitiful cover the forest might provide.

Do something!

Her anger at the brutality of the lopsided battle growing with each passing moment, Una tossed aside her useless spear and dropped to her knees. An insane, impulsive thought seized her. If this bizarre place allowed her to make objects appear and disappear, even permitting her to create functional items from nothing, then how far did that ability extend? What were the limits of this inexplicable power she now wielded?

Let's find out.

Digging her hands into the dirt before her, Una closed her eyes and cleared her mind, focusing on a single thought. Within seconds she felt a tingling in her fingers as something began to take on shape and mass within her grip. She opened her eyes and raised her hands to see that she now cradled a trio of Starfleet type-2 phasers.

"Where the hell did those come from?" Shimizu asked, his features a mask of disbelief.

"I'll explain later." She handed both of her companions a weapon. "Time to start dishing out a little of what we've been taking."

Still seething at the unchecked cruelty of the Jatohr's attack, Una stepped into the clearing and took aim at the sled nearest to Gorkon and fired. The weapon howled as its blue-white beam streaked across the clearing to envelop the sled and its pilot, and both disappeared in a pulse of energy.

"Damn," she spat, more to herself than anyone else. She had not intended to kill, but instead to disable. Selecting another target, Una forced herself to rein in her anger as she aimed at a second battle sled and fired. This time the results were far less harsh as a section of the sled exploded, destroying its power supply and sending it crashing to the ground. Satisfied with that result, she repeated her attack on a third sled, scrapping that vehicle and sending its pilot lumbering for cover.

For the first time, Una realized Joanna and Shimizu had not joined in her defense. "What's wrong?"

Joanna held up her phaser. "It doesn't work."

"Mine's dead, too," added Shimizu. "Every setting."

Realizing what was wrong, Una grabbed the phaser from Joanna's hand, aimed it at a retreating Jatohr soldier, and fired. She was rewarded with the sight of the phaser's beam striking the Jatohr and sending hir rolling onto the ground.

"I know this sounds crazy," she said as she handed the

weapon back to Joanna, "but just trust it. Focus on the phaser hitting its target. You'll get the hang of it, if you let it. I . . ." She shook her head. "Just trust me."

Not waiting for her comrades to reply, Una set off across the clearing to where she saw Gorkon lying on the ground among a group of fallen Usildar. She flinched at the sound of phaser fire and glanced over her shoulder to see Shimizu and Joanna now providing cover for her.

I'll be damned.

Reaching Gorkon, she knelt beside him and saw that the Klingon was unconscious. She placed a hand on his shoulder, tried to rouse him, and a moment later saw his eyes open.

"Keep fighting, human," he sputtered, between coughs. "For me, it appears that today is a good day to—"

"Not yet it isn't." She turned at the sound of running footsteps and saw Shimizu and Joanna running toward her. Around the clearing, the remaining battle sleds all had been disabled, their pilots either stunned or retreating into the forest. Joanna proceeded past Una to crouch next to Gorkon.

"They gave up once we started hitting back," said Shimizu. "I don't think they've ever had to deal with that level of resistance. Two of the sleds withdrew completely, and we let them go."

Una nodded. "It won't be long before Woryan knows the game's changed. We can't stay here."

Looking up from her examination of Gorkon, Joanna said, "He's dead. Just based on what I could see, he likely had massive internal injuries. There was nothing we could've done for him out here."

Her gaze lingering on the fallen Klingon warrior, Una nodded in resignation. Whatever Gorkon's ultimate fate might be in this existence, he was lost to them in the here and now. "He fought to the very end." Assuming they ever found a way out of this place, she resolved to communicate back to the Klingon Empire and Gorkon's family of his brave and noble sacrifice. Though such a gesture likely would do little to soothe any tensions between the Empire and the Federation, it might still bring a loved one some measure of peace.

Leaving Shimizu to assist Joanna in helping Le May and Stevens as well as the Usildar treat their wounded, Una made her way back to the camp. There she found Sarek waiting for her, and the Vulcan was not alone. Standing next to him was an unarmed and unarmored Jatohr. Slowly, she tucked her phaser into her waistband at the small of her back, pulling her tunic down to conceal the weapon. Her eyes narrowing as she scrutinized the new arrival, she moved to Sarek.

"Gorkon is dead," she said.

Sarek nodded. "I know." Before Una could even respond to that unexpected answer, the ambassador said, "Captain, this is Anadac. S/he means us no harm."

"How can you be sure?" she asked.

"The same way I know Gorkon is dead."

Una turned her full attention to the Jatohr. The oversized gastropod shifted hir bulk, and Una realized s/he appeared nervous, if not outright scared.

"I am a scientist, not a soldier," s/he said. "I tried to stop them, but Woryan commands them." Una found it interesting that she now comprehended the Jatohr's gurgling speech patterns without the aid of technology. It had to be another byproduct of their odd surroundings, and Una was growing increasingly uninterested in questioning such things.

"And what about you?" she asked. "Aren't you under his command as well?"

Anadac replied, "No. I abhor violence, and I am not alone. Our kind used to value all life universally, but it was with the implied conceit that Jatohr were the most intelligent form of life we ever would encounter. Once it was learned that other life existed and possessed similar if not greater intellect, many of my people began to fear the implications of such a discovery. Woryan and others like hir leveraged that uncertainty even as the scientific community struggled to prepare us for transition to your universe. It was hoped that we could find a new world and live in peace, but Woryan and his ilk have other agendas."

"Unlike Professor Eljor," said Una, recalling her first meeting with the Jatohr scientist back on Usilde. "I knew hir. S/he helped us once, long ago."

Anadac seemed to brighten at her comment. "You do understand, just as you must understand that I am here with you now at great risk to myself. If it is learned that I am here, I will be reported as a traitor and my life will be forfeit, but I had to find you."

"Why?" asked Sarek.

"Woryan has commanded me to attempt re-creating Eljor's work. I have developed a device capable of transferring all beings from this realm to yours. However, it is dependent upon energies expended by the transfer-field generator Eljor constructed in your universe. Once in position and activated, my device will harness those energies, allowing safe passage for anyone." S/he paused, then added, "You understand what this means, yes? My device is not selective, as Eljor's is."

Una replied, "So, you're saying you can get us home,

but you can't keep Woryan and his armies from follow-ing us."

"Precisely. Woryan possesses the working device, al-though he is not aware that it is operational. He is sure to demand it be used once I am dead, so if you want to return to your world, and perhaps prevent Woryan from doing so as well, you must act."

"What can we do?" asked Una.

"I have observed you," replied the Jatohr, "and Sarek as well. It is obvious that you are different from your companions, at least in some ways. You command abili-ties here that are beyond the others' comprehension. I also have seen that you respect life as we do—at least, the majority of my people. I hope you will be guided by that regard for all living things as you seek a peaceful solution to this dilemma, for all our sakes."

Una looked upon Anadac's alien features, realizing that s/he carried within hir the same selflessness and nobility that had driven Eljor during their first meeting on Usilde. The professor also had lauded hir people's nor-mally peaceful nature and how some among the Jatohr had become so consumed by the ever-present crisis of their dying universe that they were willing to cast aside their values and respect for all life and even one another in a desperate bid for survival. Anadac, on the other hand, was prepared to freely hand over hir own life in service to hir people.

We have to make sure that's not in vain.

"We'll do what we can," she said. "I promise.

"That is all I can ask," replied Anadac. The Jatohr took hir leave, after which Sarek instructed a pair of Usildar rangers to escort hir away from the camp and ensure hir safe passage from the forest.

Once s/he was gone, Una turned to Sarek. "Well, how about that?"

"Yet another piece added to an already intricate puzzle," replied the Vulcan.

Nodding, she said, "Speaking of that, you said you knew Gorkon was dead. How?"

"His perceived injuries were too great for him to accept the possibility of survival."

"So, he's like Holstine and the others?"

"Perhaps," replied the Vulcan, "but there is no way to be certain. At least not without more information."

Una gestured toward the forest where Anadac had made hir departure. "Maybe we have a way to get more information. Do you think hir portal device will work?"

"What I believe," replied Sarek, "is that there is only one means of finding out."

Seventeen

Spock entered the astrophysics lab to find Chekov and Uhura already waiting for him. He had arrived ten minutes ahead of the scheduled launch of the probe expecting to find the lab unoccupied. He was pleased to see that the other two officers had exercised their own initiative and were already at work.

"Mister Spock," said Chekov, nodding in greeting from where he sat at one of the control stations along the lab's forward bulkhead. Across from the ensign, Uhura turned from where she was scrutinizing a bank of monitor screens set into the wall above the lab's primary computer interface.

The communications officer smiled. "You're early, sir."

"As are you, Lieutenant."

Chekov said, "I just checked with Mister Scott, sir. The probe is ready to be launched whenever we're ready."

Spock nodded in approval. Given the uncertainty of what they were about to attempt, including how the probe might react to being relocated from one universe to another, he and Captain Kirk had agreed that the safest course of action was to launch the probe away from the ship before attempting to lock on to it with the Transfer Key. To that end, a pair of *Enterprise* engineers under Montgomery Scott's supervision had taken the probe from the astrophysics lab to the cargo bay from which unmanned survey drones and other probes were launched.

"I have reviewed the final set of diagnostic results,"

said Spock. "All readings are well within our anticipated parameters." He moved to the station where Uhura stood, which was still opened to reveal the improvised power cradle Montgomery Scott had fashioned to house the Transfer Key. The panels of controls and indicators were of a configuration similar to his own workstation on the bridge, though mounted higher on the bulkhead and affording him access to its controls and hooded sensor viewer. As for the alien device, it was little more than an unassuming rectangle, fitted with an array of translucent controls that presented a simplicity belying the true complexity of its intended function.

Uhura said, "The computer's analysis shows the same thing, sir. Ship's sensors and communications systems are operating normally, and I've completed the configurations for detecting gamma ray transmission."

"Excellent," said Spock. Holding up the tricorder he had brought with him, he aimed the unit at the improvised patchwork of cables and other components in which the Transfer Key was positioned. The power readings were within the acceptable range he had determined would allow the alien device to function while drawing energy directly from the *Enterprise*'s warp engines, but in a manner that would not subject the starship to dangerous feedback or power surges.

Satisfied with the scan results, Spock deactivated his tricorder and laid it on a nearby worktable. "I believe we are ready to proceed." He reached across the workstation to press its intercom control. "Spock to Mister Scott."

"Scott here, sir," replied the chief engineer, who Spock knew was manning his station on the *Enterprise*'s bridge. *"We're standing by to launch this wee beastie at your command."*

Spock replied, "You may launch at your discretion. Lieutenant Uhura and Ensign Chekov will monitor all onboard systems."

"Aye, sir. Here we go."

Another voice, Captain Kirk's, added, *"Keep this channel open, Spock. We're all keeping an eye on everything from up here anyway."*

"Acknowledged."

Turning from the console, Spock looked to where Chekov was manning an adjacent station. On the bulkhead before the ensign, an image on the large viewscreen depicted the underside of the *Enterprise*'s secondary hull. As they watched, a circular hatch opened and a small object appeared. The modified sensor probe, propelled from its launch bay inside the ship, shot into open space. Maneuvering some distance before its own small impulse engine flared to life, the probe surged forward, away from the *Enterprise*.

"All systems functioning normally," reported Chekov.

Spock nodded. "Thank you, Ensign." At his own station, he studied the indicator that monitored the probe's distance from the ship, waiting until the automated device executed its preprogrammed instructions and brought itself to a halt after traveling one thousand kilometers.

"The Klingons are getting curious," reported Kirk over the open communications frequency. *"We're picking up their sensor scans of the drone. They're holding their position, and they haven't activated their weapons."*

Uhura said, "If they're interested now, just tell them to keep watching."

"Indeed." Spock moved his hand to one set of controls, which so far had been left ignored, and pressed a blinking green button. "Activating Transfer Key."

The alien component's response was immediate, emanating a pale glow from within as its control interface came to life in shades of blues and greens.

Over the intercom, Scott said, *"Aye, it's drawing power from the warp engines. Nothing too severe. Looks to me like it's working just as you anticipated, Mister Spock."*

"Mister Chekov, activate the probe's onboard sensor transceivers," ordered the first officer. "I am initiating the transfer." He pressed another control.

On the viewscreen, a white flash of light enveloped the probe, the effect seeming innocuous, as it lacked sound in space. The effect lasted less than two seconds, by Spock's reckoning, before the expanding sphere of energy dissipated, leaving behind nothing but the void of open space.

The probe was gone.

"There was a small power surge," said Chekov, "but it's gone now, and all warp power levels are steady."

"We all saw the probe disappear, Spock," said Kirk. *"Anything yet on whether it survived the transition?"*

Spock replied, "According to the readings from the Transfer Key, the transition itself appears to have been successful. We are waiting for the probe's modified communications protocols to initiate and begin transmitting telemetry."

"Hold on," said Chekov. The ensign was leaning forward in his chair, hunching over his controls. "I think I've got something." A moment later he tapped his fists on the console. "Sensors are detecting a new power reading. It worked!"

Uhura was smiling. "Well, how about that?"

"Captain," said Spock, "the transition was successful, and we are receiving initial telemetry from the probe. Its onboard power systems appear to be functioning normally."

Having returned to her own workstation, Uhura reported, "Scanning all communications frequencies." She was holding a Feinberg receiver to her left ear and using her free hand to enter varying series of instructions to her console. After a moment, she nodded. "There's a spike in gamma radiation on a modulated frequency. It's definitely one we programmed into the probe."

Chekov asked, "That's good, right?"

"Affirmative, Ensign." Turning from his station, Spock said, "Are we recording all incoming transmissions?"

Uhura nodded. "Absolutely, sir."

"What can you make of the sensor data?" asked Kirk.

Raising her voice so it could be picked up by the intercom, Uhura replied, "This is going to be a rather slow process, Captain. Slower than normal, I mean. Gamma-radiation properties don't make them the most effective carrier waves for information. The computer will have to receive and translate any incoming signals into something we can understand, but the rate of transmission is much slower than we're used to. There's also the possibility that we might lose some of the data during the transfer. We won't be sure until we've collected enough for the computer to give us an idea of what exactly we're receiving."

"Captain," said Spock, "I have dedicated a significant portion of computer high memory to processing the incoming data, but it will still take some time to interpret it."

As he spoke, the science officer studied the streams of computer data scrolling across two of his workstation's display screens. Pieces of the probe's data puzzle were already beginning to coalesce into recognizable patterns, though he knew it would be some time before he was able to fully understand what the computer was giving them.

"Keep me informed," said the captain. *"Excellent work, everyone. Kirk out."*

With the communication ended, Spock left the computer to decipher the incoming data stream. "Mister Chekov, what is the status of the probe?"

Shifting in his seat, the ensign replied, "Its structural integrity appears sound, Mister Spock. All sensors are active, though of course Lieutenant Uhura has already explained why we'll be waiting a bit." His report was interrupted by a beeping tone from his console, and Spock watched as the young officer turned to inspect the new reading. After a moment, Chekov frowned.

"Is there a problem, Ensign?"

"I'm not sure, sir." He gestured to the status indicator. "This suggests the probe is consuming power at an elevated rate. If I'm reading this correctly, its power cell will be drained in less than an hour."

Spock's gaze shifted to the monitors on Chekov's console. It took him only a moment to confirm the ensign's conclusion. "Interesting. The onboard power cell should be sufficient to support the probe for at least twenty-four hours, even with the energy requirements of the equipment we added."

"The power utilization protocols we programmed into the onboard computer will prioritize sensor data collection over transmission back to us," said Uhura. "Those procedures have likely already kicked in. We need to calculate how much time we have based on this revised power curve."

Spock replied, "I have already done so, Lieutenant." He had performed the calculations while continuing to study the incoming sensor stream. "Communications should cease within twenty minutes." However, he realized that was only an approximation, as the data indicated the probe's energy consumption was not increasing at a steady rate. There were surges that served to complicate such an estimate.

"Obviously," said Chekov, "the probe will continue to collect sensor data until it powers off altogether." He pointed to one of his station's displays, which was providing a complete breakdown of the probe's internal systems. "The backup battery is still showing a full charge. We may be able to rely on that for the comm system to receive our signal when we attempt to retrieve the probe."

"Perhaps." Spock had not anticipated this turn of events. Then again, it was hard to plan for every contingency when dealing with the physical laws of an entire universe that was separate from this one.

Stepping away from Chekov's console, Spock turned his attention to the continuing stream of still unreadable sensor data being received by the probe. Where had it journeyed? What might it be seeing? Had it found Sarek or any of the others? What else might it encounter?

Could they retrieve it?

Eighteen

"So, should I keep this phaser you pulled out of the ground, or do you want it back?"

Una did not realize Joanna McCoy was speaking to her until the nurse tapped her on the arm. Blinking several times, she turned her attention to the younger woman. Joanna lifted her shirt to reveal the weapon tucked into the waistband of her trousers.

"You should probably keep it," said Una.

It was the first time they had spoken since abandoning the camp following the Jatohr attack. Una had made no attempt at conversation as they made their way from the forest, heading for the salt plains. Their numbers were now drastically reduced. Sarek was leading the column, and following her and Joanna were Commander Martinez and Ensigns Shimizu, Stevens, and Le May. Only fifteen Usildar had survived the skirmish.

Following their unexpected meeting with Anadac, Una and Sarek had determined that their best chance for leaving this place was to return to the wasteland that had heralded their arrival. The obvious concern was that Woryan also would see the virtue of that location when he decided the time had come for him to test Anadac's transfer device. If that were the case, then at least it would simplify the task of finding the Jatohr leader.

Well, it's about time we got a break.

"You didn't have these the whole time, right?" asked

Joanna. "I mean, if that's the answer, then that's good enough for me, because it's a lot easier to believe than what I know I saw."

After considering possible responses for a moment, Una replied, "You know what you saw." She gestured around them. "This place . . . it's obviously quite different from our own universe." As they continued to walk, following Sarek as he led a path through the thinning forest, Una took several minutes to explain her experiences since transporting here from Usilde.

"Even Sarek can't explain it," she said after detailing the peculiar abilities she had learned to harness.

"Can we all do this?"

Una shrugged. "I'm not sure. At least, not without practice and probably some kind of advanced mental disciplines." She gestured to Sarek. "Vulcans and other species who have telepathic and other mental abilities seem best-suited, but my Illyrian upbringing seems to have given me a slight advantage."

"But the phasers," said Joanna, tapping the weapon concealed beneath her shirt. "Ensign Shimizu and I were able to fire them."

Una nodded. "I've thought about that. Simply taking a desired action here—one that might normally be impossible—seems simple enough, but the idea of being able to manifest objects or remove others? That looks to be at least a bit more complicated."

"I don't think I've seen Sarek try anything like . . . like what we saw you do," said Joanna, nodding to the ambassador who walked alone and in silence ahead of them.

"He believes it might be a dangerous practice," Una replied, "but it obviously has a few advant—"

The rest of her response was lost as her body seemed to freeze in place. She felt her muscles tightening and an odd tingling sensation beginning to course across her flesh. A wave of nausea swept over her as well but faded as quickly as it came. Within moments, it seemed that all of the abrupt effects had disappeared, with the exception of what Una perceived as a low whine in her ears. Looking to Joanna, she saw that the nurse appeared similarly troubled, and even Sarek stopped his advance toward the salt plain that now was visible through the dwindling expanse of forest undergrowth.

"Did you feel that?" asked Joanna. "It happened before, when Sarek and I first arrived here." She reached up to her right ear. "I've got this odd ringing in my ears."

Una replied, "So do I."

"Any idea what it is?"

"It seems to happen whenever someone or something is transported here from our universe," Una said. "After the first time I felt it, Ensign Shimizu said he believed that to be the cause. I've felt it enough since that I'm sure he's right."

Her eyes widening, Joanna said, "But the only people who can send someone here have to be in possession of the thing . . . the Transfer Key, right?"

"Supposedly." If that was still the case, and Una had no reason to believe otherwise, then it might possibly mean that Captain Kirk and the *Enterprise* had returned to Usilde. They might be hard at work at this very moment, trying to retrieve her and everyone else trapped here.

Echoing her thoughts, Ensign Shimizu called out as he approached them, "Did you feel that? Somebody's here, but that's the strongest I've ever felt it."

"Maybe it's because we're closer to the source," suggested Una. Rubbing her ears, she added, "That might explain this persistent ringing too."

Something above them caught her eye, and she looked up to see a brilliant, multihued tendril of energy shooting across the clear blue sky. A second strand of similar iridescence cut its own swath, followed in rapid succession by still more wisps of dazzling color.

"What the hell is that about?" asked Joanna.

Una, seeing Sarek staring up at the sky, called out, "Ambassador?"

"The transfer generator," replied the Vulcan. "It has been activated."

Worried about the possible implications of such a simple statement, Una said, "It couldn't be Woryan, could it?"

"Improbable, given what Anadac told us." Sarek continued to stare at the odd light show in the sky. "A more likely explanation is that the generator has been activated by someone in our universe."

"That's what I was thinking. Are you hearing a ringing in your ears too?"

The ambassador replied, "Yes. Given the acuity of Vulcan hearing, I am quite sensitive to the effects. It is not at all a desirable feeling."

Another abrupt wave of nausea caught Una off guard and made her double over in pain. At the same time and without warning, her head began pounding from the onset of an extreme headache. What was causing this? The sensation, while somewhat comparable to her previous experiences, was still quite different and much more distressing. Further, while the nausea seemed to come and go, now the pain in her head was lingering just like the ringing that continued unabated in her ears. She focused her thoughts on willing away the dull ache behind her eyes, but it was a futile attempt.

Her own distress was interrupted by the sounds of screams coming from behind her, and Una jerked herself around to see the various Usildar. All of them were consumed by frenetic motion, leaping and screeching as they turned upon each other with unchecked aggression. Punches and kicks, bites and slashes with weapons, wrestling each other to the ground.

"What are they doing?" asked Joanna. "It's like somebody flipped a switch or something."

Una held out a hand, signaling caution. "Stay back. Don't try to stop them."

"*Klingons!*"

Both women flinched at the sudden cry of rage from behind them, and were startled to see Raul Martinez rushing past them and heading for the Usildar melee.

"Commander!" shouted Shimizu. His face an expression of shock and confusion, he asked, "What the hell is he on about? Klingons? There are no Klingons down there."

Ignoring the shouts to stop or turn around, Martinez charged forward, running headlong into the impromptu fight. He slammed into the nearest Usildar, knocking the gangly being to the ground. Not waiting, the commander found and advanced on another would-be enemy, throwing kicks and punches. Within seconds, two of the Usildar had grabbed his arms and pushed him to the ground, where they commenced to pummel him.

"No!" Joanna started forward, halted only when Una grabbed her right arm. The nurse struggled to break free. Una, her headache increasing with each passing moment, pulled on Joanna's arm with sufficient force to yank the other woman off balance.

"Wait," Una said. "We can't just go running down there. We don't know what's causing all of this."

Joanna tried once more to free her arm. "We have to help him!"

As though reacting to the scene below it, the blue sky began to darken, the strands of colored energy now standing out with even greater intensity. This was accompanied by a maniacal, piercing scream from Ensign La May, who turned on Shimizu and slammed into him, sending them both to the ground. She was faster rolling to her feet, but Shimizu, still on his knees, was able to grab her lower legs and pull her back down.

"Ensign!" shouted Una. "Stand down. That's an order!"

Instead of replying, Shimizu regained his feet. Even as Le May was pushing herself off the ground, he drew from underneath his tunic the phaser Una had given him. Le May had only an instant to register surprise at the sight of the weapon before Shimizu fired at point blank range. The phaser beam washed over her, and her body was trapped within it for a moment before going limp and collapsing to the ground.

Shimizu was searching for someone or something to shoot when Una, her skull pounding from the incessant headache, tackled him. They tumbled to the ground, and she knocked the phaser from his hand. Instinct made her close a fist and swing it at Shimizu's jaw, snapping back the ensign's head. She felt his body relax beneath her as his eyes closed.

"Terra's dead," said Joanna, and Una rolled away from Shimizu to see the nurse kneeling beside Le May's unmoving form. Then movement in Una's peripheral vision made her lurch to her left in time to see Ensign Cheryl Stevens dashing forward to scoop up Shimizu's dropped phaser. No sooner did her hand close around the weapon than she was firing indiscriminately into the handful of Usildar who were still on their feet. One after another, those targeted by the phaser beam fell to the ground.

"Stevens! No!"

How was this possible? How was it that Shimizu and Joanna had experienced initial difficulty upon being handed one of the phasers Una conjured, but Stevens had adapted with no trouble? It made no sense, but at the moment neither did anything else.

Her mind all but clouded by unending torrents of pain, Una lunged toward the ensign, who was continuing to fire at the now scattering Usildar. Focusing her tortured thoughts on the eruptions of energy from Stevens's phaser, Una pushed the weapon out of her mind. An instant later it also vanished from the ensign's hand, dissolved from existence.

"Traitor!"

Somehow comprehending that it was Una who had disarmed her, Stevens turned on the captain and ran toward her. Una was not ready for the attack and took the strike's full force, which sent her stumbling backward until she tripped and fell. Una rolled over and tried scrambling to her feet, but by then she felt Stevens at her back, the ensign's arm around her throat and a hand pressing against the side of her head. Within seconds Una felt herself on the verge of blacking out as Stevens applied force to the sleeper hold. She coughed and sputtered, the throbbing in her mind only growing as blackness began creeping into the edges of her vision.

Then the hold loosened, and the arm dropped from her throat. Sagging forward until she caught herself with one hand, Una turned and saw Stevens being lowered to the ground by Sarek, whose right hand rested on the junction between the ensign's neck and shoulder.

"Thank you," Una said, coughing between the words. Still kneeling on the ground and supported by one hand, she wiped her mouth before pushing herself to her feet. "What the hell is happening?"

The Vulcan replied, "I do not know. My initial hypothesis is that we are all somehow engaged in a most painful mass hallucination."

"Are you affected too?"

"Quite." The ambassador seemed to look into space for a moment before adding, "I just concluded a conversation with my father and my grandmother."

Frowning, Una said, "But it wasn't something that moved you to violence?"

Sarek shook his head. "No. I do not claim to understand it, though I suspect that my greater mental control and discipline has imparted an advantage to me in this regard as well." The ambassador seemed ready to say something else, but then paused as though in midthought. His gaze turned toward the maelstrom of energy strands illuminating the sky.

Una did not even have time to process this notion before a new cry of anguish greeted them. Both she and Sarek looked for the source and found Joanna still kneeling next to the fallen Ensign Le May. Tears streamed down the young woman's cheeks.

"Dad! You can't die now! You can't leave me all alone. Dad!"

Looking to Sarek, she saw that he was still mesmerized

by filaments writhing in the sky. "Sarek? Ambassador? Are you all right?"

He lowered his gaze until it fell upon her. "Fascinating. I . . . seem to have seen some new things."

"What does that mean?" Una gestured to Joanna and the others from their group who were still moving about the area. "What do we do?"

Sarek replied, "We must push past the boundaries of this perceived reality, Captain. It is our only hope to leave this place. So long as we remain trapped within this fiction, we are lost, and no one may ever find us."

Her brow knitting in confusion, Una said, "What are you talking about? What things have you seen? How did you see them?"

"I cannot explain," replied the Vulcan, "for I do not possess the correct answers. I must seek to understand those answers before I can do anything more for us."

Now hopelessly confused, Una winced against a new onslaught of pain beneath her temples. "I don't understand. You're leaving? Where are you going?"

Shaking his head, Sarek said, "I honestly do not know. All I am able to convey is that I must focus on leaving this place. I believe that is the only way to understand how we might return to our own universe."

"But how do you know this?" A sudden thought occurred to Una. "Is someone or something communicating with you?"

Sarek seemed to consider the question for a moment before replying, "I am not sure. I suspect I will soon know, and once I do, I will share it with you." He closed his eyes as though attempting a meditative trance. As Una looked on, dumbfounded, the Vulcan ambassador slowly faded from sight.

"Wait! What am I supposed to do?"

Una shouted the words, first to the spot where Sarek had been standing, and then to the sky with mounting fury, only to see the incandescent light show continuing to unspool with all fervor. The strands seem to pulse with the unrelenting pain behind her eyes. Were the two somehow connected? In this place, Una was finding it increasingly hard to be surprised by anything.

"Number One."

The voice was behind her, but when Una turned she saw only the bodies of her shipmates, along with the fallen Usildar. Beyond them, standing at the first of the trees marking the dense forest that was the way she and her companions had come, was a lone figure. A human male, he was dressed in an older, obsolete Starfleet uniform with gold tunic and dark trousers and boots. Completing the ensemble was a fitted, gunmetal-gray field jacket. He stood looking at her and waiting.

"Captain Pike."

Gone was the scarring of his face that was a consequence of his accidental exposure to delta radiation. His thinning hair, which had turned almost stark white from that same incident, was now rich and black with just a hint of gray at the temples, the way he had looked well over a decade ago when she had served with him on the *Enterprise*. His entire form was enveloped in a gleaming aura.

"It's good to see you again," said what by all evidence appeared to be Christopher Pike, her former commanding officer. "You're seeing me because I'm apparently a deep-seated thought, one that comes to you during times of stress." He looked around before returning his gaze to her. "You know you can leave this place if you want. Just like Sarek did."

"I can't just leave," replied Una. She glanced to the bodies of her fallen comrades. "I can't leave *them*. Not again."

Pike—or his representation, at least—regarded her. "They're gone. They're all gone. You don't owe them anything anymore."

"That's not true." Wincing at renewed pain beneath her temples, Una shook her head. "I have to find out what happened to them. I need to learn the entire truth, but I can't trust what I see here."

"Do you trust me, Number One?"

As the pain in her head reached its worst level, she felt a tear fall from the corner of her eye. "I don't know, Captain. I just don't know. I don't know what to think about anything here."

"You will."

When Pike or whatever he was smiled again, he opened his mouth not to speak, but instead to emit a steady, shrill electronic tone. It immediately began burrowing into her body and mind, and within a moment Una was overcome by a sudden urge to leave this place, to follow after Sarek and perhaps find the answers to all their questions.

I just have to trust him and trust my own mind. Can I do that?

An abrupt weakness seized her body, and Una felt her muscles relaxing as she fell backward to the ground. Still consumed by the near-debilitating pain in her head, she nevertheless felt sleepiness beginning to work its way into her psyche. Looking up, all she saw was dark sky illuminated by the odd, chaotic points of streaking light. Her last waking thoughts were of her former captain and mentor, and Sarek, who perhaps held the key to the answers they sought.

I have to find him.

Una tried not to flinch when the darkness above seemed to drop down upon her, pushing away everything else until nothing remained but the black.

Nineteen

Pavel Chekov was sure he could feel his brain turning to mush.

"I know I've only been looking at this for ten minutes," he said, "but it feels like I've been here for hours."

Alone in the *Enterprise*'s astrophysics lab—at least for the moment—Chekov pushed away from his console and leaned back in his chair. Raising his arms, he reached above his head and relished the stretching of the muscles in his lower back. He rotated his arms to work the kinks from his shoulders, and made a note to ask the ship's quartermaster about more comfortable workstation chairs.

With a small grunt of resignation, Chekov returned to the sensor viewer mounted to his console. Now that the probe had ceased transmitting data as it prioritized its limited remaining power reserves, and the ship's computer was continuing to process the information it already had received, Lieutenant Uhura had returned to station on the bridge. This allowed her to resume her normal duties while continuing to assist Mister Spock with decoding the communications being received from the probe. Meanwhile, Chekov's own duties remained focused on the operation of the device. It already felt like an endless cycle: observe, classify, sort, then feed the larger aggregates of data to Spock and Uhura, who would actually analyze the information. Chekov knew he was doing important work, but he could not help thinking it was a step down from the responsibilities he had had in creating the very device responsible for collecting all of this new data in the first place.

Some creator. The first piece of genuinely innovative equipment I create ends up banished irretrievably into who knows where.

"Ensign, do you have an updated systems status report?"

It took Chekov a moment to realize that it was the second time he had heard the question. With a start, he turned from his console to see Spock standing before him. Spock's hands were clasped behind his back, regarding him with his usual stoic expression. How long had the first officer been standing there? Chekov felt blood rushing to his cheeks. Had he done something stupid, like fall asleep at his station? A quick glance to his console's chronometer told him that could not be possible. So he had merely been daydreaming when his superior officer wandered into the lab. Perfect.

"I'm sorry, Mister Spock. I was . . . lost in thought." Taking a moment to consult the sensor readings, he said, "Backup battery power's continuing to drain and is now at five percent. I estimate total shutdown with reserves exhausted within ten minutes."

"Thank you." As he returned to the workstation at the rear of the room, Spock asked, "Ensign, based on the process we have been required to employ to collect the probe's data, have you drawn any conclusions about the other universe?"

Frowning, Chekov replied, "I'm not sure I understand, sir."

"I am asking if you had deduced any differences between our universe and the Jatohr's, based on the nature of how we are forced to collect the probe's sensor information."

Chekov considered the question. "Well, there's the use of gamma radiation to carry the data from the other universe to us. That itself is rather unusual."

After spending a moment in silence studying the status indicators and display monitors at his own station, Spock turned and moved back to Chekov's console. "There is something else to consider. I must admit that I did not notice it at first, as Lieutenant Uhura and I were immersed in our monitoring of the computer's deciphering of the probe data." Stepping closer to Chekov's station, he entered a series of commands, in response to which another of the monitors began to display a new stream of telemetry.

"This reading should show us the probe's relative distance from the *Enterprise*," he said. "You will note that there appears to be no variance in that distance, even though our relative position has not remained constant due to our orbit around the planet."

It took Chekov a moment to realize what the first officer was saying. "It's as if the probe is keeping station with us. How can that be?"

"I do not know, Ensign. I would expect such measurements to be all but meaningless, except for one thing." Spock entered another command string and the sensor data shifted. "These readings indicate life signs detected by the probe."

As this was the first time he had seen the probe's scan data converted from the original format, Chekov found himself leaning closer to the screen. "Jatohr life signs, of course, but also human, Klingon, and Vulcan?"

"Correct," Spock replied. "The readings are indistinct,

but still identifiable, and each carries with it an interesting quality. Do you see it?"

Feeling put on the spot as he studied the sensor readings, Chekov realized he was being tested by the science officer, or perhaps Spock was formulating a hypothesis of his own and was using this conversation to test it.

Is he trying to get me to poke a hole in his theory?

"At first," Chekov offered, "the data suggests that the other universe might occupy the same space as our own, but on another dimensional plane." That alone was enough to make his head hurt. "Can we even prove something like that with the data we have?"

"I am not prepared to make such a claim without more data and research," replied Spock. "However, the evidence we have does suggest that the other universe likely follows a different set of physical definitions that are presently beyond our ability to understand. However, we have at least surmised that the probe was likely transported to the same realm as Sarek and everyone else affected by the Transfer Key. Further, it would seem that anyone transitioned from our universe is deposited in the same relative location within the other universe, regardless of their origin point in our universe. This is fortunate, as it should considerably narrow our search efforts."

"Search efforts?" asked Chekov. "Are you suggesting we attempt to follow the probe into the other universe?"

Spock nodded. "That may be our only course of action, Ensign. However, given the speed with which the probe's power systems were depleted, it is reasonable to assume that the *Enterprise* would be similarly affected."

"But now that we've determined there are life signs over there," said Chekov, "shouldn't we be able to configure the Transfer Key to retrieve them and bring them back

herc? After all, the whole point of the transfer-field generator was to bring the Jatohr over from their universe. Surely
we can do the same for our people."

"We require more information before attempting such
a retrieval," Spock replied. "Doing so without conclusively
identifying individual life signs could prove hazardous.
There is also the fact that we simply do not know how to
employ the Transfer Key for such an action."

Studying the sensor readings, Chekov could not help
releasing a small sigh. "The life-form readings are the most
difficult to sort, Mister Spock. They all seem jumbled."
The information seemed to swim together, with different
streams blending in a manner that defied easy extrapola-
tion. To Chekov, it all appeared as though the environment
surrounding the probe was behaving as an organism.

That doesn't make sense. Maybe I'm just tired.

A series of alert tones sounded from his console, and
Chekov scowled as he noted the new readings. "That's it,
Mister Spock. The probe's power cells look to be drained."
There was no way to know what additional sensor data
it had managed to collect before depleting its energy reserves. That would only happen if they could figure out
how to return it from the other universe.

"We have collected considerable information," said
Spock. "It should prove sufficient for continuing our research."

What must he be thinking?

The question came unbidden, coursing through Chekov's mind. To this point, Spock had been quite successful
in not appearing preoccupied with concern for his father,
though the ensign knew the Vulcan's human mother was
very despondent over the current situation. Likewise,
Doctor McCoy also was worried about his daughter, who

had been transported with Sarek from Centaurus. It made sense that even with his superior emotional control, Spock still would feel anxiety about his father's well-being. That likely was compelling the first officer to work as hard as he had been doing to this point. Chekov knew that Spock was on his third consecutive duty shift and showed no signs of slowing down.

He needs your help. That's why you're here. So, get back to it.

That was all the motivation Chekov needed. The fatigue that had been teasing the edges of his awareness would just have to wait. Blowing out his breath, the young ensign returned to his workstation. Even with the probe's transmissions now halted, there remained volumes of sensor data to review.

Somewhere in the midst of that mess was an answer.

Twenty

"Captain, we have lost all sensor contact with the probe."

Eschewing his command chair, J'Teglyr had taken to stalking the bridge of the *Vron'joQ*, pausing at each station and staring over the shoulder of the Klingon officer manning each console. Everyone here was on alert, their attention riveted to the controls and actions for which they were responsible. Even J'Teglyr was feeling the heightened awareness, his every nerve seemingly alive with the rush of anticipation.

"What are you talking about?" Coming abreast of the tactical station, he peered past an anxious Lieutenant G'peq to the fire-control system displays. It took him only a moment to assess the situation as conveyed by the ship's sensors. As his tactical officer had reported, the Starfleet probe appeared to no longer be anywhere within sensor range. As for the Starfleet ship, it was doing as its commander had promised. The scans showed that the *Enterprise* was keeping to its orbit above Usilde while maintaining an interval from the *Vron'joQ* that was well away from anything J'Teglyr might see as close proximity or an attempt at provocation.

"Our sensors were tracking it from the moment it was launched, my lord," said G'peq. "After it began emitting that odd signal, our scans began to experience some disruption, but I was able to reconfigure our systems. Then the probe simply vanished."

J'Teglyr frowned. "Could it be a cloaking device?" The very thought was troublesome. Had the Earther captain deceived him by launching a covert weapon that could strike the *Vron'joQ* at any moment? "Has the Federation stolen such technology from the Romulans or someone else?"

"I do not believe that is the case," replied G'peq. "The disruption to our sensors was inconsistent with the effect associated with known forms of cloaking devices. Also, according to the latest intelligence reports, the Federation has not been developing its own stealth technology."

A student of Federation and Romulan affairs from his earliest days as an academy cadet, J'Teglyr had studied the unvarnished reports and other historical records of both powers as provided by decades of history professors, military commanders, and intelligence agents. Because of those studies, he was well aware of the conflict between the Romulan Empire and the Earthers from more than a century ago, and even the continuing skirmishes that had lasted into the early years of this century. One of the agreements contained in the peace accords between the two warring parties, the Treaty of Algeron, outlawed the Federation's ability to develop cloaking technology such as that employed by the Romulans.

To J'Teglyr, it seemed both a courageous and a foolish stipulation on the Federation's part. Why would one purposely limit a sound tactical option when preparing for war against present and future enemies? Even with everything he had read and come to know about the Federation, questions such as those still perplexed him. Such decisions would seem to invite more trouble than they were intended to prevent. Would it be a stance like this that ultimately proved the Federation's undoing? J'Teglyr thought not. After all, despite whatever gracious facade they might put forth for the purpose of formal diplomatic posturing, it was easy to imagine, somewhere in a dark room hidden deep in the heart of all that Federation nobility and sensitivity, someone was hard at work attempting to circumvent such "civilized" agreements in favor of strategic advantage.

Earthers are more like Klingons than they care to admit.

Glancing back to the tactical display, J'Teglyr saw that the *Enterprise* was continuing to maintain its position relative to the *Vron'joQ*. Farther away, though only a distance of minutes at impulse speeds, was the *I.K.S. Qo'Daqh*, still on its inbound course. What were its captain's intentions? J'Teglyr knew Commander Visla only by her tarnished reputation: a disgraced officer who acted as nursemaid to a collection of malcontents and other dregs of Klingon society. Why was she here now? If Visla harbored any lingering vestiges of honor, she would do well to set her vessel's self-destruct mechanism while still far enough from other ships to inflict damage or inconvenience.

"There are new readings from the planet's surface, my lord," reported Commander D'jorok, who had taken to manning one of the bridge's other sensor control stations. "Power levels within the alien construct are increasing far above anything we have seen since our arrival."

J'Teglyr turned his attention once more to the tactical station. His gaze lingered on the computer-generated representation of the Federation ship. "It has to be the *Enterprise*. They have learned how to manipulate the alien technology." It was obvious that Kirk and his crew had benefited from their ability to study the Transfer Key, the field generator's singular crucial and apparently irreplaceable component. The very notion had seemed outlandish when J'Teglyr first heard it, but the evidence now before his eyes would seem to prove that the Earthers held control over the Jatohr citadel.

"They go to all this trouble," he said, "they face so much risk, and for what?" He at first had not believed Kirk's assertions that Councillor Gorkon and others might be rescued from whatever "parallel universe" connected to their own via the transfer generator. With the *Enterprise* probe having now vanished from all modes of detection, perhaps this idea was not so implausible after all.

"If they have learned the secrets of the Transfer Key," said D'jorok, "then we must seize it."

J'Teglyr grunted. "And how do you propose we do that? Attack their ship? Send a boarding party to snatch it and any other goods like common pirates?"

"My lord," said G'peq, "the *Qo'Daqh* is on final approach, but it is maintaining full impulse speed."

His eyes narrowing with suspicion, J'Teglyr asked, "What is its course? An approach for orbit?"

The tactical officer shook his head. "No, Captain." Leaning over his console, he consulted the sensor readings again before adding, "It appears they are . . . they are assuming an attack vector against the *Enterprise*!"

———

Red alert sirens wailed across the bridge. On the viewscreen, the Klingon D5 battle cruiser was sailing into the frame, its forward disruptor ports already glowing with emerald power.

"Deflector shields activated!" called out Lieutenant Sulu at the helm.

Clutching the arms of his command chair, Kirk ordered, "Ready phasers and photon torpedoes. Lieutenant Rahda, stand by to fire on my command."

Seated in front of him at the navigator's station, Naomi Rahda replied, "Weapons ready, sir." The lieutenant had been summoned to the bridge to substitute for Ensign Chekov, who was still assisting Spock belowdecks. She was a seasoned officer, recently transferred from the *U.S.S. Potemkin* and rated for both helm and navigation as well as weapons and sensors. Rahda had only been with the *Enterprise* for . . . what was it? Less than two weeks, and here she was, hip deep in an emergency situation?

Welcome aboard, Lieutenant.

The arrival of the new ship had not been unexpected. Long-range sensors had detected its approach well enough in advance that Kirk and his crew had ample warning of any attack. Like the *Vron'joQ* in orbit above Usilde, this new ship had maintained a peaceful posture, running without active weapons or shields. Only in the last moments before it entered range for an expected orbital insertion had it assumed a more confrontational profile.

And what the hell is that about?

"Definitely targeting us, Captain," reported Lieutenant Michael Medeiros, the young officer manning the science station while Spock was off the bridge. "They're going for target lock and moving into position to fire."

Kirk said, "Evasive maneuvers, Sulu. Phasers, lock on."

"Evasive, aye."

Turning from the sensor controls, Medeiros shouted, "Incoming!"

An instant later the weapons ports at the front of the Klingon ship spat forth a pair of pulsing energy orbs. On the viewscreen, the disruptor bolts grew larger and angrier with each passing heartbeat. Sulu pushed the *Enterprise* away from its opponent, and the Klingon vessel disappeared up and out of the viewscreen's frame. The helm officer was fast, but not fast enough to completely avoid the attack.

Everything around Kirk shook and rattled from the impact of the disruptors against the *Enterprise*'s shields. The overhead lighting flickered as did a number of the display screens and control consoles around the bridge. He felt himself lifted from his seat but maintained his grip on the chair's armrests, preventing himself from being thrown to the deck. Everyone else managed to maintain their positions as well.

"Indirect hit to our port shields, aft," said Lieutenant Medeiros. "I'm reading several circuit overloads and power fluctuations in the port warp nacelle and engineering sections twelve and fourteen. No hull breach."

Knowing Mister Scott and his people would have that situation in hand, Kirk kept his focus on the more immediate problem. A glance to the astrogator between Sulu and Rahda showed him the relative positions of the *Enterprise* and their attacker. He noted that the *Vron'joQ*, which had been lurking at the edge of the scanner's display, was maintaining its position in orbit above the planet. Whatever this new arrival was doing, it appeared Captain J'Teglyr wanted no part of it, at least for the moment.

How lucky we are.

"Bring us about, Sulu," he said. "Rahda, don't wait for my order. Fire the second you have a clear shot."

The Indian officer spared only a glance over her shoulder. "Aye, sir."

"They're coming around again, Captain," said Medeiros. "They're trying to get in behind us."

Kirk leaned forward in his seat. "Don't let them do that, Sulu."

The lieutenant did not reply, his attention focused on his controls. His piloting prowess was evident both on the viewscreen and the astrogator as the *Enterprise* maneuvered over, under, and around the Klingon vessel, searching for an avenue of attack while denying it to its adversary.

Medeiros warned, "They're firing again!"

The effect of the second strike was not as pronounced, thanks to Sulu's skill, but the *Enterprise* still trembled beneath the force of at least one disruptor striking its shields.

"Glancing blow to starboard shields," said Medeiros, who was gripping the edge of the science console with one hand while using the other to brace himself against the station's sensor viewer.

Sulu cast a quick look over his shoulder to Kirk. "Bringing us about."

"Firing!" called out Rahda.

On the viewscreen, the Klingon ship rolled into view as the *Enterprise* approached it from below and behind just as twin beams of blue-white energy lanced across the space separating the two vessels. Energy flared at the phasers' point of impact against the enemy ship's deflector shields, and Lieutenant Rahda followed this initial strike with a second salvo even as the other ship moved to evade the attack. Her targeting was perfect, as Kirk saw the phasers slam into the shields just before a third shot pushed through and tore into the battle cruiser's hull. Without waiting, Rahda fired again and this time both beams struck the ship's aft section. Kirk noted the momentary burst of released atmosphere signifying a hull rupture.

Medeiros reported, "Direct hits on their aft hull section, Captain. Their aft shields are also down, sensors show damage to their main engines, and at least one compartment has been breached. I'm also picking up a series of massive overloads and circuit failures across the ship." He turned away from the sensor viewer. "I think we hit their primary power plant, sir."

Kirk looked to Rahda. "Nice shooting, Lieutenant."

The Klingon ship had altered its course and was now moving away from the *Enterprise*, and Kirk could see that the enemy vessel was not attempting to reacquire a target.

"Hold your fire, Lieutenant," he said. "Mister Medeiros, what's their status?"

Still hovering over the sensor viewer, the young lieutenant replied, "More surges in the ship's main power systems. Secondary systems are also fluctuating."

Rahda turned in her seat. "I was targeting its engines, but just to disable its propulsion, sir."

"I know, Lieutenant." Kirk gestured to the viewscreen. "It's an older ship. That might have as much to do with it as anything." Looking to Medeiros, he asked, "Was anyone in that breached compartment?"

The lieutenant replied, "Negative, sir, but scans are picking up more power fluctuations, and now I'm reading a failure in their life-support systems."

Turning his chair toward the communications station, Kirk said, "Uhura, hail them and ask if they require assistance." He glanced back to the viewscreen, which now showed the Klingon ship in obvious distress as it drifted and began to tumble to starboard. "And contact Captain

J'Teglyr. I want to let him know we're not pursuing the fight. Mister Sulu, hold this position."

"Aye, sir," replied the helm officer.

After a moment spent working her controls, Uhura said, "The other ship isn't responding, but they are receiving our hails. Captain J'Teglyr is coming through now, though."

"Put him onscreen."

Kirk turned to face the main viewer in time to see the image shift from the damaged Klingon vessel to J'Teglyr. Dispensing with any attempt at pleasantries, Kirk said, "Perhaps you know why your fellow captain launched an unprovoked attack on my vessel, Captain."

The Klingon had been preparing to say something when he was cut off, and Kirk watched his mouth shut, then open again. His eyes widened in obvious surprise and annoyance at the veiled accusation, and he pushed himself from his chair and stepped forward until his face all but filled the viewscreen.

"I was not aware that the Qo'Daqh *would attack, Kirk. Its captain did not provide me with any advance warning of her intentions. She was acting on her own."*

What the hell was all this about? Kirk forced his expression to remain neutral as he considered the possibilities. Who was this female Klingon commander? Was she some kind of rogue officer with a vendetta?

At the science station, Medeiros said, "The *Vron'joQ's* shields are still down, Captain."

"Of course my shields are down!" snapped J'Teglyr. *"I told you I would not take any aggressive action so long as you did the same."* He paused, looking at something Kirk could not see. *"However, I note that your defenses are still active, Captain."*

Rising from his chair, Kirk placed his hands on his hips. "Yes, they are, and they'll remain that way until I'm satisfied that this little skirmish is over, but we're holding our present position. I have no intention of moving unless provoked. Your other ship has damage to its life-support systems. It will require repair or an evacuation. We stand ready to assist if you want our help."

"*Maintain your distance, Kirk,*" replied the Klingon. "*I will deal with the* Qo'Daqh." After a moment, he added, "*Though your offer is appreciated.*" While it was a reluctant addendum, Kirk noted the hint of genuine gratitude it also possessed.

Wonders never cease.

Kirk nodded. "My pleasure, Captain. Kirk out." He gestured to Uhura to sever the communication. Once J'Teglyr's face vanished from the viewscreen and was replaced with an image of the *Qo'Daqh*, the captain shook his head as he let himself drop into his command chair. "Lieutenant Uhura, have all department heads forward damage reports directly to Mister Scott in engineering."

"Aye, Captain," replied the communications officer.

After a moment spent studying the wounded Klingon vessel, he activated the intercom panel on his armrest. "Kirk to Spock. What's your status? Anything new on the probe?"

Several seconds passed before the Vulcan's voice replied, "*Unchanged, Captain. It appears to have lost power, and we are no longer receiving telemetry. We are analyzing the data we have collected in the hopes of determining a way to reestablish contact or perhaps retrieve it. I was going to ask Mister Scott to assist us, but it is likely his skills are now required elsewhere.*"

"Your gift for understatement never ceases to amaze

me, Spock. Whatever you're going to do, you'd better figure it out fast. Now that the Klingons know for sure that we can access the transfer generator, I don't expect them to sit idly by and wait this out." Though he did not believe the unexpected attack from the *Qo'Daqh* was born from that concern, there was still Captain J'Teglyr, who was continuing to play his cards very close to his vest.

Kirk closed his eyes, shaking his head.

"Things can never be simple, can they?"

Twenty-one

Visla knelt beside Koveq, staring into eyes that no longer saw anything. Somehow they remained undamaged despite the ruin visited upon the rest of his face and chest. Ignoring the blood and the stench of his burned flesh, she placed her palm along the tattered, burned skin of his left cheek.

"I am sorry, my dear friend."

She had already carried out the ritual, staring into Koveq's open, lifeless eyes before releasing a raucous scream toward *Sto-Vo-Kor*, warning its denizens that a fine warrior was due to arrive in their midst. All that remained was to see to the disposal of his body. Would there be time to do even that before she was forced to abandon ship?

With him positioned behind her during the brief, fierce skirmish with the Federation ship, Visla had not seen the explosion from the overloaded console that had taken Koveq's life and injured another of her bridge officers. The precision phaser strike from the *Enterprise* had triggered massive overloads throughout the *Qo'Daqh*, overwhelming its overstrained, underpowered electrical relay systems. It was yet another indictment of an aged vessel that should have been refurbished or scrapped long before Visla had reached adulthood. The explosion had been enough to singe the hair on the back of her head, and shrapnel had peppered the back of her chair and her exposed skin. She had swiveled around in time to see Koveq fall from his station, dead before his body even collapsed to the deck.

From that point the battle's end was a foregone conclusion. The *Enterprise* had scored devastating hits on the *Qo'Daqh*, disabling its main engines and hampering a number of internal systems. Had its commander been of a mind to do so, the Starfleet vessel would have been able to destroy her ship with ease. Instead, Kirk had chosen in typical Earther fashion to spare her and her crew, and Visla now loathed him for it.

Finish us, you worthless targ. *Send us from this life with some shred of dignity.*

It was not to be. There would be no honorable death this day.

"Commander."

It was Woveth, who had come up behind her. Turning away from Koveq, Visla regarded her first officer and for the first time noticed the near silence of the *Qo'Daqh*'s bridge. Nearly every station and display monitor was inactive, and only emergency lighting cast any illumination into the cramped space. The rest of her bridge crew was gone, having been ordered to the ship's transporter room as part of the evacuation to the *Vron'joQ*.

"What is it?"

Woveth replied, "The last of the crew has left the ship. We are all that remain, except for the dead."

Nodding at the report, Visla considered the eleven other Klingons who, like Koveq, had died in the battle. Most of the other casualties had come from the explosion in the ship's aft portion, while two had suffered fatal injuries similar to Koveq's. "Have the dead been sent on their way to *Sto-Vo-Kor*?"

"Yes, Commander. I saw to it myself."

"Good. It is the least we can do for them. Despite whatever disgrace they may have carried, they served with honor until the end." That her crew had followed her commands and never wavered in their loyalty to her was without question. What remained unanswered was whether the lives of the dead had been sacrificed in service to a noble goal. That would be a matter of much discussion once she and the rest of the *Qo'Daqh* survivors were returned to High Command, where she would face a full accounting of her decisions and actions.

So be it.

"He was a fine warrior," said Woveth.

"Yes, he was." Visla rose to her feet, pausing one final time to study Koveq's unmoving form. In addition to his status as a loyal soldier of the Empire and her most trusted confidant, he had been a great deal more, but those were thoughts she could revisit at a more appropriate time. For now, there was the unpleasant prospect of presenting herself and her crew to Captain J'Teglyr. Was the shame she now felt the same as that experienced by her son upon his rescue from the doomed *HoS'leth*? If he could carry such a burden while awaiting retrieval on Centaurus, she could compose herself and face what was to come.

J'Teglyr waited just long enough for Commander Visla to step through the hatch and onto the *Vron'joQ*'s bridge before he stepped forward and slapped her across the face.

"Who gave you authorization to attack the Starfleet ship?" His bellowing question echoed off the room's metal bulkheads and deck plating.

For her part, Visla took the full brunt of the strike, her only reaction being the snapping of her head to the left. When she looked back to face him, a small rivulet of blood had appeared at the corner of her mouth, courtesy of the ring on J'Teglyr's right hand. She did not reach up to wipe at the blood. Standing just behind her, a male Klingon with lieutenant's rank, presumably her first officer, stepped forward, reaching for the disruptor on his hip. He froze in midstep when Visla held out a hand, and her unspoken order was complemented by Commander D'jorok drawing his own weapon and aiming it at the lieutenant's chest.

"Move again, and I will kill you where you stand."

Waving his first officer to step back, J'Teglyr returned his attention to Visla. "Was it your intention to start a war with the Federation?"

"Is war against the Federation not what the Empire has always wanted?"

J'Teglyr clamped his fist at his side. The temptation to strike again was almost overwhelming, but he resisted it. His initial fury was already beginning to ebb, but there remained the very real situation this fool may well have exacerbated.

"Such a decision is not yours to make." He forced every word between gritted teeth. "Once you arrived in the system, you fell under my authority as the senior officer present. I could kill you right here and now, and the High Command would give me a commendation."

Visla snorted. "Doubtful. Such awards are reserved for actions of true worth. We both know High Command thinks so little of me. Even killing me would be viewed as little more than disposing of a nuisance."

"Then maybe I'll do it for my own amusement." J'Teglyr took a long look at her, making no attempt to conceal his obvious, wanton stare. She was certainly attractive, and he had no doubts the passion and anger she had exhibited during her brief battle with the *Enterprise* would translate to other, more recreational pursuits.

She understood his leering for what it was and lashed out. J'Teglyr let her land the blow, feeling the sting as her hand snapped across his cheek. He even smiled in response.

"Dream all you want, J'Teglyr," she said. "Were I to allow your fantasy to come to pass, it would only be in service to putting my blade through your eye."

J'Teglyr released a hearty laugh, nodding in admiration. "Worry not, Commander. Despite whatever failings you might observe in my personal conduct, I am first and foremost an officer sworn to duty. There will be no dishonorable actions or liberties taken here today." His smile faded. "You are guests aboard my ship. Do not make me regret my decision to rescue your worthless hides."

"What of my ship?" asked Visla. "Can it be towed to a repair base?"

Turning from her, J'Teglyr eyed the image of the *Qo'Daqh* on the viewing screen as it drifted in space. The wounded vessel was tumbling on its long axis, its maneuvering and positioning thrusters offline like so many other of the ship's systems. Its starboard warp nacelle appeared inert, and numerous portholes were dark.

Looking to Visla, he asked, "Were all the survivors retrieved?"

The commander nodded. "Yes." She indicated her companion. "Lieutenant Woveth and I were the last to leave."

"How many casualties did you suffer?"

Visla cast her gaze toward the viewing screen. "Twelve, including my weapons officer."

There was a definite change in her tone, and when he looked back at her, J'Teglyr realized from her expression that Visla must have enjoyed a personal relationship with this other officer. His initial impulse was to make some snide remark to that effect, but he quashed the urge. Though it might provide a moment's petty enjoyment, there was nothing else to be gained from such a childish taunt. Instead, he redirected his attention back to the viewing screen and the *Qo'Daqh*.

"Lieutenant G'peq, lock all weapons on that ship."

He heard Visla step toward him. "What?"

"It is a relic," J'Teglyr said without looking at her. "It is not worth the effort to tow it to a spacedock, let alone the resources necessary to restore it. Better to remove it and its stain of dishonor altogether." To his surprise, Visla offered nothing more in the way of resistance. Perhaps she was already resigning herself to whatever fate the High Command had reserved for her and realizing that her time and energy were better spent on things other than the distraction of an unsalvageable vessel, regardless of whatever sentimental value it might hold.

"Weapons are ready, my lord," reported G'peq.

"Fire."

A pulsing tremor surged through the deck plating and into J'Teglyr's boots in response to his command as the tactical officer unleashed the full fury of the *Vron'joQ*'s disruptor cannons and torpedo launchers. The lighting as well as most of the bridge consoles dimmed, the result of power being drawn to feed the ship's weapons. An instant later J'Teglyr watched a maelstrom of disruptor energy and photon torpedoes streak across the screen, surging through the space separating the *Vron'joQ* and the *Qo'Daqh*.

The first disruptor bolts slammed into the wounded vessel at its midpoint, boring into the reinforced hull plating and weakening them just enough for the torpedoes to strike with full, unfiltered force. G'peq was already repeating the onslaught, and the targeted ship buckled in the face of the second barrage. The *Qo'Daqh* began to come apart, its primary hull and part of the boom section pulling away from the larger engineering section. Both warp nacelles also were torn off, and the engineering hull started to crumple before the entire ship was enveloped in a massive explosion signaling the collapse of the warp drive's antimatter containment system. The *Qo'Daqh's* death throes lasted mere heartbeats before the effects of the blast faded and all that remained of the stricken vessel was an expanding cloud of debris.

"Well done, Captain," said Visla, her words all but dripping contempt. "No doubt your many glorious victories in battle allowed you and your crew to hone the skills you bring to bear against a derelict vessel. You are truly a credit to the Empire."

Rather than respond to the obvious verbal jab, J'Teglyr instead directed another wide smile at her. "Even the least challenging of targets can prove useful on occasion. Now, it seems our most pressing matter is what to do with you and your crew while you are guests aboard my ship. Will you conduct yourselves like proper warriors of the Empire, or will I be forced to throw you into a holding cell or perhaps out an airlock?"

"I think you are mistaken, Captain." Visla pointed to the viewing screen. "Have you forgotten the Federation ship?"

"You are referring to the vessel you attacked without provocation?" J'Teglyr shook his head. "No, that has not ventured far from my thoughts. What do you suggest we do, Commander? Attack the Earthers again? Setting aside the point that you still do not have authorization to carry out such actions, are you not aware that we are in territory that is governed by the Organian Peace Treaty? Do you not understand the ramifications for breaching the treaty, and the risk this presents to the very security of the Empire?"

Still standing next to Visla, Woveth snarled. "A treaty enacted and enforced by ghosts? This is what guides our actions? Does it fuel our cowardice, as well?"

Once more, Visla jabbed a finger at the screen. "Kirk possesses the crucial component we need to exploit the alien technology. Why are we not doing everything in our power to take it from him?"

Whatever she or her family had done to earn the Empire's wrath, Visla was still a Klingon of courage. This, at least, J'Teglyr could respect, and he saw from the faces of his bridge crew that he was not alone in this regard.

"Yours is not the first voice to speak of such things." He glanced to D'jorok. "My first officer shares similar views." J'Teglyr looked to the viewing screen, on which G'peq had switched to an image of the *Enterprise* in orbit above Usilde. "Kirk is no fool. He knows that we want the Key. He is not about to let it fall from his grasp so easily, and he will fight if provoked. As you have witnessed for yourself, he is also a formidable opponent. However, none of this matters. Even though I share your desire to take the Key from Kirk, my orders on this matter are plain and inviolable. I am not to attack the *Enterprise* for any reason, unless or until a clear, unmistakable opportunity to retrieve the Key presents itself."

"A keen warrior creates such opportunities," replied Woveth, "instead of waiting for them like a child pining for his supper."

"And a loyal warrior finds a way to do that while not shirking his duty or disrespecting his superiors."

Another glance to a few of his own subordinates told

J'Teglyr that this conversation, carried out in their presence, might become troublesome if he allowed it to continue. Spirited disagreement he could abide, depending on the situation, but outright defiance of his status as the captain of this ship could not be tolerated. To so openly challenge a commanding officer was to contest the target as unfit to lead. Such action might even imply a possible attempt at mutiny and forcible removal of the beleaguered officer from command.

J'Teglyr glared at Visla. "I do not know how order and discipline were maintained on your vessel, but here subordinates keep their insolent tongues still or else they lose them to my blade."

Stepping away from her and Woveth, he stalked around the bridge's perimeter until he was standing directly before the viewing screen. His gaze focused on the *Enterprise*, trying to imagine its commander's thoughts. What was Kirk's ultimate goal with the alien technology? Even if his presence here was motivated by purity of purpose, what would happen if and when he was successful in rescuing his comrades and Councillor Gorkon? What would happen then? How far were the Earther captain and his superiors willing to go to keep the field generator out of Klingon hands or those of the Romulans or anyone else who expressed similar interest? Would they risk war? J'Teglyr doubted the Federation would initiate such a conflict, but despite all propaganda to the contrary, he knew they were more than capable of answering such a threat. Most experts agreed that despite the troublesome Organians and their interference, war between the Empire and the Federation was inevitable.

And won't that be glorious?

Twenty-two

Sarek opened his eyes and saw nothing. What he sensed, however, was far from void.

In this space of presence within emptiness, he assessed what he knew rather than dwelling on what he did not. He felt light rather than heavy, warm rather than cold, dry rather than wet. He was aware of his own heartbeat and respiration, both of which seemed slowed, though not to the point of alarm. It was as if his metabolic processes had been reduced in a manner similar to what might be done to achieve medical stasis, and yet there was no questioning his awareness of himself and his surroundings, such as they were. An attempt to reach up and touch his face yielded nothing. He felt no movement of his arm or the sensation of his fingertips brushing his cheek, and yet this did not trouble him.

Most interesting.

"Is anyone there?"

Sarek was certain he perceived the sound of his own voice. It seemed to echo first in his ears and then within his mind, but before he could speak again there were other voices, emerging without warning from the void. A multitude of thoughts—flashes and fragments of ideas and memories and emotions—were all around him. The sensation was not dissimilar to a mind-meld, and he recoiled from the uncounted minds that seemed eager to speak to him all at once. He closed himself off, shielding his own thoughts using skills and mental disciplines he had honed after years of practice.

Within a moment, the voices faded to a dull murmur, held at bay and allowing him space to think. Now he heard only dozens of voices rather than hundreds or thousands. Focusing his attention on a single source, Sarek was able to isolate a specific thought or feeling, likening it to over-hearing a lone conversation within a crowd. Even then, such separation was fleeting, as unwelcome interruptions abounded. The thoughts he perceived were little more than random comments offered from passersby, including unexpected bursts of insight or the natural rise in volume from a voice speaking with passion or a need for attention.

At the edges of his perception, Sarek sensed light beginning to infiltrate the darkness. The black turned to gray and then to white, but there was nothing else. He saw nothing of substance, but instead only variations in brightness or shadow. Still, the change was enough to provide him with a new confidence to reach out into the void—not with his arms but with his mind. Listening to the voices he had permitted beyond his mental barriers, he sensed what he surmised were memories, each laced with an emotional resonance. Others offered beliefs or theories about their own existences. There were many questions, Sarek realized, but no answers.

Emerging from the chorus of disjointed murmurings and thoughts, most of which were muffled and indistinct, was a single voice that seemed to beckon for attention.

"Hello. Hello . . ."

It did not feel incoherent, or lacking of purpose, Sarek decided. Instead, it carried an insistent tone, as though refusing to fade away while going unanswered. A reply seemed the logical course of action.

"Hello," he said. At least, he thought he did.

"You have joined us," replied the voice, now much stronger and closer. To Sarek, it seemed focused directly on him and his mind. He could not be sure if it was verbal communication or a form of telepathy, noting also that the void seemed to brighten with each word.

"I am called Sarek," he offered. "I am not of your planet or your universe. I am from a world called Vulcan."

The voice replied, "I am Edolon. I am of . . . this place."

"And what is this place?"

Instead of a direct response, a rush of unbidden thoughts coursed across his consciousness, as though hundreds of Edolons were speaking simultaneously. Almost overwhelmed by the sensation, Sarek instinctively restored his mental defenses. The voices dimmed, along with his perception of the void's brighter illumination.

"You are not of us, Sarek." When Edolon spoke this time, it was as a single voice delivered in a low, soft pitch. "I distinguish as I discover. You are not yet ready, but I know you can be."

"Ready for what? To be of you? Of this place?"

"No," Edolon said. "You are not of us, but you are not of them. You cannot be of us because when I am not this, I am instead this."

Sarek's mind filled with disjointed images of spotted and glistening skin, pairs of writhing tentacles, a large, flat foot gliding on its own secretions, and other randomized parts of what he knew to be the genderless gastropod Jatohr. The indiscriminate sequencing led him to conclude that Edolon's sense of self was quite distant from what he surmised it would be outside of this realm. It was an insight Sarek found most curious. To return the gesture, he projected a mental image of himself that he hoped Edolon might perceive.

"I am instead this," he offered.

"Yes," replied Edolon. "You are of the others, but unlike them. You are unlike any of them, Sarek. This pleases me, as you bring balance to this. You bring good to this as the object brings bad."

Confused, Sarek tried to parse the statement, but could make no sense of it. "I do not understand. What is this object that brings bad?"

"It came to this as you came to this," replied the disembodied voice. "The object has no life. It has no being, and it spreads pain through this. We must end the pain."

Edolon's thoughts confirmed to Sarek that something had changed for the worse here, but what? How was it able to influence not only the space he now occupied, but the place from which he had come? Seeking answers, Sarek lowered his mental defenses. The void around him brightened once more, though he remained unable to see. He searched for Edolon, hoping to strengthen that connection, and was rewarded with a new, greater sense of clarity.

"I was correct," said the Jatohr. "Unlike the others, you are able to acclimate. I have a better sense of you now, Sarek."

"And I perceive you as well. What I do not understand is what distinguishes this place from where I was before. Was that merely illusion?"

Edolon replied, "It is a difficult concept to comprehend. It is a point of transition, intended to assist the minds of the newly transferred. Moving from one realm to another can be traumatic for the unprepared or the unsuited. For the Jatohr, this is helpful as we prepare for transition, but such is not the case for those unlike us. Your kind seems most ill-suited for this place, which is why they remain in the other space. Or their minds eventually give up, and they are reunited with their physical forms, all of which are separate from time as we experience it outside of this place. You, however, appear to be unique."

"Perhaps I can assist their transition," said Sarek. "However, I must admit some confusion. What of the Jatohr we have encountered there? Do they exist both here and in the other place?"

"As we have awaited a time for transition, some of us have become adept at moving between the two spaces. Others, like you and your kind, become immersed in that place, to the point that they perceive everything that occurs there as being akin to reality. Complicating matters is the fact that there are some among us who dread the intrusion of those like you. There is concern that you may become even greater masters of our universe than the Jatohr, and that we then would be at your mercy."

Sarek said, "We are not your enemy. We seek only peace. The people I represent would offer to assist the Jatohr in their transition from this universe. We would find a world suitable to your species. You would be allowed to live your lives as you see fit, and we would welcome new friends."

"That may be possible, provided those who live in fear can be convinced. First, we must end the pain from the object. This place can accommodate the living, but not the inanimate. It arrived from beyond our realm, the place from which you came. We are attempting to deplete its energy so that the pain can end."

Sarek asked, "May I examine this object?"

"At your own risk," replied Edolon. "It is too painful for me to do so again, but I can show you the way."

At the Jatohr's prompting, Sarek lowered his mental barriers and cleared his mind. In a moment, he sensed

Edolon's consciousness mingling with his own, though not merging as he might expect with a mind-meld. After a moment, the white haze dominating his perception began burning away. He found himself suspended within a vast gray ocean that harbored innumerable life-forms. Most of the beings appeared to be Jatohr, at least from his vantage point, though he did also see the occasional Usildar humanoid interspersed among them. Slicing through the abyss were filaments of writhing, twisting light that spanned the color spectrum. Each string seemed to emanate from the head of a Jatohr, although there also were specimens with no such tendrils who appeared left to drift in the emptiness. The strings weaved among one another, entwining in groups of varying sizes. At an instinctual level, Sarek understood that each multihued strand somehow represented a distinct consciousness separate from its physical self, unencumbered to explore not only this place but also the distinct awareness of each of the realm's other occupants.

"Fascinating."

Edolon said, "This is but a representation we have constructed for our own understanding. We exist in a community of shared concepts and insights, and each of our minds perceive all the others to the extent that we personally desire. You could also share in this, Sarek. You could reach greater levels of understanding than you ever imagined. First, we must deal with the object. You should be able to find it."

Following the Jatohr's direction, Sarek opened his mind, pushing outward in all directions. His consciousness began to expand, spreading like ripples on a still pond. As he encountered other beings, he sensed their thoughts but did not engage them. Still he was able to perceive expressions of aspiration and heartbreak, fulfillment and passion, and even failure. When he sensed a familiar presence, he moved to explore it and was surprised to find some of his companions here, as well. Captain Una and Joanna McCoy, drifting as though in limbo. He found Beel Zeroh, his military adviser, and pondered whether the Izarian's mind had found peace in this place. There were the other *Enterprise* crew members, those Una had come to rescue, also floating listless in the void, and here too was Gorkon. For his comrade in diplomacy, for the warrior willing to die in order to protect him, for the Klingon who carried what might be a singular vision for his people, Sarek diverted from his quest.

Rather than the soiled, bloodied, and battle-weary Gorkon of the Jatohr's psychically applied environment, here the Klingon appeared just as Sarek had last seen him on Centaurus. The white coarse-napped cloth of his outer robe contrasted with the thick leather covering his shoulders and accenting his sleeves. His eyes were closed, giving him a look of serenity that to Sarek seemed at odds with a Klingon's typical disposition. Was he truly at peace, or was this merely a fabrication of the void?

A pulse of energy called to him, and Sarek realized he must be nearing the target of his search. The mental energies of numerous inhabitants of this space seemed affected by this new sensation, and Sarek realized with some effort that he could use their reactions to locate the source of this discomfort. Emerging from the void's dull gray mist was a mass of amber tendrils, coiling and twisting around a dark, cylindrical object. As he drew closer, he saw that the tube possessed many components affixed to it, highlighting its obviously artificial construction.

"It is a sensor probe," he said. Specifically, he recognized it as a model employed by Starfleet. Did that mean Spock was on the other side of whatever barrier separated the two universes? That would seem to be a logical deduction.

Edolon, silent to this point, replied, "What does that mean?"

"This is a device used by my people to collect information. It is dispatched into space, perhaps to orbit a planet or other spatial object or phenomenon and study it in detail. What it learns is recorded and transmitted back to the probe's origin point."

Realizing he could examine the probe without benefit of physical form, Sarek pushed his thoughts into the device's computer memory core. How intriguing, he decided, to merge sentient thought with stored information, without any discernible line of separation. How was that possible? Was it a byproduct of this realm or something that might be duplicated in his own universe? It would, he thought, be an interesting topic of conversation with his son.

There were others present, Sarek realized. His was not the only consciousness.

"Who are you?" said an unfamiliar, strained voice. "You must not stop us."

"I believe I can help," replied Sarek. "End your attack on this object. It is not a weapon."

"We cannot," said a second voice. "It is poison. Its emanations burn through our thoughts. We must cease its function."

"Wait," Sarek said, knowing the probe's continued operation might be his only hope for returning him, his companions, and others displaced to this dimension. "I may be able to assist you without damaging the probe."

He considered that Edolon had referred to the probe's activities as "emanations." It was safe to assume that such a device, if it had been delivered by Spock and the *Enterprise*, would not be intended to cause deliberate harm. Either the Jatohr were misinterpreting whatever signals the probe was transmitting, or else the device's actions were disruptive to this realm. Did carrier wave signals work differently here, with different causes and effects? Might such effects be hurtful or even hazardous to the Jatohr and others in his universe? It was possible, Sarek reasoned. It might also explain the discomfort suffered by Captain Una and the others, and even the mild irritation he had experienced prior to his transfer to this space.

"I do not believe it necessary to destroy the object," he said. "Instead, we can cease its transmissions to prevent further pain to your people."

Channeling his thoughts into the device, he envisioned its components. Circuitry, and energy moving between conduits and processors and storage modules. In short order he found an energy pattern that was both constant and aimed outward, away from here. The probe's sensors, it seemed. Collecting his consciousness, he directed his perceptions on that signal. He was about to focus on ending it when he realized that an opportunity had presented itself, though he was uncertain how to exploit it. Might he be able to co-opt the signal? That seemed beyond his abilities, at least for any sizable measure of time, but how much did he need? Even a short message, some clue offered to whoever was receiving the transmission, could be of benefit, but what to say?

Amanda.

Just as he had been trying to call to his wife, to somehow reassure her that he was alive and searching for a means of returning to her, so now did he compel the probe's signal to act on his behalf. He sensed the device accepting his command and felt the merest twinge in the constant flow of energy as his small message was added to the stream of transmitted information.

And then everything faded.

"What have you done?" he asked. For the first time, he recognized the toll his interaction with the probe had taken on his mental energies. Fatigue was already clouding his thoughts, urging him to sleep, but he fought to keep the impulse at bay.

"The matter is finished," said Edolon. "The emanations are no more."

His energy and awareness fading, Sarek once more tried listening to the probe, but it was now silent. He detected some residual energy, but it was limited. The device's power cells were almost exhausted. It might be possible to reactivate it, but he suspected he might have but a single opportunity. If he chose that course, it would have to be at the right time, and for the right reason. For now, his only other option seemed to be learning about this new realm, his place in it, and what might assist him in escaping from it.

Had his message gotten through? There was no way to know. As his remaining awareness dissolved, he reached out with a last, feeble attempt at connection.

Amanda.

Her name echoed as Sarek's consciousness surrendered to darkness.

Twenty-three

Despite hir best efforts, Anadac could not keep hir eye-stalks fully extended in the face of the intense, blinding spotlight shining down on hir from above.

Standing on the dais in the Grand Hall and flanked by two armed guards and stripped of hir protective shell, Anadac was unable even to shield hirself from the unforgiving light. S/he could only stand, vulnerable and quivering, before an enraged Woryan. Throngs of similarly outraged Jatohr filled the platforms surrounding hir as well as the atrium floor below. This exposure was just the next phase of an extended session of psychological torture to which s/he had already been subjected while being held in an interrogation cell. There s/he had not been subjected to questioning, but instead endured an emotionally draining process in which s/he had been forced to experience an unrestrained flood of memories incomprehensibly woven together from numerous Jatohr and pushed directly into hir mind. Death would have almost been a preferable alternative.

"I do not understand. Why am I being treated like this?"

Before hir on the dais, Woryan shifted hir enormous bulk on the dais and gestured toward Anadac. "Why? Because you have failed your mission, you have betrayed your supreme leader, and you have doomed your entire race!"

The charge struck Anadac with the force of a physical blow. "This is outrageous! I have done no such thing!"

"You have!" Woryan shifted from hir perch on the dais, gliding across the smooth floor toward Anadac. "What have you brought upon our kind?" Hir voice, amplified into to a raucous baritone that resonated throughout the massive chamber, seemed to bore directly into Anadac's consciousness. "You decimated our invasion force. How do you explain this treachery?"

"Treachery? How could I have done such a thing?"

"Your meddling has unleashed an unstoppable force upon us!" Woryan screamed. "Half of my invasion legion—half of our kind—is dead, because of *you*! What have you brought upon our land? What have you done to destroy our minds?"

Anadac struggled to connect the scant pieces of information to be mined from Woryan's tirade. Was it possible that the psychic turmoil s/he had experienced was not a torture method? Had it been a phenomenon that reached much farther than hir cell, inflicting damage upon uncounted Jatohr? Whatever had happened to wreak such havoc, s/he concluded, evidently it was beyond Woryan and hir advisors to comprehend or explain.

"Is this about the portal?"

The portal had been Woryan's foremost priority, superseding all other concerns. It had driven the Jatohr leader to bring before this very Hall Una and two other outsiders—"humans," as Una had called them—for interrogation and judgment. The entire proceeding now seemed as humiliating and pointless to the detainees as hir own treatment. Despite that, the questioning did serve to yield information Anadac had used to refine the transfer portal's process of exploiting the enormous energies initiated in the other dimension. In that regard, Una had assisted in creating the device Woryan now intended to use for leading hir legion of Jatohr soldiers to the other realm, saving them from the destruction of this one.

Was Woryan blaming the portal, and by extension Anadac hirself, for some catastrophic event?

"I am loyal to our people, Woryan. I have done nothing to harm anyone. Also, have you forgotten that I have been in your custody since the incident with my research team? Even then I thought I was upholding your wishes and carrying out your orders. If I could be allowed into my laboratory, I assure you I can find answers to—"

"Silence!" Woryan shouted. "Do you believe for a moment that I would give a traitor such as you the means to attack us again?"

"Woryan, please!" Anadac could not keep the quaver of confusion and fear from hir voice but s/he did not care. While s/he at first had wanted to understand the nature of this questioning and the treatment s/he had suffered, s/he now began to fear for hir life. "I ask again: Does this involve the portal? Was it activated without my supervision?"

"My portal has nothing to do with your betrayal."

It was the first of Woryan's statements that made sense, Anadac realized. A psychic wave of the magnitude to which the supreme leader had alluded would be impossible for the portal to generate. Without a transmission from the other dimension to provide power, the portal could not even have been operational.

"Countless cycles of work adapting our technology for the other universe, training pilots and soldiers to fight the outsiders, all of it for nothing. Was this your plan all along, Anadac? Did you intend to betray me at your first opportunity?"

"How can you believe that?" Anadac felt as if s/he were pleading for forgiveness when what s/he wanted to do was ridicule Woryan for such irrational thought. "Why would I betray my people this way? Are we all not working toward the same goal? Saving our people from annihilation?"

Woryan glared at hir, eyestalks boring into Anadac. "I used to believe that. Then, I saw the evidence for myself." S/he turned hir gaze to the assembled audience, hir voice carrying across the Hall. "Behold for yourselves, the truth of Anadac's treachery!"

The chamber's interior dome flashed to life, with swirls of colors coalescing into an image s/he quickly recognized. It was the outsiders' encampment, likely recorded by sentry drones sent to covertly monitor the strangers. S/he watched the image sharpen and enlarge until s/he could see Una and others moving about the area, just as Anadac had observed from her sled. After a few moments, the scene shifted to depict Anadac hirself, in the camp and speaking to the outsider Sarek. The two were joined by Una.

A chorus of disapproving calls echoed through the Hall, and Anadac turned to see Woryan's reactions to the images. The supreme leader unleashed a deep, muffled groan that shook the entire chamber, serving not only to hush the crowd but to further unsettle Anadac's internal sensations.

"You see betrayal, Woryan, but I tell you that is not what happened!"

Woryan snorted. "Tell us, Anadac." The leader's tone was as derisive as it was contemptuous. "Explain yourself and your collusion with our enemy, that you had hoped to keep secret from your kind."

"It was not collusion, as they are not our enemy!" Anadac felt hir entire body shivering with mounting fury. "I was attempting to negotiate with the outsiders, Woryan. Though they possess great power in their own universe, they also are quite benevolent, and they can even help us once we relocate there." Grunting in frustration, s/he added, "If you attack them, they will fight back, and they may well destroy us all if they feel so threatened. They stand ready to assist us, but your pride and anger have blinded you into believing you can dominate the other universe as you believe yourself to dominate this one. You will be proven utterly, catastrophically wrong."

In the wake of hir mistreatment at Woryan's command, the effort to unleash hir frustration with the supreme leader and this tyrannical regime had all but exhausted Anadac. If s/he was to die, then s/he could no longer deny hir feelings of outrage and shame s/he had suppressed for so long.

Woryan said nothing for several moments. It was a far longer silence than Anadac might expect, given the circumstances. When the leader did speak, hir words were not carried with the reverberation or volume that s/he had been employing to this point.

"You appear to have great faith in your new friends, but that confidence is gravely misplaced. We will be using the portal to cross to the other universe, but before that, we will hunt down the outsiders who dare to pollute our realm." Woryan returned to hir place on the dais, leaving Anadac with hir two guards.

"I urge you to reconsider, Woryan. Battle and conquest are not our only options. Please, for all our sakes, the action you are about to undertake is a decision you will regret."

Woryan laughed. "Perhaps I will, but I can assure you of one thing, Anadac: you will not live to see it."

S/he gestured to hir guards, and Anadac turned to see the soldiers stepping closer, each wielding a spear at hir. Anadac's last sensation was one of agony before everything disappeared into brilliant white light.

Twenty-four

Ensconced within the solitude of his quarters, Spock sat at the chair behind his desk. With his hands clasped together before him, his forefingers extended and touching in a meditative pose, he allowed his mind to drift while scrutinizing the constant streams of sensor data scrolling on his computer monitor. Unlike the astrophysics lab and, in particular, the bridge, the atmosphere here was conducive to quiet contemplation. It allowed him to consider the volumes of information collected by the probe and unscrambled by the ship's computer, and he could ponder not just the presented facts but also any deeper meanings to be found.

Of course, this presupposed that such significance existed in the first place, and based on his findings, Spock believed this to be true.

It had taken him hours to peruse the complete set of telemetry gathered by the probe's sensors and transmitted to the *Enterprise*, that effort following several more hours spent just waiting for the drone to supply that information via the gamma-radiation carrier wave devised by Lieutenant Uhura. Additional data would likely not be forthcoming, as he and Ensign Chekov had come to believe that the probe's power supply had been exhausted for reasons unknown following its transfer to the other realm. If there were answers to be found, they would have to be discovered within the volumes of information already at their disposal.

The sound of his door chime shifted Spock's gaze away from the computer monitor. "Enter," he called, then rose to his feet at the sight of his mother and Leonard McCoy entering the room. Amanda smiled when their eyes met.

"Spock. I hope I'm not intruding."

The Vulcan shook his head. "No. I am merely continuing my analysis of the probe data."

"Well, I've been analyzing the emptiness of my quarters. I thought a stroll around the ship might do me some good." She nodded toward McCoy. "The good doctor was kind enough to accompany me."

Glancing to McCoy, Spock said, "I trust there are no concerns regarding your health."

"Nothing like that," replied the doctor. "We've been catching up and passing the time while we wait for you to get us all the answers."

Amanda said, "You've been working for hours, Spock. That's not healthy. Would you like something to eat?"

"I do not require nourishment," replied the first officer, though when he looked again to McCoy, the doctor offered what Spock recognized as a mock frown.

"According to my dietary records, you haven't eaten since yesterday, Spock."

Knowing that McCoy was prepared to take this discussion to its ultimate conclusion and order him to eat by virtue of his authority as the chief medical officer, Spock decided there was no logical reason to reach that point. "Very well, Doctor. I will eat following the end of this duty shift."

McCoy nodded in apparent satisfaction. "Fair enough."

"Have you found something?" asked Amanda as she moved to stand next to him.

Spock said, "I am not certain. Our analysis of the sensor probe's data indicates unexplained energy patterns, which seem to intermingle on some level with the life-form readings we have detected. It is as though energy and living matter are interacting, though I am unable to determine to what extent or for what purpose."

"What about the life signs?" McCoy asked.

"Jatohr and Usildar, of course, but there are also indications of human, Vulcan, Klingon, and Izarian life signs. As with the energy readings, these life signs seem to be intertwined in a manner that is . . . interesting. Some of the readings indicate individuals, whereas others present the appearance of a single, joint consciousness."

"Sarek and the others," said Amanda. "They're alive."

Nodding, Spock replied, "It appears so, though I cannot assess his current condition."

"A joint consciousness, Spock?" asked McCoy. "How would that work?"

"I am unable to speculate without further information, Doctor." Spock gestured to his computer monitor. "I am still reviewing the remaining data sent to us by the probe, in the hopes that a clue will present itself."

Something amid the scrolling strings of data caught his eye, and he touched a control at the monitor's base. "Computer, halt data review." Not seeing what he now sought, he added, "Present previous three hundred blocks, one-half speed."

"Working," replied the stilted, feminine voice of the *Enterprise*'s main computer. Leaning closer, Spock reviewed the selected block of information with a more critical eye. To his surprise, the data making up one of the final recorded transmissions was logged not as a sensor reading but instead a communication.

"Stop," he said after a moment. Using the terminal's

manual interface, he selected and highlighted a single line of encrypted data. Amid the encoded symbols that were decipherable only to the computer as well as anyone who had troubled themselves to memorize the complete character, a single word rendered in Federation Standard stood apart from the rest of the data:

AMANDA

Still standing next to him and watching as he worked, his mother pointed to the screen. "Spock? What is that?"

His gaze still focused on the highlighted text, Spock replied, "Aside from the obvious, I believe this to be a message from Sarek."

"Are you sure?" asked McCoy. The doctor's expression only punctuated the disbelief that was evident in his question. "How is that even possible?"

"Logic suggests Sarek must have found the probe and found a way to insert this message into its telemetry stream. One is left to wonder about the message's brevity and lack of context."

McCoy shook his head. "You can ask him all about that once we get him back, Spock, along with my daughter and the others."

"That is our goal, Doctor," said Spock, "but understanding the nature of this message may be critical to facilitating their return." Had Sarek been operating with limited time or resources? How had he managed to add the message to the data stream in the first place? Each question begat others, with precious little information to help in formulating answers.

"Oh my god."

His train of thought interrupted, Spock turned in his

seat to regard his mother, who now exhibited a shocked expression. "Mother?"

"Sarek. He . . . he's been trying to contact me." Looking to McCoy, Amanda said, "Before, when you came to visit me in my quarters, I'd just woken up. I'd been dreaming, and in that dream I thought I heard Sarek calling to me. It wasn't much, just, 'My wife,' over and over." She gestured toward the computer terminal. "I don't think it was a dream."

"Mother," said Spock, "are you suggesting Sarek called out to you via the bond you share?"

Amanda frowned. "I don't know if that's it, but what if it is? Sarek melded with me when we were first married, and we've had a connection ever since. It's more him than me, of course, but when we're close, I can read the thoughts he directs to me, and if we touch, I can share with him." Her gaze fell back to her name on the screen. "He's never contacted me like this before."

"Interesting." Spock pondered the implications of what his mother had told him. "Your bond with him would be stronger than anyone with whom he had previously joined. Even I do not enjoy such a connection, as we have never melded."

"Why can't you try reaching out to him now?" asked McCoy.

Spock shook his head. "The Vulcan mind-meld requires a physical connection, unless the participants have previously joined their thoughts. As I indicated, that link does not exist for Sarek and me." To his mother, he said, "However, you alone may be able to reach him."

"Do you really believe that?" asked Amanda. "I'm not sure, Spock. I've never tried anything like this. I don't even know what to do."

"I will guide you."

McCoy said, "Now, hold on just a minute here." He indicated Amanda with a nod. "Spock, after all she's been through, I'm not sure she's up for something like this."

"Leonard, I'm fine." Amanda reached out and took Spock's hand. "If what Spock's proposing can help find Sarek and the others, then I want to try."

Spock added, "Your concern is noted and appreciated, Doctor. With that in mind, and even though a mind-meld is usually a very private experience between the participants, I would ask that you remain here to monitor my mother's condition."

Apparently mollified by this request, McCoy replied, "All right, Spock. I can do that. I appreciate your trust."

"Excellent." Still holding his mother's hand, Spock guided them both to sit on the edge of his bed. Once situated, he touched her face with his right hand, the tips of his fingers moving to the points on her face that facilitated the physical connection.

"As Sarek and I have never melded, it is unlikely that we will be able to sense one another's thoughts, even if you are successful in reaching out to him. You may well have to guide me through whatever you share."

Amanda said, "I'll try."

Instead of replying, Spock pressed his fingertips against her face, and she closed her eyes. Drawing a deep breath, he focused his thoughts.

"My mind . . . to your mind. My thoughts . . . to your thoughts."

Yes, Spock. I know you're here.

"Mother. I see what you see."

Smoke. So much of it.

"From Centaurus, the last time you were together."

Yes. Sarek was with me, then he was gone. Gone!

"And now he calls to you."

Yes, from the smoke. No. From somewhere . . . else.

"Call to him."

Sarek? Are you there? Can you hear me?

"Do you hear him?" Spock probed deeper, but sensed nothing beyond his mother's thoughts. If Sarek was there, he could not feel his presence.

I cannot see him. Sarek!

"Keep trying, Mother."

Sarek. My husband . . .

"You can do this."

I don't hear him. I . . . wait. Sarek? Sarek!

Though he heard nothing save his mother's thoughts, Spock was certain that he sensed for the briefest of moments another presence. It was communicated as little more than a ripple within the link he now shared with Amanda, appearing and fading in the space between two heartbeats. It had come and gone almost before he realized what had teased the very edge of his consciousness, but now it was clouded by his mother's increasing emotional reaction at having apparently made contact with her husband.

Sarek!

His fingers lost their connection as Amanda slumped, her head and shoulders drooping. Spock caught her before she fell back onto his bed, holding her steady as McCoy moved in to help. Together, they assisted her in lying down.

"She's exhausted, Spock," said the doctor. "Mentally and physically. She needs rest, especially if you're going to try this again."

"Yes, of course."

Looking up at them, Amanda said, "I'm sorry, Spock."

"There is no fault, Mother. When you are rested, we will make another attempt."

McCoy stared at him. "So, you think it worked?"

"I did sense something," said Spock, "though I cannot be certain it was Sarek."

Amanda replied, "It was him. I'm sure of it." Releasing a heavy sigh, she closed her eyes and shook her head. "He just seemed so far away."

"That has to be enough to go on, Spock," said McCoy. "What are we waiting for? Let's get on with bringing them back."

Spock said, "Ascertaining their status is one thing, Doctor, but using the Transfer Key to retrieve them requires more. We do not know where my father and the others are within the other universe. Our understanding of the transfer-field technology precludes conducting extensive tests, as we are uncertain how that action might affect anyone trapped there. We must be cautious." He cast a glance to his mother. "If we do attempt another meld, then I worry for my mother's well-being, but I know of no better way to contact Sarek."

He just seemed so far away.

"I know that look," said McCoy. "You're thinking hard about something."

The Transfer Key.

———

His forearms resting on the briefing room's conference table, Kirk rubbed his temples. The headache he had been fighting for the past several hours showed no signs of fading, and listening to his first officer only made it worse.

"You want to beam down to the planet, while we have Klingons in orbit, Klingons on the surface, and more Klingons on the way, so that you can try mind-melding with Sarek?"

Seated across from him and between McCoy and Amanda, Spock nodded. "That is correct, Captain."

"It sounded a little less crazy before we called you," added McCoy.

Kirk pushed himself from the table and leaned back in his chair. "You understand that the instant he realizes we've sent down a landing party, J'Teglyr could very well head to the surface and attempt to take the Transfer Key from you."

"I have considered that possibility, Captain," replied the first officer. "The Klingons on the surface have already been forced from the citadel. Once we beam down, we can take protective measures to ensure they cannot return to it."

"But why risk beaming down at all?" asked Kirk. "Why not just activate the field generator from up here, like you did with the probe?"

Spock said, "The Transfer Key does not possess a scanning or targeting system that would be needed to locate anyone transported to the other universe. That technology is part of the transfer-field generator, to which we must have direct access. I also believe that our proximity to the generator once it is activated may facilitate our efforts to contact Sarek. If we establish a connection with the other universe, that may well provide a conduit through which my mother can sense him and communicate." He paused, glancing to Amanda. "I also think the strain on my mother may be at least somewhat mitigated."

She replied, "If it helps rescue Sarek and the others, I'm willing to try."

Not for the first time, Kirk admired the courage this woman displayed. Her compassion was on par with her determination, and it was easy to see where Spock had acquired such traits.

"I appreciate your willingness to help, Amanda," said Kirk. "I also know that Mister Spock isn't prone to wild ideas. Even his most outlandish theories are based on whatever facts he's able to collect. I trust him implicitly, but that doesn't mean I'm thrilled with this plan." He reached up to wipe his forehead. "That said, I'm hard-pressed to suggest a better one, and I don't know that we'd even have the time to come up with anything else. J'Teglyr's been playing nice to this point, but I think he's just stalling while waiting for reinforcements to arrive." Support was coming for the *Enterprise*, too, in the form of the *Defiant*, but it was still hours away. For now, Kirk and his crew were on their own, and the last thing he wanted was any of his people on the surface if a Klingon armada dropped out of warp.

"If the Klingons arrive before we are able to make contact with Sarek and use the transfer-field generator to retrieve them," said Spock, "we may never get another opportunity. Either they will destroy the citadel to keep it from us, or we will be forced to do the same in order to deny them the Jatohr technology. We must therefore make our attempt before Captain J'Teglyr or any Klingon reinforcements elect to take action."

The first officer's justification was cold and business-like, and to Kirk it was missing a key element. "I'm worried about you and your mother, Spock. Sending a civilian into a potentially hostile situation isn't something I'm keen to do."

"Funny how you never seem to have that problem

when you send me," said McCoy. The doctor offered a small smile to indicate he was attempting to lighten the mood.

Amanda said, "For the record, Captain, I'm volunteering. I can't very well just sit up here and do nothing." Her gaze dropped to the conference table for a moment before she once more looked at Kirk. "Besides, I'm the one who can contact Sarek."

"I know," said Kirk. In truth, he had known from the beginning, but had been hoping Spock, McCoy, or even Amanda herself might have discovered an alternative to carrying out this insane scheme.

I'm never that lucky.

Twenty-five

Aside from the sounds of birds and insects, along with the cry of what likely was some form of carnivore lurking in the nearby jungle, and the sound of water lapping at the base of the citadel, the area around the Jatohr construct was quiet. Farther away, Spock heard the sounds of activity from the encampment, which sensors had revealed still harbored more than a dozen Klingons who had yet to be retrieved by Captain J'Teglyr and the *Vron'joQ*. There were no clouds in the sky, and the sunlight of midmorning in this part of the world provided brilliant illumination to the lush vegetation and the gleaming hull of the citadel itself. The lake, though dulled by the rampant algae infesting its waters, still seemed to be more alive in the light of day.

"Even with the changes you say they made, it's beautiful," said Amanda Grayson, from where she stood next to Spock. They, along with McCoy and Uhura, now looked out over the chest-high parapet that formed one of the Jatohr citadel's outer protective barriers and across the lake to the shoreline forming the Klingon encampment's near boundary. "It's a shame the Jatohr and the Klingons see fit to ruin it."

Spock replied, "If we are successful here, neither the Jatohr nor the Klingons will have any further reason to remain here."

Standing on the other side of Amanda, Uhura said, "Do you really think we can convince the Jatohr that we can help them, Mister Spock? Or that they'll even let us help them?"

"There is but a single way to find out, Lieutenant."

On Uhura's opposite side, McCoy asked, "Do you think we can expect any trouble from the Klingons?"

Adjusting the equipment satchel he carried slung over his left shoulder, Spock shook his head. "Perhaps, though I doubt it. The remaining group appears to be in a state of disarray, following the loss of Professor B'tinzal and members of her science team. However, we should not rule out the possibility of whoever has taken charge of the group attempting to interfere with us."

Spock had been surprised not to find a Klingon welcoming committee waiting for the landing party as they materialized in an open expanse along the citadel's exterior. There remained components of Klingon technology scattered around the immediate area, including cargo containers and a field transporter pad. The first order of business after beaming down was to ensure the pad was disabled, which only partially countered the possibility of an armed Klingon party transporting over from their encampment or from the warship. Anticipating that scenario, Spock had brought along the *Enterprise*'s veteran security chief, Lieutenant Commander Barry Giotto, along with a team of five security officers to maintain watch. Giotto and his people had already deployed portable transporter scattering fields at key points along the citadel's exterior, mirroring the tactic utilized by the Klingons during the *Enterprise*'s previous visit to the planet. Sensors had shown that those obstacles were no longer in operation, allowing the landing party to transport directly from the starship to this area within the citadel's perimeter.

Gaining entry to the complex had proven only slightly

more challenging, now that the alien fortress had activated its own series of protective countermeasures. The underwater docking bays that had been the primary point of ingress and egress were, at least according to Spock's tricorder readings, no longer an option. That entire area of the citadel appeared to be sealed off, and the sizeable docking compartments were now completely flooded. Adjoining sections appeared to have been rerouted in order to facilitate the transfer of water from the lake to the structure's interior sections. Scans also had revealed faint signs of Klingon biomatter in another part of the complex, but no life signs. It presumably was in that area that Professor B'tinzal and some of her people had met their final fates. That loss of life was unfortunate, but Spock also regretted not having the opportunity to talk with B'tinzal and perhaps learn from her what she and her team had discovered during their examination of the structure and its technology.

Forced to find another means of entering the citadel, Spock fell back upon the access codes they had acquired during the *Enterprise*'s previous visit to Usilde. Those codes had proven ineffective, likely due to the construct's ongoing, seemingly automated internal reconfigurations, and Spock had needed time to scan the door locks and acquire a new cipher.

"I'm still waiting for those robot guard dogs to come after us," said McCoy, his voice carrying a tinge of worry.

Spock replied, "I have detected no signs of their presence within the citadel, at least as far as my tricorder can penetrate the interior sections." There had been a few moments of uncertainty while the landing party waited for any of the Jatohr sentry drones to come after them, but the roving devices seemed nowhere to be found. "I would advise caution as we make our way to the control room. I suspect whatever is overseeing security inside the citadel will take a very keen interest in our activities once we attempt to use the Transfer Key."

Sensor scans from the *Enterprise* had revealed that the transfer-field generator ensconced deep within the Jatohr fortress had already taken apparent note of the Key's proximity even before the starship's arrival in orbit. Spock did not yet understand the nature of that awareness, and how, or if, the Key was communicating with the base equipment. It was but one more mystery demanding further examination, provided time and opportunity presented itself.

Using his tricorder to relay the proper code sequence to the door's locking mechanism, Spock watched as the massive circular portal dilated, offering the landing party unfettered access to the alien complex. He employed hand gestures to direct the rest of the group to follow him as he led the way through the door. Opting not to draw the phaser on his right hip, the first officer instead held his tricorder in both hands, aiming the device ahead of him as he proceeded down the cylindrical corridor. Though the entrance to the master control room was now cut off thanks to more of the citadel's internal reconfiguration, Spock found another access point from the chamber above that area.

"This was the laboratory used by Eljor," he replied when his mother asked him about the room. Thankfully, the ramp leading down from the lab had not been removed or otherwise blocked, and within moments the landing party found themselves in the alien complex's control center. In the middle of the room sat the oversized cylinder that Spock knew from his previous visit contained the primary control component for the transfer-field generator and the interface for the Transfer Key.

"This is incredible," said Amanda, standing a pace behind Spock. When he turned to regard his mother, he saw her unabashed expression of wonder as she beheld the room's array of complex alien technology. He conceded that the equipment here held a certain beauty and succeeded in melding form with function.

Standing to Spock's other side, Uhura said, "It's the most amazing thing I've ever seen. You can feel the power being harnessed here."

Spock nodded in agreement. As was the case last time he was here, the immense mechanism seemed to pulse with energy, resonating throughout the chamber and the entirety of the citadel. He knew this central component had come online only recently, reacting to the arrival of the *Enterprise* in the Libros system and the proximity of the Transfer Key. Around the room, numerous stations and monitors were dark and inert, and Spock recalled that many of these consoles had only been active when the Transfer Key was connected to the transfer-field generator. As for the rest of the complex, it had carried on for years without that vital piece, executing its various automated tasks and preparing for . . . what, exactly? The Key's return? How would it react when Spock restored the Key to its proper place?

We are here to obtain an answer to that precise question.

"I don't mind telling you that I'm a bit frightened, Spock," said Amanda after a moment. "This . . . this isn't the sort of thing I'm used to dealing with."

Feeling her hand on his arm, Spock turned and saw the trepidation on his mother's face. She had never been one to conceal her emotions from him, even on Vulcan, where such displays by "outworlders" were discouraged. As a child, he had strived to learn and maintain strict control over his emotions, a tall order, given his mixed Vulcan-human lineage. When he was less than successful in that regard, his mother had always been the voice of understanding. Rather than simply tell him where he had failed to meet his society's exacting standards and instruct him to strive harder, Amanda Grayson had encouraged him to embrace the best aspects of his dual heritage. It was a sentiment that would be echoed many years later by others, people he had come to trust, such as instructors and advisors at Starfleet Academy, Christopher Pike, Captain Una, James Kirk, and even Leonard McCoy, who stepped closer and placed a hand on his mother's shoulder.

"Don't worry, Amanda," said the doctor. "We're right here with you." He offered a knowing smile. "We've had some experience with things like this."

Uhura added, "There's an understatement."

Moving to the master console at the center of the room, Spock removed his equipment satchel from his shoulder and laid it atop the workstation. It took him but a moment to reacquaint himself with the alien controls, which he had last seen used by Captain Una. He had reviewed her notes regarding the transfer-field generator's operation, and while he had not invested the same time she had to understand the unfamiliar technology, he was comfortable he could operate the equipment well enough.

Satisfied with his assessment, Spock opened the satchel and removed the black protective case it held. Inside the case, cradled in a shock-proof cushion, was the Transfer Key.

"I guess this is the moment of truth," said McCoy. The doctor, along with Amanda and Uhura, had moved to stand with him at the console.

Without replying, Spock extracted the Key from the carrying case and inserted it into the slot on the console that matched the component's rectangular shape. The effect of his action was immediate, as the collection of dormant control stations and displays all activated in unison. Within the central column, swirling patterns of energy pulsed and rippled, and Spock heard a dull hum emanating from within the contained space.

"That was the easy part," said Uhura. "Wasn't it?"

Spock turned his attention to the alien control console. "Relatively speaking, yes." He pointed to an adjacent console, which was out of reach from where he stood. "Lieutenant, I require your assistance. The upper row of controls will require manipulation. On my signal, please press the controls I indicate, in the order I prescribe."

"Seems simple enough," replied the communications officer as she moved to the workstation.

Recalling what he had studied from the tricorder readings and other notes collected by Captain Una during her initial encounter with the citadel, Spock began pressing a series of controls on his own console. The string of commands was lengthy, but Spock had memorized the sequence. In response to his actions, several of the monitors around the central column shifted to display images of a planetary landscape, depicted from different angles. Within the central cylinder, the harnessed energies were forming into a three-dimensional holographic representation of the same terrain.

"What are we seeing?" asked Amanda. "Is this . . . ?"

Spock replied, "If I am correctly operating this equipment, these are images of the last known location used by the Transfer Key to deposit individuals transported from this universe. Unfortunately, Captain Una's reports do not include information on selecting new coordinates, so she transported herself to this location when she elected to search for her former shipmates."

"And this is where you and Jim agreed to look for her?" asked McCoy.

"Affirmative." Spock keyed one of the controls that he recalled from Una's notes, and the images on the monitor began to pan from left to right. After a moment, he realized that whatever was supplying the visual feed from the other universe had made a complete circular sweep of the surrounding area. Aside from a distant mountain range, there was nothing but unyielding pale soil in all directions.

"They're not there," said Uhura. "None of them."

Spock regarded the monitors and the holographic image. "It is as I suspected. We will have to attempt contacting Sarek again. He may be able to give us his location as well as that of the others." Turning from the console, he looked to his mother. "Do you feel able to try again?"

Nodding, Amanda rested her hand on his arm. "Of course."

"I'll keep tabs on you the whole time," said McCoy.

Satisfied with that, Spock looked to Uhura and pointed to her console. "Lieutenant, this station is used to scan the target area. It is not connected to the system that selects origin or destination points for transferred individuals, and I therefore believe we can alter its settings to search for our people and perhaps even the probe." He held up his tricorder. "I have the sensor data transmitted to us by the probe, which we should be able to use as a reference." He was not altogether certain of this, given his earlier difficulties with interpreting the wash of telemetry sent to them by the probe, but it was a start.

"Just show me what to do, Mister Spock," replied Uhura. "I'll take it from there."

A low, deep rumbling surged upward through the metallic flooring, and at first Spock thought the transfer-field generator might be engaging after having finally locked in on Sarek or anyone else trapped in the other universe. It was an additional moment before he realized that the tremors were coursing up through the bulkheads and even the console beneath his hands.

"What in blazes is that?" asked McCoy.

Spock saw that new displays were coming online at various workstations around the control room. Rows of indicators were shifting through a spectrum of colors, and the rumbling was continuing to build.

"Do you feel that?" Uhura reached for the adjacent workstation as though to prevent herself from falling to the floor just as Spock sensed the floor under his feet shifting. It was pushing against him, and his knees bent as he felt a twinge in his gut.

Now gripping his arm, Amanda said, "We're moving!"

Steadying himself against the console, Spock activated his tricorder, setting the device to a wide scan field. It took him only a moment to confirm his mother's statement.

"It appears the citadel is rising from the lake."

"Rising?" McCoy glared at him, his eyes wide with surprise. "Where the hell does it think it's going?"

With his tricorder to assist him, Spock moved to another of the workstations. "According to my scans, the entire structure is being pushed upward by thrusters using a form of hydrogen-based chemical propellant."

"Our speed's increasing, Mister Spock." Holding her own tricorder, Uhura was pointing to a large circular indicator on the console. "At least, if I'm reading this right."

"Yes," said Spock, before he pointed to another status gauge. "An artificial gravity and inertial damping system has also been activated." That was fortunate. Without those features, he and the rest of the landing party would already be pressed to the deck, powerless against the increasing thrust as the citadel continued to push upward.

Retrieving his communicator from the small of his back, he flipped open the unit's antenna cover. "Spock to Commander Giotto."

"Giotto here!" came the harried voice of the *Enterprise*'s security chief. *"Mister Spock, you need to see this, we're lifting out of the water!"*

"Bring your people inside immediately, Commander," ordered Spock. "Leave any equipment. It is imperative that you not delay."

"We're on our way! Giotto out!"

Still standing beside him, Amanda asked, "Spock, what's happening?"

"Based on our increasing speed and trajectory," replied the first officer, "the force being generated by these thrusters is sufficient to push the entire structure into low orbit."

McCoy stepped closer. "Are you saying this thing's heading into space?"

"It would appear so, Doctor."

"Heaven help us." McCoy braced himself against the nearby console. "Jim and the Klingons are going to love this."

Twenty-six

Light greeted Sarek as his clarity slowly returned. He lowered his mental defenses and reached out into the gray void. He felt the presence of other beings surrounding him, most of which seemed as inert as cocoons on a branch, their minds unwilling or unable to accept the intellectual expansion this place offered. Among them, Sarek sensed those few who had embraced this realm and traveled it as conscious entities. He perceived their minds as streaks of light and energy, intertwining themselves in pairs and groups and communes to weave a plane of awareness unlike any he had ever imagined. It called to him, its lure as palpable as if it were reaching out to grasp his arm and pull him toward it.

You must not succumb to it.

There also was something else here; something that had not been present before now. Not a living thing, but it still harbored an energy and intensity that commanded attention. Like the collected consciousness that yearned for him to join it, this new presence also seemed determined to direct him, but to where?

There also were other familiar minds present here. Pushing outward, Sarek coursed through the void, focusing on what he felt was the closest such presence. He was pleased that the first awareness he found belonged to Gorkon. Though the Klingon's body remained as still and expressionless as before, his body having succumbed to the injuries he perceived himself to have suffered within this realm, his mind was active. Sarek probed deeper, and the surrounding gray faded to black, and the silence gave way to . . . music?

"Pektu-Keltz," said Sarek, into the darkness and over the sounds of guttural screeching and near cacophonic brass and percussion.

Gorkon's voice boomed in his mind. "Who dares?"

"Sarek, Councillor. As I said, this is Pektu-Keltz, if I am not mistaken."

"The greatest Klingon performer of any time," Gorkon replied. "Unmatched in vocal strength and endurance. He once sang the complete *Shevok'tah gish* cycle for Chancellor M'Rek without interruption for food or rest. That's sixteen repetitions, Ambassador! He sang from dusk until the break of dawn without missing a note. It was glorious!"

"A notable occasion to be sure, Councillor," Sarek replied. "A fine choice to accompany your thoughts."

Gorkon snorted. "My thoughts are all I have left to me. Is this death, Sarek?"

"No, this is not death. This is a place of your own making, Gorkon, but there is a way to leave and perhaps return to where we belong. Open your mind to me."

"You speak in riddles, Vulcan."

"I can help you. Open your thoughts, Gorkon."

There was a momentary hesitation before Sarek sensed the music fading and a dim glow beginning to penetrate the darkness. Shadows flickered as though cast by candlelight, and a warm presence grew more prominent. Then came the flood of emotion. Sarek braced against the wave of tempered rage, loneliness, and hesitation tinged with . . . concern? No, there was something else.

"Trust me, Gorkon. Release your fear."

"I have no concerns!" Gorkon's voice rang in Sarek's mind. "A warrior fears nothing and regrets only the time squandered between battles!"

"This bravado serves no one. Trust me. Share my thoughts. Together, we can find the way home."

"Home. Yes," Gorkon said. "What must we do?"

"We must bind our thoughts together. Then we will bind with the others and return as one." Sarek realized now the new presence he had felt coursing through the void. Somewhere, beyond the limits of the realm in which he and the others found themselves, something was looking for them, but he perceived no threat. "I believe there is a way out of this place."

He conjured an image of the probe, offering it to Gorkon. As before, he sensed that it remained inert, suspended as they were within this realm. "This tool needs our total concentration if it is to work. If we can activate it, it may be able to help us return home, where we belong."

"I sense your determination, Vulcan!" Gorkon laughed. "You stir us to action! Within your chest beats the heart of a Klingon! Lead on, Sarek. I grow weary of this place, and I stand ready to help."

Sarek replied, "Focus your thoughts on me as I guide us. You will experience it as I perceive it."

"Where are we going?"

"To find our next ally. Be ready to follow me."

Clinging to the image of Gorkon that was now fully coalesced among his own thoughts, Sarek pushed himself back into the gray void. A burst of tension pulsed from the Klingon's presence.

"We are moving!"

A moment later Gorkon's anxiety faded, and Sarek pushed farther into the void. Other streams of thought loomed closer, but he ignored them, as they possessed no familiarity. Farther ahead, he perceived something more recognizable.

"I feel it too," said Gorkon.

Sarek replied, "We must move quickly if we are to gather the others." He was pleased with how rapidly the councillor appeared to be adapting to this new reality, however fleeting it might be. It was obvious the Klingon possessed a keen, fervent intellect that demanded perhaps far more challenge than even his exalted position within the Empire might offer. Though Sarek had known many Klingons of similar stature, Gorkon was the first who seemed not only a worthy adversary but also a formidable ally.

"I feel the same way about you, Vulcan. You embody all that is good and noble about your people."

"I appreciate that, but now is not the time. We have arrived."

A new presence was forming within his perception: Timothy Shimizu. As was the case when he found Gorkon, Sarek saw that the gangly Starfleet ensign appeared motionless, his features devoid of expression as though he were locked in stasis. Like Gorkon, Shimizu's visage belied his true state of being, and Sarek could sense the man's mind alive with activity.

"Ensign Shimizu."

Reaching into the young human's thoughts, Sarek felt himself awash in a stifling fog of despair. Dread and hopelessness welled up around him, and Sarek called forth a barrier to deflect the unwanted emotions. It was a tenuous defense, compelling him to reach back to ensure his bond with Gorkon remained intact.

"Ensign Shimizu, I am Sarek." He pushed deeper, immersing himself within the other man's consciousness.

"I'm dead," said a new voice. "I'm dead in this place, and I can't even make it back out to go to Hell."

Sarek replied, "This is not death. You are alive, and I am here to help you, but first you must assist me. Follow my voice."

"I . . . feel you, Sarek," replied Shimizu.

"Open your mind. Share my thoughts."

A new wave of calm rushed forth from Shimizu, pushing through the thick veil of vapor. Black brightened to rich blue as Sarek began to reclaim the man from the depths of his innermost mind.

"I don't understand," said Shimizu.

While Gorkon had seemed more at ease with his mental imprisonment prior to Sarek's finding him, Shimizu presented a much more vulnerable mind. Convincing him required greater care, and Sarek pressed forward with thoughts intended to ease the ensign's uncertainty. Feeling the other man beginning to relax, he refocused his own perceptions back to Gorkon. He visualized the filaments of energy that were their thoughts in this realm and wove the strands together. The three ribbons danced over and around one another, tightening and bonding.

"Gorkon," he said. "Do you sense us?"

"Yes," replied the Klingon. "Human! Are you ready to join us so that we might leave this forsaken place?"

"A Klingon!"

A new wave of fear surged over Sarek, laced with shock and contempt, and he felt Shimizu attempting to withdraw.

"You want me to help a Klingon? They're our enemies!"

"Not here," replied Sarek, feeling Shimizu pulling away from the connection they had forged with Gorkon. "Here we must work together, if we are to leave this place. You must trust me, Ensign."

"But, he's—"

Sarek said, "He is lost, as are we all. Like you, he simply wants to return home."

Just as he perceived Shimizu extricating himself from their bond, Sarek sensed another surge of emotion: empathy. It was Gorkon offering his own memories. There were images of a child, working with adults Sarek understood to be the Klingon's parents, assisting with a harvest at the family farm on *Qo'noS*. He saw impressions of artisans talking with shoppers in the Old Quarter of the First City. Other recollections coursed through the link at a rapid pace. Sarek beheld classrooms, museums, celebrations, laughter, affection.

"This is my life, Ensign Shimizu," said Gorkon. "This is my home. I wish to return there, and I cannot do so without your help."

"I . . . want to go home, too," replied Shimizu.

Feeling the strength of their bond increasing as each of them committed their focus to the link, Sarek said, "We must work together, Ensign. Otherwise we all fail."

Shimizu pushed closer, the energy of bond surging. "I understand."

"Another warrior joins the fight," said Gorkon. "What of this probe of yours, Sarek?"

"It is not yet time," said Sarek. "First, we must find the others and make sure that they are ready to depart just as we are." He was already feeling the first hints of strain from maintaining this braided connection of psyches. How much greater would the demand be as they gathered Captain Una, Joanna McCoy, and the others?

And once they had collected everyone, what then?

Spock.

Yes, of course. His son, who already had found a way to reach out to him from across the boundary separating two universes. Sarek had no doubts that his son, somewhere on the other side of that barrier, was doing all that could be done to help him and everyone else trapped here.

Spock will guide us. He will know what to do.

Twenty-seven

An alert tone from the tactical station made J'Teglyr turn in his chair to see G'peq bending over the console. The lieutenant's expression was one of confusion as he studied the sensor readings.

"What is it?" asked J'Teglyr.

"Energy readings are spiking, Captain. They are far more powerful than anything we have seen."

J'Teglyr pushed himself from his chair, and a visibly anxious G'peq stepped aside at his captain's approach, allowing J'Teglyr to take control of the console. It did not take long for him to interpret the sensor readings and see for himself what his tactical officer had reported.

"The energy signature is massive."

G'peq nodded. "There is more, my lord." He indicated one of the controls next to the central sensor monitor. "Our scans are detecting indications of thruster activity."

"From the citadel?" asked Visla, who along with her first officer, Woveth, was standing at the rear of the bridge. "How is that possible?"

"It is as we have been saying all along," replied G'peq. "The structure continues to block our sensors to a significant degree. There remain areas of its interior that are still unknown to us, and without B'tinzal and her scientists to reconnoiter, we are blind."

The implications of this new development were staggering. "Are you telling me that thing truly is a vessel of some kind?"

"That seems to be the case, my lord."

"Does it have weapons?" asked Visla.

Returning to his sensors, G'peq replied, "None that our sensors can detect."

"But your sensors did not detect the thrusters before now." Visla grunted in irritation. "That entire construct could be one massive weapon for all we know."

J'Teglyr could not disagree. Was the citadel in reality some form of dreadnought or other battleship? If such a vessel was able to reach space, it would prove a formidable opponent.

"Captain," said D'jorok, "there is also another possible cause for concern. If Kirk and his crew have somehow taken total control of the citadel, they may use it against us. After all, they know we still want it for ourselves."

"A valid point." If that indeed was the explanation, then this situation had just taken a turn for the worse. J'Teglyr turned to G'peq. "What about the *Enterprise*? Have you detected anything that indicates the Earthers might be responsible for this?"

The tactical officer shook his head. "It is possible, my lord. There are communications between the ship and their people on the surface, as well as readings like those we detected earlier that indicate the field generator is interacting with the key component, which now appears to be inside the citadel."

"What are you waiting for, J'Teglyr?" snapped Visla. "Is it not obvious that the Earthers have seized control of that device? Must we sit here and wait for Kirk to deploy it against us?"

Why was he waiting? J'Teglyr knew his orders offered

some latitude in this situation, particularly if he decided that the alien fortress was out of the imperial grasp and in danger of being taken away by the Federation. If this construct was a massive weapon, and Kirk had determined how to control it, then the Empire might be at risk.

"Prepare to attack," he ordered. Looking to D'jorok, he added, "Once we've dealt with the *Enterprise*, we will transport the key component from the citadel."

"That may not be possible," said G'peq. "If my sensor readings are correct, the device is housed within its own protective shield that will block a transporter beam."

J'Teglyr suppressed an irritated growl. "Then we will go and take it. Retrieval of the component by any means necessary is the first and only priority. G'peq, you will provide its exact location."

"Why not simply destroy the *Enterprise*?" asked Woveth.

Spinning on his heel, J'Teglyr pointed a finger at the disruptive lieutenant. "Question my orders again, and you will die, here and now."

"My first officer's question is valid," said Visla. "Why do you insist on these half measures? The alien fortress is lost. That much is obvious to everyone here but you, Captain. It is time to take decisive action for the good of the Empire."

J'Teglyr took a step toward her. "Was it the good of the Empire that motivated you into an ill-advised attack on the *Enterprise*? A child can see what drives you, Visla. You hope to reclaim your honor, and you saw defeating Kirk as a way to do that, only to discover too late that he is no typical Earther. He fights like a Klingon, except in one regard: a Klingon would have finished you while you drifted helpless in space and granted you some small sliver of dignity by dying at the hands of a superior adversary. Surely, that would have been far more preferable than having to be rescued by me, after your moronic actions cost you the lives of twelve of your crew, including the one with whom you shared your bed."

His last comment evoked the reaction he wanted, as Visla's eyes narrowed and her mouth opened in momentary shock. Then the moment was over, and she regained her composure, though J'Teglyr saw that her fists were clenched as she held them at her sides.

"You," he continued, "whose very existence dishonors every warrior who has ever pledged loyalty to Kahless and all he stands for, dare to lecture me about the good of the Empire?" His threshold for enduring this impudence had been reached. He did not care how he would be viewed by the High Command or anyone else. Any punishment they might mete out would pale in comparison to suffering this fool any longer. With a howl of unchecked fury, he reached for his disruptor.

Visla's movements were far quicker, and within the space of a heartbeat J'Teglyr found himself staring at the muzzle of her own weapon.

———

J'Teglyr's attempt to draw his disruptor was as slow as it was clumsy. Visla's sidearm had cleared its holster and was aiming at the captain's face before his hand rested on his weapon's grip. During the instant in which all of this took place, she considered giving him a chance to reconsider his action, but in the end decided it was a waste of time and energy better spent elsewhere.

She fired.

Though the disruptor's power setting was well below maximum, at this range it did not matter. The energy bolt harnessed more than sufficient force to obliterate the better portion of Captain J'Teglyr's head. Everything above his chin vanished, and the shot continued on to strike the bulkhead just to the right of the viewscreen.

The reaction around her was immediate. Even as J'Teglyr's body fell backward and tumbled across the arm of his captain's chair, the six Klingons manning stations around the bridge were turning from their consoles and reaching for weapons. Beside her, Woveth had already drawn his own disruptor. He shot the officer standing at the engineering station without warning before turning and placing his weapon's muzzle against D'jorok's cheek. The *Vron'joQ*'s first officer sneered in derision, but he had the good sense to keep his hands away from his sides.

"Think about your next actions very carefully," said Visla, eyeing the commander as her disruptor pointed at G'peq. Raising her voice, she said to the rest of the crew, "Your captain was unfit to lead you. You heard and saw his hesitation, demonstrated right here before you. Yes, it is true that you were pledged to obey him, but only so long as he showed he was worthy of your loyalty." With her free hand, she gestured to J'Teglyr's body. "Through his own inaction and cowardice, he showed you all that he was undeserving of that respect, and honor demands only one course of action."

She pointed to the viewing screen. "Out there, an enemy of the Empire now controls a weapon that places every Klingon at risk. We are warriors, bound by honor, and sworn to do everything in our power to prevent that weapon from being used against us. And yes, Kirk is a formidable adversary; that much should be obvious to each and every one of you. My vessel was unequal to the task of challenging him, but this ship?" She let the question linger in the air for a moment. "It just may be able to take him, but we must act now, before Kirk can use the alien citadel against us. If that thing is a vessel, then once it reaches orbit it may well prove too much for us to fight alone. Reinforcements are on the way, but they will not arrive in time. Until then, it is up to us. Will you stand with me?"

There was hesitation in the eyes of the remaining bridge crew, which was understandable. Loyalty to any commanding officer always was hard-won, and keeping it was an even greater challenge. J'Teglyr, for all his many faults, had found a way to inspire that commitment. Could she replace him, if only for long enough to carry out this one final quest?

It was J'Teglyr's first officer who provided the answer.

"We will stand with you, Commander."

She fixed her gaze on D'jorok. "Do you?"

"Make no mistake. My loyalty is and remains to J'Teglyr, and my duty requires that I look after the interests of those under my command. For that reason alone, I will obey you, as will they, until the current crisis is past." With his left hand, he reached across his body and pulled his disruptor from its holster before extending it grip first to Visla. "Once that is done, and my crew is safe from the situation you have caused, I promise nothing."

Accepting first the disruptor and then his *d'k tahg*, Visla believed him. The prudent course here would be to kill D'jorok now, but the truth was she needed him. There was no time for a proper transition of command, and the *Vron'joQ*'s crew outnumbered her own. She could not afford the prospect of mutiny until this business with the *Enterprise* was concluded. Assuming they survived, there would be time later for her to indulge D'jorok's desire to avenge his captain's death.

"That is fair," she said. "I would expect nothing else from a Klingon of your character."

Turning his attention to the rest of the bridge crew, D'jorok raised his voice. "You will obey Commander Visla as you would Captain J'Teglyr or myself. Anything less, and you will answer to me."

Visla answered the statement by lowering her disruptor. "Your loyalty to J'Teglyr and the Empire is notable, Commander. Perhaps one day, I will be worthy of such devotion."

His eyes still narrow with simmering anger, D'jorok replied, "It is unlikely."

"Then at least I can admire your honesty." She gestured to Woveth. "My first officer will assume your duties. You will see to your crew."

Glancing at Woveth, D'jorok said nothing, but Visla could see that he was not pleased with the new arrangement. This was expected, given that Woveth was junior in rank, but right now she needed a first officer she could trust without doubt.

D'jorok nodded. "I understand."

"Good." Stepping past him, Visla moved to the command chair. "Have two of your men see to your captain," she said, gesturing to J'Teglyr's body. She waited until she had lowered herself into the command chair and for two of the *Vron'joQ* bridge officers to remove J'Teglyr before issuing her next order.

"Prepare to attack."

Twenty-eight

Despite the distance separating the *Enterprise* from Usilde, the main viewscreen was doing a commendable job depicting the citadel as it rose up from the planet. The image had been set to provide a close-up view as the alien vessel—as it was without doubt a vessel—pushed through the atmosphere on its way to space. As beautiful as the construct had looked to Kirk when it sat in the massive lake on the planet's surface, now that it was free of its earthly confines, the ship appeared nothing short of majestic.

"That's incredible," he said, realizing as he did so that he was leaning far enough forward in his command chair that he was almost ready to topple out of it.

The captain had come within a hairsbreadth of leading the landing party back to the planet and the citadel. With a Klingon ship in orbit, he decided instead that his place was here on the bridge. Spock was more than capable of leading the team to the surface, but now Kirk could not help the pang of guilt coursing through him at the thought of his people being in danger and without him there to lead them.

Spock can handle it. Do your job.

"What's powering it?" he asked.

Now manning the science station in Spock's absence, Ensign Chekov reported, "A form of chemical-propelled rocket thrusters, sir. Based on the readings from the exhaust plumes, it looks like the main element is hydrogen, likely extracted from the lake water." The junior officer shrugged. "It's not the most efficient alternative for creating fuel, but for a one-time use? Why not?"

"The thing's been sitting in that lake for decades," Kirk said. "It's had plenty of time to figure out how to make fuel as part of its overall preparations for launch. What about weapons?"

Chekov replied, "None that I can detect, sir. According to Captain Una's original reports from eighteen years ago, it did not possess weapons at that time."

"But Captain Una also didn't know the whole thing was a ship," said Kirk, "and it's had eighteen years to modify itself. Want to bet it learned some things from us and the Klingons during all that time? Keep checking."

"I do have a sensor fix on the landing party. It's fuzzy, but I can track their movements, and the readings are improving as the citadel gets closer. The transporter room reports they're still unable to lock on. We lost the signal the instant that dampening field activated."

That was an expected yet still unpleasant development, given the difficulties encountered to this point by the starship's sensors, and during numerous attempts at penetrating the citadel's hull. While the alien vessel was on the surface, the landing party could simply exit from its interior spaces. Now that it was on the move and ascending toward orbit, tracking Spock and the others had become an even greater priority, and one hampered by the activation of a powerful new dampening field that was playing havoc with sensors, communications, and transporters. Spock had reported that he had attempted to track the field to its source and disable it, to no avail. Along with this new wrinkle, there was also potential danger to the *Enterprise*. If the citadel decided the starship and anything else in its way was an enemy, then things were about to become very complicated in rapid fashion.

Tapping the intercom control on his armrest, Kirk said, "Engineering. Scotty, we need a solution for the sensors and the transporters. Things are about to get crazy up here, and we may need to pull back the landing party fast."

There was a pause before the *Enterprise*'s chief engineer replied, *"Aye, sir. We're working on it, but I can't make you any promises. It took almost every trick I had to beef up communications to punch through the interference from that thing. Transporters are a bit more delicate. I'll send any ideas I have to Mister Chekov."* The fatigue in the man's voice rang in Kirk's ears, but there was nothing to be done about that now.

"Keep at it, Scotty. If anybody can figure it out, it's you. Kirk out." Turning back to the science station, he said, "Mister Chekov, keep monitoring the Transfer Key and the field generator. I want to know the moment there's the slightest change." The captain glanced over his shoulder to Lieutenant Palmer. "Get me Spock."

The communications officer replied, "Aye, sir."

Within seconds, the Vulcan's voice could be heard over the bridge's intercom system. *"Spock here, Captain."*

Shifting in his seat, Kirk said, "Mister Spock, I don't have to tell you we're getting a little jumpy up here. What's your status?"

"We have not yet attempted to reestablish contact with Sarek. With the citadel now making its way to orbit, I do not know how this will affect our efforts at communication or retrieval."

Haunting images of Captain Una and everyone else materializing in open space outside the citadel began to fester in Kirk's mind, but he pushed away those disturbing thoughts. "Spock, surely the technology involved here had to foresee something like this, particularly if the plan was always for the citadel to be a ship of some kind. Wouldn't that make sense?"

"*That is my hope, Captain.*"

Another nagging thought was fighting for Kirk's attention. "Do we know what's behind all of this? Can you tell us anything new about the citadel's internal configuration? Does it have a warp drive?"

"*We are unable to access those areas which house or support anything resembling a propulsion system. However, energy readings suggest the vessel does not possess interstellar travel capabilities. Then again, we did not even think it was a ship until a short while ago.*"

None of this made any sense. At least, not yet. "But why, Spock? The Jatohr were terraforming the planet; why would they need a ship, and particularly one that couldn't get them beyond this star system?"

There was a pause, as though Spock were considering the various possibilities. Then he said, "*Without more facts, offering a hypothesis may prove counterproductive.*"

"Humor me, Spock."

"*A craft of this size and power, in orbit or in the vicinity of the planet, could prove useful as a way station from which to launch future probes and ships to the system's outlying planets. Also, should the citadel prove to harbor weapons, it might make it a formidable defense for any permanent settlement on the surface. If it does reveal itself to be capable of interstellar travel, then it could be rooted in something as simple as finding additional planets that can provide a home for their species.*"

"Or it could be a combination of any of those ideas." Rising from his chair, Kirk moved around Lieutenant

Rahda at the navigator's station and closer to the viewscreen and its image of Usilde. "Spock, what do you think would happen if you deactivated the Transfer Key?"

Kirk imagined Spock's mind turning over that question before the Vulcan replied, *"At the very least, it would sever the link between the two universes and prevent Sarek and the others from returning to our side."*

"That much I guessed. What about the citadel itself? What do you think it would do if we pulled the Key? Would it return to the planet, continue to orbit, or do something else entirely?"

"Without more information, I am unable to make a proper hypothesis, Captain."

Kirk rested his forearms atop the bridge's forward railing. "We're still having trouble with the transporters. Scotty's working on it, but anything you can do from your end could be a huge help."

"I shall continue my efforts to disable the dampening field, Captain."

From the science station, Chekov said, "Captain, the citadel has ascended to the upper limits of the planet's mesosphere, and its speed is slowing. Based on its trajectory, its orbit will be well below our own."

"Spock," said Kirk, "did you get that?"

"Affirmative. We are able to monitor the citadel's progress, speed, and trajectory, though we are unable to access its navigation system."

Stepping away from the viewscreen, Kirk moved to the rail separating the command well from Chekov. "Ensign, can you get me anything more on the citadel's interior?"

The young officer had already turned back to his instruments. "I've been working on that, sir. Engineering gave me a few pointers for reconfiguring the sensor arrays, and I'm making those adjustments now." Kirk let the man work without interruption, his fingers moving with speed and purpose across the rows of controls on the science station before him. Then, appearing satisfied with his efforts, the ensign nodded as though to himself before leaning once more over the station's sensor viewer.

"We can make out those areas housing the thrusters used for the launch," Chekov said after a moment, "along with the fuel reservoirs feeding them. I'm also picking up indications of new power conduits we couldn't see before, routing energy from a central core to various points along the hull." The ensign stiffened, and he pulled his face away from the viewer. "Captain, I think it's a type of ionized plasma generator."

"Ionized plasma?" Kirk frowned. "For propulsion?"

Chekov shook his head. "I don't think so, sir." He tapped another of his controls and one of the larger screens on the bulkhead above his console flared to life. On the screen was a computer-generated depiction of the citadel, with numerous points along its outer hull highlighted by blinking red dots.

"Weapons ports," said Lieutenant Rahda from where she sat behind Kirk, and he turned in her direction.

"I think you're right, Lieutenant."

Over the open comm channel, Spock said, "*It would seem that those are just one more facet of the citadel's ongoing modifications and reconfigurations. Such a development would seem logical, if the Jatohr felt the citadel required defending once off the planet's surface. We will attempt to collect more data, Captain.*"

"There's something else, sir," said Chekov. He pointed to the citadel schematic. "The reservoirs I mentioned? They appear to contain far more liquid than was used to supply fuel for the launch. If I'm reading the sensors correctly, nearly three-quarters of the stored amount has yet to be expended."

"*Even if the ship was designed for multiple launches and landings,*" said Spock, "*it seems most inefficient to carry such excess weight into orbit.*"

Kirk frowned. "I was thinking the same thing."

"I agree, sir." Chekov tapped a series of controls on his console, which had the effect of activating another group of highlighted locations on the diagram. Studying the revised image, Kirk noted that all of these new indicators were located on the citadel's underside, but were different from the thruster ports used to lift the alien structure from the planet.

"What are those?"

"These ports along the lower hull are also linked to the reservoirs," replied Chekov, "though the conduits feeding them all extend from a separate compartment inside the ship." Once more, he pointed to the screen. "The reservoirs look to supply water and whatever else was taken in from the lake, run it through this section, then route it through the conduits to these new points."

Kirk studied the schematic. "They're not thrusters. Spock?"

"*We will attempt to investigate that, as well, Captain.*"

"First things first. I want a way to get you out of there. Everything else is secondary. Understood?"

"*Affirmative. Spock out.*"

With the connection severed, Kirk turned from the railing. "Mister Sulu, raise deflector shields and take us to within normal transporter range." Moving to his command chair, he tapped the armrest's intercom control. "Bridge to engineering. Scotty, I'm going to need another miracle."

"*Just one?*" replied the engineer.

"Transporters. They just became your top priority. Get me something, even if it's just a single compartment near the outer hull. I'll take anything that's accessible to the landing party."

Scott replied, "*We're already on it, sir. Even if I can route more power to the transporter system, we'll probably have to get a might closer to that thing, just to be on the safe side.*"

Safe side? Kirk forced himself not to comment on that. Instead, he asked, "How close?"

"*Close enough to read hull markings and warning labels, sir. It's likely the only way to keep the transporter beams from scattering during any sort of retrieval process. That would be . . . messy.*"

Forcing away the unwelcome images Scott's report conjured, Kirk said, "I'll work with whatever you give me. Just make it happen."

Any next comments Kirk may have had were squashed by the sound of the red alert klaxon blasting across the bridge.

"Incoming fire!" Sulu shouted.

On the viewscreen, plumes of green-yellow light pulsed from seven points along the citadel's hull. Writhing spheres of undulating energy plasma surged away from the alien construct, growing larger as they closed the distance separating the ship from the *Enterprise*.

Kirk slammed his fist against his armrest intercom panel. "All hands! Brace for impact!"

That was all the time he had to warn his crew before the plasma bolts slammed into the starship's shields. The view on the main screen wavered and blinked, slicing apart as the imaging sensors struggled to compensate as power was automatically drawn from every available system to support the shield generators. Kirk felt the deck heave beneath him and he gripped the arms of his chair to keep from being thrown from his seat. All around him, his bridge officers fought to keep their stations as the ship's artificial gravity and inertial dampers fought back against the attack.

"It's firing again!" Sulu warned.

"Evasive! Rahda, return fire! Target those weapons ports!"

The image on the viewscreen was once again stable, and Kirk saw the new energy discharges as the citadel unleashed a second assault at the same time Lieutenant Rahda released a barrage of phaser fire back toward the alien ship. Then the angle shifted as Sulu maneuvered the *Enterprise* up and away from the incoming fire, and the citadel disappeared from view. The ship shuddered from a new impact against the shields, but the effects this time were far weaker.

"Direct hit on three of the weapons ports," said Chekov. "They look to be offline. We suffered only a minor hit to our aft shields, but the forward shields took a beating during the first strike. They're firming back up, but the shield generators seem to be lagging."

Sulu said, "I've maneuvered us well away from the citadel, sir. Do you want me to take us back?"

"Get ready," replied Kirk. Pushing himself from his seat, he moved to grip the back of the helm officer's chair. "Do you think you can stay ahead of it if it starts firing again?"

"I think so, sir."

"Do whatever you have to do, but I want to keep us as close as possible to the landing party."

Chekov turned from the science station. "Captain, I'm picking up a new reading. The citadel is venting something into the planet's atmosphere. It has a chemical composition I've never seen before. There's a large percentage of nitrogen and a few other things I recognize, but other elements don't match anything in our records."

"Let's see it," said Kirk, stepping away from Sulu and moving around the helm console to stand before the viewscreen, which now depicted the citadel hovering at the very edge of Usilde's atmosphere. Pale white plumes emanated from numerous points across the vessel's underside, aimed toward the planet. From the distance between the *Enterprise* and the citadel as inferred by the screen's imaging sensors, Kirk noted how the compound spread and seemed to dissolve, lost amid the haze surrounding the lush green world.

"What's it doing?" he asked.

Chekov replied, "The compound is mixing with the atmosphere, sir. So far the effects are almost miniscule, but they are there."

Before Kirk could respond to that, Lieutenant Palmer said, "Captain, we're being hailed by Mister Spock."

"Put him on."

A moment later, the science officer's voice said over the intercom, *"Captain, are you detecting the new readings from the citadel?"*

"Chekov's on it, Spock. What do you make of it?"

"It is the new compound created from the water and other resources taken from the lake. The citadel's own refining process has added elements brought from the other universe and mixed it with the raw materials to create a new chemical agent designed to be introduced into the planet's atmosphere. This is apparently the next step in the auto-

mated terraforming efforts put into motion by the Jatohr eighteen years ago, though I suspect this aspect of the operation will take far less time to complete."

Turning to the science station, Kirk said, "Chekov? Can you make any sort of estimate?"

The ensign had already returned to the sensor viewer. "At the present rate of dispersal, the reservoirs aboard the citadel will be depleted within hours."

"The actual reconfiguration of the atmosphere will take considerably more time," added Spock. *"Weeks, at least, likely longer. I am unable to be more precise without additional information."*

"I don't understand," said Kirk. "The Jatohr are able to breathe the same air we do. Their environmental requirements can't be that different. And they were already making smaller changes to the atmosphere just from their efforts on the surface." He recalled from his review of Captain Una's mission reports that the Jatohr terraforming efforts had produced an increase in the levels of nitrogen present in Usilde's air. She had noted her own speculations as to whether this was a byproduct of the changes being made to that area of the planet's ecosystem or a deliberate alteration on the Jatohr's part.

"What about the Usildar?" asked Sulu. "Are they in danger?"

"At present," replied Spock, *"I am unable to answer that question."*

Kirk said, "See what you can find out." He had no intention of standing by while the Jatohr's attempts to salvage whatever remained of their own civilization inflicted genocide upon the Usildar and every other living thing on the planet.

"Understood," replied Spock.

"We're working the problems on our end," said Kirk. "If necessary, we'll start targeting the ship to try and stop the spread of the compound."

His words were answered by yet another sounding of the alert siren. The alarm indicator at the center of the helm and navigation console drew Kirk's gaze, pulsing bright red in time to the audible warning.

"What now?"

"It's the *Vron'joQ*, sir," reported Sulu. "They've broken from standard orbit and are on an intercept course."

Twenty-nine

Once more, awareness returned and Una realized she was lying prone and exposed on the barren salt plain. The rays of the twin suns beat down upon her, and she held up a hand to block their light. As before, however, she felt no heat. It was yet another byproduct of this mysterious realm. Looking toward the sky, she saw that the captivating aerial display of the bizarre energy ribbons had vanished.

What had happened? She tried to recall the events that had led to her being deposited here, but saw only chaos in her thoughts, which defied her attempts to untangle them. Then she recalled her last memories before losing consciousness—the brutal fighting between the Usildar, her former shipmates hallucinating or summoning all manner of odd or perverted memories before turning on one another, and then Sarek. Of course the ambassador had found something discernible only to him in this crazy place. He had latched on to a substantial clue as to the reality of this universe, and had somehow managed to remove himself from this realm and transport to . . . something else, but what?

Una pushed herself to a sitting position, scanning the surrounding terrain for signs of life. As had been the case during her previous visit here, there was nothing. The salt flats remained unchanged and seemingly unimpressed by the passage of time. She was alone. Where was everyone else? What had become of her shipmates Joanna McCoy, Ambassador Sarek, and even Gorkon?

Also absent, Una noted with great thanks, was the pain in her mind. She seemed to be free from the urgent, persistent discomfort that had plagued her consciousness. All of that had faded, leaving no residual effects. How had that happened?

Captain Una, do you hear me?

"Sarek?" She jerked herself to her feet, searching for the source of the voice and realizing only after a moment that the words were not in her ears, but within her thoughts. "Ambassador? Is that you?"

Yes.

"What happened to us? Where did you go?"

I have moved into the true reality of this universe. Where you are, where I was, is but a state of altered consciousness. It is a "thoughtspace," serving as a means of acclimating the mind of a living being until they are prepared to accept the reality of entering another dimension. Time here remains still. Nothing here is real.

Una looked around the salt flats. "So, this is an anteroom? A way station, of sorts, but only for the mind? If that's the case, then why were Martinez and the others still here, even after all these years?"

Their minds are largely incompatible with this universe. The thoughtspace protected them from that. Though I am able to discern between it and reality, even I am under strain. Your companions remain here, as they have all this time. Unless we act, we will remain here forever.

Realization, laced with fervent hope, gripped Una. "Does that mean no one we've seen die here is really dead?"

That is correct. Everyone here is alive, and we can all return to our universe. To do that, I require your assistance.

"To get us back? How? What can I do?"

The disturbance we all felt earlier was caused by the introduction of a probe from our universe, sent by the Enterprise. The Jatohr deactivated it because its transmissions to our universe caused them great pain and spilled over to this realm. I believe we can reactivate the probe and use it to initiate a transfer back to our universe. To do that, we must work together, and you must join me here.

Una remained unconvinced. "And you think you can do all of that?"

My mental abilities and disciplines appear to be of great advantage here. It seems to have surprised some of the Jatohr I have encountered.

Considering her options, Una came to the conclusion that there was nothing to lose and little else she could do if she hoped to get her friends home.

"How do I get to you?"

You must will yourself beyond the thoughtspace, just as I did. The transition is somewhat unpleasant, but I will help however I am able.

The thought of finding an experience less pleasant than remaining alone in this odd, inexplicable realm almost made her laugh. "All right, Ambassador. What do I do?"

Movement across the plain, low on the horizon and almost blocked by the distant mountain range, caught her attention. A mass of individuals and small vehicles was making its way across the open terrain, heading for her. Behind it were great clouds of dust dispersed by the procession's passage.

"Sarek, I've got company." As the horde drew closer, she recognized antigrav sleds, to say nothing of the ponderous bulks of legions of Jatohr. Then her gaze fixed on one being at the center of the group.

"It's Woryan," she said, "and he's got a lot of followers. What the hell are they doing all the way out here?"

Una watched as the small army drew ever closer. Overhead, flying craft of varying sizes dotted the sky. Dozens, perhaps hundreds of antigravity sleds blanketed the salt plains, each carrying individual Jatohr. Leading them all as he sat atop a battle sled festooned with weapons and ornamentation that made it seem more ceremonial than functional, was Woryan.

The enormous gastropod's sled slowed as it approached her, allowing Una to get an unfettered look at hir. Then the sled lurched to a stop, and Woryan's eyestalks straightened as they beheld the sight before hir.

"Hold!"

Hir voice rolled across the open ground. As the rest of hir band slowed to a stop, a pair of battle sleds broke away from the procession and glided toward Unal. Standing her ground, Una watched the sleds until they moved to flank her, hovering perhaps ten meters to either side. Forcing herself to ignore them, she directed her attention to the group's leader.

"Hello, Woryan." As she spoke, she held her hands away from her body, to demonstrate that she was unarmed.

"Outsider," replied the Jatohr. "You dare to challenge me, on the verge of our salvation?"

"Of course," she said, directing her comments to Sarek. "They're massing for transfer to our universe."

A logical deduction, said Sarek, his voice ever composed and calm. *Captain Kirk and the* Enterprise *are working to rescue us. Now that they have activated the transfer-field generator, Woryan and his followers are moving to be ready when it reaches into this universe to find us.*

"Can we stop them?"

I do not know. Possibly. Perhaps not. You cannot stay there, Una. You must join me here.

"It is good that you are here to see the beginning of our invasion of your worlds," said Woryan, "just as it is a pity that you will not live to see its conclusion. Behold, creature!"

In response to his apparent command, another pair of battle sleds rose from the amassed Jatohr. Trailing behind them were thick, metallic cables, and as the sleds lifted toward the sky the cables became taut. Their far ends were attached to the opposing corners of a massive, opalescent arch-shaped portal. Within moments, the portal stood upright, towering high and wide enough to provide passage for any craft or being in the assemblage.

"So," said Una, "this is what Anadac told me about. It's your answer for transferring to my universe."

Woryan shifted his bulk on the battle sled. "It may not be as noble in purpose as what Eljor created, but it will serve our needs well enough. Now we no longer need to wait for rescue. Instead, we will seize the opportunity as it is presented to us. When your people activate the Transfer Key, we will be ready, and there will be no stopping us."

Studying the construct, Una noted that it was fitted together from a number of components linked together to provide strength and support for the entire arch now that it was assembled. Even across the distance separating them, she felt its power.

"It's basically an antenna," she said. "It draws energy from the transfer-field generator that's channeled over here, but redirects it to you rather than whatever the Transfer Key is targeting."

"Impressive, creature," replied Woryan. "Perhaps I should

spare your life, so that you can watch the power we now wield."

Una shook her head. "I don't think so." She could not see how such a device would even function here, being a manifestation of the thoughtspace. How would Woryan react when hir great plan unraveled before hir very eyes?

Let's find out.

Clearing her mind just as she had done with the wall in the prison cell, Una visualized the arch before her and tried to imagine its internal workings. Where would its power source reside? The base, she decided. It was squat and flared out to each side of the arch itself. What would happen if that piece just . . . ?

Una nearly laughed aloud when the arch's base disappeared, leaving the rest of the construct to tumble forward. Jatohr soldiers scattered in all directions, trying to avoid being caught beneath it as it crashed to the ground, kicking plumes of dust into the air.

"The insolence!" Woryan's amplified voice filled the air as s/he gestured wildly toward hir soldiers. "Seize her!"

"Sarek," said Una, "if you can help get me away from here, now would be a good time."

You must focus on me, Una. Concentrate on finding me.

She ignored the sounds of Jatohr soldiers gliding across the open ground toward her. Forcing away all those distractions, she honed in on Sarek's voice, listening as the Vulcan guided her.

Leave the thoughtspace, Una. Come to me.

An odd sensation played across her skin, and Una opened her eyes in time to see the approaching Jatohr soldiers along with everything around her fading from her vision.

Una plunged into pale white nothingness.

The light faded, replaced by unending blackness, though she sensed she was not alone. It took but a moment to focus on the familiarity of the other presence.

"Sarek?"

In response to her query, the darkness ebbed, and Una's vision filled with uncounted forms suspended motionless within a vast, gray void. Looking down, she saw nothing. There was no perception of depth or height, but instead only the gray, though she also was surrounded by a mass of multicolored filaments, each pulsing with energy as they twisted, twirled, and intertwined with one another. It was as she had seen in the sky before chaos erupted. Some of the beings in her midst appeared to be generating still more of the filaments, casting them upon unseen currents to traverse the void around her.

"Una, you are safe."

She heard Sarek's voice, but he was nowhere to be seen. She searched among the indistinct beings gathered here, but there was no sign of the Vulcan.

"Where are we?"

"The reality of this universe," replied the ambassador, "and not the visions we all were experiencing within the thoughtspace. We exist outside time and the physical laws that govern our own universe. At least, that is how I understand it. I am still learning."

Gripped by concern, Una said, "I hear you, but I cannot see you."

"I am elsewhere, suspended as everyone you now see. Here, we connect and communicate not physically, but rather consciously. We share each other's intellects and thoughts, along with our dreams and ideas."

"And our emotions and nightmares," Una countered.

Sarek replied, "For some, it can be an overwhelming experience. I regret that we do not have time to fully explore this place, but ultimately we are incompatible with this universe. We can exist here for a short time, though it strains our mental faculties and our ability to reason. Each individual's reaction is different. You and I appear better able to face the challenges we find here, but others are not so fortunate."

"You mean Martinez."

"Yes, and my advisor, Beel Zeroh. Their minds are still active, but they have entered a protected state in order to prevent further damage. If they are to survive, we must return with them to our universe."

Una did not pretend to understand everything Sarek was telling her, but she had no reason to distrust the Vulcan. "What do we do?"

"You must reach out with your mind. It requires total focus, and we must combine our own energies toward a joint purpose."

"The probe," said Una. "I remember now. It came here from our universe."

Sarek replied, "Yes. It is the key. Together, we must all find it and restore its power so that it can communicate with the *Enterprise*. I have already seen its components and protocols. Once activated, its will send a signal back to our universe and provide a path home."

"How can you be sure?"

"I trust in my son, Captain. Before we can proceed to the probe, we must find the others. Our minds must all join as one, if we are to leave this place together. I have already found Beel Zeroh, but I feel you are better able to collect your former shipmates."

"How do I do that?" Even as she asked the question, she sensed a new presence that also was familiar; more so than Sarek.

"Tim?"

"I'm here, Number One," said the voice of Ensign Timothy Shimizu.

Una felt a rush of renewed hope and confidence washing over her. "It's good to hear your voice, but damned if I know how this is happening."

"I don't have a clue either, but I don't care," replied Shimizu. "For now, I'm trusting in you and the ambassador. I knew you'd find a way to pull us back. All this time, I never gave up."

Sarek's voice sounded in her mind. "The others, Captain. Go."

Driven by new resolve, Una pushed herself into the void, seeking out any familiar presence. How could she find them, among all these uncounted perceptions? She visualized images of each of her former *Enterprise* shipmates, their faces playing across her consciousness. No sooner did she consider an impression of Ingrid Holstine than she was sure she felt the lieutenant looming somewhere nearby. It took Una only a moment to find her form, drifting in repose in the gray ocean.

"Holstine," said Una. "Ingrid, can you hear me?"

"Lieutenant Una? Is that you?"

Una forgave the outdated reference to her rank. "I wish I had time to explain, but right now I need you to follow me. Can you concentrate on staying with me?"

There was a pause, and when Holstine replied, it was with an air of uncertainty. "I think so. I don't . . . I think I understand what to do. It's good to see you."

"Likewise. We'll explain everything later. Follow me."

Repeating the exercise one by one, and with Sarek helping to guide her, Una retrieved each of her comrades. With every addition, she felt the collective consciousness growing stronger and more confident. Voices and thoughts intermingled as reunions took place, at least on some level. How had her friends been trapped here so long without any concept of time's passage? Or perhaps their minds simply rejected that reality in order to preserve their sanity. There was no way to know, at least not until they all returned to their own universe.

Her familiarity with each of her people made the process much easier, and it was interesting to Una how they bonded together as each new person was added to the group. The security officers, Cambias, Le May, and Griffin, found one another with ease, their energies melding together as though forming a security perimeter in order to protect the rest of the group. Then there were Stevens, Craig, and Goldberg, the members of the *Enterprise*'s bridge crew, who, along with Holstine, chose to connect, remaining together in this universe in the same manner in which they had been pulled from their own.

Then there was Raul Martinez.

She sensed from the beginning that the commander would prove to be the greatest challenge. Even with Sarek's help to guide her through the void, he was difficult to locate. Unlike the others, Martinez did not respond to her calls, forcing her to rely on conceptualizations of past memories they shared. It was disconcerting, not being able to hear the strong, confident voice of the man who once had been her superior officer and a gifted leader respected by all who served under him.

Finally, after what seemed like interminable silence, she sensed a faint presence she knew to be his. He was weak and his mind disjointed, but there nevertheless. Una delved ever deeper into the void.

"It's gone," said a voice, barely registering in her consciousness. "All of it. I can't take this anymore."

"Raul?" She flailed in the gray abyss, trying to reel him closer. "Where are you?"

She became aware of a small, feeble point of light, and followed it. The closer she approached, the stronger the sense of familiarity. A figure began to take shape before her. Martinez, floating limp in the void.

"Raul, it's me. Una."

"I can't," replied Martinez. Defeat laced his voice. "I'm tired. I tried to stay strong, but it never ended. I can't fight anymore."

Sarek said, "We can still save him, but we must work together."

"I'm not leaving him," said Una. "Not after all this."

"We are not leaving him, but his mind is not up to the task of assisting us. We must join the others and combine our self-energies. Then we will come back for Commander Martinez. We cannot proceed without you, Captain."

Another voice said, "I can stay with him."

It took Una a moment to recognize the new arrival. "Joanna?" She drew strength from the warmth of the new consciousness, recognizing the comforting, soothing presence of Joanna McCoy.

"It's nice to see you," said the nurse. "I have no idea what the hell is going on. Hopefully one of you big-brain types can explain it at some point."

"Can you help Martinez?" asked Una, directing her perceptions to her friend. His body remained lifeless, his expression flat. She could sense his thoughts, weak as they were. Still, there was something she could grasp.

Joanna replied, "I don't know if I can help him, but I can at least be here for him, and make sure he knows he's not alone."

Una could already feel Joanna's consciousness reaching out to embrace Martinez's, two minds weaving together as two filaments of pulsing energy. Almost immediately, she thought she felt a small spark of life from her old friend.

Yes!

"I can feel him getting stronger," said Joanna. "Just a little, but it's there. We won't lose him, Una. We'll get him home."

"We're getting all of us home."

With a final probe of Martinez's thoughts to assure herself that he was not lost, Una turned her attention back to the void. She now had the tools to reach her goal.

"All right, Ambassador," she said, seeking out Sarek's consciousness. "We're all yours. Let's get the hell out of here."

Thirty

Spock turned at the sound of the running footsteps outside the master control room in time to see Lieutenant Commander Barry Giotto and his five-person contingent of security officers coming through the doorway. At first, Spock thought the security chief and his team might be under attack, and he reached for his phaser. The group, consisting of three men and two women, all human save for a single Vulcan, Ensign Valren, followed Giotto into the room and began spreading outward in a semicircular formation facing the door.

"Commander?" prompted Spock as he pulled his phaser from his waist.

Giotto replied, "Sorry, sir. We ran into one of those sentry drones you warned us about. We took it out, along with another one that showed up out of nowhere. That's when I decided we should get here and make sure you're okay."

"You could have contacted me by communicator," replied Spock.

"I prefer the personal touch, sir." Turning to Ensign Nick Minecci, the next most senior member of his team, Giotto said, "Minecci, you and Hawthorne on this hatch." He gestured toward the ramps leading to the expansive room's upper levels. "The rest of you spread out up there. I want this entrance and the one from the upstairs lab covered. Keep your eyes open, and call out if you see or hear anything."

His team dispersed in accordance with his instructions, leaving Giotto alone with Spock. "I'm sticking with you and the others, Mister Spock."

"Your prudence is appreciated, Commander."

The first officer had been expecting some kind of reaction to the landing party's presence, but nothing had presented itself even after the citadel's launch from the planet. Now that the alien structure had achieved its low orbit over Usilde and had begun expelling the terraforming compound into the atmosphere, Spock was surprised that there had not been more active resistance to the landing party being in the control room. They had not faced constant harassment by the sentry drones during their previous visits. He could only guess that the automated security protocols overseeing the citadel's interior were monitoring the intruders in their midst and determining the most efficient measures when circumstances warranted taking action. Perhaps the fact that Spock and his people had confined themselves to this single room and their activities to the transfer-field generator had mitigated their threat potential. That seemed odd on the face of it, but then Spock considered that the primary purpose of the citadel was to facilitate the transfer of the Jatohr from their universe to this one.

"Any luck finding Captain Una and the others, sir?" asked Giotto.

Spock shook his head. "Not yet, Commander." He made his way back to the center column where Lieutenant Uhura, Doctor McCoy, and his mother still stood before the control consoles, their attention fixed on the array of status monitors that now were divided between depicting the odd, barren landscape from the other universe and views of Usilde from orbit. One angle showed the citadel's underside and the white plumes being directed toward the planet. The effect of the terraforming chemicals was already evident, with the atmosphere in the immediate vicinity of the citadel adopting a faint yellow hue.

"Mister Spock," said Uhura from the adjacent console, "these readings are confusing." When he moved to join her, the communications officer pointed first to the tricorder in her left hand and then the workstation. "According to the data on life-form readings we received from the probe, I'm able to understand this equipment's scans of the other universe, and it is detecting life-forms. Most of them are Jatohr, but there are also other readings these sensors don't seem to understand. Based on my count, there are thirteen anomalous readings. Those have to be our people, sir. Captain Una, Ambassador Sarek, Doctor McCoy's daughter—everyone."

"All alive?" asked McCoy.

Uhura nodded. "Yes, Doctor."

"Why can't you retrieve them?" Amanda stepped closer, and Spock noted the deepening concern on his mother's face.

"I'm not sure if we can or can't, ma'am," replied the lieutenant. She gestured to the screens and the holographic representation of the landscape. "This is where Captain Una said we should look, and according to the scan readings, we're picking up life-forms that may or may not be in that area." She frowned. "The Transfer Key seems to be locking on those readings, but we're still not seeing anything. It doesn't make any sense."

"Why not just try to pull in whatever this thing is supposedly scanning?" asked McCoy. "Wait. That would mean the Jatohr too."

Spock replied, "It would seem so. The process appears

to share only some similarities with our own transporter technology, but there are obvious differences, owing to the nature of transferring individuals and objects across dimensional planes."

"But I thought the Transfer Key could target specific individuals," said Uhura.

"That was the case in our universe. Apparently, things work somewhat differently in the other realm."

Pausing, Spock examined the readings as conveyed by the alien status indicators and gauges. "One set of sensor data informs us that life-forms are in this location, while others show that the region is unoccupied. Logic suggests that at least one of these readings is inaccurate. That, or we are simply missing a key piece of information as we attempt to understand what we are seeing."

"I think my head hurts," said Giotto.

The sound of his communicator chirping for attention interrupted Spock's reply. He retrieved the device from his waist and activated it. "Spock here."

Kirk's voice sounded clearly. *"Things are starting to get tense up here, Spock. It's looking like the Klingons have decided to make a move. Scotty's still trying to come up with a way to get you out of there, but it's not going to happen before the Klingons are on us. Any luck finding Una and the others?"*

Spock said, "We have encountered difficulties with the Jatohr technology, Captain. Apparently, retrieving someone from the other universe is far more complicated than sending someone there."

"Of course it is. So, what do we do?"

"We could activate the Transfer Key, and allow it to do what it is already programmed to do." Spock studied the readings. "If I understand these readings, the transfer-field generator seems poised to do just that. However, that would mean any Jatohr selected by the Transfer Key would be included in the transfer."

"You're not talking about all Jatohr, everywhere, are you?"

"Not if I understand these readings correctly," said Spock. "The number is actually rather limited, but I am also concerned about the unknown risk to any non-Jatohr life readings."

"Spock, if the Klingons press the issue, there may not be time to be picky later." The tension in the captain's voice was becoming more evident. *"For all I know, they're thinking if they can't have the citadel, then no one can, and they'll just destroy it rather than leaving it for us."*

Feeling a hand on his arm, Spock looked down to see Amanda, her eyes wide with concern. "Spock."

"It has to be worth the risk," added McCoy. "If we lose this chance, we might never get another one."

Their emotional appeals were not lost on him. Spock understood the desire to retrieve Sarek and the others. His loyalty to Captain Una was equal to what he felt for James Kirk and his predecessor, Christopher Pike, and gave him insight to what McCoy and his mother were feeling, but he could not make a decision of such importance based purely on emotion.

Not purely, Spock reminded himself. *The risks appear to be negligible and are outweighed by the real danger we now face. What does logic dictate?*

"Very well. We will make the attempt."

Uhura said, "Where will all those people end up when they're transferred?" She looked around the room. "It doesn't make sense that they'd all show up in here."

"A reasonable conclusion, Lieutenant," replied Spock.

"There are areas within the citadel that are large enough to accommodate such numbers. Any of those are logical destinations."

"Is that supposed to be a guess?" asked McCoy.

Spock shook his head. "A deduction, based on available facts."

"Where are these larger areas?" Giotto gestured to his two security officers at the doorway. "I can send people to check."

"Lieutenant Uhura will provide that information." Spock moved to the console that held the Transfer Key. Still holding his communicator, he raised the unit back to his lips. "Captain, we are proceeding with the transfer."

"I've got my fingers crossed."

Without further discussion, Spock pressed the controls on the Transfer Key.

The immediate effect was the noticeable increase in activity within the room's central core. Swirls of contained energy pulsed and flared, mixing in and around one another as the hum of large equipment increased. All around the room, lighting as well as various workstations blinked and flickered as though power within the citadel was being directed away from them and fed to the transfer field generator, which hummed even louder as it absorbed this increased energy. The noise continued to grow until it became uncomfortable, followed by what sounded to Spock like a single, massive burst of compressed air rushing forth through an opened valve.

And then the noise faded. The chaos unfolding inside the center column abated, and the room's illumination returned to normal.

"Okay, that was pretty annoying," said McCoy. "Let's try to not do that again."

Spock turned from the console and saw that his mother looked pained. "Are you all right?"

Nodding as she rubbed her temples, Amanda replied, "It felt like a spike being jammed into my ears."

"Mister Spock," said Uhura, who had returned to the console he had instructed her to oversee. "According to these readings, the transfer was successful." She tapped one of the controls as he had instructed her to do. "The large concentration of life-form readings is gone. I mean, from the other universe. I think."

"*We've found them,*" said the voice of Captain Kirk over the still open communicator. "*They're down on the planet. There's a glade west of the Usildar village, between it and the lake where we originally found the citadel. Looks like everyone was transferred there.*" There was a pause before the captain added, "*Hang on. Chekov's scanning that site. The only life signs he's picking up are Jatohr. No human, Vulcan, Klingon, or Izarian readings.*"

"Where are the others?" asked Commander Giotto.

Moving back to the console with the Transfer Key, Spock inspected the workstation's cluster of status readings, before using his tricorder to collect more detailed information.

"The Key appears to have worked in response to its programming," he said. "That is to say, its default, preprogrammed instructions."

McCoy grunted in irritation. "Meaning only the Jatohr."

"It would appear so."

"What do we do?" asked Amanda. "We can still reach out to Sarek, can't we? Find him and get him to where he and the others can be rescued?"

"The probe," said Uhura. "If you can contact Sarek,

maybe we can get him to alter the probe's harmonic frequency again and give us something to lock on to."

Spock nodded. While their experiments with the probe had showed promise, they had failed to retrieve it with this method before the device deactivated, presumably from a power drain as an effect of its presence in the other universe. Even if Sarek could find the probe, there was no guarantee the device would be functional.

There seems to be no alternative.

From his communicator, Kirk's voice said, *"Spock, check your readings over there. The citadel looks to be increasing the rate it's spitting out the terraforming compound. Can you confirm that?"*

"Just a moment, Captain." Spock moved to another console, which he and Uhura had determined was a station with many displays and indicators devoted to a number of onboard systems. Their tricorder readings had shown that a small collection of such controls was devoted to the conduits feeding the compound to the vent systems, but their attempts to interrupt that process had to this point been unsuccessful.

"You are correct," he said, after examining the indicators. "The rate has increased by approximately sixteen percent and is continuing to rise. A logical deduction is that the process has been accelerated due to the arrival of the Jatohr on the planet."

Kirk said, *"We have to stop it, Spock."*

"Acknowledged." With his tricorder, he studied the alien console yet again. "The rate of increase has risen a total of twenty-three percent and is holding at that level."

"What's that do for your estimates?" asked McCoy.

Spock considered the calculations. "The chemical will have been completely deployed within three hours, but effects to the planet's atmosphere likely will be damaging to non-Jatohr life-forms as well as indigenous wildlife and vegetation well before that. Captain Kirk, I do not see a means for us to disable the system that cannot be over-ridden by automated processes, but there may be another option."

Returning to the console with the Transfer Key, Spock again consulted his tricorder, checking his readings against the information Captain Una had recorded during her initial examination of the citadel. It took him only a moment to confirm his theory.

"Captain, we may be able to redirect energy drawn by the transfer-field generator back to its central power relays, bypassing its internal safety mechanisms and oversight systems in an uncontrolled manner."

Kirk said, *"You're talking about an overload."*

"A forced chamber explosion, yes." Spock glanced again at his tricorder. "If we are to successfully avert per-manent environmental damage to the planet, the process must be initiated within fifteen minutes."

"That's not a lot of time. Scotty still doesn't have the transporters ready, and I've got a Klingon ship coming at me." There was a short silence before Kirk added, *"Unless we find a way to disable that dampening field, we may not be able to get you out of there in time."*

Spock turned his attention to the console, beginning the process of entering instructions to the citadel's power systems. "The dampening field appears to be overseen by a protected system, as are its power generators. We are un-able to reach them in the time available, as they have been blocked by the ongoing reconfiguration of various interior spaces."

"Chekov's identified a section near the citadel's outer hull

that Scotty thinks he can punch through," said Kirk, before relaying a set of coordinates.

Uhura input the information to her tricorder. "I've got it, Mister Spock. If I'm reading this correctly, it'll take us a few minutes to get there."

"And there are no guarantees of a successful retrieval," said Spock.

"It's all we've got," replied Kirk. *"Start the overload procedure."*

Amanda stepped forward. "Spock, wait. What about your father?"

"Joanna," added McCoy, "and everyone else still over there. Spock, we can't . . ."

"There is no choice, Doctor." He paused, his gaze locking with his mother's. "The needs of the many must take precedence." With a final set of instructions entered, a new indicator flared to life on the console. To Spock, it appeared as a collection of densely packed, multihued dots on a black background. The graphic began pulsing, and with each iteration a few of the dots faded. Spock checked the indicator against his tricorder readings.

"We now have twelve minutes before the overload occurs."

"Start making your way to the extraction point," said Kirk.

Spock replied, "We are not quite finished here, Captain." He turned to Amanda, whose expression was one of anguish, and extended his hand.

"Come, Mother. There is still time. We will try to contact Sarek."

Thirty-one

Kirk stared at the main viewscreen, watching as the *Vron'joQ* moved across the image of the planet Usilde, growing larger with each passing moment.

"They're arming weapons, sir," said Chekov from where he still stood hunched over the science station's sensor viewer. "And they've raised their shields."

Damn it!

There was no time for this nonsense, not with Spock and the rest of the landing party still aboard the citadel and a very ominous clock now ticking.

"How can they not see what's going on? Captain J'Teglyr has to at least think his own people might be at risk down there." Dropping the heel of his hand onto his armrest, Kirk activated the chair's comm system. "Kirk to engineering. Scotty, where are my transporters?"

"*We're still working at it, sir.*" The chief engineer's voice was taut with strain, as though he were engaged in physical effort, and Kirk pictured the other man entrenched inside one of the ship's Jefferies tubes. "*That damned dampening field is giving us fits. We're reconfiguring the targeting scanners through the navigational deflector to increase power for the matter stream and the annular confinement beams. We'll still have to get pretty close, though, sir. It's going to be tricky.*"

"Tricky's going to have to be good enough," replied Kirk. "We're running out of time. Just get me a way in there."

"*Aye, Captain. Stand by.*"

No sooner was the connection severed than Chekov said, "Captain, the Klingon vessel is closing to optimum weapons range."

"Maintain evasive, Mister Sulu. I don't want to give them an easy shot."

The helmsman glanced over his shoulder. "What about the citadel, sir?"

Kirk shifted his gaze from the viewscreen to the astrogator between Sulu and Lieutenant Rahda, noting the relative positions of the *Enterprise*, the *Vron'joQ*, and the citadel. The alien ship had settled into its low, stationary orbit, all but daring anyone or anything to approach it as it continued to expel chemicals into Usilde's atmosphere. The citadel's proximity to the planet's mesosphere would make getting near it trickier, as the massive vessel's orbit would limit possible approach vectors.

"Mister Chekov," Kirk said, "if necessary, could we destroy the citadel?"

"Not completely, sir," replied the ensign, "but we could definitely do some serious damage. According to our sensor readings, its hull won't stand up to an extended attack with photon torpedoes. If we can breach it at the right points, we can definitely target power systems and whatever else might look vulnerable. That might trigger total destruction, but the more likely outcome is that whatever remains will simply fall back to the planet."

Kirk grimaced at the unpleasant thought. "That could be dangerous for the Usildar and even the Klingons. There's no way to know what kind of ecological damage a crash might cause, considering its cargo." They needed a way to disable or destroy the citadel that was not hazardous to Usilde, its indigenous population, and anyone else down on the planet.

You may not have a choice. Not anymore.

"Lieutenant Rahda, start plotting possible firing solutions." Swiveling his chair, Kirk turned to Lieutenant Palmer. "Open a channel to the *Vron'joQ*."

The communications officer tapped a sequence of controls at her workstation before replying, "Frequency open, sir."

"J'Teglyr, this is Captain Kirk. From where I sit, Captain, you appear to be taking provocative action. Please explain the nature of your intercept course."

After a moment, Palmer said, "They're definitely receiving, sir, but I'm not getting any response."

"Captain," Kirk said into the open channel, "perhaps you haven't noticed, but the Jatohr citadel has launched from the planet's surface and assumed orbit. It's armed, and we've already taken fire. You can see for yourself that it's introducing a compound into the planet's atmosphere that will continue the Jatohr terraforming process. The Usildar may be in danger, and you have your own people down there, and now the citadel is building to an overload of its power plant. Are you really going to do this *now*?"

To his surprise, Palmer said, "They're transmitting, Captain. Audio and visual."

"Onscreen."

The *Vron'joQ* and the planet behind it disappeared from the viewscreen, replaced not by J'Teglyr but instead a female Klingon whom Kirk did not recognize, sitting in the high-backed chair at the center of the warship's bridge. He noted from her uniform insignia that she carried a commander's rank.

"I am Visla, now in command of this vessel."

Scowling, Kirk asked, "What happened to J'Teglyr?"

"I . . . relieved him of his duties." Visla leaned forward

in her seat, her expression hardening. *"He was unwilling to do all that might be necessary to defend the Empire and its interests. Rest assured that I do not share this failing."*

What the hell was going on over on that ship? Was J'Teglyr dead, executed for any number of real or perceived offenses? The Klingon captain had at least appeared uninterested in battling the *Enterprise*, but this Visla seemed driven by some other agenda.

As he stared at her image on the viewscreen, Kirk realized who she was, and why she seemed so determined. "You commanded the *Qo'Daqh*, and you attacked us earlier. An unprovoked attack, I might add."

"Unprovoked?" Raising her right hand, she pointed to something Kirk could not see. *"You control that alien machine, which has now risen from the planet. Your people are aboard it, Captain. Are you trying to tell me you have no intentions of seizing it for your Starfleet to exploit? To use it against your enemies?"*

Kirk felt his jaw tightening, but he forced himself to keep his tone level. "Didn't you see the thing firing at my ship? I have a team trapped over there, and I can't get them out of there if you insist on facing off against me." Rising from his chair, he glared at her. "Don't get between me and my people, Commander."

"Bold words, Captain," replied Visla. The Klingon offered a menacing smile. *"Let us see if your actions are worthy of them."*

She made a gesture and her image dissolved, returning the forward view of the *Vron'joQ* as it continued its approach.

"They've accelerated to full impulse, Captain!"

Kirk grabbed the back of Sulu's chair. "Evasive maneuvers." Even before the lieutenant could move to execute the order, he said, "No, wait." He leaned closer to the helm officer. "Take us in closer to the citadel."

"Closer, sir?" Sulu shot him a skeptical glance.

Nodding, Kirk replied, "Right. Why should we have all the fun getting shot at by the citadel?"

Sulu smiled. "Aye, sir."

A moment later, the lieutenant was inputting the necessary commands to the helm console, and Kirk watched the *Vron'joQ* curve up and away beyond the viewscreen's upper right corner as the *Enterprise* changed its trajectory. Within seconds, the citadel was centered on the screen, depicted from above with the starship angling toward it.

"The citadel appears to be tracking our approach, Captain," said Chekov, his face all but buried in the sensor viewer. "Their weapons ports are coming to bear."

His attention divided between his instruments and the tactical scanner that had emerged from his console, Sulu asked, "How close do you want us, sir?"

"Close enough to scratch the paint," replied Kirk as he returned to his seat. "Get us close enough, and maybe it'll look for something else to shoot at."

It took only a moment for the Jatohr construct to announce its displeasure at the *Enterprise*'s return, with Chekov calling out a new warning as the first volley of plasma energy bolts spat forth from ports along the spires festooning the citadel's upper hull. Sulu's evasive tactics saw to it that the starship suffered only glancing blows as he closed the distance, but Kirk felt the effects of every impact against the deflector shields channeled through the vessel's structure. At the same time, Lieutenant Rahda was continuing her quest to target and disable any weapons ports that presented themselves. Phaser fire streaked across the citadel's hull, and Rahda was rewarded as some of the strikes found their mark.

"We hit three ports on that pass, sir," reported Rahda.

Kirk nodded. "Nice shooting, Lieutenant. Keep it up."

"Here comes the *Vron'joQ*," warned Chekov. "They're coming right at us." A moment later, he called out, "They're targeting us!"

"Sulu," Kirk prompted. Rather than replying, the lieutenant responded by executing yet another shift in the *Enterprise*'s trajectory, and Kirk tried to ignore his stomach's objections as the citadel rolled to starboard on the viewscreen. Along its hull, weapons ports flashed, each one unleashing another barrage of disruptor energy. This time the aim was true, and the screen dissolved in a brilliant white light with enough intensity to overstress the imaging processor. A heartbeat later, the ship trembled and protested as the shields bore the brunt of the violent attack.

"Sorry, Captain." Sulu cast a guilty grimace over his shoulder as he gripped his console to hold himself in his seat. His apology was punctuated by a second series of strikes against the shields, though these impacts were not as severe.

Chekov said, "That's the *Vron'joQ*, maneuvering in behind us. We took heavy damage to the port shields from the citadel. The generators are lagging on getting them back to full strength."

"Take us in closer," ordered Kirk, his attention split between the viewscreen and the astrogator as he judged the position of the *Enterprise* and the Klingon vessel. "Rahda, stand by on phasers."

The viewscreen image shifted again in response to Sulu's maneuvering the starship toward the citadel. Stars and the curvature of the planet all but disappeared, blocked out by the alien structure's gleaming exterior. Kirk saw the dark openings of the weapons ports, and movement inside, as the plasma disruptors took new aim and prepared to fire.

"Now, Rahda," said Kirk. "Fire!"

The navigator executed the command and twin beams of blue-white energy lanced across space, striking a pair of the weapons ports as the *Enterprise* passed overhead. Without waiting for orders, Sulu guided the ship along an evasive course across the citadel's outer hull, giving Rahda additional targets of opportunity. A few of the ports survived the strike and were continuing to fire, and Kirk watched the energy bolts streak past the edges of the viewscreen.

"The *Vron'joQ* has taken direct hits to its aft shields," said Chekov, his voice rising in volume and pitch. He leaned closer to his sensor viewer, almost pressing his face against the viewfinder. "Another hit. Aft shields are buckling!"

Kirk shifted in his seat. "Sulu, bring us around, and watch our backs. Rahda, target the *Vron'joQ*'s propulsion system and fire at will."

The citadel disappeared from the viewscreen and Kirk watched Usilde swing into view, before which was the silhouette of the D6 battle cruiser. Flares of energy were visible near the ship's stern, a clear indication that its deflector shields had been compromised. Not waiting, Rahda fired again, and the *Enterprise*'s phasers sliced through the faltering shields to strike the Klingon ship's starboard warp nacelle. The lieutenant followed with another barrage, this time scoring a direct hit on the cruiser's aft hull.

"Hold your fire, Lieutenant," said Kirk. "Chekov, damage report?"

The ensign replied, "They're moving off, sir. Their warp drive is offline, and their impulse engines also appear damaged. They've still got weapons, but I'm picking up other system overloads throughout the ship." Looking away from the sensors, he added, "Their life-support systems appear damaged, too, Captain."

"Critical?"

"Not at the moment sir, but they'll definitely need major repairs."

Kirk nodded. "Leave them be, but keep an eye on them. We've got bigger problems right now. How much time until the overload?"

"Nine minutes, forty seconds, sir," replied Chekov.

Turning his chair, Kirk looked to the communications station. "Palmer, get me Spock."

Thirty-two

Having moved to a quiet corner of the control room, away from the rest of the landing party as well as the central column and its workstations, Spock directed Amanda to sit on the floor. He then settled into position, and she mimicked his movements as he adopted a meditative pose, sitting with his legs crossed and arms resting on his lap.

"Are you certain you can do this?" asked Spock. "The discomfort you experienced last time was formidable."

Her lips pressed together, Amanda nodded. "I have to do this, Spock. I'm the only one who can. I'm ready." To emphasize her reply, she reached out and took his hands in hers. "But I can't do it without you."

The previous meld had proven difficult for Amanda, due mostly to the extra strain to which she had been subjected as part of attempting to make contact with Sarek across whatever barrier separated the two universes. Spock surmised that the level of difficulty was further amplified by whatever Sarek himself was experiencing in the bizarre realm.

Leaning toward his mother, Spock reached out and placed the fingertips of his right hand against her left cheek. He pressed against the contact points to initiate the meld, and her eyes closed. Spock followed suit, forcing his mind clear of all thoughts save Amanda.

"My mind to your mind. My thoughts to your thoughts."

Thanks to their earlier joining, navigating this meld was far easier, and within moments Spock sensed his mother's presence in proximity to his own. An image of her face coalesced before him, and she smiled. It was that confident, knowing smile she exuded throughout his childhood, a comforting expression that always accompanied some words of encouragement or counsel. Living on a world among Vulcans, Amanda Grayson had always comported herself in the finest traditions of her adopted home, impressing even his father's exacting, uncompromising standards of conduct. Even then, she still found ways to assert herself as a human and an individual, instead of remaining satisfied being known only as the wife and partner of a prominent diplomat. Though it had taken many years, Spock now understood he carried within him the best qualities of both his parents and the dual heritage that was his birthright.

It was that joint nature, and his connection to both his mother and his father, which would now serve them.

Beyond the image of Amanda that now was fully formed in his mind, Spock once again saw the barren plain representing the other universe. In the distance, standing alone on the wasteland, was a figure. Spock could not discern any recognizable features, and yet he sensed a familiarity.

"Father?"

Spock heard nothing from the figure, but there was another voice.

"Sarek? Do you hear me?"

I hear you, my wife. Is Spock with you? I think I sense his presence.

"Yes," said Amanda. "He's here. Sarek, you must come. Time is running out. If you don't leave soon, you and the others will be trapped. We tried to find you, and here you are, but we can't get the transfer field to lock on to you."

I am not where you think I am. Nothing here is what it appears to be. All that we see here is illusion. We must fight to break through to reality. It is difficult.

Though he heard Sarek's words, Spock felt none of the connection he shared with Amanda. It was as though a wall had been erected between them, blocking his consciousness from that of his father's. There was no joining, no connection. It was like hearing an echo carried forth from a vast abyss.

"You have to try, Sarek," said Amanda, and Spock sensed her plea resonating in and around his own thoughts. "There isn't much time."

———

"Now, everyone! The time is *now*!"

With Amanda Grayson's impassioned entreaty still ringing in his mind, Sarek summoned each of the dozen minds he had woven into this joint consciousness. All responded to his call save Commander Raul Martinez and Beel Zeroh, his military advisor whom Sarek had thought dead upon finding him in this realm. He was grateful to have been proven wrong, as was the case with the other members of Captain Una's former landing party. All were alive, the transitory thoughtspace having never allowed them to pass through to the Jatohr universe and possibly saving them from irreversible mental trauma and death. However, it remained to be seen whether any or all of them would suffer lasting effects from their time trapped here.

First, we must leave this place.

Sarek felt himself wavering under the mental strain,

but before him was the manifestation of his achievement: the multicolored strand of psychic energy he guided through sheer force of will. He sensed the group mind lurching into motion, already accelerating as each mind resolved itself to their mutual success.

Among the cacophony of disjointed thoughts running the gamut of emotions, he heard a single, clear voice.

"I feel your exertion, Sarek. Let me help."

Of all his companions, Una with her advanced mental acuities was the one most able to assist him. It was she who had come forth to help him complete the task of amassing her former shipmates and the rest of the group, including Joanna McCoy and Beel Zeroh. Once they were assembled, she had guided her companions into the joint link, their thoughts weaving together and forming a single commune. This had freed Sarek to prepare for the trial of navigating them all through the thoughtspace. Now they were under way, and he relaxed his thoughts, allowing her to advance until they were united within the twisting, undulating filament of drive and desire.

Pushing outward, he sought the probe. It was there, where it had remained since its arrival in this place. Sarek's thoughts still echoed with the pain the device had caused, and its reaction to the realm in which it found itself. In order to leave this place, the probe would once more be required to disrupt it.

"We are here," he said to the commune as the probe solidified before him. The group responded with an outpouring of thoughts and emotions Sarek almost found difficult to absorb. Pushing aside the distracting perceptions, he concentrated instead on the new task before him.

"We have to work together," he heard Una say. "Concentrate on the probe."

The inert cylinder hovered at the forefront of his consciousness even as Sarek sensed the collected push of his companions, amplified by the thoughtspace itself, aiding him to focus on the probe. He delved into the artificial construct, visualizing its internal systems, which were inert, but there was energy in abundance here, now that he knew how to employ it. His companions were a prime source, as was the ambient, encompassing glow of the thoughtspace itself. Even he could direct a flow of purpose, translating it for the probe's use.

"I can sense it," said Joanna, her voice distant. "I feel a warmth."

Sarek conjured images of electrical current flowing across reenergized power cells. He made himself a conduit, channeling life into the inert systems and willing them back to life.

Then he sensed a surge of presence forcing itself into his thoughts.

"You seek to restore the pain, Sarek of Vulcan." The voice, like the consciousness, was familiar.

"Edolon," said Sarek, struggling to remain centered on the probe. "I can stop the pain, as I told the others."

"Why do you do this?"

"As you have already determined, we are not meant for your realm." Sarek pushed ahead, directing his self-energy forward. "This is our way home."

Edolon replied, "You dismiss this too quickly."

Ignoring the rebuke, Sarek concentrated on solidifying his visualization of the probe's internal circuitry. He felt the same warmth Joanna perceived, and a dim glow now teased the edges of his perceptions, but it was weak. Sarek realized he was losing his focus, due to his unwelcome companion.

"This place offers much. You simply do not see it yet."

Sarek said, "I do see it." He also noted the strain on his psyche. There was an urge to raise his mental barriers to thwart Edolon's insistence, but he knew that would come at the expense of his link with the probe. Only Una, bringing her own mental discipline to bear, prevented him from losing his connection to the group. He sensed her calming Joanna and the others, and for a moment he even felt Gorkon's haughty presence attempting to rumble forth.

"I see it, Edolon. More clearly than you know."

"You are without question a unique being, Sarek. There is so much we could learn from one another."

Edolon's admission was enough for Sarek to draw renewed purpose, and he called upon every remaining reserve of self-energy he could muster. Una and the other minds in his commune were there, supporting him, and he sensed their moving to surround him and offer even more of themselves to their joint effort. The probe became more distinct, its own presence growing more overt, and Sarek imagined power flowing across circuits and conduits.

"The others are waiting, Sarek," said Edolon.

"Waiting to see if we are successful?"

Edolon replied, "Waiting for me to put an end to this before you bring more pain."

"Then stop us." It was a bold challenge, but Sarek's consciousness was set on his goal. There would be no further uncertainty.

"What makes you so dedicated to that realm?"

Instead of answering, Sarek summoned images of his home world, Vulcan. Stark, gray mountains clashed with harsh, red deserts. Lava boiled and belched across the Fire Plains. The Voroth Sea churned foam along the shores of Raal. Sand-fire storms swept and raged through its deserts.

Heat baked and cracked its plains, and yet all of it possessed undeniable beauty.

Images of a life spent in service to others, of the even greater collective that was the Federation, and his people's place in it. A commitment to peace, to the expansion of knowledge, to the cooperation of countless beings representing myriad beliefs and purposes.

Amanda, his wife, and their steadfast, loving bond. How her thoughts and perspectives informed his own, and his greatest desire to enrich her life as she did his.

His son. Even with their past differences and conflicts, Spock was the one thing in the universe about whom Sarek was most proud. Such emotional confessions were not the Vulcan way, but that did not mean he did not harbor them. His pride at his son's accomplishments warmed his heart and even his soul, as Amanda had once said.

"We are so different," said Edolon, "and yet so alike, in many ways."

Sarek imparted his commitment to *Kol-Ut-Shan*. Infinite diversity, to be celebrated within the universe's infinite combinations. Differences in thought and being were aspects to be honored, even celebrated among all life, wherever it may be. To believe such could be achieved at the exclusion of even a single individual was illogical. Consideration of all perspectives through communication of belief and mutual respect was the path Sarek saw toward advancement and improvement for all.

"All of this awaits us," said Sarek. "You would deny it to us?"

Once more, he felt himself weakening. Sharing with Edolon had left him empty and vulnerable, but Una and Joanna McCoy and even Gorkon along with the others were rallying to his side. The unified thoughts pulsed and surged through him, but would it be enough?

"You have shown us much, Sarek."

He sensed Edolon pulling away, extricating hirself from Sarek's perceptions even as he sensed power emanating at long last from the probe. Energy pulsated, chasing away the darkness.

"You should not be denied this home of yours, Sarek of Vulcan. Go."

"Come with us," said Sarek. "Salvation awaits you."

Edolon replied, "Our time has passed. Others have made the transit, but there is no fleeing our fate."

Before Sarek could respond, the probe came fully to life. It resumed its transmissions, casting its signal into the void, striking out across the limits of this universe and perhaps even to points beyond. Had they been successful?

"Sarek," said Una. "Can you feel it? I think—"

Her voice, along with the thoughts of her companions and Joanna McCoy and the others, vanished as the psychic link connecting them all exploded, cascading outward in an explosion of blinding white light.

Thirty-three

Amanda Grayson gasped, jerking backward and pulling away from Spock's hand, the fingers of which had been placed along the mind-meld contact points on her face. Sensing the shock to her mind but unable to explain it, Spock reached for her as she threatened to slump all the way to the floor.

"Mother," he said, holding her steady. "Are you all right?"

Drawing a deep breath, Amanda opened her eyes, which were reddened. "I'm so . . . weak. Sarek. I felt him and then something blocked me. I don't . . . I don't know what happened."

Still seated in front of her on the floor of the control room, Spock looked up as McCoy approached, already kneeling next to his mother and placing a gentle hand on her shoulder. "Take it easy, Amanda." With his other hand, he retrieved a small medical scanner from a compartment on his tricorder and activated it. The compact device made a warbling sound as he held it before Amanda's body. "Pulse, respiration, and blood pressure are all elevated, and she's had a form of neurological shock." He deactivated the scanner. "The strain of that mind-meld, Spock. It's too much for her."

"I understand," replied the first officer. Pushing himself to his feet, he said, "Mother, I sensed you were able to contact Sarek. Was he able to make the adjustments to the probe?"

Amanda's expression darkened. "I . . . I'm not sure."

"The field generator acted up while you two were under," said McCoy. "Nothing like before, but it was still something."

Behind them, Uhura turned from the console that still hosted the Transfer Key. "I think it worked, Mister Spock. I'm showing a reading here that's very similar to the gamma-ray emissions we picked up from the probe during our trial runs."

The beep of his communicator punctuated her report, and Spock retrieved the device and activated it. "Spock here."

James Kirk's voice burst from the communicator's speaker. *"We've got them, Spock! Fourteen life signs on the planet, near where the Jatohr were put down. Everyone's accounted for."*

"Captain," said Amanda, leaning close to Spock, "my husband. He was injured on Centaurus."

"We don't know everyone's condition," replied the captain, *"but I've already got a medical and security team heading to the transporter room. They're being taken care of, and now it's time to get you the hell out of there."*

"Amen to that," said McCoy. "What do we do?"

"Scotty's finalizing his adjustments to the transporter. It's our only shot. Start heading for the location we gave you."

Having located the selected compartment with his tricorder, a location near the citadel's outer hull and in an unshielded section of the massive structure, Spock had also determined the shortest route to that point from the control room. With only minutes remaining, the landing party would be cutting it very close.

"Commander Giotto," said Spock. "Take your security team and head to the extraction point. If Mister Scott is able to modify the transporters, there will be precious little time to waste. You should be at the designated location and ready to beam out at a moment's notice."

The security chief frowned. "Sir, my job is to protect you and the other senior officers."

"We're right behind you," said McCoy. "But I don't want to have to wait in line to get off this thing."

"The doctor is correct, Commander." Spock gestured for the door. "Proceed to the extraction point."

Though obviously displeased with the directive, and no doubt motivated by a sincere desire to oversee the safety of those in his charge, Giotto offered a curt nod. "Aye, sir, but don't make me regret not disobeying your orders."

"I second that," said Uhura.

With Giotto and the security team running ahead of them and McCoy and Uhura flanking him, Spock took hold of Amanda's arm and ushered her out of the control room.

Walking at a rapid pace next to Amanda so that he could support her by holding her other arm, McCoy said, "Spock, remind me not to tag along with you the next time you decide to go traipsing around inside an alien contraption."

———

Kirk's grip on the armrests of his chair was so intense that he noticed a dull tingling sensation in his fingertips. Lifting his hands, he watched the tint of the skin on his fingers go from pale to pink as blood flow was restored.

Control yourself, Captain.

"Coming up on target," reported Sulu from the helm. Under his skilled hands, the *Enterprise* had braved the turbulence that came with low-orbit maneuvering and guided the starship beneath the citadel for a second time, providing access to the massive structure's underside and the vents that continued to discharge the compound. It was not a smooth ride, as indicated by the buffeting to which the ship was subjected as Sulu navigated the limits of the planet's upper atmosphere.

Seated next to him, Lieutenant Rahda said, "Firing." She tapped her controls, and another barrage of phaser fire spat forth. Both beams struck the target vent and Kirk watched the brief puff of fire and expelled air as its housing was destroyed.

"Incoming fire!" warned Chekov.

Kirk did not have to say anything as Sulu piloted the *Enterprise* away from the citadel. Within seconds the low rumbling of the ship's hull faded as the starship returned to normal space.

"This is taking too long," he said. On the bridge's main viewscreen, the citadel still hovered over Usilde, continuing to vent the terraforming compound into the planet's atmosphere. There were too many vents to address and not enough time. Meanwhile, sensor readouts were still processing the effects of the chemical composition on Usilde's natural environment, and the fact that such calculations were taking so much time was all Kirk needed to know about how much damage the Jatohr technology was inflicting on this innocent world.

In truth, the citadel's imminent destruction was something of a blessing, as it would occur well before this aspect of the terraforming process could be completed. Kirk hoped whatever changes had been introduced to Usilde's ecosystem could be mitigated if not reversed, for the good of the planet's indigenous population. He had no doubts that the best scientific minds in the Federation could be called upon to resolve this situation, no matter the level of difficulty or the time required to accomplish that goal.

We'll fix it. We owe it to the Usildar, but first things first.

"Chekov," he asked, "where are they?"

Glancing away from his sensor readouts, the ensign replied, "The landing party is within fifty meters of the extraction point, sir. Sensor readings are much clearer than they were even just a minute ago."

Kirk nodded. The adjustments to communications and sensors needed to circumvent the citadel's dampening field had taken time, but not as much or with the same level of difficulty as the transporters. Because of that, he was able to see and hear his people as they moved through the Jatohr ship even while standing powerless to help them.

"How much time do they have?"

"Just over two minutes," replied Sulu. The helm officer was hunched over his console, his hands resting on the controls and waiting for the order to take the *Enterprise* on yet another run toward the citadel. Their previous pass had given Montgomery Scott an additional opportunity to evaluate his transporter modifications by beaming a test cylinder to the location designated for the landing party's extraction. That experiment had occurred with the starship taking fire from the citadel just as it had during its attack runs, and Kirk knew that his luck for taunting the Jatohr ship's weapons had to be running low.

He activated his chair's intercom control. "Kirk to engineering. Scotty."

"I know, Captain," replied the harried chief engineer. *"I think I've almost got it. I need to make one more adjustment, and then we can run another test."*

"Forget the tests," snapped Kirk. "This is it, one way or the other. We won't get another chance. Are you ready?"

Scott sighed over the open channel. *"I can't make any promises, Captain."*

"Ninety seconds, sir," reported Sulu.

Kirk tapped the arm of his chair with his fist. "Then we don't have anything to lose, do we? Sulu, take us in."

"Aye, sir," said the helm officer, turning once more to his controls.

Pushing himself back in his chair, Kirk watched the citadel grow to fill the viewscreen. It was going to be close, but there was no more time to wait, or waste.

It was now or never.

All but carrying Amanda between them, Spock and McCoy entered the chamber, on the heels of Lieutenant Uhura. The room was a circular affair, filled with all manner of conduits and what might have been cargo containers, stacked in odd configurations along the curved bulkheads. A circular hatch, larger than the others he had seen and appearing to be much thicker, was set into the room's far wall.

"Looks to be an airlock, sir," said Lieutenant Commander Giotto, who stood waiting in the room with the other five members of his security team. He tapped the tricorder slung against his left hip. "At least, that's what this says."

McCoy grunted. "End of the road."

Instead of replying, Spock activated his communicator. "Spock to *Enterprise.*"

"Kirk here. We're reading you at the extraction point. Stand by. We're coming for you right now."

"How much time do we have?" asked Uhura.

"Sixty-four seconds," replied Spock. He deduced that extracting ten people via transporter, particularly one experiencing the apparent problems described by the captain, would consume most of that remaining time. Upon reflection, he decided this was an observation that did not need to be shared with the others.

"Closing to transporter range," said Kirk. *"Get ready."*

Two seconds later, Giotto and his security team were enveloped in the familiar gold shimmer of transporter beams. The six officers faded and dissolved, and Spock exchanged glances with his mother.

"That's a good sign, I hope," she said.

Several more seconds passed, during which McCoy and Uhura moved to stand next to each other. The doctor placed his arm around her shoulder.

"It'll be all right," he said. "Jim won't let us down. He'd die first."

Uhura smiled. "I know."

Recognizing the sentiment, Spock also noted the conviction with which his companions spoke. Though logic suggested that such statements were fraught with emotion rather than reason, he realized that they also were declarations from which he found comfort. The doctor was correct in at least one regard: James Kirk would without hesitation give his own life in service to the well-being of those under his command. He would never quit, would never succumb, would never surrender so long as they were in danger.

McCoy's unwavering belief was confirmed when Kirk's voice exploded from the communicator.

"They're safe! Hang on, Spock. It's your turn."

Only then did Spock realize that Amanda was holding

his hand, and he had but a fleeting moment to notice her grip tightening before he felt the welcome tingle of the transporter beam. The last thing he heard before the beam consumed him was Leonard McCoy's voice.

"Told you."

_____

"Bridge, we've got them all!"

Kirk pushed himself from his chair, lunging toward the helm console. "Sulu, get us out of here."

The lieutenant was already feeding the necessary commands to the helm console, and Kirk watched as the citadel dropped below the viewscreen's lower edge as the *Enterprise* pushed its way toward space. Kirk counted down the precious few seconds remaining to them.

"Chekov, is the *Vron'joQ* at a safe distance?"

At the science station, the ensign replied, "They're holding position four hundred thousand kilometers from the planet, sir. That should be sufficient." He paused, then added, "If it's not, then we've likely got bigger problems."

Checking his count against the chronometer on Sulu's station, Kirk saw that only seconds remained until detonation. "Full power to aft shields. Maintain speed until further notice. Reverse angle on viewer."

The image on the screen changed to show the citadel, still hovering above the planet, but only for a moment before the entire vessel shuddered as though racked by massive internal explosions. Kirk watched as great fissures opened in the ship's hull, belching fire as the entire structure began to come apart. An immense ball of energy expanded outward from the ship's core, growing within seconds to consume the entire citadel. Debris was cast in all directions, including no small amount shunted toward the planet. Kirk winced at that, hoping the falling wreckage posed no threat to anyone on the surface. There were also the environmental concerns posed by the explosion occurring within the planet's atmosphere, but there was nothing he could do about that now except hope that any damage could be repaired later.

As the explosion faded, leaving behind only a cloud of wreckage, Kirk allowed himself a sigh of relief. He closed his eyes, feeling the strain of the past hours only now beginning to ebb.

"Well done, everyone."

As his bridge officers continued to watch over their stations, assessing the status of the ship's various systems and determining the scope of any damage, Kirk was left to ponder the beautiful green world. Usilde, despite all it had suffered, beckoned, but what of the Usildar, or the Jatohr for that matter? What was to become of them? Their fates, now seemingly intertwined, remained unknown.

Break's over, Kirk chided himself. *Back to work.*

Thirty-four

Her fingers slick with green blood, Captain Una tore at Sarek's burned, tattered robes until she laid bare the ambassador's torso. Multiple wounds from shrapnel marred his flesh, and he was in obvious pain. He looked to be slipping into shock. What the hell had happened?

Wait. His injuries from Centaurus. They were arrested, somehow, in the other universe, but now we're back. Damn it!

"I need help here! Hurry!"

It was only when she moved to readjust the small pack slung across her back that she realized she was carrying all of the Starfleet equipment she had taken with her when she had transferred herself to the Jatohr universe. Her phaser and tricorder were all here.

And the survival kit!

Pulling the pack over her shoulders, Una dropped it to the ground and pulled out the Starfleet field medkit that was part of her survival provisions. She was attempting to fumble open the kit when she saw a shadow fall across Sarek's body.

"Captain," said Joanna McCoy as she rushed toward her, dropping to the ground next to the wounded Vulcan and pushing her way past Una to assess his injuries.

"He's the same way he was before we were transported to the other universe," McCoy said. She snatched the medkit from Una's hands and opened it. "He's in a bad way. This kit won't be enough."

Reaching to the small of her back, Una sighed in relief when her hand wrapped around the communicator she found there. She flipped it open.

"Una to . . . Captain Una to whoever's up there. We have an emergency. Vulcan male in critical condition requiring immediate attention. Lock on to this signal and transport now!" To her great relief, a familiar voice replied.

"Captain Una, this is Jim Kirk. Transporter room is preparing to beam him up now. Stand by."

"I'm going with him," snapped Joanna, who had availed herself of Una's tricorder and was now holding a portable scanner over Sarek.

Una nodded. "No argument." Into the communicator, she said, "Captain Kirk, two to beam up. Then send down a medical team and security people. We've got a lot of disoriented people down here."

"On it. Prepare for transport."

Placing the communicator on Sarek's chest, she pushed herself away from him and Joanna mere seconds before she heard the telltale whine of transporter energy flaring into existence. Joanna and Sarek were enveloped in the glowing gold sheen, and their bodies faded into nothingness, leaving Una standing alone.

"Good luck," she said to the air.

Una allowed herself to assess her current situation. She had regained awareness to find herself standing in what she recognized as a forest on Usilde. Her first sight had been the wounded Ambassador Sarek, at which point instinct took over. Now that he was gone, transported to the *Enterprise* and hopefully receiving the best possible care from the starship's chief medical officer, she had time to absorb a most important realization.

We're back.

Turning from the spot where she had found Sarek, Una took in her surroundings. Scattered around her were her former *Enterprise* crewmates, as well as hundreds of Usildar. A short distance away, more Jatohr than she could easily count occupied a large clearing at the edge of the forest on the far side of the lake that she realized was no longer home to the citadel. What had happened to it? As for the Jatohr, from what she could see, they appeared confused and even more lethargic than she remembered from her previous encounters.

Moving among the group of returnees, Una first found Lieutenant Ingrid Holstine and Petty Officer James Cambias. Both of her comrades were sitting on the ground, dazed and disoriented.

"Lieutenant," said Holstine. Then she shook her head and blinked several times. "I mean, Captain. It's going to take me a little while to get used to that."

Una smiled. "It's all right."

Reaching up to rub his temples, Cambias said, "Thank you for coming after us, Captain, and for never giving up on us."

"You'd have done the same for me."

Cambias exchanged looks with Holstine. "So, eighteen years. Think they'll give us retroactive promotions?"

"I'll see to it personally," said Una. She placed her hand on the petty officer's shoulder. "Just sit tight. A team from the *Enterprise* is on the way."

After checking on the other members of her former crew—Le May, Griffin, Stevens, Goldberg, and Craig—Una made her way to where Ensign Tim Shimizu sat next to Commander Raul Martinez.

"Tim," she said as she approached. "Are you all right?"

Pushing himself to his feet, Shimizu moved to her

and they embraced. She heard and felt his deep sigh as he gripped her, and for a moment Una thought she might cry. She had waited years for this moment, and the feeling of success was all but overwhelming.

The victory had not come without cost.

Pulling back from her, Shimizu wiped his eyes before gesturing to Martinez. "The commander's still out of it. I think he needs help."

Una knelt next to Martinez. The other man's eyes were open and staring at some fixed point in space, though she suspected he saw nothing. His lips were moving, though she heard no words.

"I don't get it," said Shimizu. "Aside from Captain April, he's the strongest, toughest man I've ever known, but something over there was just too much for him."

"It's not his fault," said Una. "None of us should've been over there. We weren't suited to that universe, and we each reacted in different ways. Somehow it just was worse for Raul. We'll get him all the help he needs."

Shimizu nodded. "He'll be okay. I just know it. It's still Raul Martinez in there, right?"

"I hope so," said Una. "This isn't what I wanted when I came to get all of you."

"It's not your fault." Shimizu put a hand on her arm. "You kept your promise. Even after all these years, you never forgot us. You gave us back our lives, Una. That's got to give him some strength to fight with." He looked to Martinez. "Somehow he knows that. I can feel it."

Tears welling up in her eyes, Una gripped his hand. "Thank you, Tim."

"No, Una. Thank *you*."

"*This is Captain James T. Kirk of the Federation Starship* Enterprise. *Our sensors show that your vessel is crippled and your life-support systems are failing. If you surrender, you have my word that you will be well-treated and turned over to your people when their ships arrive. In the meantime, we will assist you in making emergency repairs so that you don't have to abandon your ship. Please respond.*"

Hot fury burned Visla's eyes. Staring at the static-filled image of the Starfleet captain that dominated the *Vron'joQ* bridge's viewscreen, she seethed. His expression, though deeply serious, could not completely mask his arrogant sense of superiority. This was the face of an adversary who knew he had won. He might appear magnanimous, but Visla knew that in short order he would be standing in a bar, drinking and regaling his friends with stories of his victory. The very idea only fueled her anger.

Just as she was considering drawing her disruptor and shooting the screen, the Earther's face faded, sputtered, then flared back to full brightness before disappearing altogether, and the viewscreen went dark. All around her, Visla heard the sounds of other stations shutting down. Display monitors and consoles deactivated, each one robbing the bridge of a bit more illumination. After a moment, there was only the feeble illumination provided by the battery-operated emergency lighting. Beneath her, the ship itself groaned in protest as it drifted helpless in space.

"I have no control," reported K'darqa from the helm station. The lieutenant slammed his fists into the now useless console. "We are easy prey for our enemies."

From where he stood at one of the bridge's rear stations, Woveth said, "Weapons systems are offline. Shields are down."

"They will not kill us," said Commander D'jorok. He

was standing next to the helm console and trying to assist K'darqa, but looked over his shoulder. "If they wanted to do so, we would already be dead, but that is not the way of Earthers."

Slamming her fist against the arm of her chair, Visla activated the internal communications channel. "Engineering, damage report. Are you able to make repairs?"

There was a long pause—too long, in fact—before the voice of Morval, the *Vron'joQ*'s haggard engineering officer, said over the open channel, *"Primary propulsion is offline, Commander, and it is beyond our ability to repair. We will require towing to a repair facility."*

"At last report," said Woveth, "the *D'ghaj* was proceeding here at maximum speed and is due to arrive within the day." He grunted. "I do not believe we will be able to wait for them without assistance from the *Enterprise*."

"That is unacceptable!" Her fists clenching, Visla wanted to pound the chair's armrests, but managed to restrain herself.

"Impulse engines are also damaged, but I may be able to restore them, given time. However, my priority is repairing life support. The artificial gravity field was simple, but the rest is in much worse condition. Our list of needed repairs is extensive, and will require much time to address."

"Is that due to your lack of will, engineer, or your lack of ability?"

"The ship was operating at full efficiency at the time you took command of it, and after we rescued you from your own foolhardy action against the Earther starship, Commander. Did you not learn anything from that earlier attempt?"

Snarling with mounting rage, Visla pushed herself from the chair. She spun on her heel and leveled an accusatory finger at D'jorok. "Your crew is as insubordinate as it is incompetent. I want that *petaQ*'s head on my wall."

D'jorok regarded her with open contempt. "Perhaps you might wait until he has saved the rest of us from asphyxiating before you kill him."

"You insolent dog." Woveth moved from the rear of the bridge, and as he stepped into her view, Visla saw her first officer drawing his disruptor.

"No!" she snapped, but it was too late.

An accomplished marksman, Woveth cleared the weapon from its holster and was bringing it up to aim at D'jorok. The *Vron'joQ*'s first officer was faster, brandishing a smaller disruptor from beneath his baldric and raising it in a single, fluid motion. Visla winced at the howl of energy as D'jorok fired in the bridge's confined space, and the orange flash from his weapon's muzzle was bright enough to make her reach up to shield her eyes. The disruptor bolt slammed into Woveth's chest, and he shrieked in pain as his body was torn apart by the hellish energies unleashed upon him. The echo of his screams was still ringing in Visla's ears even after her first officer vanished. Without missing a beat, D'jorok moved his arm so that the compact disruptor now pointed at Visla's face.

"You have tainted this ship and its crew with the stain of your dishonor," he said, sneering. Around the bridge, Visla saw other members of the *Vron'joQ*'s crew, undoubtedly loyal to D'jorok and their slain captain, taking those few of her own men who still survived. Glancing to where K'darqa had moved from the helm console to take her sensor officer, Bakal, under guard, D'jorok motioned with the disruptor toward the bridge's rear hatch.

"Take them to the brig. I will deal with them later."

Visla, standing within easy reach of D'jorok's weapon, sneered at him. "What are your intentions, Commander?"

"First, I am taking charge of this vessel. As of this moment, you are officially relieved of the command you stole." There was no hesitation, no doubt, in D'jorok's voice. Visla saw that this was a Klingon driven by conviction and unwavering loyalty to the captain she had killed. She had underestimated J'Teglyr and those he commanded.

Visla glared at D'jorok. "You are arresting me? What then? Offer me as a gift to the Earthers? That is your vengeance for your fallen captain?" She saw his hand tighten on the grip of his disruptor, and she was certain a flicker of anger crossed his dark eyes, but that was the extent of his reaction to her verbal jab.

"My personal preference is to kill you where you stand," he said, "but I am a soldier of the Empire, sworn to obey no matter how unpleasant that duty may be. You and the remaining crew from your ship will be delivered to the captain of whichever vessel arrives to assist us."

"Give in to your urges. Kill me." Thoughts of her son clouded her mind. K'tovel, along with the other *HoS'leth* survivors, still waited for her on Centaurus. How much time would pass before she saw him again? What would become of him once she met whatever fate awaited her?

D'jorok replied, "I am well aware of your family's dishonor. I can even understand you wanting to reclaim that which you thought was wrongly taken from you, but your actions here were not justified. We have paid a heavy price for your bloodlust, and we have nothing to show for it. Now we must ask for help from the Earthers. I would rather die than do that, but it will be worth it if I live long enough to see you thrown into the deepest, darkest hole in the Empire."

Shaking her head, Visla almost gave in to her urge to

spit at him. "You are no less a coward than your captain. It disgusts me even to look at you." The very idea of surrendering to this insignificant *pujwl'* was loathsome to every atom of her being.

D'jorok remained silent for several moments, and the two of them stared at each other along the length of his disruptor. Then his expression seemed to soften.

"Perhaps you should have killed me when you killed my captain."

Snarling, Visla nodded. "Yes."

Without another word, D'jorok smiled and lowered his disruptor to his side.

"Commander?" said one of his officers.

Neither Visla nor D'jorok looked to the source, each keeping their gaze locked on the other. It was obvious to her what he was doing, leaving himself exposed to her attack. Something in his eyes had changed, and now she was certain he had no intention of fulfilling whatever duty or obligation had kept her alive to this point. From somewhere in the depths of whatever passed for his coward's heart, D'jorok had summoned enough loyalty and devotion to his dead captain that he now openly challenged her on the bridge of his ship and in full view of his subordinates.

Only one option remains.

Visla reached for the disruptor on her hip, but even as her hand wrapped around the weapon's grip, she saw the harsh orange flash as D'jorok fired.

Thirty-five

Standing at the entrance to the mining camp, Kirk listened and noted the relative quiet. What had been a thriving hub of forced labor was now still. The machines and other equipment were silent, the mines had been emptied of their workers, and most of the dormitories that had housed captive Usildar were abandoned. For the first time in decades, the people who called this planet home answered to no one, and neither were they forced to live with the constant interference or reminders of their oppression. They had wasted no time acting on that freedom, throwing off the figurative and literal shackles of their oppressors and even now were plundering both the mining compound and nearby Klingon encampment. The process would take days, but the Usildar now had nothing but time.

And maybe we can help speed things up a bit.

A transporter beam sounded behind him, and Kirk turned to see a lone figure coalescing into existence. It did not take long for him to recognize Spock as the Vulcan's body solidified and the beam faded. Kirk noted that his friend wore a tricorder slung from his left shoulder, but like him carried no phaser. The need for weapons had thankfully passed.

"Captain," Spock said, by way of greeting.

Kirk nodded. "Mister Spock. I didn't expect to see you down here so soon. How are your parents?"

LEGACIES: PURGATORY'S KEY

"Doctor McCoy reports that they both will make complete recoveries. My mother is resting in guest quarters while my father already transported to the surface with Councillor Gorkon."

Surprised to hear that, Kirk said, "Already? I would've thought he'd take a little time, particularly with your mother also recuperating."

"You have met my father, Captain," replied Spock. "Surely you recall that he is not prone to long periods of convalescence."

The deadpan comment made Kirk chuckle. "Point taken. As long as he's feeling up to it, we can certainly use his help. There's going to be a lot to do here. Speaking of that, what's the latest with the Usildar?" He gestured toward the mining camp. "How are our friends? At least I hope we can call them that."

"Commander Giotto reports that all Usildar laborers have been freed at all locations," replied the first officer. "The Usildar know they are free to make use of any of the facilities and equipment left by the Jatohr and the Klingons, though most are electing to return to their homes, and many families are banding together to create temporary shelters until new homes can be constructed."

"What about our own shelters and other supplies?" asked Kirk, glancing to his friend. "Where are we on that?"

Stepping closer, Spock replied, "Lieutenant Uhura reports that engineering and supply teams will have deployed our entire complement of emergency shelters at the location for the new Usilde village as well as the surrounding areas by nightfall. She adds that Captain Blair and the *Defiant* are adding their supplies to that effort. The Usildar have been most welcoming of the assistance."

"Excellent. It's the least we can do."

Upon their release, many of the Usildar had asked to be relocated to the site of their original village, much of which had fallen to disrepair and destruction thanks to the actions of their former Jatohr and Klingon masters. An *Enterprise* survey team had concluded that the area would be usable once debris and other waste were cleared to make room for new construction. With the arrival of the *Defiant* just hours earlier, there now were two starships' worth of personnel to assist the liberated Usildar in establishing new villages throughout the region, at least until the *Enterprise*'s scheduled departure.

Kirk still could see individual and small groups of Usildar moving about the compound, their darkly tanned skin and bright, jade hair contrasting with the encampment's darkened, polluted gray soil. Even from this removed vantage point, he recognized that they carried themselves with new purpose. Stacks and piles of cargo containers, building materials, and other items were being staged at different points around the camp. According to the reports from *Enterprise* security and survey teams, the Klingons, in their haste to depart Usilde, had apparently left all but the most essential or sensitive equipment, abandoning everything else. Much within the compound would be of value to the Usildar, along with the assistance that soon would be provided by the Federation. To Kirk's eye, there was enough materiel to rebuild and expand the nearby village. Such supplies would be augmented first from the shipboard stores of the *Enterprise* and the *Defiant*, followed later by more comprehensive shipments as Starfleet dispatched dedicated engineering and colony support staff to the planet.

Resettling the Usildar and helping them get back on their feet and readjust in the wake of their liberation from

Klingon rule would take time. Then there was the work necessary to undo the harmful effects of the Jatohr's terraforming, both the extended effort here on the surface as well as the limited contamination of the planet's atmosphere. The damage from the combined endeavor, though extensive, was not irreversible, and some of the best minds in Starfleet and the Federation were already en route to Usilde to lend their expertise to what was sure to be a lengthy recovery operation.

"As for the Jatohr who were stranded in our universe after the citadel's destruction," said Spock, "many of them remain disoriented following the transfer from their universe. Doctor McCoy has requested assistance from Starfleet Medical, and a team of xenobiology specialists is now en route. In the meantime, Mister Giotto reports that they also have been resettled here in the camp. His counterpart from the *Defiant* has already established a security rotation to oversee our guests."

Kirk nodded at the report. Though a few Jatohr had attempted to stand against the security team he had sent from the *Enterprise*, the majority of them had offered no resistance. A team from the starship's sociological department had transported to the planet surface and taken the lead on communicating with the displaced aliens, attempting to convince the Jatohr that all would be done to aid in their acclimation to this universe.

"According to the last message I received," said Kirk, "a colony support and relocation team is part of the group Starfleet's sending out to us. They should be here in a couple of days." Though the *Enterprise* was due to depart the Libros system to Starbase 6 for much-needed repairs, the *Defiant* would remain in orbit and with personnel here on the surface to assist the Usildar and the

Jatohr, and handle the transition to the dedicated support team that would establish a long-term outpost here. The plan was for the group of Starfleet and Federation civilian engineering, science, medical, terraforming, and colony support specialists to remain here on the planet until the Usilde were completely resettled and as much of the damage inflicted upon them and their world was treated or reversed. Then there was the matter of the stranded Jatohr, who also would need a home. None of this was a simple proposition by any means, but Kirk knew the Federation and Starfleet would devote the required resources and people until the task was completed. The Usildar deserved nothing less, and even the Jatohr could not be dismissed, despite the bizarre circumstances that had brought them here.

It's what we do.

"Captain Kirk!"

Kirk heard the voice just before he detected movement beyond where Spock stood, and he looked past the Vulcan to see Lieutenant Sulu approaching, along with a trio of Usildar. The small party was making its way along the narrow footpath cut into the side of the hill on this side of the valley. Kirk eyed the Usildar walking alongside Sulu, guessing him to be the apparent leader of the village, or what remained of it. He was using a polished staff as a cane, and Kirk noted that he walked with a limp. Kirk thought his clothing seemed ceremonial, including the ornate, carved wooden helmet adorned with polished seed shells.

"Captain," said the Usildar as the group moved to stand before Kirk. "I am Onumes, and I speak for all you helped free. It is an honor to finally meet you."

"The honor is mine, sir," replied Kirk. "I must say, your

people are very resilient. They seem to be adapting very quickly to their new situation."

"We are a simple people, Captain. The world around us provides all we require, and we take from it only what we need." His expression faltering, Onumes cast his gaze toward the mining camp. "It is a pity others do not share such harmony with whatever world they call home, and are therefore forced to plunder the homes of others."

Kirk nodded. "It's not an uncommon story. We had to learn that same lesson ourselves, a long time ago."

"I am told that you can help us return our world to what it was before the Newcomers came. You can change the soil and the water as they did, but not hurt it. You can clean the air?"

"That's right. We have people who are well-trained in such methods." He gestured to Sulu. "In fact, my crew has been working on just such a measure to help you. Lieutenant?"

The helm officer cleared his throat. "Yes, sir, that's right." To Onumes, he said, "We've been researching the Jatohr terraforming efforts. The ecological considerations here are unique, due to the influence of the Jatohr's techniques and their origin from the other universe, but given enough time and working with our own terraforming experts, we think we have a means of reversing the effects without causing any further damage. I've already transmitted my findings to Starfleet Command, and our research divisions are going over our data. By the time the first terraforming teams arrive, they should have a better idea of the work involved."

"It will take some time, but when it's finished," added Kirk, "your world will be as it was before the Newcomers arrived. That's a promise, sir."

Onumes asked, "And your people will leave us?"

"If that's what you want, then yes. We'll leave you in peace and never return, if that's your wish."

The Usildar leader seemed to ponder this for a moment before responding, "There are those among my people who would be pleased with that. However, I feel that is not the best course. We should be welcoming of friends, and you have more than proven yourselves as such. It is my hope that we can extend that friendship."

"I hope for that, as well," replied Kirk.

"And what of the Newcomers?" asked Onumes. "Those who remain here after the destruction of their citadel; what is to become of them?"

Kirk sighed. "That's a very good question, and I don't know if the answers are simple. They need to be relocated, of course."

"Ideally, they can be moved to a world that is better-suited to their form of life," added Spock, "or that requires only a minimum of ecological modifications to better support them. Starfleet is studying the issue and will hopefully have an answer in the near future."

"Until then," Kirk said, "We'd like to keep them here, at least until we have a relocation plan in place." He indicated the mining camp with a wave. "We can make use of these facilities to shelter them and ensure they're treated well."

Onumes replied, "We have discussed this with your ambassador." He gestured to Spock. "The one who looks like you. He said that there would be measures taken to ensure security and peace between our two peoples until the Newcomers can be moved. We have agreed to honor his request."

"That's very generous of you," said Kirk. "Thank you."

"We understand that their reasons for being here were

not malicious," said the Usildar leader. "It is unfortunate that their forms are not harmonious with our world as it was, and as it once again will be. We would have welcomed them."

Kirk smiled in genuine admiration. If Onumes was representative of all Usildar, then these were people of tremendous strength and character. It was regrettable that the tranquility of their existence had been disrupted by the Jatohr and the Klingons and even the Federation. That could not be undone, but at least now the Federation could see to it that the damage inflicted here was healed and the Usildar left in peace. Still, their innocence had been shattered, and they now were aware of other civilizations among the stars who might seek to do them harm. It would fall to the Federation to see to it that the Usildar were once more afforded the opportunity to live their lives as they saw fit.

That doesn't seem like too much to ask, does it?

After accepting Sulu's invitation to join him, Onumes excused himself, following the lieutenant back down the path to the Usildar village and the lake that had served as the citadel's decades-long home. Kirk smiled as Sulu's animated descriptions of the terraforming techniques that would restore the lake and the surrounding areas to its former beauty echoed through the trees even after the pair disappeared from sight.

"Sometimes I wonder if Sulu made a mistake," said Kirk, "switching from the sciences to operations."

Spock replied, "Mister Sulu is a man of many talents."

Proceeding farther into the encampment, it did not take long for Kirk and Spock to find the set of dormitory buildings that had been selected to house the dozens of displaced Jatohr.

"Per your orders," said Spock, "the Jatohr are not being confined, and they have agreed to remain in the compound until such time as we enable a relocation plan. Also, Doctor McCoy and the *Defiant*'s chief medical officer have researched Jatohr dietary requirements, and the galley staffs from both ships are working to provide an ample food supply."

Kirk nodded. "Good. There's no reason they can't be as comfortable as possible and practical until we can figure out what to do with them." He sighed. "Of course, I know that's an unpopular opinion right now, both aboard ship and back at headquarters."

"It is fortunate that there were no deaths aboard the *Enterprise* or the *Defiant* as a consequence of the battle," said Spock.

"But there were casualties. There are those who think that's something for which the Jatohr need to be punished."

"There are, of course, mitigating circumstances."

Kirk nodded, his gaze on the ground ahead of him. "I know. That's why I'm glad your father is involved in making sure we get the best possible outcome for everyone involved in this entire mess." Sensing movement ahead of him, Kirk looked up to see a small group walking toward them. Ambassador Sarek was crossing the mining camp's open courtyard, accompanied by a single, bulky Jatohr escorted by one of the *Enterprise*'s security officers, Ensign Nick Minecci. "Speak of the devil."

"Captain," said the ambassador, before raising his hand and offering the traditional Vulcan gesture of greeting.

"Ambassador, it's good to see you well."

Sarek nodded to his son, though maintained decorum for both their sakes. "Nurse McCoy's timely intervention on my behalf played a large part in my treatment, along with the work of her father and Doctor M'Benga. They both are most efficient physicians, and I am grateful for the superb care they have given my wife and the other injured."

"Captain," said Ensign Minecci, from where he stood next to his Jatohr charge, "Edolon has requested to speak with you."

Kirk's attention shifted to the Jatohr who had been designated as the leader of hir people now being housed in the mining camp. Hir predecessor, Woryan, had suffered a neurological incapacitation during the transition between universes, resulting in hir removal from command of the Jatohr forces that now were in disarray.

"Edolon, what can I do for you?"

"You have already done much for us, Captain," replied Edolon. "I simply wanted to thank you for your treatment of our people. You are as your Ambassador Sarek and Captain Una described you, and you honor us with your words and deeds."

Kirk said, "There will be questions, of course." He indicated Ambassador Sarek. "However, you have a very formidable ally. I don't anticipate too many problems."

"Two allies," said Sarek. "Councillor Gorkon has informed me that with this world being in disputed territory and with possible violations against the Organian Peace Treaty, it is in the Empire's best interests to see this matter resolved quickly and efficiently. He intends to address the High Council, and anticipates no difficulties eliciting their agreement on this matter."

"That's good to hear," said Kirk. He had not had the opportunity to speak with the councillor following everyone's return from the other universe, as Gorkon had been transported to the *Vron'joQ* by then. As for the Klingon ship and its crew, they were free to leave at any time, so far as Kirk was concerned.

"According to my chief engineer," he said, "the *Vron'joQ*'s life-support systems are back online, and the wounded members of its crew are being treated."

Spock added, "It still requires extensive repairs to its warp drive that cannot be addressed here, but the *Vron'joQ* itself can be safely towed to the nearest Klingon facility as soon as another ship arrives."

"Until then," said Sarek, "Councillor Gorkon has assured me that there will be no trouble from the *Vron'joQ* or its crew."

Returning his attention to Edolon, Kirk said, "Many of your people were affected by the transfer from your universe. We're doing all we can, but I'm afraid your physiology is very different from anything we've encountered, so we've requested additional help."

Edolon replied, "Not all of our people were affected. If anything, the transfer seems to have served as a reminder to them of why we opted to journey here. We are not conquerors, and we regret the actions of those who took that course." S/he paused, shifting hir bulk. "I understand that efforts are already under way to find us a suitable world. That is most gracious, Captain. My people and I will endeavor to be worthy of that consideration and assistance. We promise to cause no further trouble." Though it was difficult to read the Jatohr's facial expressions, Kirk saw that Edolon looked despondent, and he thought he could guess the reason.

"You are likely experiencing feelings of isolation," said Sarek. "Given what you taught me about your universe, I feel I can at least somewhat understand and appreciate what you now face. My experiences in your world were fascinating, and I very much look forward to discussing them with you at length."

"I would welcome such a conversation myself," added Spock. "Based on what my father has told me, the role telepathic and psionic abilities play in your universe would make for enlightening discussion."

Edolon said, "I appreciate your offer, but it is not myself with whom I am concerned, or even those who are here with me. With the citadel destroyed, the rest of the Jatohr remain trapped there. The device's destruction has likely doomed my civilization to eventual extinction."

Spock said, "Not necessarily. Though the citadel is gone, it is possible that the transfer-field technology can be re-created. According to Captain Una's descriptions of your scientific accomplishments, you may be able to contribute to that effort yourself. In time, we may be able to reconnect to your universe and bring the rest of your people here. Or you and they can be moved to another realm that is better suited to your species."

"Perhaps, but you cannot be certain."

The Vulcan shook his head. "No, but we will still make the attempt."

"We can ask no more." To Kirk, Edolon said, "Thank you, Captain, for everything."

At Kirk's direction, Minecci guided the Jatohr back into the compound. The captain watched them go, noting how those Usildar they encountered chose to offer greetings as they passed. He detected no lingering animosity or other negative feelings.

"Remarkable," said Sarek. "Their capacity for forgiveness is encouraging."

Kirk replied, "It certainly is."

The ambassador took his leave and walked out of the

camp. Once the elder Vulcan was on the path leading back to the Usildar village, Kirk regarded his first officer.

"I have to say, Spock, that it's encouraging to hear about your father and Gorkon working so well together." He briefly considered asking Gorkon what, if anything, the Empire might do to recompense the Usildar for occupying their planet and enslaving them, but he opted against giving voice to that impulse. There was nothing to be gained by it, and the councillor was not to blame for the decision that led to the Empire's involvement on this world. Indeed, Kirk regretted that he likely would not have the opportunity to meet Gorkon, if for no other reason than to thank him in person for his role in averting what had threatened to become an interstellar incident.

Maybe one of these days.

Spock replied, "It will require dedicated effort from invested parties on both sides, Captain. I do believe that Councillor Gorkon is such a person."

It was hard to argue his friend's point, Kirk decided. Indeed, it was obvious from his words and deeds that Gorkon was not a typical Klingon, certainly not when compared to their warrior class and even to the other diplomats Kirk had encountered over the years. Gorkon possessed a quality he found refreshing and even promising. Here was someone who did not seek war, or even concessions in order to refrain from waging war. Kirk sensed the genuine desire to do what was right, and perhaps find a way to bridge the gulf separating the Empire from the Federation and other adversaries. If there was to be lasting peace between the two interstellar rivals, it would be thanks to the efforts of individuals such as Gorkon and Ambassador Sarek.

The future, Kirk decided, could not be in better hands.

Thirty-six

While it might be the end of his scheduled duty shift, Leonard McCoy knew he was not going anywhere.

With a sigh, he dropped into the chair behind his desk, which in actuality was little more than a small nook tucked into the outer office of the *Enterprise*'s sickbay. Lifting his feet, he placed them on the corner of the desk and leaned back in his chair.

"You look tired," said Joanna McCoy as she emerged from the sickbay's examination room carrying a data slate. "When was the last time you slept?"

Tapping the fingers of his left hand on the desk, McCoy replied, "You're starting to sound more and more like me all the time."

"If you mean gruff and irritable, I learned from the master." Joanna smiled, taking some of the sting out of the verbal jab. "Seriously, though. You could use a break."

McCoy nodded in agreement. "No argument there." He gestured over his shoulder, in the general direction of the patient care ward. "I want to make one more round here and the other wards before I grab a nap."

"Doctor M'Benga and Nurse Chapel can do that for you," said Joanna. She moved to perch herself on the edge of his desk, near his feet.

"They need a break the same as I do. It's been a long day."

Her smile tightening almost to a grimace, Joanna reached up to rub her temples. "Closer to two, you know."

"Don't remind me." In truth, McCoy had lost track of the hours that had elapsed since the battle with the Jatohr, so occupied had he been with its aftermath. First, there had been Ambassador Sarek's injuries, inflicted back on Centaurus and somehow arrested by the odd properties of the Jatohr universe. Once returned to this dimensional plane, those wounds still required treatment, though it was a routine matter for McCoy and his assistant medical officer, Doctor Jabilo M'Benga, to tackle. The process had been even smoother thanks to the expertise M'Benga had acquired during his period of study and internship at the Vulcan Science Academy's hospital.

In addition to the ambassador, everyone who had been retrieved from the other universe had been brought to sickbay for assessment of their condition. Due to the odd nature of the other realm and the virtual existence to which Captain Una and everyone else had been subjected, there had been no further physical injuries. Mental trauma, on the other hand, had run the gamut from simple disorientation and short-term memory loss to total catatonia, though that was limited to a single case. Otherwise, fatigue of one flavor or another had been the most common malady affecting everyone who had endured the Jatohr universe.

Small favors, I suppose.

"Doctor McCoy," said a new voice. "Leonard."

Looking toward the doorway separating the office from sickbay's patient treatment areas, he smiled at the sight of Amanda Grayson. Even dressed in a standard Starfleet-issue pale blue patient's coverall garment, she still managed to affect an air of grace and distinction. Despite that, McCoy noted the dark circles under her eyes, which were still red and puffy from a lack of sleep.

"Amanda," he said, rising to his feet, "what are you doing out of bed?"

"To be honest, I'm looking to escape." She glanced toward the doors leading to the adjacent corridor. "I thought about sneaking out the other door, but that didn't seem fair to you." She regarded him with a small, knowing smile. "I'm hoping my honesty will buy me a favor, and you will let me return to my quarters."

McCoy looked to Joanna, who made a show of raising her hands. "Don't look at me. I didn't put her up to it."

"You were subjected to a tremendous mental strain," said McCoy. "Besides, I don't know that I've ever heard of anyone enduring a mind-meld the way you did. I'd like to make sure there are no unexpected side effects."

Amanda replied, "I'm told you released my husband from sickbay, and he's already wandering around down on that planet. Surely if he's fit for duty even after everything he went through, I can be trusted to sleep in a different and more comfortable bed?"

"Okay, that I did tell her," said Joanna.

"You're not helping, Nurse," snapped McCoy, but he offered her a sidelong glance to let her know he was not being completely serious, and received a mischievous grin for his trouble. Returning his attention to Amanda, he said, "I had prescribed bed rest for the ambassador, but he insisted that he felt fine, and my diagnostics agreed with him."

Joanna added, "The ambassador was most impressed with his care. I believe he used the words 'adequate' and 'efficient.' High praise from any Vulcan, but from Sarek?" She shook her head. "That's pretty amazing."

"You're having just a bit too much fun at my expense, offspring." Stepping away from his desk, McCoy reached out and laid a hand on Amanda's forearm. "As my daughter so eloquently pointed out, the ambassador's a Vulcan, whereas—"

"I'm an older, weaker human woman?" As she spoke the words, Amanda's eyes narrowed, but McCoy caught the gentle teasing in her tone.

"I'm not going to walk into that trap." McCoy frowned. "To be honest, I was going to release you later today; I don't think it makes much difference whether you're here or in your quarters."

Nodding, Amanda replied, "I'm grateful, Leonard." After a moment, she added, "There is one other thing. As I said, my husband is down on the planet."

"He's helping with the Usildar and the displaced Jatohr," said Joanna. "It's going to take a while before the effects of the Jatohr terraforming are reversed, and the Jatohr themselves will be relocated."

McCoy added, "According to the captain, the ambassador could be here for a bit." Realizing where this was going, he asked, "You'll want to stay with him, of course."

"Of course." Again, Amanda smiled. "We have been apart far too long."

"Can't argue with that." McCoy made a gesture as though he was waving an imaginary magic wand. "By the power vested in me as the chief medical officer, I hereby vacate your sickbay sentence. You're free to go." He held up a finger. "On one condition. I'm going to let Doctor Hamilton on the *Defiant* know that I'd like her to check up on you before her ship leaves. I'll be asking the *Lexington*'s doctor to look in on you when they get here, too."

"Fair enough," said Amanda. "Thank you, Leonard."

Releasing a mock sigh, McCoy looked toward the overhead. "I'm getting soft as I get older."

Amanda leaned toward him and left a small kiss on his cheek. "You're a good man, Leonard McCoy. My son is lucky to have you as his friend."

"Please tell him that." McCoy grinned. "It's been a pleasure seeing you again."

"Likewise." With a final farewell to him and Joanna, Amanda Grayson exited the sickbay, leaving McCoy and Joanna alone.

McCoy waited until the doors were closed before saying, "Adequate and efficient. I want that in my official obituary."

"Adequate to a Vulcan is pretty impressive," replied Joanna.

The response made McCoy chuckle. "That reminds me of something I should've said before. You were a tremendous help. Thank you."

With McCoy and M'Benga focused on Ambassador Sarek and his injuries, it had fallen to the rest of the *Enterprise* medical staff to see to Captain Una and everyone else who had come back from the other universe. There also were a few minor injuries among the ship's personnel as a consequence of the brief yet fierce battle with the Jatohr citadel. Nurse Chapel had taken the lead on that effort, but Joanna had wasted no time pitching in wherever she could be of assistance. Working together, they had assessed Una and the other former *Enterprise* crewmembers and released most of them to guest quarters for bed rest. Thanks to those efforts, only Amanda Grayson and two of Una's shipmates had remained here in the patient care ward.

"I have to admit," he said, moving back to his desk, "I was worried sick about you. Not knowing for sure what happened." Forgoing his chair, he opted instead to lean against the desk itself. "Even with Captain Una deciding to transport to the other universe, and Spock saying there was a way to get all of you back, there was still a part of me that . . ." He could not bring himself to finish the sentence, so instead he reached up to wipe his face. "Well, you know."

Joanna moved closer. "Yeah, I know."

Changing the subject, he asked, "How are you holding up?"

"It's no worse than clinical rotations at school," replied his daughter. "The big difference working there is that I didn't know all of the patients."

McCoy said, "You got to know them . . . over there?"

Joanna nodded. "Some better than others."

"Well, I guess I'll never understand what they went through. What *you* went through."

Shrugging, she replied, "I don't know that I will either. Maybe none of us ever really will." She gestured toward the patient ward. "Captain Una and a few of them are in there, with Commander Martinez. I've talked to a few of them since we got back. I know they were all together for a lot longer than I was with them, and I get the feeling it helps for them to see someone else who went through at least some of what they experienced. They can talk to me without having to explain themselves, because I get it, you know what I mean?"

"I think I do," said McCoy. "And who do *you* have to talk to?" When Joanna looked at him somewhat plaintively and shrugged, he felt his heart sink. "You know you can talk to me, right?"

Reaching up to rub the corner of her left eye, Joanna said, "I know that, Dad. I do." She paused, staring at her hand as though she had wiped something from her face. "I mean, we say it and we know it but it never really happens. It's not that I don't want it to but . . . I'm just not used to you being available, so I guess I don't count on it."

The words were not unfamiliar, and neither was the quick surge of defensiveness he felt rise within him, but he quashed it.

No. Not this time.

Every agonizing moment between her disappearance on Centaurus and her retrieval had been interminable, racked with worry, far more difficult than anything he had endured since becoming a parent. The gratitude he had felt upon first seeing her was perhaps the most joyous feeling he had experienced since the day of her birth. Indeed, his happiest memories and his greatest joys involved her.

That feeling of relief was short-lived, replaced soon afterward by elation and unfettered pride as McCoy watched his daughter assisting Chapel and the rest of his staff. In that moment, watching her exude a passion for her patients that rivaled his own seemed to wash away the barriers erected between father and daughter. The lengthy separations, the frayed emotions, the fighting, all of it seemed so pointless. Now their shared zeal for helping others seemed to be forging a bond they had been unable to fashion for themselves. McCoy did not question it, but instead turned such queries inward, taking himself to task.

What the hell took you so long?

"I'm sorry," he said. When Joanna started to reply, McCoy held up his hand. "No, for real. I need to say it out loud. After your mother and I divorced, I chose a life in Starfleet, and back then I know you thought I chose it over you. I didn't, but I did think you were better off with your mother and without me mucking things up. What I never told you is that I wasn't better off without you. I can't fix what I did back then, and I can't do anything about the lost time between us, but if you're willing, I'd like to try to make up for it, starting right now."

Her lips trembling, Joanna reached up to wipe away the lone tear trailing down her right cheek. "I'd like that. I want to try, too, Dad. We'll do it together."

McCoy pulled her to him, feeling her arms around his waist and her face against his shoulder. Reaching up, he placed a hand on the back of her head, holding her as the emotions surged forth. He had carried the burden of sadness, guilt, and regret for far too long, and now he felt it lifting ever so slightly from his consciousness. It would take time before he pushed it away forever, but at least now he would not be undertaking the task alone.

Pulling away from him, Joanna wiped at her eyes, and McCoy did his best to compose himself.

Joanna said, "I . . . I told Nurse Chapel I'd update the patient logs for the official report. She was looking pretty tired, and I thought she could use the break."

"That was very thoughtful." McCoy swallowed the lump in his throat. "I'm going to check on Martinez."

They exchanged a final look, each smiling at the other, before Joanna turned and headed to the small desk used by Chapel for her administrative work. Taking that as his cue, McCoy made his way to the patient care ward. The first thing he saw was Lieutenant Commander Raul Martinez, lying unconscious in his bed. He had not moved since the last time McCoy had looked in on him. Standing beside him was Captain Una. Ensign Timothy Shimizu was sleeping on his side in an adjacent bed. Una was dividing her attention between her friend and the patient monitor above Martinez's bed, and McCoy noted that the panel's readings had not changed since his last check. Unlike Shimizu and Martinez, Una was in her Starfleet uniform.

"Captain," said McCoy, "how are you feeling?" He had

recommended but not ordered her to bed rest in guest quarters.

Turning from Martinez, Una replied. "I'm feeling much better, Doctor. Sleep did wonders, but I couldn't stay in that room any longer." She gestured to her friend. "I wanted to check on Raul."

McCoy shook his head as he stepped into the room. "No need to explain. I understand completely." He waved toward Shimizu. "I was going to send him to guest quarters, but I can do that when he wakes up."

Una once more looked down at Martinez. "Has there been any change in Raul's condition?"

"No." McCoy pointed to the monitor. "On the plus side, he hasn't gotten any worse. There's no way to know how long it might take for him to pull out of whatever this is, but we'll do everything we can for him." McCoy had begun the process of composing the report he would soon be filing to Starfleet Medical, requesting special assistance and treatment for Martinez.

"When I set out to bring them home," said the captain, "I was prepared to find some or all of them dead, but I never considered anything like this."

McCoy replied, "The best medical minds in the Federation will be consulted. There are any number of treatments to be tried. I've even talked to Ambassador Sarek and Doctor M'Benga about possibly discussing the commander with Vulcan High Masters." He shook his head. "I used to be a skeptic about that sort of thing, but Spock's convinced me. If there's a way to help Martinez, I promise you we'll find it."

"Even if he's helped, what then?" Una's gaze was fixed on the unconscious man. "Will he be able to return to Starfleet? Will he even want to? So much time has passed.

Everything has changed so much." She blew out her breath. "I can't help thinking I did this more for myself than for any of them. All things considered, maybe they were better off there, in the other universe."

"I don't agree with that at all," said McCoy. "From what I understand about what happened over there, none of you had much choice about your fate. Only you and Sarek were able to figure a way out, while everybody else was left in the illusion, or whatever the hell it was. You gave them all a chance to regain control over their lives, to chart their own paths, the way we're meant to live. You gave hope. Our futures will be better with these people playing a part in it, and I for one am damned grateful to you for that."

Still staring at Martinez, Una said, "Thank you, Doctor. That's very kind of you." She folded her arms. "However, I put a lot of lives at risk. I'll have to answer for that."

"I've got a hunch more than a few people aboard this ship will be ready to vouch for you, starting with those two men up on the bridge. Spock will do it because you and he served together, and you and I both know he never forgets that sort of thing. Jim Kirk will do it because he'll always support Spock, and because it's the right thing to do."

McCoy paused, feeling emotion once more welling up within him. "And I'll do it because you brought my daughter back to me."

Thirty-seven

"Thanks again for everything, Tom. I owe you a drink the next time we're at the same starbase."

On the main viewscreen, Captain Thomas Blair smiled from where he sat on the bridge of the *Defiant*. "*Not a problem, Jim. I'm just sorry we didn't have a chance to really catch up.*"

Leaning against the bridge's forward railing, Kirk returned the smile. "Duty calls, and when it does it always has lousy timing."

"*I appreciate you leaving all those extra supplies and equipment. That should help to tide us over until the Lexington and the Masao arrive in a few days. Your people were a huge help with the initial resettlement. We'll be able to hold down the fort until everybody else gets here. I imagine things will be pretty quiet until then.*"

Nearly forty-eight hours had elapsed since the battle with the citadel and the return of Captain Una, Ambassador Sarek, and the others. It had taken far less time for Kirk to start getting antsy about moving on to their next assignment, or in this case a diversion to Starbase 6 for the *Enterprise* to receive a much-needed inspection and repairs. With his chief engineer asking, if not outright begging, for the *Enterprise* to put into a starship maintenance facility for a good going-over, Kirk had requested another ship be sent to Usilde to relieve them. Another trusted friend, Commodore Robert Wesley, was now en route aboard the *U.S.S. Lexington*. Kirk knew that this world and its people who had already endured so much would be in good hands. If there was anyone else who could oversee the delicate situation faced by the Usildar and the displaced Jatohr, it was Bob Wesley and Tom Blair. As for the *Masao*, Kirk only knew the ship and its crew by reputation as one of three vessels dedicated to Starfleet's Corps of Engineers. He and the *Enterprise* had worked with another of those crews on occasion and found them to be a resourceful group who could accomplish anything if they set their mind to the task. The Usildar would want for nothing once their new or restored villages were constructed or repaired.

Stepping down from his science station, Spock crossed the command well to stand next to Kirk. "Captain Blair, I understand that you play chess. My father does as well, and would welcome a formidable opponent, should the opportunity present itself."

Blair's smile widened. *"Chess against a Vulcan? I've never had the pleasure. I just may look into that, Commander. Thanks."* To Kirk, he offered a mock salute. *"Until next time, Jim. Fair winds, following seas, and all that."*

Returning the gesture, Kirk replied. "Fair winds, Tom. Kirk out."

The connection was severed and Thomas Blair's image was replaced by a view of Usilde, slowly rotating as the *Enterprise* maintained its orbit.

Seated at her communications station, Lieutenant Uhura turned in her chair. "Captain, I've just received a message from Ambassador Sarek, conveying his thanks for the provisions and other material we provided to him and Councillor Gorkon."

"Thank you, Lieutenant. Please pass on my acknowledgment. I'll send a long message in a little while."

From where he sat at the navigator's station, Ensign Chekov said, "All departments have reported in, Captain. All personnel are back aboard, and we can depart."

Lieutenant Sulu reported, "According to Mister Scott, we can go to warp at any time, though he requests that we 'take it easy.' His words, sir."

Kirk smiled. "We'll do our best. Carry on, gentlemen."

Turning back to the viewscreen, Kirk continued to lean against the bridge railing while allowing himself one last, long look at the lush, blue-green world. After a moment, he glanced at Spock, who remained nearby. "Your father volunteering to stay behind was a good thing, I think. He's just the right person for a job like this. He and Gorkon both."

Spock nodded. "Perhaps this is but the beginning of a stronger relation between the Federation and the Klingon Empire."

"That'd be something to see." After a moment, Kirk asked, "I approved your mother's request to transport to the surface less than an hour ago. How's she doing?"

"Doctor McCoy was pleased enough with her recovery to discharge her from sickbay earlier this morning, though he did recommend bed rest in her guest quarters. As you have learned, she was not amiable to the doctor's treatment regimen."

Kirk could not resist a small smile. "I've noticed that sort of thing tends to run in your family."

"Indeed. It is her intention to remain on Usilde with my father, and I have already taken my leave of them."

"Then I guess we don't need to head to Vulcan after a stop at Centaurus. Scotty will be happy to hear that."

As if on cue, the turbolift doors opened, and Kirk looked over his shoulder to see Captain Una walking onto the bridge, followed by Montgomery Scott. While the chief engineer proceeded to his station, Una paused just outside the lift doors. As she had done during her previous visit to the *Enterprise* months earlier, she was taking a moment to look around the room as though soaking in the scene. Kirk noted a wistful, faraway look in her eyes as she inspected the different stations. Everyone on the bridge had turned in their seat to regard her, and each offered a silent, respectful nod. There was no animosity or disapproval here. To a person, his crew was telling Una, each in their own way, that they respected what she had done for her shipmates, and they harbored no regrets about the role they had played in helping her.

For her part, Una seemed to understand the unspoken acknowledgments, for after a moment she reached up to wipe the corner of her right eye. "Thank you. Thank you all. I could not have done this without your help, and I'm forever grateful." Looking to Kirk, she added, "You have one hell of an outstanding crew, Captain. Bob April and Chris Pike would be proud."

Uncomfortable with the public praise in the presence of his subordinates, Kirk turned from the railing as Una moved around the bridge and stepped down into the command well. She extended her hand to him.

"I can't ever thank you enough, Captain."

Taking her hand, Kirk shook his head. "No need to thank me. Captain Pike would have done the same for us if the situation were reversed, and I know you'd have supported him just like Spock was there for me."

Turning to Spock, Una smiled. "And you, my old friend. What would I have done without you?"

"I am confident you would eventually have devised

your own solution, Captain. My presence merely facilitated that process."

Una laughed. "One of these days, I'll have to teach you how to accept a compliment when it's offered."

"When you do," Kirk said, "let me know the secret."

"I'll do that." After a moment, Una's smile faded, and she drew herself up, reasserting her military bearing. In a lower, more formal voice, she said, "Captain, now that everything's done, I'm presenting myself to you for arrest. I figure we should play it by the book from here on out. There's no sense adding trouble to what's already going to be a pretty large pile when I get back to headquarters."

Shrugging, Kirk replied, "Well, they'll have to throw us both in the brig, then. I went along with the plan. I'm not about to let you stand there by yourself."

"It is possible that Starfleet Command will understand and appreciate the very unusual and unique circumstances that compelled you to act as you both did." Spock, his hands clasped behind his back, punctuated his comment with a raised eyebrow. "Of course, this likely will be contingent upon their review of what I assume will be the very lengthy and detailed reports each of you submits about this affair."

"After all," Kirk said, "we did mitigate an interstellar incident and perhaps even prevented full-scale war by rescuing Gorkon. I can't imagine anyone who's commanded a starship could sit on a review board and take issue with an officer doing everything in their power to make sure that no one is left behind." He turned to Una. "You'll have people on your side, Una, including me."

Spock added, "I stand with you, as well, Captain."

After a moment, Kirk said, "Doctor McCoy told us about Martinez. I'm sorry."

"Your doctor is hopeful that, given time and proper care, Raul might emerge from his catatonia." Una's expression softened and she dropped her gaze to the deck for a moment. When she looked up again, Kirk noted the moisture at the corners of her eyes. "I just wish I could've gotten in there sooner or done more."

"You can't keep punishing yourself," said Kirk. "You had no way to know they were even alive, or if it was possible to retrieve your comrades."

"The whole time, we had the answer. We held it in our own damned hands. All those years, wasted." Una shook her head. "I don't know that I'll ever be able to forgive myself."

Kirk could sense that pushing the captain further on this point would be a mistake. She needed time to work through her feelings of despair on her own terms. Whether Una undertook that task alone, sought the aid of a trusted friend like Spock, or even a therapist, only time would tell.

"If I can be of assistance," said Spock, "please do not hesitate to tell me."

"Whatever you need," added Kirk.

Forcing a smile, Una replied, "You've both done so much already. Let's see what Command has to say about our little adventure, and we'll go from there. Now, if you're not going to toss me into the brig, I'd like to rejoin my shipmates."

"By all means, Captain."

With a final appreciative nod, Una turned and left the command well. The turbolift doors parted at her approach, and Kirk saw Doctor McCoy standing in the car. The physician stepped aside to permit Una to enter the lift, offering her a muted greeting before walking onto the bridge.

Moving to join the captain and Spock, McCoy sighed.

"With the exception of Commander Martinez, I expect everyone to make a full and speedy recovery. The help he needs is way outside of my league, Jim, but I've reached out to a few friends of mine at Starfleet Medical and made them aware of the issue. They're already making arrangements for treatment and therapy as soon as we can get Martinez transferred there. He's got a long road ahead of him, that's for sure."

"At least Martinez will have a chance, thanks to Captain Una." Kirk knew that her shipmate's condition would wear on her. She had spent all these years trying to prove that a rescue of her comrades was possible, had taken on the risk of finding and retrieving them, and returned with everyone, which made the reality of Martinez's condition all that more painful to witness.

McCoy laid a hand on the red railing, tapping it with his fingers. "You don't really think they're going to throw the book at Una, do you? After everything she and her people went through, and everything she risked to get them back?"

Shaking his head, Kirk replied, "Not if I have anything to say about it."

The doctor's expression was a mask of doubt. "Be sure to talk loudly, then."

"Captain," said Uhura, "incoming message from Starbase 6. Commodore Enwright reports that they've received our request for a docking facility and an inspection team, and they'll be ready for our arrival."

"Bless the maker," replied Scott as he rose from his own station. "It'll be good to give the old girl a proper checkup."

Turning from the viewscreen, Kirk rested his back against the railing, crossed his arms, and offered a wry grin. "Scotty, I don't think I've ever heard you like this before. Do you have so little confidence in your own skills?"

"It's not like that at all, sir," replied the engineer. "But we've been through quite a wee bit, as you know, and I'd just like to make sure everything's shipshape." He rested a loving hand on his console. "You can't ever be too sure, Captain."

Kirk said, "Well, I'm sure Commodore Enwright will be thrilled that you of all people have such confidence in his staff."

"Speaking of the commodore," said Uhura, "he also sends his regards, and says that he's looking forward to seeing us."

"Well, I'm glad somebody is."

McCoy eyed him. "You're not worried about Starfleet Command, are you?"

"There is just cause for concern, Doctor," replied Spock. "Concealing the Transfer Key is a serious matter, as is the fact that its existence was left out of all official reports submitted by three different command-grade officers. Captain Una's complicity, along with the rest of the *Enterprise* crew under Captain April's command, and even myself and Captain Kirk, cannot be ignored."

"They can't throw us all in the brig," said Kirk. "Besides, with the Transfer Key and the citadel destroyed, there's nothing left for the Klingons or anyone else to worry about."

Spock replied, "There remains the possibility that someone, either the Klingons or even someone within the Federation, might succeed in re-creating the Jatohr technology."

"Maybe," said Kirk, "but given that it originated in a different universe that operates under a somewhat different set of physical laws, that someone has quite the challenge ahead of them." Despite these facts, and what he had told Captain Una, he still harbored reservations about how Starfleet Command would view her actions and his own. At best, they would be considered "unconventional" and at worst mutinous, though his gut told him that given sufficient information and time to process it, Command would come to understand and appreciate all that had been done, both in the name of loyalty and Federation security.

Sounds good in theory, anyway.

Pushing off from the railing, Kirk began moving toward his command chair. "Mister Chekov, lay in a course for Starbase 6."

"Aye, sir," replied the ensign, his fingers already moving to carry out the order.

Kirk settled into his seat, resting his elbows on the chair arms as he took a final look around the bridge. Everyone had returned to their duties, and the status screens and indicators he could see from where he sat told him that the *Enterprise* and its crew were ready for departure. Closing his eyes for a moment, he drew a deep breath, then released it slowly.

"You okay, Jim?" asked McCoy. The doctor had taken up his customary position to the left of Kirk's chair. Mirroring his friend's actions, Spock now stood near Kirk's right arm.

"I'm actually relieved, Bones. I'd been carrying the secret of the Transfer Key for years. Hiding it in my cabin, not able to tell anyone, worried about what might happen if the wrong people somehow found it. I'm glad it's over."

Spock said, "Do you believe you acted correctly in preserving the secret?"

"Yes." Though he blurted out the reply, Kirk realized he

was questioning his response even as the word left his lips. "It was probably the safest of several undesirable choices, and I understand why Bob April did what he did. Based on the information he had at the time, there was too great a risk to allow the Jatohr to continue what they were doing, and he was honoring the dying wishes of the transfer field's creator. Eljor didn't want it used as a tool of aggression, and leaving it for the Klingons or some other enemy certainly wasn't an option."

Kirk paused, drawing another long, calming breath. "If I have any regrets, it's that we weren't able to understand the Jatohr's plight sooner, and we weren't able to help them. We might take issue with their methods, but they were and still are fighting to save themselves from extinction."

"Given the differences between our dimension and theirs," said Spock, "it is entirely possible that time is measured in a different manner throughout that dimension, and not just in the realm in which Captain Una and the others found themselves. What might sound immediate to us may in fact be a significant interval from the Jatohr's perspective."

"But there's no way to know for sure," replied McCoy.

The Vulcan nodded. "Unfortunately, Doctor, you are correct."

"And that's the tragedy." Kirk said nothing for moment, content to contemplate the planet still rotating on the bridge viewscreen. "But at least we can help the Jatohr who are here, and the Usildar as well."

Then a less unpleasant thought occurred to him. "I guess there is one downside to all of this. An *Enterprise* tradition's been broken." He smiled. "There's no secret to pass on to whoever ends up replacing me one day."

"I'm okay with that," replied McCoy. "Besides, you look pretty good sitting in that chair."

Spock said, "Agreed. The mission of the *Enterprise* is one of discovery, not secrecy. Let that be its tradition for generations to come."

"That's very profound, Mister Spock," offered McCoy.

"I always endeavor to provide meaningful counsel."

"You do quite well." Sitting up a bit straighter in his seat, Kirk said, "Mister Chekov, are we ready with that course?"

The young ensign shifted in his chair and nodded. "Course for Starbase 6 laid in and ready, sir."

"Mister Sulu, take us out of orbit. Once we're clear of the system, proceed at warp factor two."

The helm officer nodded. "Warp two, aye."

Discovery.

Kirk let the notion roll around in his mind as he watched the planet Usilde grow smaller on the viewscreen, disappearing from sight amid the vast, uncounted stars visible in the interstellar void. *A tradition for generations to come.* They were indeed very powerful words, evoking an even greater challenge and the potential to forge a legacy for all time.

It was a challenge James Kirk, with the help of his friends, crew, and his ship, would always be ready to face.

Space . . . the final frontier.
These are the voyages of the Starship Enterprise.
Its five-year mission: to explore strange new worlds . . .
to seek out new life and new civilizations . . .
to boldly go where no man has gone before.

ACKNOWLEDGMENTS

As always, we are grateful to Ed Schlesinger and Margaret Clark, our editors at Pocket Books, who toil behind the curtain to make sure we authors behave ourselves and play well with each other. The entire *Legacies* trilogy was a rather sizable undertaking with a lot of moving parts, and our editors were there to make sure we kept the trains on the tracks, the balls in the air, the ducks in their rows, and all those other things that keep projects like this moving.

Thanks very much to fellow wordsmiths Greg Cox and David Mack, with whom we conspired to bring about this little slice of celebration for *Star Trek*'s 50th Anniversary. The collaborative process—the emails, the brainstorming, the plotting and planning and evil laughing—was our favorite part of the entire project, fueled as it was by our mutual love for the little television show that started it all.

We tip our hats to John Van Citters at CBS Television Licensing. More than just the guy who approves our stories, he's as much a fan as any of us: fiercely protective not just of the *Star Trek* brand but also its legacy, and unwaveringly supportive of our efforts. While we literally could not do what we do without his approval, we also can't do it without his encouragement and enthusiasm. Thanks for being in our corner, John.

We owe a special shout-out to our copyeditor, Scott Pearson. Given the chaotic circumstances under which this book was written, Scott ended up shouldering a larger burden than even he likely anticipated when he took the job. He saved our bacon a couple of times with his eagle-eyed review of our various blatherings, and we figure we also owe the guy a bottle or two of his favorite wine, or at least the stuff we can afford.

Finally, there's you, our faithful readers. We're here because of your continued good graces, particularly for something like this, and you're never far from our thoughts whenever we hatch these crazy schemes. *Star Trek*'s 50th Anniversary is your party too. Live long and prosper, and thank you.

ABOUT THE AUTHORS

Dayton Ward has been modified to fit this medium, to write in the space allotted, and has been edited for content. Reader discretion is advised.

Visit Dayton on the web at www.daytonward.com.

Kevin Dilmore is universally specific and easily sendable. If you have questions about postage rates, contact your local post office.